BY KATHY REICHS

Two Nights
The Bone Collection (novellas)
Speaking in Bones
Bones Never Lie
Bones of the Lost
Bones Are Forever
Flash and Bones
Spider Bones
206 Bones
Devil Bones
Bones to Ashes
Break No Bones
Cross Bones
Monday Mourning
Bare Bones
Grave Secrets
Fatal Voyage
Deadly Décisions
Death du Jour
Déjà Dead

YOUNG ADULT FICTION (WITH BRENDAN REICHS)

Trace Evidence
Terminal
Exposure
Code
Seizure
Virals
Spike (novella)
Shock (novella)
Swipe (novella)
Shift (novella)

TWO NIGHTS

A NOVEL

KATHY REICHS

PUBLISHED BY SIMON & SCHUSTER
NEW YORK   LONDON   TORONTO   SYDNEY   NEW DELHI

SIMON &
SCHUSTER
CANADA

Simon & Schuster Canada
A Division of Simon & Schuster, Inc.
166 King Street East, Suite 300
Toronto, Ontario M5A 1J3

This Simon & Schuster Canada edition January 2018

The U.S. edition of this book is published by Bantam Books, an imprint of the Random House Publishing Group, a division of Random House, Inc.

SIMON & SCHUSTER CANADA and colophon are registered trademarks of Simon & Schuster, Inc.

For information about special discounts for bulk purchases, please contact Simon & Schuster Special Sales at 1-800-268-3216 or CustomerService@simonandschuster.ca.

Book design by Carole Lowenstein

Manufactured in the United States of America

1 3 5 7 9 10 8 6 4 2

ISBN 978-1-4767-2645-8
ISBN 978-1-5011-9239-5 (pbk)
ISBN 978-1-5011-4652-7 (ebook)

For
Hazel Inara Reichs,
born July 20, 2015

CHAPTER 1

My right-hand neighbor thinks I'm crazy, so she brings me cheese. I heard the one-two crunch of her boots on the path. A pause, then the oyster shells crunched again.

I lifted a corner of the towel covering my kitchen window. She was already five yards off, a shadow-laced smudge among the live oaks.

Six years, and I still didn't know her name. Didn't want to. Had no desire to exchange recipes or comments on the tides.

I cracked the door, snagged the plastic-wrapped package, and shoved it into the fridge.

Truth is, I don't mind the cheese. What I hate are the sharp little eyes plumbing my soul. That and the pity.

And the goats. When the wind is right, the bleating bullies into my dreams and I'm back in Helmand with the blood and the dust.

Or maybe I'm reading the old gal wrong. Maybe the cheese is a bribe so I don't murder Billie or Nanny.

My left-hand neighbor hanged himself from the end of his pier. His dog curled up and died by his head. Double suicide. Maggot jamboree by the time the bodies were found.

Arthur was a wood-carver, Prince a collie. I prefer their silent company. Fits my two-pronged plan for life. Need no one. Feel nothing.

I ran six miles and put in time with my free weights. A beer and a sandwich for lunch, then I spent the afternoon shooting Cheerwine cans off a dune at Gray Bay. The beach was deserted and not far away. Nothing is.

Goat Island is a skinny strip of sand just a monkey's spit wide, uninhabited until Henry and Blanche Holloway rowed over to escape the stresses of 1930s Charleston. Legend has it they spent decades in a hole covered with driftwood and palm fronds.

Now *that* sounds warp-speed psycho to me.

But Henry and Blanche had one thing right. For solitude, Goat Island is the cat's meow. Even today there's no ferry, no paved road, ergo no cars or trucks. No access except by private boat. Outsiders rarely find reason to come.

The few scrappy residents live in cottages cobbled together from wreckage ignored or tossed ashore by Hurricane Hugo. My porch roof is the ass end of a disemboweled rowboat. Goat Lady's shed started life as Arthur's latrine.

Don't get me wrong. I don't live hole-in-the-ground au naturel batty. I've got electricity, a septic tank. All the advantages.

The downside to Goat is the spring mosquitoes, some large enough to carry off St. Bernards. By six the bloodsuckers were organizing into squadrons, preparing to strike. Over and out for *moi*.

I was home rubbing aloe on bites when the bell above the stove jangled its jerry-rigged warning.

The moths did their frenzied dance in my chest.

I dug the shotgun from my duffel, thumbed shells into the chamber, and crept to a window. The sun was low, flaming the waterway orange and making me squint.

Far below, a figure crouched on my dock, securing lines. Both human and boat were featureless black cutouts against the tangerine glow.

My grip tightened on the stock, ready to pump.

The figure straightened and headed my way. Male. Barrel-chested. Not big, but muscular in a scrawny-arms-and-legs way.

I recognized the confident drill-sergeant stride. The contour of the ragged Tilley hat. Not vintage, just old.

Shit!

I snapped into action. Ammo out and into the duffel, guns into the closet. Liquor bottles, glasses, and dirty dishes under the sink. Yesterday's clothes and flip-flops heave-ho into the bedroom.

His knock was hard enough to rattle the screen in its jamb. One last look around, then I hurried to undo the inner door locks. Two, then the deadbolt.

He stood with hands on hips, looking left toward the marsh. His eyes were blue, his face weathered as the month of March.

"What's wrong?" Mouth dry. No one ever came uninvited. No one ever came.

"Something's gotta be wrong for me to drop by?" Gravelly. Gruff.

"Of course not." Plastic smile molding my face. "You usually give a heads-up."

"How? Send a pigeon?"

I said nothing.

"You gonna leave me out here till I need a transfusion?"

I lifted the hook and stepped back. Beau entered, gaze skimming. A cop gaze. One spin around the cottage, then it settled on me, running the same critique I resent in my neighbor.

The scar burned an itchy path below my right eye.

"I didn't recognize the boat." Concentrating on normal.

"Getting the gel coat repaired. But what? You were maybe expecting Bowie?"

"He died."

"Yeah?"

"Yeah."

"Gonna offer a man a beer?"

I got two Palmetto Ambers from the fridge and we moved to the living room, a small hexagon accessed through a wood-trimmed arch. Ceiling fan, sofa, two threadbare chairs, three beat-to-hell tables. No need for décor. Only Beau and one other were allowed in my home.

Beau dropped onto the sofa, sloughed off the hat, and took a long pull of his beer. His hair was gray and buzzed to the scalp. Had been since I'd known him. Probably since his mama first shaved it with clippers at a kitchen chair.

I sat opposite, knees jutting, feet under my bum. The five-window view wrapped us like an IMAX featuring the Atlantic seaboard.

A picture formed in my head. Beau with a younger man's face. Hiding his frustration, his pride. Not pleading, but close. Asking a fellow cop to give his foster kid yet another break. Red-blue pulsing his badge and the honky-tonk shack at his back.

Beau raised his right ankle to his left knee. Cleared his throat. Levered the foot up and down several times.

"Had an interesting call today." Eyes on a Top-Sider as old as the hat. "Lady name of Opaline Drucker."

That triggered a ping in some remote brain chip.

"Who is she?"

"I'll leave the telling of that for after."

"After what?"

"Hearing me out." Tone a million miles from drop-by casual. "Mrs. Drucker has a problem. I think you can help her."

"Why would I want to do that?"

Beau took another swig, then set the bottle on the floor. Uncrossing his legs, he leaned forward and looked me full in the eye. "You're in a bad place, Sunnie."

"I'm happy as a clam out here." Arms uplifted to emphasize the level of my joy.

"We both know that's not what I mean."

"What *do* you mean?"

"Look, I get it. You overreacted, you killed the bastard."

"PSO ruled it a justified shoot." Curt. The incident was the final straw for the Professional Standards Office, Charleston PD's version of internal affairs. The end of my career in law enforcement. And ancient history.

"Damn straight it was." Beau flicked dirt from jeans too faded to qualify as blue. Maybe a bug. "The scumbag nearly took out your eye."

"No way I'd ride a desk." Cheeks burning.

"Hell no. I'd have quit, too."

"You here to remind me what a loser I am? First the Corps, then the job? News flash. I already know." Meaner than I intended. Or not.

"Knock it off."

"Get to the point."

"It's been six years."

"Ah. You've come to enforce some kind of self-pity statute." Arm-wrapping my chest and tucking my hands into my pits. "Oh, wait. You're off the force, too."

Beau breathed deeply. Exhaled through his nose. Chose his words.

"You can't hide on this island, talking to no one, doing God knows what to yourself."

"Yes. I can."

"You've withdrawn from the whole goddamned human race."

"I have a bestie that lives in my bedside table. Want to meet him?"

"See. There you go. The least little pressure and out come the jokes."

"I have you."

"I'm about *all* you have."

"And you think I'm nuts." God knows I did.

"Of course you're not nuts." Frustrated, trying for patient. "But you can't just sit out here doing nothing."

"I run, I shoot, I fish, I read." Gut rolled tight as an armadillo under threat.

"It's not normal."

"I've tried normal. Too many rules. Too much constraint." Too much rage? I'm a big girl. I can own it now.

"Why are you so goddamned stubborn?"

"It's a gift."

I detest explaining myself. To Beau. To the therapists with their gentle eyes and nonprobing questions that probe. To anyone. I changed the subject.

"What's this got to do with Orphaline Drucker?"

"Opaline. I think helping her could benefit you."

"Wow. I'm your new project."

Beau ignored that. "Drucker's granddaughter's been missing for over a year."

"Kids run off. They're famous for it." I knocked back some beer.

"She was only fifteen." A beat, then, "Opaline thinks she's been grabbed by a cult."

Unbidden, another cerebral barrage. I sent the images to the place where I keep them all buried.

A full minute. Then I said, "Let me get this straight. I'm to be this kid's savior because I need saving?"

"Something like that."

Beau's eyes were now blue-laser-focused on mine. I stared back, every neuron in my brain ordering retreat.

Still, I bit. "Where's she being held?"

"No one knows."

Silence on our side of the window screens. On the other, animated gull conversation about crabs or fish. Maybe trash.

"I don't know shit about finding MPs," I said.

"You were SERE." Beau used the military acronym for Survival, Evasion, Resistance, and Escape.

"That's different." It was. But I got his point.

"And how was it you were chosen to teach those courses?"

"Lottery?"

"Right. And the other intel 'duties' we don't talk about?" Air-hooking quotes around the purposely vague noun.

I took another swallow.

The curtains lifted on a breeze smelling of salt and pluff mud.

The room crept a few nanometers from orange toward amber.

Other memories bubbled up. Uneaten bologna sandwiches, blown-off guitar lessons, a lipstick-ravaged wall, once painted pink to please a teenage girl.

Beau tried hard the three short years that he had me. Never got a thank-you from his surly, copper-haired ward.

"Talk about the kid." I broke the silence.

"Better you get the facts direct from Opaline."

"A face-to-face meet?" Blood pulsing in the little shallow beside my collarbone.

"You can use my car."

Taking my silence as consent, Beau pushed to his feet and handed me a blue-lined page ripped from a spiral notebook. Eyes pointed elsewhere, I flipped it onto the table beside me.

When Beau was gone, I tossed the paper into the wastebasket by my bathroom sink. An icy shower, then I armed the security system, checked for creatures outside my windows, and hit the rack.

Sleep was evasive, which is normal for me. But this was different. I've spent so long trying not to think about the past, about those two nights, that my insomniac mind tends to focus on the present. Buy butter. Clean the guns. Change the porch bulb.

That night I was visited by a million ghosts.

Experts say it's healing to contemplate loss. To talk about it. Bullshit. Revisiting the past makes me nauseous and costs me rest.

After hours of futile twisting in sweat-damp sheets, I got up, padded to the bathroom, and dug Beau's paper from among the jumble of tissues, Q-tips, and wadded-up hair. A glance at the scrawled address, then I crumpled and returned the page to the discards of my daily toilette.

The living room was dancing with shadows and still as a tomb. I settled on the couch and lowered my lids. Like five black eyes, the hexagon windows watched me force my mind blank.

CHAPTER 2

Opaline Drucker's home occupied one side of a small spur shooting east from Legare Street. The stolid two-story brick Georgian faced off across the cobbles with the only other occupant of Poesie Court, another stolid two-story brick Georgian. Both addresses were South of Broad, a location befitting Opaline's social status. Which I'd discovered via a quick Internet search.

Neither house gave a rat's ass about curb appeal. Two windows up, two down, each with shutters to the sides and a flower box below. Both ran narrow and deep, away from the street, and both had double-decker terraces spanning one side. Though mirror-image walls hid what lay behind, I knew each upper terrace overlooked a garden.

I parked and got out of Beau's Audi. At the *thunk* of the door, a squirrel hotfooted up the trunk of a magnolia. A tail-twitching pause, then it shot to the ground, cut right, and disappeared into a bed of peonies the size of Rhode Island.

The day was humid and far too warm for April. The air smelled of sun on moss-covered earth and stone. Of grass cut by workers speaking languages other than English.

Somewhere out of sight, a sprinkler spit out a rhythmic *tic-tic-tic*. A church bell rang. No other sound broke the stillness. Poesie Court dozed as though traffic and tourists hadn't yet been invented.

But it went beyond quiet. The little enclave felt like a time warp. Like a place whose inhabitants had for centuries shunned the scrutiny of strangers.

A quick scan of number five, then I headed up the flagstones toward number seven. I could picture the grande dame's interior, all wainscoting and cornices and carved balustrades. Not my style. But what the hell. I never hold a good balustrade against anyone.

A thumb to the bell triggered a trill worthy of a Vatican chapel. I wondered about the nature of the minion who would answer the door.

The woman who greeted me was black and probably in her sixties. She wore a short-sleeved gray dress with white collar and apron, all starched stiffer than a British upper lip. I gave her my name. She listened, expressionless, eyes never meeting mine.

"Mrs. Drucker is expecting you. Please follow me."

I did. Across gleaming marble, beneath a convoluted crystal chandelier, past an elaborately designed staircase swirling with great drama toward a second story. Beyond the foyer, we continued down a wood-paneled hall to a set of glass doors at the back of the house.

"Please wait here." The maid disappeared to announce my presence.

I looked around. More polished marble underfoot. More twisting crystal overhead. Through a partially open door to my right I could see a sliver of grand piano, above it the top half of an oil portrait, a man posing with one hand on his chest. Not a smiley guy.

I checked my image in a full-length mirror to my left. Jeans slim enough to fit my ass with legs long enough to reach my feet. With my height and lack of poundage, finding pants that fit takes serious searching. Not that I care much. White blouse roomy enough to hide the bulge at the small of my back. Hair doing unruly.

I was adjusting my ponytail clip when the maid returned and held the door wide with one fleshy arm. I followed her through to the outside.

A woman sat on a dark wicker sofa at the far end of the terrace, hair a wavery white beacon in shadows cast by flora hanging above her and potted palms flanking her sides. Despite the sticky weather, a patchwork quilt covered the woman's lap and legs. A small dog, maybe a Pomeranian, slept curled on the quilt. The woman was stroking its back.

The maid crossed to the woman and said, "She here, ma'am."

The woman showed no indication of having heard. The maid gestured me forward and spoke more loudly. "Mrs. Drucker?"

"There is no need to shout." Without raising her eyes from the dog.

"Yes, ma'am. Ms. Night—"

"I heard you, Miranda. Lord in heaven, I think my dear dead mama heard you." The vowels were broad, the voice cool as honey on ice.

"Yes, ma'am. Will y'all be needing something?"

"Have you asked our guest what refreshment she wishes?"

Miranda reoriented one shoulder toward me.

"Water, please," I said.

Drucker flapped a blue-veined hand, as though swatting a fly. "Bring sweet tea."

Miranda withdrew, eyes still on her shoes.

"Sit." The hand indicated a chair, then resumed stroking the Pomeranian. Which, like the maid, didn't grace me with a glance.

I sat. Seconds passed. A full minute. The dog was a snorer.

"Mrs. Drucker?"

Nothing but stroking and snoring.

"You contacted Beau Beaumonde about a problem you have."

A tiny breeze toyed with the overhead baskets, tickling the petunia tendrils curling over their rims. I waited what seemed a very long time.

Silence.

"Mrs. Drucker?"

More silence.

I didn't need this. I stood.

Drucker dragged her gaze from the dog to look up at me. I braced for the predictable. Some were shocked by the scar. Some repulsed. Most, uncomfortable, pretended it wasn't there. A few stared, kids mostly.

Drucker's face remained placid. It was what I expected, the flesh pooling below the orbits and sagging along the jawline, the wrinkles far too gentle to fit with the rings on her neck. A plastic surgeon had clearly been working the scene.

It was Drucker's eyes that startled—red-rimmed near the ducts and lids, with irises so faintly tinted they appeared almost transparent. But it wasn't the absence of color that chilled me. It was the absence of reaction. Or emotion. Or something I couldn't identify then. Something I would later come to understand.

"I know who you are," she said.

Finding the statement odd, I waited.

"Making contact does require diligence. No email. No phone. Really, sweetheart. It is the age of instant communication."

"You managed."

"I am a woman not easily deterred."

"Congratulations."

"Please sit."

I did. Immediately regretted it.

"Sunday Night. Such an odd name."

I felt a prick of annoyance. Not because the comment was untrue. Because I'd heard it so often. I said nothing. The dog slept.

The rheumy eyes looked me over. "I don't understand your appearance. No makeup, black nails. Is that what's meant by Goth?"

"OPI Black Onyx." Knowing that wasn't her question.

"You're very tall, young lady. Bless your heart, in today's world you *are* considered young. In my day, an unmarried woman of your age was called a spinster."

"You wished to discuss a problem?"

"I know its origin. Your name, that is. It must have been difficult growing up in such circumstances. No forenames or surnames? Born on a Sunday so that's what you're called?" Drucker sniffed in disdain. "Truly inexplicable."

The annoyance edged up. I drew the prescribed breath. Let it out slowly. Drucker rolled on.

"So very sad. I fear it is the children who suffer most."

The gnarled hand continued caressing. The dog continued snoring. I continued saying nothing.

"How unbearable to have everyone you know die all in one swoop. To be left alone at a most delicate point in your life."

"This is clearly a mistake." I reached for my purse.

"Please, Miss Night. Spare me the drama. Given sufficient resources, anyone's past is knowable."

"Then use those resources to find someone else." I started to rise. Which this time woke the dog. Drucker shushed it. The dog resettled, chin on its paws, sleepy eyes on me.

"Given your history, I believe you are most suitable for my purposes. But I've heard that you have a temper. That you are impetuous, impatient, and very poor at taking direction."

"Is that so?" It was.

"My dear Miss Night. I've known Perry Beaumonde a very long time. Beau." Drucker's forehead creased. It was the first I'd noticed her eyebrows, which were scraggly white and now tight with disapproval. "I don't like nicknames, but the world is what it is. Perry's a fine man, was a fine officer. It's not surprising he took you to raise."

"For high school."

"Which didn't go well. Dropout. GED diploma. Arrest at age eighteen, record expunged. Administrative discharge from the military. Although, frankly, I'm not certain what that means. And, of course, there is the matter of not killing yourself on command."

I stared, face a mask, heat prickling the back of my sternum. No way I'd do any favors for this bitch.

"How good are you at discretion?" Drucker asked.

"I'd give myself five stars out of five." Terse.

"At survival?"

"Ten out of five."

"If I hire you, will you see the job through to completion?"

"Hire me?"

"I wouldn't ask anyone to work without pay."

"I don't think I want to work for you."

"I'm offering one hundred forty thousand dollars plus expenses."

"What is it you want done?" Not querying the large and somewhat odd figure.

"Twenty thousand dollars up front."

"To do what?"

"The rest as the job is completed."

"I find it tiresome to have to repeat my question."

"Some people will do anything for that sum."

"I'm not one of them."

"You don't care about money?"

"Not much."

"Yes." Drucker nodded once, as though mentally correcting herself. "I've heard that, too."

Again, I fought the desire to get up and walk out. Wasn't sure why I stayed.

"Should you not wish to sully your hands, the money can go to a charity of your choosing." Thick with genteel sarcasm. "Anonymously, should your morals demand."

Behind me a door opened, then footsteps crossed the terrace. Miranda placed two glasses on a low table between us, withdrew. Neither Drucker nor I went for the tea.

Instead she reached for an envelope to her right. Displeased with the jostling, the dog hopped from her lap, padded a few feet, and curled up on the far end of the sofa.

Drucker held the envelope out to me. I leaned forward and took it. She circled one gnarled finger, indicating that I should examine the contents.

Inside was a single photograph. Good-looking woman, maybe

mid-forties, two kids, one of each gender. The boy was all sunshine blond, smiling, unashamed of a mouth full of metal. His turquoise eyes gazed confidently into the lens. The girl had copper hair and freckled skin, and carried more weight than she probably liked. Her chin was up, her arms crossed defiantly on her chest.

The boy wore a pink designer polo and tan chinos. Mother and daughter wore pink linen sundresses and gardenia blossoms behind their left ears. The three were standing on a boardwalk, a beach at their backs.

I looked at Drucker, brows lifted in question.

"My daughter, Mary Gray Bright, and her children, Stella and Bowen. The picture is several years old." Again the scornful sniff. "Taken long after her loser husband was finally gone. Alex. No loss."

"You must be very proud of your family."

"I was. Until a pack of vermin wiped them off the map." Like the window-glass eyes, Drucker's voice was devoid of emotion.

"Excuse me?" Shocked reflex.

"Mary Gray and Bowen were slaughtered in cold blood. God knows what they did with poor Stella."

"I am sorry for your loss." Lame. But all I could manage.

"I was able to hold a funeral at First Baptist. Closed casket, of course. Mary Gray had only half of her face. Bowen had no head at all. I bought them new outfits. Waste of money. No one could see."

"When did this happen?"

"One year ago last week. No arrests were ever made."

"The task you want done has to do with their deaths?"

"I want those responsible found."

"I'm not a PI."

"You were a cop. In the military you did investigative work." Drucker handed me a second envelope. "You saw my grandson." Another finger. "Now look at him."

I lifted the flap. The envelope held six three-by-five color prints. I slid them out, winged the stack like a deck of cards. Included in each photo was an identifier. Slightly different from the format I knew, but familiar. I skimmed the data. The photos were part of a series taken by a Chicago PD crime scene unit.

Knowing the images would be grim, I braced myself. Tipped my head to accommodate my good eye. Looked at the first shot.

Grim. But dear God.

I drew a breath to fight slippage from the vault in my brain. Not quick enough. A montage detonated, headlight bright, cruel. A white disk moon. Blackened bodies arranged like radiating spokes. Talons of red on clapboard siding.

I swallowed against the curdling in my belly. Clamped my teeth. Continued my walk through the photos.

The images captured the remains of the horror that had taken Drucker's family. A headless torso, the child shoulders a starburst of shredded flesh. A severed foot, sneaker still laced tight. A small, pale hand beside a boulder spray-painted with names. A woman faceup on grass, one eye wide and fixed, the other a raw crater, foamy red spittle flowing upward from what had once been her mouth. Tissue blasted onto a stone façade, dark and white and shiny and red.

I stared at the carnage. At the graffiti-covered rock. Something was wrong. What?

I glanced at Drucker. She was watching me, eyes silent crystals of ice.

"What did you mean about Stella?"

"She vanished in the melee."

"You think she's being held by those who did this?" A little memory bell was pinging. A bombing. A missing kid. Out on the island, I don't follow news. But I'd caught snippets during supply trips to town.

"I do."

"Her body wasn't recovered at the scene?" Nervous, a dumb question.

"Would I be asking you to search for Stella if I had her remains?"

"Tell me about her," I said.

"Ah, dear Stella. Always the sarcasm, the wisecrack, the witty retort."

"A happy kid?"

"Far from it. Resentful, rebellious. I believe my granddaughter was deeply troubled. That there was a darkness inside her she worked hard to keep hidden. I'm not putting this well. Do you gather my meaning?"

Drucker's description had cut right to my soul. I nodded.

"You've heard the saying 'sad clown'? Well, that was my Stella."

Sad clown. Mad clown. Bluster and sarcasm to hide the fear.

The bright ginger hair.

The pull to this kid felt visceral.

Placing the images facedown, I pushed myself up from the table and crossed the terrace. Back to Drucker, I spread my fingers and leaned into the house. The brick felt warm on my palms. It was red-brown and chipped, the mortar mushroom and flecked with black.

My vision blurred. I blinked it clear and returned to my chair.

"Do you know the names of the people who did this?"

"I do not."

"Do you know why your family was targeted?"

"I'm not certain they were. Others died in the incident. My poor lambs may have been collateral damage. Such an inadequate term for human death, don't you agree?"

"Please explain."

"These butchers had their agenda. They cared not a toot for the people I loved."

"Surely there was an investigation."

She nodded, tight. "The police thought the bombers were terrorists targeting Jews."

"Are you Jewish?" First Baptist?

"Good lord, no. The attack happened at some sort of Hebrew school."

"What else do you know?"

"I know there were four of them, three men and a woman. Surveillance footage survived. The faces are unclear, but enhancements were done."

Drucker handed me a third envelope, this one brown and larger than the ones lying on the table between us. In it was another series of prints, each a blowup of a frame taken at some distance from the subject. I flipped through them.

The images were grainy, the features barely recognizable. The four were in a vehicle, the woman riding shotgun. She was caught turning to her left, hair winging, mouth a dark circle in her face. One arm was outstretched. Reaching toward the driver? The others were looking straight ahead.

I returned the photos to their envelope, lifted the other two from the table, and started to hand all three back. Drucker stopped me with a raised palm.

"You keep them. They are not the originals."

"You want me to find Stella. You think finding the bombers will lead me to her."

Again the quick nod. "I'll pay twenty-five thousand a head, an additional forty thousand to learn the fate of my granddaughter."

"I'm to do what if I locate these people?"

"Such evil doesn't deserve to suck air from the planet."

"I won't execute them."

"You've never taken a life, Ms. Night?"

"Bunnies and kittens. But I eat what I kill."

"Yes. I've heard you find yourself droll." The folds under Drucker's eyes twitched twice. "Your choice. Either way you get paid."

"After so much time, there may be insufficient evidence to prosecute."

"I know that. I want them caught. I would do this myself, but I am too old."

"Your granddaughter may be dead."

"I know that, too." The scraggly brows dipped low over the crystalline eyes. Drucker studied me from below them, perhaps undecided. Then, "Two days ago an attempt was made to access funds at the Bank of South Carolina, a small account I established to teach Stella responsible finance. Besides myself and my accountant, the only persons with knowledge of the money were Mary Gray and Stella."

"A withdrawal was made?"

"Do I look like a fool? Following the bombing, all log-in information was changed."

"But you left the account in place."

"Frankly, I forgot all about it. Until notified of the recent activity."

"Did you tell the police?"

"The police did nothing but waste my time."

"You think Stella tried to access the money?"

"I think it's a possibility."

"The bombing took place in Chicago?"

"Yes."

"Is that where you'd like me to start?"

"Really, Miss Night. Would Shanghai seem more logical?"

I slid free the family photo and studied the faces. Stella looked awkward, angry. Myself at her age. A fellow member of the tiny human tribe with fiery hair.

Was she alive? Being held captive?

I picked out the crime scene photo that had troubled me. Studied it a very long time.

Drucker must have seen something in my eyes, read it her way.

"Do we have a deal, Miss Night?"

I'd considered PI work after leaving the force. Private security. Running skip traces and spying on cheating spouses held no appeal. Ditto babysitting millionaire tycoons and their cronies.

But Beau was right. I had the skills. I could find these bastards. If they had Stella, I could bring her home.

Did I want to do it? Mixed feelings.

I had no desire to leave my solitude and rejoin the world. Still, I could nail those responsible. Maybe free a kid who was living in hell.

Decision. I didn't like Drucker. But I'd do it for her daughter and grandson. For Stella.

For the thrill of the hunt? Hell no.

The buzzing adrenaline told me otherwise.

"I'll need expense money up front," I said.

"Have you something with which to make notes?"

I took a pen and small tablet from my purse.

"Peter Crage." Drucker provided a phone number and address. "Mr. Crage is my financial adviser. He will give you the twenty thousand plus whatever you require."

"For now, just expenses." Not wanting to be obligated.

"Go to him. Provide a figure. He will be expecting you."

"Talk about your granddaughter."

Heart pounding, I thumbed to a clean page.

CHAPTER
3

"Ms. Night, such a pleasure." The sapphire on Crage's finger must have weighed five pounds. "Mrs. Drucker advised me you'd be stopping by. Might I offer you something? Iced tea, perhaps?"

"No, thank you." I'd hit a Starbucks on the way. More caffeine and sugar and I'd be photo-bombing the Hubble.

"Please." Arcing the hefty sapphire toward a grouping of love seat, armchairs, and marble-topped coffee and end tables. "We'll be more comfortable by the window."

The love seat positioned me with my back to a wall. I chose it and placed my purse by my side. Crage sat opposite and crossed his legs. He was elderly, but trim and tanned. His double-breasted blazer was blue, his bow tie fuchsia, his trousers cream.

I could see Broad Street through the glass behind his head, some of Meeting. The sidewalks along each were filled with tourists moving in both directions.

"Perhaps a drink?" Crage winked, as though suggesting something terribly naughty. "The sun is nicely over the yardarm somewhere in the world."

"Why not," I said.

"Cognac?"

"*Bien sur.*"

Crage crossed to a wet bar and poured from a decanter that looked like a chem lab beaker. Except for the gold stopper.

"Frapin Cuvee 1888." Handing me a crystal snifter. "It's French."

"Beats my usual Copper and Kings. It's American."

Unexpected humor wasn't Crage's strong suit. "Would you prefer something else?"

"Not a chance."

I raised my glass in salute, then took a mouthful. Smoke and flowers exploded on my tongue.

"Yours is such a lovely name, Ms. Night. May I call you Sunnie?" Vowels thicker than caramel on a Granny Smith.

"Ms. Night works for me."

"As you wish."

"You know why I'm here."

"Please." Crage spread his hands. "From your perspective."

"Opaline Drucker wants me to find the people who killed her daughter and grandson. And to determine what happened to her granddaughter. She says online access was recently attempted for a bank account known only to Stella and her mother."

"And to me."

"Mrs. Drucker believes that attempt might have been made by Stella herself."

"Or by error, by hackers, by delinquents phishing from Beijing."

I couldn't disagree. "Our arrangement includes payment of a fee and expenses."

"You will be going to Chicago."

"For starters."

"How much do you need?"

I quoted a figure.

"Would you prefer that in cash or wire transfer?"

"I'll take five thousand in cash now. Direct deposit will work for the rest. Later." I handed him a paper with the account number and routing information.

Crage's lips and brows displayed something I couldn't interpret, then he placed the paper on the table. "If you require additional monies, simply let me know."

We each took a hit of cognac. The stuff could have made Bonaparte wet his breeches.

"Tell me about Opaline Drucker." I set down my glass.

"Are you a newcomer to Charleston?"

"Not exactly."

"How long have you lived here?"

"All my life." All that I'll talk about.

"You've not heard of the Drucker family? Drucker Park? Drucker Boulevard? Drucker Pavilion?"

"I've Googled the name. I want to know about the lady."

"Opaline's assets are such that she will never want for anything. The money is inherited, of course. Mostly from land, some from phosphate mining and other interests."

"I'm not concerned she'll stiff me on the bill."

Crage missed the sarcasm. Or chose to ignore it. "Far from it. I've managed Opaline's portfolio for years. She remains one of the richest women in South Carolina." Sincerely grieved shake of the head. "Her entire fortune would have gone to Mary Gray and the children."

More about wealth. I wanted to know about character.

"But what is Opaline like?" I pressed.

Crage swirled his cognac. His nails were manicured, his cuticles trimmed with the same surgical precision as his hair. When he answered, his words were carefully chosen. Breeding? Professional ethics? Or something else?

"Opaline is the last living member of an old Charleston family. She is eighty-two and was brought up in a different time."

"Meaning?"

"She is a very strong-willed woman. And smart as a whippet. But ladies of her station were not educated as girls are today. Opaline was sent to finishing schools in Europe. She learned to embroider, play piano, speak Italian and French."

Outside the window framing Crage's head, an enterprising pigeon was grazing the sill. Below, on Meeting Street, a horse-drawn carriage was blocking a Budweiser delivery truck. A line of stalled traffic was building. Through the glass I could hear muted honking.

"That being said," Crage continued, "Opaline has outlived two husbands. And the terrible tragedy that brings us together."

Crage drew a breath as though to go on, let it out without speaking.

"What aren't you saying?"

"Don't let appearances fool you, Ms. Night. Opaline Drucker is cunning, resourceful, and tough as nails. When she wants something, there is no stopping her."

"Is that 'something' revenge?"

"I am not a psychologist. I cannot evaluate Opaline's motives."

"Say I find the people who killed her family. Say there's no way to bring charges. What would she do?"

"I cannot answer that."

"Besides wiring money, what can you do?"

"I can put you in touch with Opaline's people in Chicago."

"She has people in Chicago?"

"Her financial interests are complex."

"I thought you handled all her affairs."

"Opaline is not what I would label a hands-off client."

Not certain the meaning of his response. "You implied she's not worldly."

"I meant she is not formally schooled in areas such as law and economics. She is, however, self-educated. On many topics."

"Assassination?"

"I beg your pardon?" Affronted.

"A link to your colleague in Chicago would be helpful."

Crage pulled an iPhone from his pocket and scrolled through his contacts. "Layton Furr." He read off a phone number and address. I wrote them in my tablet.

"While I'm at it, may I have your information?" Crage raised his thumbs, ready to input data.

"No," I said.

Looking startled and less than pleased, Crage pocketed his phone.

"Have Furr book a hotel for me," I said. "I'll go early tomorrow."

"We favor the Ritz."

"That should do." We?

"Do you mind terribly flying commercial?"

"Hardship builds character."

"Shall I have my secretary arrange for a flight?"

"Yes, thanks."

"Have you a preference concerning seating?"

"Indoor."

A slight dip of the brows, then Crage walked to his desk, dialed an extension, and relayed the info. "Mr. Furr will meet you at O'Hare." When he'd returned to his chair, placed the handset on the table, and recrossed his legs: "He can provide background on the whole ugly affair."

"I'll need to meet with the cops who worked the case."

"Mr. Furr will arrange an introduction."

"And visit the school where the attack took place."

"Of course. He'll be happy to organize anything you might require during your stay."

"Maybe some of that deep-dish pizza."

"Pardon?"

"It's mentioned in all the travel magazines."

The phone rang. Crage answered, listened, pressed the handset to his chest.

"United has a mid-morning flight. It's a regional jet, I'm afraid, so there is no first class." Looking truly pained at the thought.

"I'll manage," I said.

"That will be fine, Mary." Crage disconnected.

"Tell me what you know about Stella," I said.

Crage looked at me for so long I thought perhaps he hadn't heard. I was about to repeat my request when he finally spoke.

"What I am going to say does not leave this office."

"Mr. Crage, I—"

"I will make reference to nothing illegal."

I didn't reply.

"Four bodies were found at the scene of the bombing. Fortunately, most of the students had already departed for the day. All were"—slight pause—"disfigured." Crage hesitated, considering whether to elaborate, left it at that. "The victims were identified by the medical examiner. Mary Gray, Bowen, and two members of the group with whom they were touring. Stella was not among the dead."

"Mrs. Drucker told me as much. Surely the police searched. The FBI."

"Extensively, and I believe quite competently. The problem was they had nothing to work with. Save for one woman who thought she might have seen a suspicious van, there were no eyewitnesses. No vehicle. No manifesto sent to the media. An MO that matched naught elsewhere. No clues whatsoever other than a poor-quality surveillance video shot from across the street. The group struck and vanished. In the chaos, Stella vanished, too."

I waited out another searching pause.

"What Opaline probably did not tell you is that she received a phone call at her home three weeks after the incident. A man claimed to have her granddaughter and demanded fifty thousand dollars. He threatened to kill Stella instantly and painfully should the authorities be contacted."

"Did Opaline ask for proof?"

"The man read a quote he claimed Stella had given to him. *Knowledge comes, but wisdom lingers.*"

"Alfred, Lord Tennyson." How the hell did I know that?

"Impressive, Ms. Night. The saying was one of Stella's favorites."

"Opaline paid the ransom," I guessed.

"Against my advice."

"And never saw her granddaughter."

"No."

"And the police have never been told."

"Opaline is a very proud woman. Proud and stubborn."

And rich and gullible. I didn't say it.

Crage glanced at his watch, a blue and gold Rolex Yacht-Master that reported the state of every wind and tide on the globe.

"My goodness me. How has it grown so late? You must have a million chores to complete before setting off."

With regret, I downed the remaining molecules of my cognac. Crage stood. I stood.

"Ms. Night, might I make a personal observation?"

I cocked a brow.

"I notice you are wearing a firearm."

"I'm not flying to Chicago just for the pizza."

"I understand. And I am not judging you. Quite the contrary. I find the presence of the gun strangely reassuring. I mention it only because I am certain the airlines have rules concerning that sort of thing. Perhaps the city of Chicago has laws pertaining to citizens carrying concealed weapons. Do you need help along those lines?"

"No, thank you."

"I assume you have the proper permit?"

"I'm good."

"Let's hope so." Crage's lips flicked a vanishing smile. "Should anything unfortunate occur, I further assume that the Drucker name will not be associated."

"Opaline and I chatted about discretion."

"It is essential."

"I never asked the dog's name."

"Yes."

Crage crossed to a framed landscape on the wall to the right of the door. Lots of trees, a pond, a couple of swans. After swinging the painting forward, he rotated a knob, then leaned in. A few seconds, then he closed the safe and repositioned the artwork. Returning to me, he held out a stack of bills. A thick one.

I took the money and placed it in my purse.

"Are you not nervous carrying so much cash?"

"I find the gun strangely reassuring."

"One more cautionary note. Opaline can be . . ." Again the hesitation. "How best to put it? Erratic."

"Meaning?"

"Tread carefully." Indicating the door. "Shall we?"

"Let's do."

I managed to maintain the bravado all the way to street level. Walking toward the parking deck, it dissolved.

CHAPTER 4

At one time the Windy City had some of the strictest gun laws on the books. Then came a smackdown from the U.S. Supreme Court. Now any fool can load up and stick a gun in her shorts.

Except for assault weapons. A restriction that was really going to cramp my style.

While on the job, my right cornea took the business end of a junkie's blade. Blinded by blood and Murray's Superior Pomade, I thought I felt the guy reach for a gun. He went to the morgue. I went to the ER.

Thirty percent visual loss and the finding that my collar was unarmed earned me the choice of a desk or early retirement. Not this chick. I said adios and turned in my badge. As a retired cop with a disability, thanks to the police protection bill I have the right to carry concealed anywhere in the country.

I knew that TSA regs allow unloaded handguns inside luggage if properly secured in hard-sided containers. I also knew that I'd have to declare a firearm at the counter, show my paperwork, maybe fill out a form. And check the bag. A practice I view as akin to Russian roulette.

Charleston isn't London or L.A. Still, evening rush hour can be a bitch. While slogging across town, talking myself calm, I made the decision to take my Glock 23. Small enough but big enough. If someone stole it from my suitcase, I'd be out only five hundred bucks.

Once across the Cooper River, the worst congestion was behind me. Or so it seemed. I suspect the Ravenel Bridge has a peculiar effect on the primitive parts of my brain. The high white swoop above the water always makes me mildly giddy. Or the height and soaring girders scare me shitless.

I made only two stops. At the Walmart I bought a prepaid smartphone and a thirty-day wireless Web-text-talk card. Paid cash, activated my new toy. At the Petco I snagged a three-pound bag of pumpkin seeds.

Twenty minutes later I was crossing the Intracoastal Waterway onto Sullivan's Island. A short distance, another bridge, not a pants-pisser, and I was on the Isle of Palms. The sun was dropping behind the Boathouse, turning Breach Inlet gold in a great wide triangle.

I scanned the road ahead, the shoulders to either side. A few cars at the restaurant, a scattering of pelicans and gulls on the dock. After checking the rearview mirror, I lowered my window. The mingled scents of marsh grass, salt water, and discarded shrimp casings filled my nose.

Almost home. Almost safe.

I continued on Palm Boulevard, passed the IOP Connector, two small commercial strips, eventually wound my way onto Morgan Creek Drive, then a little-used loop called Lower Waterway. Palmetto palms and live oaks skipped sinewy shadows across my windshield. Here and there, a house window glowed yellow in the deepening dusk.

Just before the end of the pavement, past all but one, I pulled into a gravel driveway beside a tilted mailbox labeled P. BEAU-MONDE. A quick three-sixty glance, then I parked and got out.

The air was still. I stood a moment, listening to the quiet.

April was too early, but soon tourists and out-of-town vacation-home owners would pack IOP. They'd slick up and hit the beaches, gorge on fried oysters and shrimp, buy plastic crap in the souvenir shops. None of that blighted Goat Island. There one heard nothing but night birds, palm fronds, and the occasional boat.

I *wheep-wheeped* the lock on Beau's Audi, then headed toward a one-story frame house with weathered gray siding and a single pair of windows looking onto the street. A carport. A shed whose longevity looked questionable and had for decades. But follow the oyster shell path around the corner and the view is kick-ass.

I looked toward the waterway. Saw two boats tied up, no one on the pier.

A three-step climb to the porch.

"Anyone home?" Calling through the screen.

A series of guttural grunts, then a bulldog waddle-charged into the room.

"Hey, Sherman." I opened the door.

Sherman hustled over, a tank meaning business. After sniffing my jeans, a process that shared at least a quart of saliva, he wagged the short stump that passed for his tail. I patted his head. He slumped onto one haunch and blew air through his nose.

"Yo!" I shouted.

Beau bellowed from somewhere out of sight. "Cool your jets. I'm coming."

"I'll be on the porch."

I patted my thigh. Sherman wheezed to his feet and joined me, pace saying the move outside was a bad idea. I sat on the swing and pushed back and forth with one foot. Was about to ask the dog about his day when Beau spoke through the screen door.

"You want a brew?"

"I do."

Footsteps retreated, returned, then the hinges *whirrped*. Beau stepped out and handed me an Amstel.

"Thanks," I said.

Beau dropped into a rocker, leaned back, and parked his feet on the railing. We both took a few moments to eyeball the water and the marsh. To down some beer. Yeah, we're predictable.

"Sherman tell you he don't like his new diet?"

"Not yet," I said.

"He will."

I watched a line of pelicans swoop high, then low to skim over the waves. Asked, "Is Opaline Drucker the piece of work I think she is?"

"She's a tough old cookie. All the Druckers are. Were," Beau corrected himself. "You met with her?"

"And her representative, a guy named Peter Crage."

"Douchebag, but a mannerly one."

"Crage's desk probably cost more than your house."

"He's well connected."

"Do you know him?"

"I know of him."

"And?" Taking another hit of the Amstel. Not as good as the mannerly douchebag's cognac, but close.

"Crage handles very few portfolios. Old clients, older money. He must sing a sweet tune, because folks tend to stick with him."

"Or sing no tune at all."

Beau tipped his head, acknowledging I had a point.

"Has he ever had complaints? Been investigated?"

"Beats me. I was planning to throw on brats. You hungry?"

"I can't stay that long."

"You need to slow down and smell the gardenias."

"I'm allergic."

"Since when?"

"Adult onset."

Beau snorted. Sherman rolled his eyes up without lifting his head.

"Spill," I said. "What do you know about this Drucker thing?"

"I can't believe you didn't connect the dots. The media slavered over the story for weeks."

"I don't have a TV. And the vics were named Bright, not Drucker. So what's the deal?"

A long pull of Amstel, then, "The Drucker money has roots. Opaline's the last of the line, wears a sash says she's riding on genes from a Confederate soldier."

"UDC?" I referred to the United Daughters of the Confederacy.

"Yep. When Mary Gray was sixteen, Opaline made her do the whole debutante thing. Balls and gowns weren't the kid's style. After her coming-out she got defiant, so Opaline shipped her off to Switzerland for her final two years of high school."

"Opaline made a comment that implied she disliked Mary Gray's husband."

"Can't fault her there. Alex Bright's a sleaze."

"I know you'll explain that."

"Bright ran some sort of real estate and mortgage scam. It was the feds busted him, not us. So I don't know all the details. He ended up doing time. Opaline did the happy dance when Mary Gray dumped his ass."

"Where was Bright when the bombing went down?"

"Scraping plates at Butner."

"The federal prison near Raleigh."

Beau nodded. "Bright was never a suspect, if that's where you're going. He went quietly after Mary Gray filed. Kids were just knee-high. He showed zero interest in 'em, before or after the divorce."

"Was Bright Jewish?"

"Didn't ask about that. But the Drucker family's WASP as Old Whitey."

"Who's Old Whitey?"

"Zach Taylor's horse."

"So how did they end up dead in a terrorist attack on Jews?"

"Mary Gray was what you might call a beatnik."

"You might. I was born after *Dobie Gillis* was canceled."

Beau turned to face me, faux offended. "How would you know about *Dobie Gillis*?"

"Read about it in a book on ancient history."

"You know what you are?"

"Young. Go on."

A few rounds on the rocker, then, "Mary Gray wasn't much older than you. In fact, all accounts, she was a lot like you."

"How so?"

"Impulsive. Hotheaded."

"I admire you, too."

"Seemed she was always looking."

"Looking for what?"

"Something beyond Charleston. At least beyond blue blood and sashes."

Beau took another sip and gazed out at the pelicans. The fliers had moved on, but a few bobbers were working the current. I made an impatient gesture. Pointless, but good practice to sharpen my skills.

"She'd converted to Baha'i," Beau continued. "Not sure that's the right term. Conversion, I mean."

"There's a Baha'i presence here?"

Now the look was one of faux indignation. "If you'd come in off your island you'd be more aware."

"Baha'i isn't Jewish." I knew little about the faith, except that.

"Mary Gray had the kids on some sort of multireligion experience. They were visiting churches, synagogues, temples, schools, cultural centers, that sort of thing. Wanting to expose them, you know."

I nodded.

"You'll have to check on this, but I think the tour was organized through a big Baha'i temple outside of Chicago. That day the group was visiting a Jewish girls' school on the north side of the city. The other vics were Jewish. Two women, both with the group."

"Stella was fifteen?"

"She was in high school, so that sounds about right."

"Drucker said she was awkward."

"Coming from Opaline, that could mean anything."

"Crage said Drucker was erratic."

"She's made some abrupt reversals that left a bad taste. Pulling out on charity events, business deals, firing folks, that sort of thing."

"What do you think happened to Stella?"

"Probably dead."

"What makes you say that?"

"An abandoned Subaru Forester was found the day after the attack. Matched the description of the SUV spotted at the scene. CSU found blood inside. DNA testing showed it belonged to Stella."

"Doesn't mean she's not alive."

"'Course it doesn't."

I debated the ethics of revealing a confidence. Decided the information was safe with Beau. "Did you know Opaline received a ransom demand a few weeks after the bombing?"

Beau's expression told me he didn't.

"Fifty thousand. She ponied up, but no Stella."

Beau gouged the label on his bottle with one yellowed thumbnail.

"What are you thinking?" I asked.

"Lowball."

"Agreed," I said. "Sounds amateur."

"The Chicago cops find out about the ransom?"

"Hell if I know. Are they still on the job?"

"Oh yeah. Bernie Clegg and Roy Capps. Guys in the squad there call them C-squared."

"Amateur operation, yet C-squared never found the kid or her body. Never nailed a single one of the doers?"

"Nope."

"Odd."

"That's why I rolled the shitball to you."

"You said it was to save me from myself."

"That too."

"I'm not a cop anymore."

"You did your time."

"About five minutes."

"I thought this child's plight might stir your juices."

Beau could always read me. Usually better than I read myself.

"Be easier if you had a phone," he said.

"I do now."

"You sleeping these days?"

"Sure. I slept last Wednesday."

"Still popping pills?"

Nope.

"Tomorrow I fly to Chicago."

"For how long?"

"I'm not sure."

"Anything I can cover?"

"Keep an eye on my boat."

"Always do."

"And check on Bob now and then."

Beau gave me a look that said he'd rather drink sewer sludge.

CHAPTER
5

I crumbled. Beau wanted company, and I owed him for the Drucker intel.

And lingering delayed going home to my ghosts.

He grilled on a Weber whose entry into the world had predated mine. We reconvened on the porch and ate the brats from plastic plates with coleslaw and beet salad purchased at the Harris Teeter. Using stealth, I violated the rules of Sherman's newly imposed nutritional regimen. The dog never left my side.

At full dark, Beau fired up his old Coleman lantern. Maybe testing the spiders nesting in my head. I willed them calm and stayed on the swing. Kept my eyes off the bright little flame. Conversation drifted from boats to booze to my choice of weapons for the upcoming trip.

We were on our third Amstel and a plate of Oreos when Beau queried my strategy for Chicago.

"First I'll meet with Capps and Clegg, get their take."

"I could request they get the file to you ASAP."

"That would be good. Then I'll talk to folks, make my interests known, hang around and see what breaks."

"Precision planning," Beau deadpanned.

"Yes."

"Could be tough churning leads on a case a full year cold."

"If nothing happens, I'll stir the pot."

"Using what kinda spoon?"

"You say the bombing and search for Stella were high-profile?"

"Until the next breaking news came along."

"I'll get online tonight, plant messages on social media to tweak some memories."

"What do you know about social media?"

"I live on an island. Not a gulag."

"Could put an ad in the paper for us dinosaurs don't tweet or twiddle or Facebook."

"Good idea." I thought a moment. "Opaline's got deep pockets. Maybe I'll offer a fat reward."

"You think a reward could get one of them to turn on the others?"

"For every participant in an assassination or bombing there's a support network of minimally three or four people." How often had I imparted that wisdom in my SERE courses? "Who knows how their group dynamics have changed. You know what Opaline said?"

"Do something with your hair?"

"She said some people will do anything for a big enough sum. Anyway, knowing there's a price on their heads might get one of them to try to make contact with me."

"Or try to kill you."

"That's contact."

"And you'll have the Glock."

"I will," I said.

"You think they're still in Chicago?"

"It only takes one. Perps like to burrow in where they feel safe." More SERE insight.

"I wouldn't hang around."

"You wouldn't blow up a school."

"Sounds dangerous."

"Yeah. I like that part."

"You joke, but I suspect that's true." Beau believes a death wish lurks in my subconscious.

"Sunday's excellent adventure." I drew a hand through the air as though highlighting a title.

"Am I gonna regret laying this thing in your lap?" Snappish.

"Jesus. I'm doing it for the kid."

Our eyes locked for a beat, then Beau looked away. We sat silent, Beau rocking, me swinging, Sherman nudging my leg.

"How 'bout I take you to the airport?" An olive branch for the lantern. For tweaking my crazies.

"I can grab a taxi," I said.

"That wasn't the question."

"Sure. A ride would be nice."

It was pitch-black and moonless when I headed down to the boat. Didn't matter. The trip was short and I knew the way by heart.

On Goat Island, I tied up, grabbed my packages, then checked the fishing line I keep stretched low across the end of my dock. Satisfied it was undisturbed, I headed to the house.

Once inside, I locked the locks and changed the alarm from "away" to "home." I'd barely turned on a lamp and popped a jazz CD into the player when I heard claws on glass. Crossing the kitchen, all of three steps, I disengaged the latch and slid the window sideways. A squirrel crouched on the ledge outside, eyes two shiny black beads focused on me.

"How's tricks?"

Bob twitched his tail but said nothing.

"Hungry?"

Bob sat up. Twitched again.

I reached out, pulled a metal bin across the sill and into the sink, filled it with the newly purchased pumpkin seeds, and returned it to the ledge. Bob scampered over and executed a Louganis into the chow.

"You're welcome," I said.

Bob's response was continued digging and cracking.

"I'll be in the bedroom." Removing the gun and holster from the small of my back. "We need to talk."

I slid the window, leaving a three-inch opening, then wedged a wooden dowel into the track. My improvised squirrel-friendly security system. Sunday Night, girl genius.

Packing took little time. Two pairs of jeans, tops, undies, socks. Two sets of toiletries. A backpack. The box for the Glock. A couple of .40 S&W thirteen-round magazines.

I paused. Reassessed. Got my Glock 17 and a spare cartridge from the gun safe, boxed, and threw them in. Better to have and not need than to need and not have. Anything else I would purchase in Chicago.

Propped in bed, I opened my MacBook Air and got online. Yeah, even on Goat. A laptop and Bluetooth-enabled phone and you're cybercooking.

I linked the burner to the computer and spent some time surfing the World Wide Web, looking for anything I could find on the murder of Mary Gray Drucker Bright and her son and the disappearance of her daughter.

For several weeks following the bombing, every TV, radio, and print outlet in America had been on fire providing minutiae and offering speculation. Then, with nothing new to report, the media moved on.

Stella's picture came up again and again. The copper hair. The petulant frown. The same frown I'd worn as a kid. With each image I felt I'd been kicked in the gut.

Irrational. But staring at those eyes, I heard a whispered call for help. Stella reaching out to me from some dark place.

After supplying an alias to create a temporary Gmail account, I considered the small rectangle requesting a username.

Diana Krall's purring vocals began conspiring with the brats and the beer. My brain grew thick, my lids heavy. I closed my eyes for a second. Just one second.

My thoughts drifted to a conversation long ago. Not a conversation, an interrogation.

Name?

Sunday.

Sunday what?

Just Sunday.

Come on, kid. You got a last name.

Pavement at my feet pulsing red and blue. Heart banging. Mosquitoes whining high and hungry in my ears.

You listening to me, girl?

Lyrics drifting from a radio far off.

"Hot August night, and the leaves hanging down . . ."

Give it up here, or give it up in jail.

Night. Sunday Night.

I snapped back. Ella Fitzgerald was urging someone to hurry home.

I entered *hurryhome* and added three digits from my Marine Corps service number. The email address hurryhome407@gmail .com was all mine.

Armed with what little information I'd gleaned, I found the *Chicago Tribune* website and placed an old-fashioned ad in the classified section. One column, three lines:

> **Info wanted re: bombing at Bnos Aliza School, Devon Ave., October 2014. Contact S. Night, Ritz-Carlton Hotel. hurryhome407@gmail.com $5,000 REWARD.**

In addition to five days in the paper, Opaline's sixty-two bucks got her three days in the Spanish-language *Hoy,* one Monday in the *RedEye,* and seven days online at classifieds.chicagotribune.com.

Finally, I opened a Twitter account. My first tweet was a two-part, 280-character version of the *Trib* ad, adding only that the attack had occurred in Chicago. That done, I repeated the process with every form of social media I knew.

Ninety minutes after starting, I logged off.

I was in the mudroom cleaning the Glock 23 when Bob scampered onto the table. I explained the upcoming trip. Said Beau would have his back while I was away. He didn't look pleased, but he didn't object.

"You staying the night?" I asked.

Bob dropped to the floor and shot down the hall.

I slid the kitchen window tight and locked it. In the bedroom, cracked another and engaged an identical dowel.

Cold shower. Bed.

As I tossed and turned in the dark, the spiders crept from their silken tunnels, all hairy legs and surplus eyes. Dragging questions, some old, some new.

Was Beau right about my drive toward self-destruction? Did that explain the lure of the military? The job? The cold hard steel of a gun?

Was the search for Stella Bright about some twisted need in me? If so, why the gut clench every time I thought of this kid?

Why *had* I withdrawn to Goat Island? Was I slowly creeping toward a replay of Henry and Blanche? In a few years would boaters skim the shoreline hoping for a glimpse of the deranged old lady who talked to squirrels?

Was I already mad? Would I end up like Arthur, hanging from a rope with gull shit on my head?

If I felt for Stella, might I start feeling for others? For everything?

Across the water, the bright spot of Beau's Coleman burned in the night.

Two Weeks

She's locked in the cellar again. The room is small and window-less, with a heavy wood door that feels rough to the touch. She won't make the mistake of pounding or scratching. The slivers will hurt. And no one will come.

She reaches out, knowing the brick will be cold. It is.

She shivers. Draws her heels beneath her. Pain flames across her raw knees.

She's done something to make them unhappy. She's unsure what.

She closes her eyes to the darkness and tries to think. She's exhausted. They were up all night. First the Testing. Then sitting stiffly on the old wooden chairs, spines straight, attentive.

She listened, knowing their goal was righteous. Her reason for being put on the earth.

Her tailbone aches. Her back. She pictures the scars, some red, some waxy white, all in a sea of pale freckled skin. She viewed them once by angling a mirror. Never again.

What did she do to anger them?

That's it. She grew restless and allowed her mind to drift. Something she heard couldn't be right. Her question seemed valid to her.

An older woman also raised her hand.

Interruptions are allowed. But hers upset them.

Her exile will be temporary. If they feed her, she'll use meals to measure the time. Two per day. It's what she always does.

She understands the punishment is her fault. That they love and value her. She vows to be better. Stronger.

She wishes she could see the sky. Imagines it blue with clouds like tendrils of gauzy white cotton.

She pictures the field. She's permitted to go there if she's good. Never alone, but she doesn't mind.

The crocuses are poking up through the soil. The redbuds have blossoms that look like crumpled little faces. She's allowed to read the book about plants that she found in the attic. She wishes she had it. A flashlight.

Stillness.

She smells mildew and dampness.

She wants to feel sunshine on her face. To run. Skip. Do cartwheels and handsprings.

Stillness.

The chill and the darkness seem to thicken around her.

She opens her eyes. Closes them again.

She trembles. Draws her legs tighter.

Stillness.

She dozes. Wakes. Thinks about birds. She likes birds, too.

Stillness.

Hinges rasp. Rusty. Unwilling.

Heavy footsteps clump down stairs.

Her heart starts beating way too fast.

CHAPTER
6

Beau wasn't chatty on the way to the airport. Fine with me. I had a lot on my mind.

He departed with one directive. "Keep me looped in."

"Copy that," I said. "Don't forget Bob."

"I don't like squirrels."

"He likes you."

"Why do you call him Bob?"

"It's what he responds to."

Charleston International Airport. I like the name. Tells you what the place is. Not who some dead guy was. CHS is user-friendly and rarely busy. I like that, too.

Checking in was easy. I filled out the firearm declaration form. They took my bag, smiled, wished me a good flight. I passed through security and went to the gate.

Dropping into a seat by a window overlooking a runway, I pulled out my book, *Anna Karenina*. Self-improvement 101. Part of my attempt to make up for all the reading I'd been denied, then later dodged, in my youth. But I found it hard to concentrate. Kept seeing the sun-kissed family in Drucker's snapshot. Two murdered, one missing.

Aviation miracle. We landed on time.

I'd just lifted my bag from the belt when I noticed a man cutting toward me through the crowd. He was a burly bear of a guy with neatly trimmed brown hair and an uneven gait. I guessed bad knees from his football or soccer days.

"Welcome to Chicago, Ms. Night," the bear man said. "I'm Layton Furr."

We shook hands. Furr's suit was a deep shade of expensive, hand-tailored to disguise the extra bulk on his frame. His tie was red, his shirt so white I almost shielded my eyes.

"Grab your bag?" Furr was tall enough to regard me nose to nose.

"I can handle it," I said.

"Good stuff." Sounding like a high school coach. "This way." Furr began to steer me with one hand on my elbow. I stepped away, out of reach. He looked surprised, then gestured toward an exit. I followed, untethered.

Outside the terminal, Furr made a call on his mobile. In seconds a black town car rolled to the curb. The trunk opened, then a dark man in a dark suit got out from behind the wheel, came around to us, and reached for my bag. I relinquished it. Furr and I got into the backseat and we started off. A brown paper bag sat in the space between us, top rolled and taped.

Furr said to the driver, "The Ritz-Carlton, please." Turning to me, "Are you familiar with Chicago, Ms. Night?" Urbanite to yokel off the plantation.

"I saw *Scarface*."

"Good one." Finger pistol point. "The Ritz is on the Magnificent Mile. That's what we call Michigan Avenue along that stretch."

"Sounds magnificent." Thinking about the last hotel I'd stayed in, a seedy dump in Kandahar that overlooked a garage and a construction site, both blocked by a window AC unable to keep the room below eighty degrees.

"My assistant booked you an executive suite. Extra bucks, extra view."

"Mrs. Drucker is very generous."

"Damn straight."

Furr leaned back and clasped his hands in his lap. His fingers were short and stumpy and seemed disproportionate to the rest of his body.

"Do you know why Mrs. Drucker is hosting me here?" I asked.

"I know some, not all." Cagey.

"Peter Crage said you could network me in locally."

"Yes."

"I want to meet with the lead investigators."

"Of course."

"Right away."

"I'll do my best."

"Will the cops be friendly to a civilian outsider?" Doubting such would be the case.

"I really can't say."

"Do you know them?"

"We've met." Furr indicated the grocery bag. "They've sent this for you."

My stomach chose that moment to protest the presence of only bad airline coffee.

"Feel free to use room service," Furr said.

"I've had nothing all morning but beer on the plane."

"Will you need anything else right now?"

"A place to buy ammo." To shock his fat ass.

Furr hooked a stubby finger onto a gold-linked cuff to check his watch. "What say we have dinner tonight, I try to set up a meet."

"Works for me."

The Ritz was located in a lofty glass and steel skyscraper named Water Tower Place. Furr asked the driver to wait, then accompanied me inside. I think he doubted my ability to survive outside the shire.

Check-in was on the twelfth floor. We rode the elevator in silence, Furr miffed that I wouldn't give him my bag. Which was on wheels and weighed maybe ten pounds.

The lobby was immense, with elaborate chandeliers and a fountain featuring giant sculpted cranes. Or maybe they were herons.

Furr waited as I went through the process of obtaining a room. When I had my key card in hand, "So, dinner tonight?"

"Sticking to the plan," I said.

Furr smiled tentatively, not sure how to read me. "How 'bout Lawry's?"

"Sounds good."

"It's in the old McCormick mansion, which is close. I'll swing by at, say, seven?" Running censorious eyes over my jeans, leather jacket, and boisterous hair.

"I'll get myself there," I said.

"Chicago is very large and very busy. Navigating can be confusing."

"I'll buy a map."

"Your call." Furr gave me the address and left.

My suite was on the twenty-fourth floor. The living room had furniture upholstered in artfully coordinated shades of mauve, a wet bar, a billion-inch flat-screen TV, and a desk. The windows overlooked Lake Michigan and Navy Pier.

The bedroom was as big as my house. In addition to a king bed it contained the usual bureaus, nightstands, chair, and another mongo TV. More magnificent views.

The bath and powder rooms involved a major investment in marble. The former had a Jacuzzi. No sauna in either. I'd talk to Furr about that.

I unpacked one set of clothes and toiletries and placed the other, along with the Glock 17, Furr's bag, my purse and laptop, in the backpack. Then I reassembled and loaded the Glock 23. Considered. Decided to leave that gun in the safe. Sliding into my jacket, I snatched the pack by its straps and headed for the elevator.

After exiting the Ritz, I walked west on Pearson, then south on Michigan. The sidewalks were thick with shoppers, dog walkers, businessmen, and tourists. I heard Old Blue Eyes singing about his kind of town. A few blocks, then I turned left onto Ohio. Beyond a combination espresso-gelato shop, I cut under a black canopy and entered the Inn of Chicago.

The lobby was done in cranberry and zebra skin, had a fireplace, and promised a rooftop bar. I paid cash for one night and checked into a room that would cost Opaline Drucker a hundred and fifty bucks. It was on the nineteenth floor.

The elevator was small, the corridor dimly lit. I wasn't sure if that was for conservation, ambience, or economy.

The room had a queen bed, nightstands with lamps, a TV, a small desk, and a lime-green chair. The extra floor space was enough to accommodate the backpack. The bathroom was clean and had soap, shampoo, TP, and a wall-mounted hair dryer. All the comforts.

I set Furr's bag on the desk, unpacked my clothes, and laid out my toiletries. Loaded the Glock 17 and locked it in the safe. That done, I dug out my laptop and a small device that looked like a shiny black mouse. Its open-source encryption technology would keep my online activities safe from prying eyes. Sitting cross-legged on the bed, I turned the thing on, then booted the Mac.

The hotel's Wi-Fi network made itself known. After agreeing to fork over six bucks a day, I watched the little fan pop up on the toolbar. Laptop connected, I repeated the process with my Walmart smartphone.

Next, I crossed to the closet and pulled a tiny motion detector from the pocket of my spare pair of jeans. A visual sweep of the room turned up few hiding places with unobstructed views of the door. Tucking the small cylinder beside a lamp, I made adjustments until I was satisfied with the positioning of its sensors. Then I opened an app on the phone. Time for a test run.

I stepped to the door. The phone buzzed in my hand. Hot damn. Paranoia had its upside.

Taking only my key, I walked to a lit exit sign at the far end of the hall and let myself through the heavy metal door. The stairwell was done in tasteful concrete. Checking my surroundings at each landing, I descended to the lobby. Satisfied, and winded, I returned to the room, sat at the desk, and opened the brown paper bag. My watch said 1:20.

Inside was an accordian folder with a flap cover. A name and number on the outside indicated it was the case file for the Bnos Aliza bombing investigation. Given the weight of the crime, I was surprised at the lightness of the folder. But grateful to Furr for getting it to me.

I unwound the little bungee tie, emptied the folder's contents onto the desk, and began sorting. There were scores of pages, all photocopies. Standard procedure. An original murder book never leaves the squad room. I thanked the hapless underling who'd been buttonholed to do the Xeroxing.

The lead detectives, Roy Capps and Bernie Clegg, were with the CPD Area Three violent crime section. But they'd worked with people from the Central Investigation Division, CID, including bomb and arson experts, and the FBI violent crime task force.

There were three packets of photos. One from the crime scene unit that had processed the scene. One from the medical examiner. The third, which was thin, I wasn't sure. I set all three aside.

Then I read everything. The scene report. The hundreds of summaries of witness interviews. The forms listing evidence and property recovered and analyzed. Capps's and Clegg's investigation notes, both on the bombing and on the search for Stella Bright. Capps's overview of the investigation. Someone named Penzer's comments on victimology. Speculation on potentially related investigations and suspects. A report on the Subaru Forester. A report on DNA found in the Forester. The match to Stella. The match to a close relative of Stella's. A report on dog hair, which was black and from an indeterminate breed.

Next, I turned to the ME reports. Sarah Ruth Gellman, age thirty-three. Judith Rachel Vance, age fifty-two. Mary Gray Drucker Bright, age forty-four. Bowen Andrew Bright, age twelve.

I was giving Bowen's report a second, more thorough read when one section caused a flashbulb image to fire in my brain.

Sudden insight, a lightning strike straight to my heart.

Wanting but dreading verification, I dug one CSU photo from the envelope in my purse. Found its match in the series I'd just been given. Laid them side by side.

The pictures showed identical stone façades coated with identical gore. Within the gore a detail logged in my subconscious.

I stared at the twin images, feeling sick. Feeling torture at my inability to change what had happened.

A fuzzy silhouette was visible amid the splatter of blood and human tissue, a cutout where the façade remained unblemished. A void created by someone to the right of the boulder. Someone upright and close to the wall.

I squeezed my eyes shut, knowing with certainty that the person standing by the school had been Stella. Knowing she'd witnessed the brutal slaughter of her brother. Knowing parts of Bowen's mutilated body had blasted backward into her terrified face.

Molten rage fired from neuron to neuron. I took a breath. Another. Opened my eyes. Recommitted to my resolve to find this kid. If she was alive. She had to be alive.

I continued with the file, every now and then stopping to gaze out the window. The sky remained overcast, the lake imperturbably gray. The surrounding skyscrapers never moved.

Now and then I dropped my chin to my chest and lowered my lids. Willed Stella to talk to me. Nothing.

At three, I turned to the CSU photos I hadn't yet viewed.

There were thirty-six three-by-five color prints, all taken by a Chicago PD photographer. Some were close-ups, others were shot at varying distances and angles. I saw a three-story stone building with a gaping, snaggletoothed hole in one side. A bicycle rack twisted into a grotesque spiral. Blood pooled on concrete. Shredded clothing, torn books, an isolated shoe visible on a darkly stained lawn. Four bodies, at first exposed, later forming still mounds under blue plastic sheeting. A moment of horror frozen in time. The gore-streaked façade.

The thin packet contained the same enhanced stills I'd been

given by Opaline Drucker. Three men, one woman, faces blurred by distance, movement, and glass. The woman was reacting to something. Stella staggering into the street? Lying dead by the curb?

Again, I wondered what had startled the woman. What she'd turned to say. Looking at the four, knowing their deadly errand, my loathing felt like a living thing inside me.

I wanted to spring into action and find this kid. To snatch her from the hands of those who would warp her reality forever. I had to talk myself calm. To accept that going off half-cocked would do more harm than good. To both Stella and me.

My watch said 5:10.

I checked my email and the social media accounts on which I'd posted requests for information. Nothing.

I researched anti-Semitic incidents in the Chicago area. Found stories about graffiti on a garage and a synagogue, vandalism in a cemetery, cyberbullying at a high school.

I looked up Bernie Clegg and Roy Capps. Both had worked the high-profile murder of a politician's son in 2008. Capps had received some sort of award from the Kiwanis in 2012. Otherwise, I found nothing on either.

At six, I returned to the Ritz, where it took no time and no money to get online. I installed a second motion detector. A quick test. I was off.

CHAPTER 7

The pedestrian crowd was changing along the Magnificent Mile—more haggard office workers, fewer nannies—but still thick. I walked south to Ontario, turned right, and arrived at Lawry's.

The interior had high ceilings, bronze lions, old-masters-style paintings, a lot of gleaming wood trim. I spoke to the maître d', who eyed me with the same look of disapproval Furr had employed. I wondered if the two practiced together.

The maître d' handed me off to an underling, who led me to Furr. He was seated at a corner table on a nail-studded, high-backed leather chair. So was a guy in a jacket and pants not purchased at the same shop as Furr's suit.

Furr rose. Cheap Jacket did not.

"You found the place." A note of surprise.

"Asked a cop."

"I took the liberty of inviting Detective Capps. I hope that's okay?"

Capps had prickly hair the color of a dime. Under the bad jacket he appeared to be fit, maybe a bit light for his height. Which I esti-mated at five four, tops.

The underling pulled out my chair. I sat. Reached over and snuffed the candle with my thumb and finger. The men exchanged a glance. Without comment, the waiter took the offending artifact away.

Capps was swirling a crystal tumbler containing something amber on ice. He didn't offer a hand.

Furr resumed his seat and asked, "Care for a cocktail?"

As if by magic, a waitress appeared.

"Vodka martini, dirty, with extra olives," I said. "Tito's if you have it."

The waitress beamed. "My pleasure." I believed her.

Furr ordered a second Macallan. Capps drained and raised his glass. The waitress smiled again and hurried off.

"I could eat a horse." Furr opened his menu, a not-so-subtle hint to move things along.

The waitress returned with our drinks. Capps and I ordered the prime rib. Furr asked for a porterhouse and a bottle of Chateau Montelena 2008. The waitress seemed thrilled with our choices.

Furr spoke when she'd gone. "I've explained your undertaking to Detective Capps. He and his partner investigated the bombing that killed Mary Gray Bright and her son. They're experts in that sort of atrocity."

"We've worked our share of hate crimes." Capps's voice was nasal and higher than I expected.

"Is that what this was?" I asked.

"It had all the markings."

"A Hebrew girls' school?"

"Bnos Aliza. On Devon Avenue, in West Rogers Park. Mixed hood, but lots of Orthodox Jews living around there. You know, women with wigs, guys with the hats and curls. There was some controversy about a year before the bombing."

"What sort of controversy?"

"A Jewish community organization claimed they'd been threatened, so they hired off-duty cops to cruise the neighborhood. The Chicago PD wasn't thrilled."

"Did you talk to those who did the patrols? Check out the alleged threats?"

Capps's scowl was his answer. His eyes were dark and looked like they rarely smiled. Or missed a thing.

"How about the school's faculty and staff? Did you background every employee? The students? Their families?"

"Yes, Ms. Night." Indulgent. "Faculty, staff, students, families, neighbors, parents' employers and employees, rabbis, orthodontists, bus drivers, ballet teachers, the guy who sold the girls their little black tights."

"People missing from school that day?"

Another tolerant nod.

"I read the case file," I said. Added, "Thanks."

Before Capps could respond, the sommelier arrived. Glasses were distributed and the wine was decanted. Our food was served.

"What about the explosive device?" I asked when we were well into our entrées.

"Garden-variety pipe bomb," Capps said. "Dime a dozen. Rudolph planted one in Centennial Park during the Atlanta Olympics. Harris and Klebold had them at Columbine."

I thought a minute. "Why not go bigger, max out the damage?"

Capps shrugged "who knows," a tight, quick lift of one shoulder. Despite the Scotch and wine, the man had a sense of tension about him like a snake, coiled and alert.

"Any lead from the components?"

Capps shook his head. "The usual crap, all easily available for purchase. Hell, there are instructions online for building the damn things. YouTube videos."

"Any prints off the fragments?"

"No."

"Opaline Drucker gave me images taken from video captured at the time of the attack. Three men, one woman. Any luck with those?"

"The images were shit. No one knew shit."

"I want to view it."

No reply.

"Tell me about the Forester."

"Stolen from the Oakbrook shopping mall, abandoned at a student housing complex in DeKalb. The plate was switched with one taken from a vehicle at O'Hare."

"DeKalb. Isn't there a university?"

"Northern Illinois. And yes, we looked at the possibility of a student or campus link."

"Any E-ZPass use? Tollbooth sightings, that sort of thing?"

"No."

"And the only physical evidence recovered from the Forester was blood, some showing a DNA match to Stella?"

"And some dog hair." Nothing in Capps's tone. "One smear wasn't consistent with Stella. Sequencing suggested that blood came from a close relative."

"Meaning what?"

"The kid was with her family and it was a bloodbath."

"You didn't find it odd that nothing else was in there?"

"They'd obviously cleaned house. The stuff was recovered from deep down below the seats."

I pictured Stella bleeding on the floor of a van driven by strangers, terrified or unconscious. My mouth went dry. My appetite went south.

"How large is the group?" I asked.

"We were never certain it was a group."

"What do you mean?"

"We ran the MO through ViCAP." Capps referred to the FBI's Violent Criminal Apprehension Program. "Looked at other bombings, other signatures, found no homegrown or foreign groups or incidents that fit our profile."

"And no one claimed responsibility."

"Nope. No outraged manifesto sent to the press, no jailhouse bragging, no drunk shooting off his mouth in a bar. Nothing. And no repeat performance. It was like these assholes hit, then vanished into thin air."

"What's your theory?"

Capps's lips hiked up at one corner and he shook his head. "Which one?"

I gestured for him to elaborate.

"The whole thing smelled like amateur hour."

"But the amateurs got away."

"You know what I love, Ms. Night? Civilians coming into my town and telling me I didn't do my job."

Capps sipped his wine. Slowly set down the glass.

"The attack seemed sloppy. For example, why not disable the security camera? Why not cover your faces? Why be on that street at all?"

"Maybe they thought camouflage or vandalism would draw attention."

"Why make no demand? Money? Turf? Firing of the headmaster? If you don't want revenge or a payoff, why blow people up?"

"Any chance of a gang or mob connection?" I asked.

"None."

"You used the term *hate crime*."

"Then why not use the media attention to further your cause? There were no anti-Israeli tirades. No pro-Palestinian histrionics. No bluster against girls learning to read."

I thought about that. "Maybe choice of the school was random."

Both men just looked at me.

"Maybe the group's goal was less well defined." I was speaking as ideas popped into my mind. "The city. Authority. Minorities in general."

"You talking some crackpot militia?" Capps sounded unconvinced.

"Maybe the goal was simply to create fear. To disrupt the establishment, the government, the cops. Maybe they viewed the attack as phase one in a broader war. A trigger. Like Charles Manson and Helter Skelter."

"Why not continue the war?"

"Who says they aren't?"

"What do you mean?"

"What if their MO is to never repeat their MO?"

"You saying they're not slack, we're just stupid?" Capps's tone now had an edge.

"How far did you get, Detective?"

"I worked with what I had. What I had was shit."

"You had a video. An IED. A vehicle. A missing kid. Did you know Opaline Drucker paid a ransom for Stella?"

Capps's eyes cut to Furr. It was clear he did not.

"How hard did you look?" I pressed.

"Hard." The edge was up a notch.

Wanting to diffuse the tension, Furr stepped in. "The police worked as diligently as any department in any town would look into a horrific crime in the national spotlight. Devoted as many resources to the case as they could. There were no informants, no witnesses, almost no physical evidence. What more could they do?"

"You still looking?" I directed my question to Capps.

"We're working on a number of theories." Steely.

"Look, I get it," I said. "Every force in the country is stretched to the limit. You did what you could, canvassed, checked the terrorist files, ran the forensics. Bottom line: One year later, a kid's still missing and you've got no solve."

For a long, cold moment Capps just glared. I understood his resentment. At one time, I'd been him.

"Stella could be dead." Capps tried to interrupt me. I didn't let him. "Or she could be out there. Captive. Abused. The case is officially open, but admit it. No one's busting ass digging up leads."

The waitress came and asked if we'd finished our meals. Only Furr returned her smile. She cleared our plates anyway.

No one ordered dessert.

It was after nine when I left the restaurant. The air felt damp and much colder than when I'd entered.

I returned to the Ritz, rode to my room, and found a ball game on TV. It was the tenth inning at Wrigley. The Cubs had been tied with the Cardinals since the fourth. I wasn't much interested but wanted to allow time before leaving.

I half-listened to the play-by-play and gazed out the window. Agitated. Unable to focus. Seeing only a blood-covered kid in an SUV.

Twenty-four floors below, the city glittered and pulsed with energy. Not like Charleston, which would be turning back her feather quilts at that hour. Chicago never sleeps.

Finally, bottom of the fourteenth, one on, two out, the crowd noise hushed, then exploded. The announcers went bonkers. A win for the home team.

I turned off the TV. After checking the motion detector, I descended and walked to my three-star inn.

Riding up in the elevator, I glanced at my watch, added an hour for Eastern time. 11:40. I wondered if Beau had crossed to the island to fill Bob's feeder.

Thirteen Days

She has no need of a clock, can tell the hour by the quality of the moonlight. By the slant and sharpness of the shadows. She figures that's how her mind does it. Isn't totally sure.

But it's different here. She doesn't trust her instincts, knows only that it's hard past midnight.

Her eyes crawl the room. The shapes are off, the corners and angles wrong in the murky gloom.

They've moved. Piled their belongings into cars and vans and driven for hours. To this place. A city place.

Outside, she hears the soft clickety-clack of a train. The fingernail scrape of a branch on the screen. From the kitchen, the muted shriek of a boiling kettle.

There are fewer people here. She's sleeping in a room with just two beds. She prefers not being in the bunks.

He comes unaccompanied to her now. Sometimes early, sometimes late. When the others are sleeping. Or busy with tasks.

She doesn't like being alone with him. The closed door. The drawn window shades. She loves yet fears him. Knows he is her only hope of enlightenment.

KATHY REICHS · 60

The Testing is one-on-one. Just them. She dislikes the way his eyes move over her body. The flared pupils if she moans or gasps. The quickened breath if she cries out.

As if he enjoys her pain.

Which can't be true. It hurts him, too. He does it for her. To ensure that she has the strength needed.

Needed to do what?

She climbs from bed, crosses to the window, and looks down. No redbuds. No crocuses. A small patch of grass, an alley, dark silhouettes she knows to be trees. Beyond the trees, a vacant lot. Beyond the lot, the low glow of neon.

Voices rise through the floorboards. Passionate. Loud.

The discussions have become more heated of late. They make her anxious. Her skin itches all the time. She's given herself a rash by scratching. The bumpy red patches keep her awake.

But she must have dozed off.

She listens. Catches random phrases. The Crossing, of course. Talk of that is constant. Of joy. Reward. A better world. But there's a new intensity that keeps her on edge. Keeps her constantly feeling as though acid's been poured down her spine.

She hears words that confuse her.

Tonight she was sent upstairs early again. He'll come soon.

Something is happening. She doesn't know what.

Though she won't ask questions, she vows to find out. But how? Eavesdrop? Poke through drawers? Trash?

Thinking of snooping causes her scalp to tingle. She knows it's a bad idea.

But she has no good idea.

There is only one person she can truly trust. She'll ask him. If the answer is no, she'll abandon the scheme.

She has to find a place where they can be alone.

CHAPTER
8

The next morning I was still the only person aware of my presence online. The *Tribune* ad was running. I wasn't too excited. Placing it was a long shot. Who reads print papers anymore?

I phoned the desk at the Ritz. No one had tried to contact me there. I called Capps, got his voicemail, left a message.

At seven, I turned in my key, left the inn, and began walking north. The sky was gray, the wind more biting than the night before. To the east, traffic whizzed by in two directions. Beyond the traffic, waves pounded boulders lining the shore of America's second-largest Great Lake. Dark questions looped in my head. Was Stella somewhere looking out at that same frigid water? Was her body putrefying within its depths?

I refused to believe it.

On Delaware Place, I entered the Raffaello Hotel. Things must have been slow. The clerk let me check in early. Accepted cash, though that took some persuasion. Seventh floor, microwave and fridge, ten bucks for Internet. Gun stowed in the safe, motion detector arranged, back stairwell checked, I again ventured forth.

My leather jacket was woefully inadequate for April in the north. En route to my room at the Ritz, I consulted the Water Tower Place mall directory, then made a stop on the sixth level. At Abercrombie & Fitch I bought a couple of turtleneck sweaters, a tan wool explorer hat, leather gloves, and a cashmere scarf. I knew Opaline wouldn't want me wearing synthetics. A quick coffee and a hunk of lemon pound cake at Starbucks, then I hummed up to twenty-four.

Another call to Capps. Clegg. Another cybercheck. Nada.

Not sure what else to do, I set up a website and started a blog, accompanying my comments about the school bombing with a photo of Bnos Aliza that I'd found online. I considered using the enhancements made from the surveillance video. Post their faces, let the bastards sue me. Decided against it. Should they show themselves, I wanted the advantage of knowing what they looked like while they were clueless about me. Besides, the images were crap.

At nine, I went to Bnos Aliza. No one would talk to me. I spent an hour casing the neighborhood surrounding the school. Discovered zip.

Next I visited the Baha'i House of Worship in Wilmette, a taxi outing that cost my employer a good chunk of change. Nice ride along the lake and through the North Shore burbs. I learned that the temple is the oldest in the world and the only one in the United States. Nothing else. No one there would talk to me, either.

I wanted to rush out and knock down walls. To waterboard someone into answering my questions. Maybe Capps or Clegg.

Back at the Ritz, my room phone was flashing. Surprised, I pressed the button. A recording told me I had something other than a voice message and asked that I phone the operator. I did. She put me on hold. Then, "Yes, Ms. Night. There is an item for you at the front desk. The instructions were for personal pickup only. Otherwise I'd have sent it up to your room."

"Thank you. I'll be right down."

The "item" was a sealed envelope with S. NIGHT penned in block letters across the front. The envelope bore no Ritz emblem. No logo of any kind. It had no stamp, no return address.

"Did this come by courier?" I asked the clerk, a fastidiously groomed African American man whose name badge said NOAH.

"I'm not sure, madam. I've just come on duty. Shall I inquire of my colleague?"

"Please."

Noah disappeared through a door to his right, returned to the desk several minutes later.

"The letter was delivered by a woman who declined to leave her name. My colleague did request it."

"When?"

"Perhaps an hour ago."

"Did the woman ask to speak with me? Ask for my room extension?"

"I wouldn't know that, madam."

"Is she still here?"

"I'm sorry, madam. I have no way to be certain."

"Thanks."

I stood a moment with the letter in my hand. Confused. Why specify personal pickup only? Why hadn't they mailed it? Or, even simpler, phoned me? Why not contact me online? A wish to be untraceable? That made no sense. For a savvy user, the Internet allows complete anonymity. So does a burner phone.

Then the lightbulb. They wanted to eyeball me. Deliver the envelope, post a watcher, wait to see who picks it up. Maybe snap a few pics. They'd know me; I wouldn't know them. Clever. But not clever enough.

I flicked a wave to Noah, casual as hell. Then I cut right, took the two steps down, walked past the fountain with the heron/ cranes, and sat in a chair in front of the windows. From there I could observe most of the lobby.

Pretending that the glare from outside bothered my eyes, I put

KATHY REICHS · 64

on my Ray-Bans. Then, faking interest in the envelope, I discreetly scanned my surroundings from behind the dark lenses.

The lobby held few people. A guy reading a paper. A woman with two kids and a mountain of luggage. A half-dozen Asian tourists waiting for the rest of the group. Or the bus.

I opened the envelope. It contained one sheet of paper, unlined, the long edge ragged where it had been torn from a tablet or book.

I read. Felt a high-speed pump of adrenaline. The message was short. It said:

> Tonight. Midnight. Foster Beach. The eastern end of the
> pedestrian underpass below Lake Shore Drive. Come alone.
> Disobey, your young friend dies.

CHAPTER
9

I lingered a moment to calm my nerves, then got up and returned to the desk. Leaning on one elbow, body half-turned, I asked my pal Noah a series of pointless questions while surreptitiously checking the activity behind me. Noting nothing suspicious, I thanked him, walked straight back past the heron/crane lobby, and stopped at a wall mirror just beyond the elevators.

I readjusted the scarf and hat, eyes on the reflected lobby behind me. Saw no one pretending not to observe. No one rising from a sofa or chair. No one speaking furtively into a cellphone.

Strung along the wall opposite the mirror, glass cases displayed goodies for sale in the Ritz shops. Far down, by the door, a woman was studying an item on one of the shelves. She wore a trench coat, boots, and a White Sox cap. As I watched she raised a mobile phone to her eye and lined me up with the viewfinder. I dropped to a squat and ran a hand across the tile as though searching for something. She got nothing.

I debated going to my room for the Glock 23. Decided against it. If someone was tailing me, I didn't want to lose him. Or her.

I exited the hotel and turned toward Michigan. Now that they'd found me, I wasn't sure what they'd do. Or who they were. If it was the Bnos Aliza bombers, they might have Stella. They'd used deadly force in the past. In the note they'd threatened to kill again. Stella?

Or they might want to take me off the board. Better to stay in a crowd.

I'm good at surveillance, know all the tricks. I spotted my tail one block south, on the opposite side of the street. The woman viewing the overpriced baubles.

I continued strolling, stopping at storefronts here and there, hoping for reflected glimpses of her. And to demonstrate what an amateur I was.

South of Water, Michigan Avenue crosses the Chicago River. Halfway over the bridge, I paused to take in the view.

The woman didn't show herself on the bridge. Knowing she couldn't risk letting me get too far ahead, I picked up the pace, then stopped again at the far end. I spotted Sox Cap moving through the pedestrians ten yards back, on the far side.

Time to up the ante. Once across the river, I fired to a stone staircase and took the treads two at a time down to the Riverwalk. If my pursuer wanted to stick with me she'd have to sprint. If not, I'd still gain information.

If Sox Cap didn't run, that meant she'd either gotten what she needed or was handing me off to a partner. If she did run, that meant she didn't care that I'd made her. Perhaps because she intended to kill me. Or her partner did. I wasn't crazy about either possibility.

Sox Cap didn't descend the stairs. I never saw her along the Riverwalk. I returned to Water Tower Place by a zigzag route. Didn't spot her. She wasn't in the lobby of the Ritz.

I went up to my room and took off my jacket, hat, and scarf. Got the Glock 23 from the safe and laid it on the bedside table. Ran my hands through my hair. Rotated my shoulders. Laced my fingers, stretched my arms, and cracked my knuckles. Felt totally pumped. A full day of getting nowhere and I was finally seeing action. And I'd outsmarted someone who thought she was outsmarting me. But who the hell was she?

I hadn't gotten a good look at the woman's face. The female bomber? If so, they thought they had an advantage. That I didn't know them but they knew me. At least the woman did. Pat on the back for not posting their faces online.

But what if Sox Cap wasn't one of the bombers? What if she was a scammer looking to score an easy five grand? One of a group of scammers? What if the note had been a ruse to test me? To see how careful I was about the reward. How smart. How armed.

Either way, points in my column. I knew what one of them looked like. Sort of. They knew nothing about me except I was tall. And that I was staying at the Ritz. Which I wasn't.

I rode the Water Tower escalator down to Abercrombie & Fitch, bought a black puffer jacket and a green cap with a red moose above the bill. A stop at the Sunglass Hut for some blue Maui Jims. Another at the Finish Line for a pair of Adidas Ultra Boosts, chartreuse with black stripes on the sides. An hour after leaving, I was back in my room. Mall shopping, also the cat's meow.

I booted the Mac and opened Google Maps. Perused street and satellite views. Then I spent some time on the CTA website, viewing options for public transit in Chicago. In minutes I had a peach of a plan.

I tucked my hair under the moose cap, which took some doing, then laced on the shoes. I attached my holster to my belt, this time at my hip, not the small of my back. I palmed in the magazine and put the gun in the holster. Finally, I put on the new jacket.

Heart hammering, I ran a quick check of the motion detector. Satisfied, I pressed the do-not-disturb button and left.

I walked south to Chicago, then west to State to a subway entrance opposite a McDonald's. Vagrants filled the sidewalk, smoking, sleeping, panhandling, doing nothing. A bearded guy in a ratty army jacket separated from a group of three and approached me on wobbly legs. His teeth were gone, his eyes crusted, his outstretched hand unsteady. I gave him a five spot. Dozens of eyes watched. I hoped he could keep the money long enough to buy a Big Mac.

I rode the Red Line north to Bryn Mawr, walked east from the station, then took a tunnel under Lake Shore Drive to the Lakefront Trail. From there I turned right. I wanted to scope out the meet site before I showed up that night. If anyone was watching, I figured they'd expect me to come from the south.

To my left ran parkland dotted with the occasional tree, beyond it a breakwater, beyond the breakwater, the lake. The area was fairly active now. Runners, skaters, bikers, and dog walkers passed me going in both directions. Kids tossed balls and Frisbees. Couples pressed together on benches, enduring the cold for the freedom to neck.

The sun was still high, the office, condo, and apartment buildings to the west throwing long, rectangular shadows across the traffic, the trail, and the grass. I knew that, come dark, the area would be deserted. That the joggers and cyclists and lovers would have fled to the safety of their dead bolts and touch-pad security systems.

My eyes roved. My ears stayed on high alert. Challenging with waves crashing, gulls cawing, vehicles whooshing by on the Drive.

As I moved south, the shoreline gradually curved in, the green space narrowed, and the trees grew denser. On spotting the rendezvous point, I felt my scalp prickle. The setup was as bad as I'd feared.

The underpass was long and straight, maybe twenty feet in width. The walls had no recesses or alcoves. No place to hide. If I entered and they blocked the ends, I'd be trapped. Stay out of the underpass.

Across from the lakeside opening was a thick stand of hardwoods. If I came up the trail, or down it as I was doing now, they could conceal themselves and take me out from the safety of the trees. Not good, either.

Or, if they were smart, they could work a tunnel-tree strategy.

Have people covering both. If they were smart. Capps thought they were sloppy. And he'd won a Kiwanis award.

I stared at the underpass. Even in midafternoon the interior was deep in shadow. A row of ceiling lights was trying but accomplishing little. Besides, if my pursuers were smart they'd smash the bulbs. If they were smart.

I walked the area, crossed the beach, stared at the lake, cold and frigid, running all the way up to join Huron at the Straits of Mackinac. I checked the parking lot, a basketball court, a small pavilion. I snapped pics with my phone.

It was after three when I got back to Bryn Mawr. Just beyond the metro station, I found a place called Hellas Gyros. Though my gut was in free fall, I knew I had to eat. While forcing down a souvlaki on pita and drinking a Beck's, I scrolled through the shots I'd taken and thought about options. About what to do.

If caught, I was dead. If I escaped, Stella was dead?

I refused to consider either possibility.

"When you find your opponent's weak spot, hammer it."

I must have voiced the thought aloud, because a kid clearing the booth to my right said, "You need something, lady?"

"Tactics," I said.

"What?" Wiping greasy hands on his apron. Which was once white.

"It's a quote from a very wise man."

"Yeah? Like Plato?"

"John Heisman."

I bunched my wrapper, drained my beer, and headed for the train. As I clicked and swayed toward my stop, the same questions kept looping in my head. Were my pursuers the bombers? Were they planning to shoot me? Was Stella alive? Did the threat toward my "young friend" refer to her? If they had her, would my actions put her at risk?

By the time I got off at Chicago and State, I had the broad outline of my three-part strategy for the upcoming encounter. First, I wanted to scramble whatever they intended for me. Second, I wanted at least one of them to bolt. Third, I wanted to follow the bolter without his or her knowledge. And I wanted not to get killed. I guess that made four.

Take a Glock? Hell yeah. These guys had used explosives. Killed a kid. I didn't plan to shoot anyone. And I wasn't luring them into a trap. If there was a trap, they were luring me. Maybe the trees. Maybe the underpass. Maybe the trail south of the rendezvous point.

If I was dealing with the bombers, I had a rough idea what they looked like from the surveillance video images. Only the woman in the Sox cap knew what I looked like. Tall, nice shades. If I wasn't dealing with the bombers, advantage to both sides.

Either way, the woman in the Sox cap would have to be there to ID me for the rest of the group. If there was a group. Any pics she might have snapped would be useless.

How large a group? If they planned to cap me in the underpass they'd need a tag team to work the ends, in addition to the woman in the Sox cap, who'd be standing lookout. Four were captured on the Bnos Aliza video, three men and a woman. Had others been hunkered down in the SUV? Waiting elsewhere? Manning an escape route? How many others?

They didn't need four. But would a lone person agree to stay behind? Refuse to participate? Not likely. Too gutless. But a lot could have changed in the group over the course of a year. People dead. Couples split, maybe hostile. New recruits.

Still, I guessed I'd be facing four. *If* I was dealing with the bombers. And if so, they'd be as wary of deception as I was. They'd be watching for signs of a trap. A police setup. The trick with the note. The tail. They were being careful. Or thought they were.

Bombers? Con artists? What I didn't know could have filled Soldier Field.

There was nothing to do but sally forth into the fray. I'd stay out of the underpass. Away from the trees. Carry the Glock on my hip.

What else did Heisman say?

When in doubt, punt.

CHAPTER 10

Feeling too amped to sit still, I checked out of the Raffaello and into the Tremont on East Chestnut. A scan of my online posts reconfirmed that I was still the only being on the planet interested in them. Though @hurryhome407 had picked up seven followers on Twitter. Go figure.

After finding the address of a wig shop on State Street, I strapped on the Glock 23, donned the black puffer, and set off for the Loop.

The selection was superb. I bought a short blond bob and a long black number that made me want to sing "The Shoop Shoop Song." I'd barely hit the sidewalk when my phone buzzed in my purse. I checked the screen. The motion detector at the Ritz had been tripped.

I raced to Water Tower Place. On twenty-four, I continued past my room and turned right at the end of the hall. Squatting low, breathing fast, I peeked around the corner.

There was no sign of a lookout. Odd. SOP for busting hotel rooms is one inside, one outside standing guard.

The privacy light was on, as I'd left it. I considered possibilities. A false alert? A cleaning or maintenance worker? A bomber wanting to blow me away?

I placed my purse, my backpack, and the wig bag on the floor and slid the Glock from its holster. Holding the gun behind my thigh for concealment, I checked the corridor I was in, then the intersecting and parallel corridors. Saw no one.

I dug my key card from my purse and clamped it between my front teeth. Clutching the gun two-handed and pointed down, senses hyperfocused, I started forward.

All sounds receded to deep background. I saw zip but the door. The numerals 2417.

At my suite, I stopped and listened hard. Heard only the hammering of my own heart. I stepped to the left of the door and, releasing one hand from the gun, swiped the key card across the lock. The little click sounded like a cannon in a cave.

I hopped left and pressed my shoulders to the wall. Again grasped the gun two-handed, muzzle now up.

Nothing happened.

I waited a full ten seconds. Took a lot of deep breaths. Strained for any hint of a presence beyond the door.

Then I reswiped and kicked out at the same time. The door flew in, hit the wall, and ricocheted. I caught it on the rebound with one boot, then scurried back around the corner, out of sight.

More nothing happening. No one shouted. No one rushed forth.

Gun again by my thigh, I edged down the hall until I had an angled view of the room. The lights were out, the curtains drawn but seeping a fair dose of afternoon glow. I couldn't remember if I'd left them open or closed.

I continued past 2417 and crossed to the opposite side. If someone came out blazing, they'd expect me in the same position as when I'd booted the door. Lowering the Glock, I waited. The partially open door waited.

Twenty minutes passed. The elevator hummed by several times. I hoped it would make no stops on twenty-four. Then it did.

The doors skimmed back and a waiter got off pushing a room service cart. Blond hair, ambitious cowlick, maybe eighteen. He didn't notice me. Or pretended not to. But he paused at the open door, looked undecided, then disappeared around the corner at which I'd crouched earlier.

I checked my watch again and again. 5:30. 5:55. 6:10. I thought about strategies if I needed to pee.

Just past seven the elevator stopped again. A man and a kid got off. The man had razor-styled silver hair and looked like he'd just come from an Armani shoot. The kid was rougher—stubble, faded jeans, a grubby jacket over a T. The man glanced at me, quickly away, regretful of having allowed his eyes to make contact with mine. The kid gave me a slow once-over, cocky. They entered a room eight digits down from 2417.

More time passed. I pictured the living room of my suite. The furniture. The entrances to the baths and bedroom. Mapped escape routes. Attack routes.

I thought about how idiotic I'd feel if it turned out no one was in the suite and I was growing older in the hall, locked and loaded. I thought about how much more idiotic I'd feel if I walked right in and got capped. I decided to be patient and grow older.

But my opponent, or opponents, were patient, too. Easier with the comfort of sofas, chairs, and commodes. Still, I guessed they'd yield to nerves sooner than I would, fearful of discovery by hotel staff or security. A wide-open door is out of the norm.

My neck and back started to ache. My hand cramped from grasping the gun. With a round in the chamber I had to hold it carefully yet out of sight.

A couple exited the elevator. He was short, with a florid face and a gut that hung over his belt. She was short, too, but lean and gaunt. Both wore Steelers windbreakers and polyester pants. Both made a point of looking straight ahead as they hurried to the end of the hall and turned left.

Next it was a guy in a blue sweater and glasses with tortoise-shell frames. An academic, or trying to look like one. I played guess the nerd. Anthropology. Economics. Poetry. An unlikely accomplice. Still, I watched him until he was safely in his room.

The light slanting from my suite slowly faded. I kept my eyes on it, watching for any sign of movement. A shadow. A flicker. A hint that those inside were making their play.

I wondered how long he or she or they could hold out. If he or she or they needed to either kill me or be at Foster Beach at midnight. Fine. I had nowhere to go until then.

7:20. Elevator traffic was picking up. Not good.

A family of four came next. Mom, Pop, Junior, and Sis. Both kids were carrying bags from the Disney Store. The Griswolds hitting the big city for culture. Junior eyed me with undisguised curiosity.

"Dad!" Grabbing Pop's arm. "That lady's got a—"

Pop shushed him with a sharp expulsion of air.

"But, Dad—"

"Shut it until we're in the room."

Junior's body language radiated what he thought of that. The bickering began as soon as they rounded the corner. Was truncated by the slam of a door.

The stress of maintaining vigilance was taking its toll. My neck was taut as the branch of an oak, my lower back on fire. My good eye throbbed. My bad eye throbbed harder. I was sweating inside the puffer.

I considered the door. It had stopped roughly two-thirds open. If a thug was waiting to blast through the gap, he'd have to come from the right, eyes and gun aimed toward the point where he'd seen me last. Or she had. Or they had.

And if it *was* a team effort? Maybe the lead thug would kick the door as I'd done, then both would blast forward, one cutting left, the other right. Or maybe they'd crouch and creep. Or dive and roll in separate directions.

Or maybe they were far more patient than I anticipated. Maybe they'd sit tight until I made a move.

What would *I* do? Probably opt for the dive and roll. Move fast. Hope I was more agile than the mope standing in the hall all day.

Or maybe the suite was empty.

7:40.

I could barely feel my right hand. Eyes glued to the gaping space between the door and the jamb, I released my grip on the Glock, rotated my wrist, and opened and closed my fingers. They tingled as though rebounding from frostbite. Circulation restored, I reestablished my hold, pointer flat beside the trigger guard.

8:08.

I thought about dialing security. Or the front desk. I could report that I'd found my room door open, say I feared an intrusion. But if an armed thug really was waiting for me, some hapless hotel employee might get killed. Maybe the kid with the cowlick. Or Noah. Better to wait. I'd give it at least until 10:30.

The guy came out upright but coiled, fired two shots down the corridor toward the wall opposite the one at which I was standing. He was big and wore a black tracksuit and knitted cap pulled low on his forehead.

He tensed when he realized I wasn't where he'd expected. Whipped around, gun pointed at me.

Crack!

My left shoulder winged backward. Fire ripped down my arm. I shot him.

The world ebbed as I squeezed off the round. I didn't breathe. Didn't blink. Didn't flinch at the recoil.

My bullet made the guy stumble but didn't take him down. He leveled his muzzle at my chest. I saw the deadly little hole in the blue-black steel, his trigger finger tense. I shot him a second time. He fell to his knees, then crumpled facedown on the carpet. I held him in my sights. He didn't move. A nine-millimeter Beretta lay by his hand.

A heartbeat, two, three.

I lunged across the hall, leaped over his body, and dove headfirst through the open door into the suite. My shoulder and rib cage hit the entry tile hard. Lungs in spasm, I rolled behind the sofa.

A few beats, then, fighting for air, I rose to my knees and peered over the sofa back. Saw a gray rectangle of sky and lake. Movement reflected in the colossal TV?

I fired again.

The bullet ricocheted and shattered the screen. The phone exploded into the window glass. The handset dropped and skittered across the floor.

A dial tone droned in the sudden stillness.

My eyes swept the room. It was empty.

I slid down to my butt, drew my knees to my belly, and tried to breathe. It wasn't working out. Maybe the bullet. Maybe the slam-dive onto the tile.

The dial tone cut off. A robotic voice said something I couldn't catch. I didn't care.

After finally managing to suck in some air, I crawled on all fours—three actually, my left shoulder was useless—toward the guy I'd shot. He lay still, the Beretta by his side.

Gun ready in my right hand, I probed the man's throat with my left. Felt no pulse. A stain was blossoming on his tracksuit and the carpet around him.

I holstered the Glock. Crawled back and snatched the handset from the rug. Heard nothing but dead air. I pressed the button, waited, tried again.

I was dragging toward the bedroom when agitated voices sounded in the corridor. I reversed toward the living room.

"Hotel security! Come out! Now!"

"It's okay," I said. "There's a dead man in the hall." As if they couldn't spot him. "I've been hit. I'll step to where you can see me." Right hand high, I walked to the door.

There were two of them, one black, one white, both short and skinny, both wearing dark suits and red ties. Black looked like he'd just graduated high school. White looked like he'd qualify for Social Security.

Both probably made fifteen bucks an hour. I stepped back. Very. Slowly.

White and Black moved into the suite. White wore a tag that said s. HARVEY. Black's said j. FIX.

"Hands clasped on top of your head!" Harvey's face was a bag of wrinkles, his jaw saggy, his eyes green half-moons under low-hanging lids.

"I've been shot," I said. "My left shoulder is whacked."

Harvey looked undecided what to do about that. Fix circled me toward the phone.

"I have a firearm in a holster on my right hip," I said.

"Don't move!" Harvey commanded. Fix was having no luck with the handset.

"I can remove it, but I'll have to lower my arm," I said.

"One finger."

I lifted the Glock as directed. Harvey pointed toward the floor. I set the Glock down and kicked it toward his feet. He picked it up.

"Are you bleeding?" Fix had switched to his own mobile to contact the desk.

"Yes," I said.

"Yes," he said into the mouthpiece. A pause, then, "ASAP. We got a probable DOA up here." Fix disconnected. "Cruiser's en route and there's a bus on the way."

"I'm feeling a little woozy," I said.

Harvey pointed to the sofa. "Keep your hands where I can see them."

I sat. Fix moved into position beside his partner. Both eyed me. The scar. The black nails. The red hair, unbound, haloing my head like a lion's mane. I could tell Fix was pumped about the tale he'd be sharing that night.

"All right." Harvey was taking the lead. "What happened here, ma'am?"

"I'm an investigator from out of state," I said. "I'm working a case involving a bombing and a kidnapping."

"You got ID?"

"Around the corner in the hall." I hoped. "A purse, a backpack, and a plastic bag."

Fix left, returned in seconds. I produced my driver's license, retired police ID, and gun permit. Harvey scanned the documents,
then handed them to Fix.

"Okay, South Carolina. We know who you are. Who's the guy
you just burned?"

"I'm guessing he didn't like me reopening the case."

"How'd you know he was in your room?" Sherlock Harvey.

"I'm a pro," I lied.

"With no clue who you just popped."

He had me there. "My shoulder is pretty uncomfortable."

"An ambulance has been dispatched," Fix said.

"For him?" Cocking my chin toward the door.

"For you." Fix thought I was serious. "ME's en route for him."

"Good call." The pain was getting sharper, my responses less
than snappy.

Time passed. Then, down the hall, I heard an elevator open.
Voices. Hurried steps. A gurney clanking, wheels humming across
wool plush.

"Could you make one more call?" I was finding it harder to talk.

Harvey and Fix said nothing.

"Could you contact Roy Capps or Bernie Clegg?"

"Lawyers?" Harvey couldn't have made his disgust more apparent.

"Detectives. Area Three."

Approximately four minutes later I was screaming toward the
infamous Cook County ER.

Twelve Days

She's found a place in the vacant lot. A patch of bare ground surrounded by trees. Sounds are muted inside her tiny cocoon. Blunted by their worming journey through needles and embryonic leaves.

She'll be punished if they learn she's ventured from the yard. She takes the risk. Sneaks across the alley whenever she can. She's even smuggled a quilt from the house.

She lies on her back, legs flexed, and gazes up at the latticework of shapes overhead. She imagines reasons the branches might be reaching out. To hold hands. To dance. To pray.

To brand her. To gouge her eyes from her head.

The scabs on her knees have reopened. They ooze and burn. Unconsciously, her fingers go to them. Explore. Tease tiny hunks of salt from her flesh.

Sun and shadow dapple her face. She forces her mind calm. She loves calm.

Too much new is coming at her of late. The move. Talk of another. Endless discourse on the Crossing. But always in code. Buzzwords she doesn't understand.

Endless Testing. Endless pain.

His eyes. His hands. His hot onion breath on her face.

Everyone seems on edge, their movements sharp, their eyes jumpy. No one tells her what's up. Or when it will happen. But she knows something is coming. She feels powerless. Flawed. Afraid that she's afraid. Terrified they will learn of her weakness.

She's jittery all day. Prickly lying in bed at night. Her skin is a watercolor in red. Her ribs throb. She thinks one may be broken.

Her mother visits in the dark, face tight, gaze lingering far too long. Thinking what? Your brother and I love you? Be brave? We will be together forever?

It's a mirage, of course. She knows she's making it up in her head.

She tries to detach from the past. From the way it used to be. Tries to balance things. To keep the good and shove the bad to a far back corner of her mind. To bury it all with the pain.

The clearing is good. And hers alone. When in it, the sense of foreboding recedes. It's not here. Not now. Not real.

But it is real.

She breathes the spice of bark, moist earth, and sun-warmed needles. Last time it was rain-soaked needles. She's uncertain which she prefers.

Beyond the green silence she hears a siren wailing, a dog barking, a garbage truck rumbling and grinding. Sounds of normal life. Not hers.

Bees whine close by. Maybe wasps. She can't see them, but their presence reassures her. She thinks of pollen. Of honey. There were bees at the farm. She pictures the fields, the barn. Less than a day's drive, but a lifetime away.

Enough, she tells herself. They are living here now. She doesn't like this place but dreads another move. The known is better than the unknown.

The unknown.

People have disappeared. She has no idea why. They're not al-

lowed to talk to one another now. Not like they did. They weren't strong?

She is strong. She will endure. She will accomplish the extraordinary.

A puff of wind noses through from outside. It feels nice on her ravaged skin. Feathery.

Across the alley, a voice calls her name.

Her heart explodes.

Blood buzzes below her ribs like the wasps.

CHAPTER 11

It's no longer called Cook County. The monster beside the Eisenhower Expressway is now the John H. Stroger, Jr., Hospital. All 1.2 million square feet of it. And it's not the ER. It's the Department of Emergency Medicine.

I didn't care about names. Or the chaos swirling around me. The guy yelling obscenities. The baby screaming. The phones ringing. The sirens announcing the delivery of yet more carnage.

Through the cacophony of misery, I was trying to make out what Roy Capps was saying. I could hear him barking on the far side of the privacy curtain. Hadn't a clue who was taking the hit.

I sat up and swung my legs over the side of the table. Felt a moment of vertigo. Dropped my chin and did some deep breathing. I'd blacked out briefly in the ambulance, been wide awake to enjoy the X-raying, disinfecting, probing, and stitching. Not a big deal. I've been patched up before.

The curtain whipped back and the doc who'd done the heavy lifting strode into the bay. Long legs, long neck, made me think of the cranes at the Ritz. His name badge said DR. TEDESCANI.

Behind Tedescani was Capps. Behind Capps was a guy in his fifties with a big square head and hair well on its way to a comb-over. His eyes were small and blue-gray and never stopped moving. I assumed this was Clegg.

Tedescani crossed to me and adjusted the sling cradling my left arm. "You burned a good hunk of karma today. And you owe thanks to that jacket." Indicating the puffer, which lay in two pieces, cut up the back.

"And to my blistering speed," I said.

"The bullet nicked muscle, tumbled, then stopped, causing no major damage. I assume you weren't sitting still. That or your assailant was the world's worst marksman."

"Have you seen bullets do that before?" Sounded like complex physics to me.

"I've seen everything before." Tedescani handed me a printout. "I've written you a script for Vicodin and an antibiotic."

"Better living through chemistry."

"Fill them, don't fill them. It's your shoulder."

"Thank you."

"Keep the wound dry. Change the dressing every twenty-four hours."

"That's it?"

"No fastballs or sliders."

"Can I go?"

"These gentlemen would like a word with you." Indicating C-squared. "I don't know about the uniforms out in the hall."

Tedescani withdrew to serve the next lucky customer.

"You want to tell me what the fuck just happened?" The flush on Capps's face matched the stains on what was left of my turtleneck.

"I shot a guy at the Ritz."

"No shit."

"He meant to shoot me."

"Bully for him."

"Did you speak to Mutt and Jeff?"

"If you mean Harvey and Fix, they gave us their version. We want yours."

"I assume this is your partner?" I indicated Clegg, who was standing with arms folded, feet spread, looking like he'd exited the womb a cop. He was taller than Capps, but who wasn't.

Clegg just stared.

"So who was this guy?" Capps asked.

"I never got a good look at his face."

Capps tossed me a red fleece jacket that looked like it might have been rejected by the homeless.

"Now's your chance. He's taking callers right down the street."

The Cook County Medical Examiner facility was minutes away. Which made me wonder about survival rates at ole John H. Stroger, Jr.

A tech met us in reception and led us to a gurney in an empty autopsy room. On the gurney was a body bag. The tech unzipped it and withdrew to lean against a wall. C-squared and I stepped close.

The bag held a male still wearing the tracksuit in which he'd died. He was white and had a scraggly blond mustache.

I got Opaline Drucker's four photos from my purse and selected the three men. C-squared and I looked from the photos to the corpse. The man in the bag had been driving the Subaru Forester at Bnos Aliza.

"Cha-ching," Capps said.

I looked at him.

"Furr told us you're paid by the head."

"This kid can't be out of his twenties." I found Capps's insinuation offensive.

"And he won't be celebrating the big three-oh."

"How much you getting for him?" Clegg's vowels were nasal and flat, Chicago all the way.

"Twenty-five grand," Capps answered, before I could deflect the question.

"This fuckwad came gunning for me," I snapped.

"Uh-huh."

"You're out of line. *I* didn't ambush *him*."

"How'd you know he was in your room?" Clegg asked.

I explained the motion detector.

"So you kicked the door open, then waited in the hall."

"Yes."

"How long?"

"A few hours."

"Tenacious."

"I'm famous for it."

"And the wigs?"

"That too."

For a few beats we all studied the man in the bag. He looked pale as uncooked fish. And far too young to be hosting rigor mortis.

"Here's the thing," Capps said. "Drucker grease or not, we can't have you running around our town shooting people you think might or might not hate Jews enough to blow up their kids."

"And collecting twenty-five bills a pop." Clegg seemed irked as much by the money as by the death.

"I'm not an assassin. I was hired to close a case you and your colleagues left open. I didn't shoot this guy for profit. I shot him because he shot me."

"And the ads you ran online and in the *Trib*? That wasn't a lure?"

So C-squared were keeping tabs on me. I said nothing.

"Let's talk about the wigs," Capps said.

"I prefer the blond look."

"You need disguises because . . . ?" Capps let the question hang.

"One of them may be able to ID me."

"ID you."

"Recognize me."

"I understand the term. I want to know how that could be."

"I think I was tailed yesterday."

"You're in contact with them?" Capps's whole little body bristled.

"Someone left a note for me at the Ritz. Maybe the bombers, maybe not."

"To arrange a meet?"

I didn't want C-squared mucking up that night's rendezvous. Perhaps sending those who'd arranged it scurrying back underground. Perhaps getting Stella Bright killed.

"Nothing like that. I think the idea was to eyeball me. See who I am, assess me as a threat. Thus the impulse to tweak my appearance."

Capps and Clegg exchanged a look. I got the sense neither was buying my story.

"They'll ink and roll this guy in the morning." I flicked a thumb at the gurney. "I'm guessing he'll be in the system."

"Names part of your deal?" Clegg asked.

"No," I said.

Capps gestured to the tech that we were done.

The tech hesitated, then, "You might want to check his hands."

"Do we?"

The tech shrugged. Uninterested, though he'd clearly been listening.

Capps rotated an impatient wrist.

The tech pushed from the wall, joined us at the gurney, and angled the man's right arm up and onto his belly. When he loosened the paper bag covering the hand, visible at the base of his thumb was a crude monochrome tattoo.

"You got a magnifier?" Capps asked.

The tech produced a handheld lens. One by one C-squared and I peered through it.

"I'm seeing a couple of *J*'s hooked together," Clegg said.

"Looks amateur, maybe a prison tat," Capps said.

"Are you familiar with the symbol?" I asked.

"No," they both said.

Capps took out his phone and shot a few pics. The tech re-bagged the hand, closed the zipper, then rolled the mustachioed corpse toward the cooler.

"Finally a lead," I said.

"Break out the bubbly," Capps said.

Down the hall, a door whooshed, clanged. The tech returned. "You need anything else?"

"We're good," Capps said.

"You able to find your way out?"

"Oh yeah."

The tech took his leave.

"How about my piece?" I asked Capps, already knowing the answer.

"We'll be keeping that for now."

"The guy was packing a Beretta."

"Same as half the gangbangers in America."

Clegg had me there.

A wall clock said 10:43. Analog, with old-fashioned black numerals and a sweep second hand. I had to hurry.

"How about a ride to the Ritz?" I smiled my most charming smile. Which contracted a multitude of muscles and reoriented the scar just so. Move number three. I had a whole repertoire.

They dropped me with an order to stay in touch. Reminded me of Beau at the Charleston airport. After watching their taillights disappear around the corner, I hurried to the Tremont.

Tossing my purse and the wig bag onto the bed, I took off the fleece, then the sling. Teeth gritted against the pain, I wriggled out of the bloodstained, newly one-sleeved turtleneck and pulled on a clean one. Then I retrieved the Glock 17 from the safe and shoved it into the empty holster on my belt.

Using mostly my right hand, I managed to don the black wig. After maneuvering back into the fleece, which involved a lot of cursing, I checked myself in the mirror. A bit Natasha Fatale, but the look would do. Different enough from yesterday that they might not spot me right off.

11:17. I checked the motion detector, descended to the lobby, and flagged a taxi.

Riding north on Lake Shore Drive, I thought about the people I was going to encounter. They were smart. And they were ruthless. They'd bombed a school. They'd arranged to meet me at midnight, all the while planning to shoot me in the afternoon. Did they know how that had gone down? They must. What would happen now? Would they even show up?

Did they have Stella? Had they already killed her?

Were the would-be assassins and the Foster Beach people one and the same? If not, who wanted me dead? If so, would they try again at the underpass? Should I go? Should I have told Capps and Clegg? Probably a big yes there.

Should I have taken time to fill the prescription for Vicodin? The local anesthesia was wearing off. My shoulder felt as though I'd walked it into an industrial fan.

I had to go. Other than the guy in the morgue, the meet was the only lead I had. Opaline Drucker had asked if I'd see it through. I'd given myself five stars out of five.

Again the flash images. The silhouette in the gore. The shock on the face of the female bomber. The autopsy photos of Bowen Bright.

Though irrational, my gut insisted that Stella was alive. If not, these people might know where her body could be found.

I leaned back. Unwise on two levels. The ratty upholstery snagged at the wig. The pressure on my spine triggered pain from my shoulder to my wrist.

I sat forward, left arm in my lap, right elbow on my knee. Outside the taxi, streetlights whipped by as disjointed peach vapor strips. Beyond the lights, the lake, a dark and forbidding void in the night.

CHAPTER 12

I spotted the Sox cap while still twenty yards north of the rendez-vous point. Rookie move. The full moon turned the white logo neon.

The woman was by an oak, on the lake side of the trail, just past the pedestrian underpass. I saw no one else around. But there had to be others. Others with guns. I guessed they were positioned in the trees and the underpass.

I cut east toward the beach and, keeping to the shadows, circled to a point behind the woman. I was the only human afoot and didn't want to test the effectiveness of my disguise.

The woman was looking south. She hadn't gotten pics at the Ritz, so only she could ID me. Though I guessed the others had been given a verbal description. I knew them only from the video stills, which were far from clear. *If* these were the people who'd bombed the Bnos Aliza School.

So we waited. She was nervous, scanning for me, for cops, for any sign of a setup. I was keeping her in my sights. And looking for her cohorts. And trying to keep the damn wig in place. An icy breeze off the lake was making that hard.

It was the Ritz all over again. This time out in the elements, not in a hall. I was wearing only the fleece. And had a hole in my shoulder that hurt like a bastard.

Flashback image. A mud-walled village holding a soldier scheduled for video beheading. An extraction team hunkered in a dung-colored desert. Frigid cold. A hunk of metal in my shoulder from an IED.

Time passed. Across Lake Shore Drive, the city hummed with all the notes of a midnight symphony. Blasts of hip-hop from passing cars. Sirens. Horns. The occasional voice raised in anger or song.

The woman was shorter than I remembered. The trench coat hung to the middle of her calves. She wore dark pants under it, running shoes. No purse. I guessed she carried her gun in a pocket.

Every now and then my gaze dropped to my watch, then bounced back to the woman. She was scanning wider now, checking her surroundings in all directions. I caught flashes of her face. Her eyes were black holes below the brim of her cap.

At 1:30, the woman pulled a mobile from her purse, spoke briefly, then disconnected. A figure appeared at the mouth of the underpass. Waved. The woman waved, hand arcing pale in the gloom. I wondered if two small *J*'s darkened her thumb.

The woman held position a few more minutes, then angled toward the underpass.

I was ninety minutes late. They were pulling the plug.

Or were they? Had the woman spotted me? Had her companion? Was it possible I'd been made from that far away? Had the woman placed or received the call? Were there more lookouts I hadn't seen?

Follow her? I didn't want to go into the underpass. Though feeble, the lights were still working. If others were waiting, I'd be a sitting duck. Give her time to clear the tunnel, then pick her up west of Lake Shore? But I didn't want to lose her. It had taken a lot of effort to find her. I'd been shot because of her. Maybe. Or maybe she was a lone scammer. Either way, I had to know.

I adjusted the wig. *Natasha, do your stuff.* I crept toward the underpass.

The woman was exiting the far end. Otherwise, the long murky space was empty. I walked through quickly, alert to every sound, a female alone in the night in a dangerous place. A black-haired female. With a Glock in one hand.

The woman wasn't hard to follow. It was late, she was probably tired, hadn't heard or seen me, wasn't expecting a tail. She walked south on Sheridan, then west on Foster, moving briskly but not in a panic. At Broadway, she turned south again. We passed small groceries and restaurants, all closed. The names suggested a Vietnamese hood. I noted the Tank Noodle restaurant, a sandwich shop called Ba Le. Stored the info.

I wondered about the woman's companions. Why had others been at Foster Beach? Were they the bombers? If so, where were they now? If not, where were they now?

As we walked, I watched the woman's gait. I noticed for the first time the hunched bearing, as if she wanted to reduce her height, perhaps minimize the amount of person she presented to the world. Still, she was stepping along smartly.

At Argyle, the woman again went west. The twisty route made me question my earlier confidence. Had I been busted? Was the woman trying to lose me? Lead me to another ambush? I picked up the pace and rounded the corner.

The neighborhood was residential and poorly lit. I stretched my eyes down the street. It had a narrow strip of parkway running along each curb, mud and dog shit now but, come summer, hopefully grass. Parked cars lined both sides. The few scraggly trees spread still-bare fingers across the night sky.

The buildings were a mix of older homes and three- and six-flats. At mid-block on the north, one large complex wrapped a courtyard centered on a fountain that had seen better days. The single-family homes had wooden porches and faded siding. All other structures were deeply committed to brick.

Many of the three- and six-flats had tiny fenced yards. The

woman entered one that did not. The door was to the left, up five concrete steps, past planters holding nothing but dead vegetation. On the right, the building bowed out into a bay. Three stories, three windows per bay. In less than a minute a light went on in a second-floor window. Not in front, but around to the side.

Stella's prison? I had to fight the impulse to rush in and sack the place.

The street was completely deserted. I imagined an insomniac neighbor, a 911 call, a need to explain my loitering to Capps and Clegg. I was freezing in my wig and turtleneck and lightweight fleece. I decided to give it half an hour.

I slipped into the courtyard and found a corner from which I could see both the door the woman had entered and the lit window. Leaning against a wall, I cradled my left arm with my right.

The light stayed on. No one left the building.

To get the lay of the land, I cupped my hands around my phone and called up Google Maps. There was a small college to the south, a big-ass cemetery just south of that. Not sure how that helped. But it passed the time.

At 2:35 the window went dark.

Bedtime, I thought. I don't know who she is or what she wants. If she's a scammer or a bomber. But I know where she lives. That's worth something.

Now what?

People think of detective work as heart-pounding, adrenaline-pumping pursuit and confrontation. The high-speed chase. The takedown. The big bust. There's some of that. But mostly detectives spend mind-numbing hours waiting and watching.

No one arrived. No one left. No one screamed. No gun was fired. No lifeless body was carried out rolled in a rug. I guessed nothing more would happen that night. I was freezing, hungry, and thirsty. My arm was throbbing. Though I craved action, I knew it was more prudent to call it a day.

I didn't stop for food. But back in my ninth-floor room, sans Vicodin, I hit the minibar. The first Scotch dropped the pain in my shoulder from a seven to a four. The second numbed me enough to allow my brain to clock out.

But not right away. The last scene to play in my overwrought mind. Eighteen-year-old me, sweat, snot, and blood on my face. Cuffs on my wrists, a cop at my side. Beau, at last out of patience, doing tough love. Pick a uniform, kid. Military or DOC. No way I was going to jail.

Eleven Days

They are trapped in a chain of dreary wet days. No one ventures out. She can't visit the clearing.

After supper, they gather as usual. The Leader preaches of salvation and a glorious new order. Of fulfillment. Enlightenment. His voice thunders. His gaze is hot enough to brand her face.

His sermons usually light embers in her chest. Make her feel handpicked. Tonight she zings with nervous energy. The words take forever to find an ending.

He senses her agitation. Or her scratching disgusts him. He sends her away. To wait. She knows it will be bad. The Testing is always worse when she has upset him.

Alone in her room, she imagines the clearing at night. Moonlight sifting through the trees. Or blackness all around, thick and velvety-soft. Shadowy creatures. Leaves winking dark and pale, depending on the serendipitous twists of their spines. Each time she paints a different canvas.

Tonight's the night. A woman named True has been sleeping in her room. True is not here, and no one will say where she's gone. Or *when she'll return. The old lady who posed questions has also vanished.*

His voice rolls on, soaring and plunging. Eventually stops. Chairs scrape the floorboards. Then come the familiar nighttime sounds. Footfalls on the stairs. Doors closing. Toilets flushing. Water trickling through pipes.

The noises seem to go on forever. She waits them out. Waits for him. No matter how much it hurts, she won't moan or flinch. Won't let a single tear escape from her eyes. She has learned to go to another place. To take herself into the make-believe canvas and away from the pain.

He doesn't come. Instead she hears voices outside. An engine revving up. Tires spitting gravel. She is grateful for the reprieve. She is also afraid. Is he so angry that he has given up on her? Will he cast her out? Worse?

Where are True and the old woman?

Should she abandon her foolhardy plan?

No. She has to see it for real.

When all is finally still she sits up in bed. Listens, blood thudding in her ears.

She envisions every inch of her route. Out the window, which she's left partially open. Butt-slide on the roof. Scramble down the ladder. Sprint across the yard.

She is petrified. She is exhilarated. The ladder is there because some mundane task was interrupted by rain. What if someone wakes and decides to stow it? What if True returns? She has planned for neither catastrophe.

Barely breathing, she changes into sweatshirt and jeans, retrieves her windbreaker and shoes from under the bed. Presses the bundle to her chest. Feels her heart drum the nylon.

She almost turns back.

No. She has to see it at night. Smell it. Just once.

She pulls on the jacket, snugs into the sneakers, ties the laces. Tiptoes across the room.

The rain has stopped and the world is now shrouded in mist. She turns and eases feet first, belly down over the sill.

The roof is steep and cellophane-slick. She skids. Fast. Too fast. Her palms rake the shingles. She almost cries out.

A terrifying plunge, then her soles slam the gutter. She balances, breath frozen, certain the clatter has give her away.

Not a sound from inside the house. No window lights up.

Palms burning, she rolls and bum-scoots to the ladder. Scrambles down the rungs, across the alley, and into the trees.

She's done it!

Lying on the quilt, spread-eagle, she gazes up through the spiky branches overhead.

The mist is a gray smear blurring the moon. It dampens her lashes. Collects on her hair and in the folds of her ears. Cools her palms.

The quiet surrounds her.

But his words seethe and boil in her brain.

In all her life she's never been so confused. So afraid.

Her suspicions cannot be true.

CHAPTER
13

The next morning I was back on Argyle Street by seven, bearing Dunkin' Donuts coffee and a half-dozen chocolate-glazed with sprinkles, fuel badly needed given my three hours of sleep, throbbing shoulder, and "screw dinner" Scotch hangover. I was a curly-headed blonde.

I did a bit more reconnaissance than I had in the wee hours after my underpass adventure. Ended up in a different corner of the same courtyard, this one boasting winter-bare shrubbery and a concrete bench.

The woman came out at noon. She wasn't wearing the Sox cap, and I could see that her hair was long and auburn. She had it tied in a loose knot at the back of her head.

She went to a Lebanese grocery on Broadway, emerged with an eco-friendly carrier bulging with goodies. At two, she walked to a dry cleaner, returned with plastic-shrouded clothing over one shoulder. She never saw me shadowing her.

At five, I hit a noodle shop on Broadway, then hurried back to Argyle. At six, the light in the second-story window went on. By then my shoulder was screaming and my lower back was cramped from favoring my left side. I hung around until ten, when the room went dark. Then, feeling Stella was safe for at least one more night and needing to do something more proactive, I treated myself to a taxi.

The cabbie dropped me at the Ritz. He was a whiny sort, bitter that Uber was horning in on his turf. Glad to part company, I watched his rig belch exhaust as it gunned from the curb. All the way up to twelve, I could taste the fumes at the back of my throat.

The lobby was packed. A lot of people wore badges on lanyards hung around their necks. I saw no one furtively watching or weaving through the crowd toward me. No one thumbing a cellphone. I pushed for an elevator.

The car was full. Had a behemoth convention overrun the place? I checked a mirror hanging high in one corner. The fish-eye effect made everyone look squat and threatening.

I felt the familiar heat in my chest. Did the prescribed deep breathing. Reassured myself that all was well.

Myself didn't buy it. Cover your ass, it warned. And get the Vicodin.

A group of five got off on twenty-four. Three turned right. I blended with them, walked to the end of the corridor, and slipped through the emergency exit. After letting a couple of minutes go by, I cracked the door and peered down the hall.

Beyond my suite was the corridor in which I'd left my belongings the previous day. On the wall where the elevator and suite hall T-boned into the intersecting hall was a gilt-framed mirror, below it a sideboard with a floral arrangement and a house phone.

Reflected in the mirror was a man standing where I had squatted, a scrawny guy in a corduroy jacket, black pants, and Nikes. He kept his left hand in his pocket. As I watched, he rolled the wall on one shoulder and peeked around the corner.

My body hunched. Instinct.

The man's hair formed a fuzzy blond ring around a disk of scalp at the back of his head. Made me think of a monk's tonsure. A furtive mouse-through-the-hole glance, then he drew back.

Were my attackers giving it another go? Or was my paranoia working overtime. I watched the corridor through my tiny gap.

The elevator stopped and two women got off. Both wore name tags. One said MILLER, the other WRYZNIAK. They went left and disappeared around the corner. Seconds later the monk took another look-see.

If the guy wasn't watching for me, what other purpose could he have? A secret tryst? A jealous lover? A husband hoping to catch his conventioneering wife in flagrante delicto?

As with Sox Cap, I wondered if the monk had a partner. That's how I'd do it. If so, the second guy should be positioned in the stairwell where I was hiding. One at each end of the hall. That way they could nail me in the crossfire.

Had this been the purpose of Sox Cap's call at the underpass? Go to plan B? They'd know who I was based on her description. And the fact that I had a key card to enter the suite.

The elevator stopped again. Two men got off, no badges. They turned in my direction. I saw the monk peek around the corner to check them out.

I watched for another quarter hour. No one approached the guy. He never used a phone, never signaled toward a room or intersecting hall.

I thought about that. About the fact that he was standing by a mirror that telegraphed his every move. The guy wasn't a pro. Odds were, he was working alone.

I had the Glock, could have taken him out. But I wanted to grill him. To learn what I could about Stella. And another shooting would not have improved my position with C-squared. Or the Ritz.

Soundlessly, I eased the door to the jamb and scampered down one flight. The layout on twenty-three was identical to that on twenty-four. I looked for the service elevator. Found it at the end of the corridor in which the monk was holding vigil.

I pushed the button. Waited. Descended one floor. Listened. Descended another. Listened. No bonging. No groaning of gears or cables. Just the whir of the motor and the hum of the door.

I returned to twenty-four and exited into a large janitorial closet similar to one I'd encountered several floors below. Buckets, mops, vacuums, carts. Adrenaline pumping, I crossed the tile and eased open the door. The monk's back was to me.

I took a deep breath and started down the hall. This had to work. I had no backup scheme.

But I did have experience in hand-to-hand combat. Training in ways to inflict as well as receive pain. Muscles ready but relaxed, I closed in on my prey.

As I crouched to hit him, the monk glanced my way. His eyes went wide. He spun, flexed a knee, and kicked out with one foot. I followed his action, moving in the same direction as his thrust. Too slow. His boot slammed my hip. I lost my balance and fell. Rolled out of his range.

With adrenaline firing, one's sense of time is distorted. The next few moments seemed to go on forever. Nothing I hadn't experienced before.

The guy pounced and grabbed my hair to yank back my head. The wig came off. He tossed it, forced me prone, and, faster than I'd have thought possible, wrapped my left arm and neck in a half nelson. My cervical vertebrae crunched. A firestorm exploded in my wounded shoulder.

The monk's face was close to mine, his breath hot and moist on my skin. I could smell garlic and stale beer from his dinner.

I went limp for a heartbeat. My opponent fell for the ploy and, overconfident, raised his upper body and loosened his fingers to regrip my right wrist. Taking advantage of his blunder, I shot my arm stiff, tore free of his grasp, and pushed up with all my strength.

The sharp reangling of my torso tipped the guy sideways. The half nelson slipped. I twisted and struck up at his nose with the heel of my hand. Cartilage snapped and blood gushed.

I ass-scooted to free my legs. We both scrambled to our knees. He came at me. I nailed him with an elbow to the jaw. His head flew sideways. He hit the carpet, rose up, and crawled toward the sideboard. He was clawing his way upright when I took him down with a kick to the kidneys. The scrawny dude was tougher than he looked. Again he tried to stand.

I pressed the muzzle of the Glock to the back of his neck.

"Not so fast, my friend."

He froze.

"Put both hands on your head."

He did.

"Lace your fingers."

He did. Right on the tonsure. Which, up close, looked scaly and pink. Ditto the fingers.

Keeping the Glock tight to his neck, I checked the guy's jacket pockets. Scored a Beretta nine-millimeter and a hotel key card. I frisked him with my free hand. The movement triggered more flames in my damaged shoulder. I found nothing else.

As I stuck the Beretta into my waistband, a door opened behind me. In the mirror I saw Wryzniak chugging up the hall, stainless-steel ice bucket wrapped in her arms. Front-on she looked like some kind of gluten-free muffin.

On seeing us, Wryzniak froze, pivoted, and scurried back to her room. I knew she'd be heading straight for the phone.

"You and I are going to have a nice little chat." My voice was low and forged of steel. "Keep your hands where they are. Don't breathe. Don't blink. Don't step sideways off a line leading straight to my suite."

The monk started to speak. I jammed the muzzle deeper into his flesh. "I've killed one of your pals. I won't hesitate going for two."

We walked quickly, me pressed to his back like a jockey on a Thoroughbred. Only I was two hands taller. Outside the door, I gave him my key card.

"Open it," I said.

"You're going to shoot me."

"I might," I said. "Open it."

He disengaged the lock but didn't budge. "Move, dickhead." I shoved him with a foot to his ass. He stumbled forward into the living room. No one opened fire or rushed out. I followed him in and kicked the door shut.

"Sit." Indicating the sofa. "And no bleeding on the rug. They cleaned it once. I'm not paying twice."

He sat. Backhanded his face. Eyed the blood, uncertain what to do next.

I crossed to the desk, unloaded and set the Beretta on the blotter. Placed my Glock beside it.

"Who are you?" I remained standing, wanting the advantage of height and the glare off the glass.

No response.

"Having to repeat makes me cross. Being cross makes me jumpy. You don't want me jumpy." I picked up the Glock.

The monk remained silent. One of his eyes was already swelling shut. His right cheek was bloody, and a fresh stream was running from his nose.

"What's your name?"

"Suck my dick."

"Ethnic. Quaint. Okay, Suck. What's the deal?"

He stared at me, stoic. I guessed his age at mid- to late twenties. Hard to tell with the bad hair.

"Fine. You're shy. I'll start. Here's an interesting factoid. I'll get twenty-five grand for your sorry ass. And my employer isn't picky about the state of your health."

"I need a doctor."

"That's good. You're sharing."

"May I at least have a Kleenex?"

I gestured at a box on the far end of the desk. Almost flinched from the pain. Almost.

The monk pushed to his feet, chin elevated, fingers pinching his nostrils. Three steps, then he feigned reaching for a tissue. At the last second twisted and lunged for my throat.

I was ready this time. I slipped behind him, crooked his arm back and up sharply while simultaneously hyperflexing his wrist.

Squeezed. The bones dislocated with a sickening pop. I released my hold.

The monk dropped to his knees, shriek deflating into a moan. His hand was hanging wrong, his thumb bent at a very odd angle. I noticed that the hairs on his fingers were blond and thick.

"Rookie move, Suck." I pointed at the couch.

He resumed his seat, wincing and gingerly cradling his arm.

"What's your name?" I asked.

He stared, face pale, jaw set.

"Maybe that one's too hard. We'll come back to it. Why are you here?"

More silence.

"I could do the other hand." No way, but I didn't let it show. "Happens a lot, I hear. People trip, snap both wrists." I didn't know if that was true, but it sounded good.

"Eat shit."

"Must hurt."

"Kiss my—"

"If you answer my questions I'll call for a medic."

"Let me leave and none of this happened."

"It's not going to play that way. What's your name?"

"Fuck you." Not as forceful as he wanted. I guessed his pain was much worse than mine.

I took the Bnos Aliza stills from my purse and chose the remaining two males. A lot could change in a year. And the image was crap. I couldn't be sure. I was still comparing features when someone pounded on the door. Wryzniak had come through.

I went to the bedroom and tucked my Glock behind the flatscreen. Returned. The monk hadn't moved.

"Come in!" I yelled.

It was Harvey and Fix, the same pair who'd responded to the shooting.

"So we meet again." Harvey actually said that.

"So we do," I replied. "This gentleman needs attention."

"What happened to him?"

KATHY REICHS · 104

"Tripped."

"You're one tough cookie." He actually said that, too.

"I am."

"Who is he?"

"He won't say."

As before, Fix manned the phone. When he'd disconnected: "The hotel doc's on her way."

"He was in your suite?" Harvey asked.

"No."

"Why'd you beat him up?"

"He doesn't like me."

"Was he armed?"

"On the desk."

"What about you?"

I shook my head. Would have pulled out the pockets of the fleece but the theatrics weren't worth jostling my shoulder.

"Your buddies are en route," Fix said.

"Capps and Clegg?"

Fix nodded.

We waited in silence until the doctor arrived. Mocha skin, short black hair, five minutes out of med school. She wore a silk blouse, pencil skirt, and carried a vintage double-handled physician's bag. Her name tag said DR. JEFFERSON. The Ritz really wants you to know the staff. I like that.

"Check that guy." Harvey gestured with a thumb.

Jefferson perched on the couch, drew latex gloves from her kit, and snapped them on. After swabbing the monk's face with a moist towelette, she palpated his nose. His jaw muscles bunched, but he didn't cry out.

She checked the wrist, said to him, "It's a dislocation, not a break. Still, you'd best be examined by an orthopedist." To Harvey, "May I administer a painkiller?"

"He has to make a statement first," I said.

"Yeah?" Harvey said.

"Yeah," I said.

The monk said nothing.

Jefferson was zipping her snazzy leather satchel when Capps and Clegg charged in. Clegg looked at me, then at the monk. "Another twenty-five bills in the bank?"

"I'm not sure," I said.

"This one got a tat?"

"Not that I've seen."

"Still, could be a pal of the one you capped," Clegg said.

"Nothing gets by you."

Clegg's lips tucked in and his head wagged slowly.

"This man should be seen by a specialist," Jefferson said. "Now. Or he may suffer permanent loss of motion."

"Would be a shame with such a great future behind him," I said.

Jefferson wasn't amused. She lifted her bag from the floor and strode toward the door.

"Have a blessed day," I said to the retreating pencil skirt.

The good doctor declined to return my warm wishes.

"You need us for anything else?" Harvey asked.

"We can handle it from here," Capps said.

"Have a good one."

"You've been keeping busy," Capps said when Harvey and Fix had gone. "What's the story this time?"

I laid it out. "Can you hold him?"

"What the fuck?" The monk came alive.

"On what charge?" Capps asked me, mostly for the monk's benefit.

"He was packing a Beretta," I said.

"That's not illegal," the monk said. Realizing his mistake, "And who says the gun's mine?"

"The weapon could be unlicensed," I said. "Or stolen. He could have an arrest record. Or psychiatric issues."

"Like that stops anyone in this country." Clegg, master of sarcasm.

KATHY REICHS · 106

"There's always assault," I said.

"Are you serious?" The monk's pallid cheeks were lighting up red. "You attacked me! You broke my fucking arm!"

"Doc says it's not a break," I said.

Capps looked to Clegg. Clegg shrugged "whatever."

"We can hold him for forty-eight," Capps said. "Then it's charge him or kick him."

"You're locking me up?" The monk was doing outraged, which really wasn't working.

"Are you staying at this hotel, sir?" Capps asked him.

The monk glared.

"No matter. Guest registration is easy to verify."

"Probably got up here with a stolen key card."

"MO for the guy you capped," Clegg said.

Capps refocused on the monk. "What's your name?"

More glare.

"What were you doing in the hallway?"

"Waiting for someone."

"Who?"

"Suck my dick."

"He likes to say that," I said.

Capps and Clegg exchanged another of their looks. "I'll call for an ambulance," Clegg said. "Wouldn't want accusations of police brutality."

While Clegg spoke on his cell, Capps took cuffs from his belt, clamped one side onto the monk's good wrist, the other onto a chrome crosspiece at the end of the sofa. Then he nodded toward the bedroom. I went in. He followed.

"You okay?"

"Ducky."

"You look like hell."

"My gimp shoulder took a hit. I'll live."

"I have a couple of thoughts I'd like to share. First off, the Ritz isn't pleased. The only reason you're not out is Drucker's pull."

"She knows?"

"Layton Furr is a very conscientious employee."

"I didn't kill this guy." Tipping my head toward the living room.

"Management appreciates that. And, truth be told, so do I. Best-case scenario, he and his buds are small-time goons with IQs lower than their moral standards."

"And bombs."

"Perhaps."

"And an abducted kid."

"Perhaps that, too."

"Worst-case?" I asked.

"They're terrorists with bigger aspirations. Perhaps part of a network that's managed to stay under the radar. Until now. We'll sweat this prick hard."

"Make him give it up on Stella."

"The kid's probably dead."

She was alive. I felt it in my soul. Didn't say it.

"I want to view the Bnos Aliza video."

Capps hesitated, then, "My partner and I don't want you here, Ms. Night. Working for profit."

I started to object. He cut me off.

"We also don't want you dead."

"Meaning?"

"These people have tried twice. In all likelihood, they'll come at you again."

"I expect so."

"I know you'll take measures. Those measures must not involve more corpses."

"You have my gun."

Capps's face shut down. I thought he was through, but he spoke again.

"We've learned some disturbing facts about you. I hope the press doesn't learn them, too. So far the hotel has kept things quiet. But think, Ms. Night. How often are people gunned down at the Ritz?"

Through the door we heard the arrival of the EMTs. Voices.

"Gunned down by a woman with an expunged juvie record and"—tight head wag—"a less than exemplary military file."

I felt my carotid throb. Willed my face neutral.

"I appreciate the trauma that a difficult childhood inflicts." Capps's voice went barbed-wire cold. "But I will not have you working out your issues on my patch. Do we understand each other?"

I didn't trust myself to speak.

Capps flicked a smile. "Have a nice day."

I heard but didn't hear the swish of Capps's soles. The clank of the cuffs. The rattle of the gurney. I stood paralyzed, heart plowing, chest burning. Face-to-face with my life. Again.

My mother's features congealed in some overwrought tangle of neurons, the few splinters of her story I'd managed to pry loose. A teen nanny lured from Dublin to Manhattan, undocumented, a pedophile's fantasy. Her flight to the streets. Her encounter with a charismatic guru, a pathological narcissist promising salvation, ultimately demanding death.

My brain offered no flashbulb images of my father. It held no memories, just fragments of his tale, reluctantly yielded. A tall black man, unholy, banished for spreading his seed. For me?

Time passed. No idea how much. Then, slowly, the quiet registered. The kind of quiet made up of empty space and a thousand sounds of the present. The minibar humming. TV dialogue floating through a wall. The muffled buzz of some unseen electronic device.

I drew the required inhalations. Got a Scotch and downed half the little bottle in one pull. Fought the fiends back into the recesses where I keep them captive.

When the Scotch was gone and my pulse was normal, I considered the big king bed. The Jacuzzi. The colossal TV. My shoulder said yes. My head said no.

After collecting my wig from beneath the sideboard, I descended and trudged to the Tremont. A long hot soak and a couple of Advil and I was feeling almost human. Propped on the bed, I thumbed a number into my Walmart mobile.

Far away, a phone rang twice. A voice answered.

"Hey."

"You busy?" I asked.

"In general?"

"The next few days. Maybe longer."

"A couple of deliveries. One boat trip. Nothing I can't rearrange if you need me. You know that."

"I do."

"That's our deal."

"That's our deal."

"You in trouble?"

"Never."

"Talk to me."

I did.

Ten Days

S ome have left, others have arrived. Strangers.
That night they drag chairs from all over the house. She sits
in one, a good girl living only for the word. The mission.

His voice thunders, a jungle drum pounding out a battle call.
Though the language is oblique, one thing is clear.
It's coming.
Soon.
The Crossing.
Again, the Leader sends her to bed before the gathering ends.
He also must leave. A few others. She wonders why. None of them
has made a troublesome query. Nor does she anymore.

His eyes meet hers as they rise to go. They tell her nothing. Since
coming to the new place he has been too busy to talk. Or, sensing
her craziness, he is avoiding confrontation. That's how he labels
her misgivings.
Is she crazy?
She has to know more.
She makes the right sounds. Washing up. Flushing. Closing her
door.

Then she creeps back to sit at the top of the stairs. She pictures herself, a small dark shadow in the gray oozing from a window far down the hall.

She listens, breath shallow, every cell still.

Just crusade.

The usual veiled rhetoric.

Future order. Return to the path.

Then her whole body goes cold.

Sacrifice of innocents. Act of love.

A question. She's unsure who poses it.

The answer is charged with anger, not love.

Death. The sole solution.

The air goes out of her lungs.

Another question.

More words she can never unhear.

No exceptions. Babies. Children. Total commitment.

She works to inhale.

Her brain pulses.

No.

No.

No.

CHAPTER 14

I woke with a shoulder so stiff I had to loosen it manually using my right hand. An exercise I did not enjoy. The wound had bled, so I changed the dressing and popped a couple more Advil before attempting to dress and tug on the blond wig. Also a less than pleasant experience. I'd decided against the Vicodin. The pain was like old times. New times.

Spring had yet to arrive in the city beside the lake. According to my phone, afternoon temperatures would soar to forty-eight. Rain was falling. Hell, maybe that *was* spring in Illinois.

I skipped breakfast, too anxious to eat. My fourth day here and still nothing on Stella. Where was this kid who was haunting my dreams by night and living in my head by day? The Bnos Aliza bombers knew I was poking around. Hell, I was shooting people. Had they murdered her because she'd become a liability to them? Because they feared testimony she might give?

Because of me?

Time was slipping through my fingers. I had to make a breakthrough.

I rode the Red Line north to Lawrence and, cautious, took a

zigzag route from the "L" station, keeping an eye out for signs I was being followed. I saw none. If they were tailing me, they were good. Based on their performances at Foster Beach and at the Ritz, I doubted that.

I grabbed two coffees to go from a café on Winthrop, added a Snickers from a pharmacy. As I passed a Chicago Housing Authority building, several sidewalk entrepreneurs offered to sell me some really good shit. It was 8:15. Though it sounded appealing, I declined. I had caffeine, chocolate, and peanuts. I also had props. If my quarry glanced into the courtyard, she'd see a badly dressed blonde reading Tolstoy in a drizzle.

By ten the second coffee was cold, a condition that did nothing to improve its flavor. Which I imagined was fairly close to Arghandab runoff. Though, full disclosure, I've never drunk from an Afghan river.

I poured the dregs on the ground, slipped the book and cardboard cups into my purse, and crossed to the bay-fronted building. Risky, but the Advil had worn off and the candy was gone. I was amped and needed to move.

I climbed the five steps to the porch and entered. The front door gave onto a small foyer with a tile floor sincerely in need of scrubbing. Four brass mailboxes formed a square on the left-hand wall. Beside each box were a buzzer and a grimy glass rectangle covering a handwritten name.

Four apartments, three up, one in the basement, I guessed. Or maybe one of the floors was divided. I read the names: B. Nakulabye, RR, T. Fugakawa, T. & F. Leighter, J. Kerr.

J. Kerr was on two. Bingo.

I pressed the buzzer. A voice came through the little round speaker, tinny and distorted but definitely female.

"Yes?"

"Mr. Hawthorn?"

"Sorry?"

"Mr. Hawthorn."

"He moved."

The intercom went dead.

I exited and crossed back to my bench. Five minutes later Kerr came out and headed west on Argyle. I tailed her until she turned left at Clark. Watched until she boarded a bus. Then I hurried back, entered the foyer, and pressed the bell for J. Kerr.

No answer. I pressed again. A third time, laying on a full ten seconds. Nothing.

I tried the door. Of course it was locked. I appraised. The building was old. The lock was old. Piece of cake.

I dug a small zipper case from my purse and took a moment to admire my purchase. Compact. Ergonomic. A burglar's best friend.

I set to work turning tumblers, listening, mostly going by feel. In less than two minutes, I was in.

The staircase had turns and landings and reflected a more prosperous era in the building's past. The banisters and newels, beautifully carved, were now coated with layers of yellowed varnish. The tread runner was in the same grubby state as the foyer tile.

The second floor had only one unit. I knocked. No answer. I knocked again, waited, then repeated the process of picking the lock. Here it took roughly forty-five seconds.

I cracked the door and called out. No one answered.

J. Kerr's apartment was totally silent. Still, I drew the Glock and did a fast sweep. Living room in front, two bedrooms down a long narrow hall, dining room and kitchen in back.

I peered out a kitchen window. Saw a small yard covered in concrete. Beyond the yard, an alley. Across the alley, garbage cans and the butt end of a row of buildings like the one I was in.

A lightning search of the cabinets and fridge told me little about the woman who'd stocked them. She bought overpriced organic everything. Liked yogurt, kale, and whole grain bread. Or at least she ate them. One drawer held a small plastic bottle of Brahmi–Gotu Kola capsules. I was clueless what that was. Beside the bottle was packaging that indicated the product had been bought online. I checked the delivery address. Using my phone, took a shot of the label.

I raced to the living room, then retraced my route, snagging details as I passed each room. The place looked like one of those
extended-stay corporate executive deals. The furniture was boring,
the art forgettable. Warehouse knickknacks here and there, artfully
arranged and meant not to offend. Sensationally bland upholstery,
bedding, and carpets, mostly in shades of tan and beige. Drapes in
the living room, venetian blinds elsewhere, all closed but leaking a
little morning light.

The bath was shared by both bedrooms. Like the kitchen, it revealed zip about J. Kerr. There was nothing girly or personal in the
shower or under the sink. No makeup, nail polish, body lotion, or
face cream. The shampoo, soaps, and other toiletries were all common pharmacy brands: deodorant, toothpaste, dental floss, razor,
comb and brush, hair binders, tampons.

The bedrooms continued the theme of early blah. One book on
the bedside table: *A Treasury of English Sonnets*. So Kerr had a
lyrical soul. Or poetry came with the place and she wasn't a reader.

A quick trip through the dresser yielded underwear, all white
cotton, socks, all white cotton, and sweatshirts, plain gray, no witty
sayings, sports logos, or college insignia. Three dark polyester
blouses and three pairs of jeans hung in the closet. Beside them,
still in their plastic sheaths, were a black skirt and two black sweaters. On the floor below, black boots, running shoes, and a pair of
black flats. On the shelf above, a black wool scarf and the Sox cap.
So much for lyrical.

The lit window I'd observed was in the back bedroom. Twin
bed, nightstand, lamp, no book. Blinds.

On the wall opposite the bed was a black printer's keyhole desk,
probably Pottery Barn, one long drawer across the middle, three
stacked on each side. On the desktop was a MacBook Air similar
to my own.

Hell-o.

I checked my watch. I'd been in the apartment almost seven
minutes. I'd promised myself thirty, max.

I hurried to the desk and began rifling drawers. Found the usual pens, tablets, envelopes, tape. The bottom drawer on the right was crammed with burner phones still in the packaging. Made sense. No landline in the apartment.

The bottom drawer on the left held a collection of mail. I flipped through. Mostly ads and flyers, crap addressed to "Occupant" at the Argyle address. I wondered why Kerr hadn't tossed the lot. Remembered the heap on my sideboard, brought to the island from the post office but never sorted.

Then I discovered the real purpose of the stack. Camouflage. Seriously?

Hidden below the mail were two passports bound together with a rubber band. Both were American. Both showed a woman with auburn hair, wide-spaced brown eyes, and a nose much too large for her face. I guessed her age at early twenties. I'd never gotten a good look at Sox Cap, but I suspected I was viewing her now. I doubted she was the woman caught on the Bnos Aliza surveillance video.

The first passport had been issued to Jasmine Helena Kerr, birth date 12/22/92. Christmas baby. Bad timing. The other belonged to Jennifer Claire Latourneau, born 10/15/94. Using my phone, I snapped a pic of each photo page, then returned both to the drawer.

Nine minutes.

Nerves buzzing, I dropped into the chair and opened the laptop. A screen saver fired to life. A lioness gazing over the savanna with her cub. The little rectangle demanded a password. Of course it did.

I shut down and, holding the command and S keys, switched to single-user mode, entered a few commands, rebooted, and set up a new administrator account, inputting the minimal amount of info requested. After creating a username and password, I went to system preferences, reset and verified the password for the original administrator, logged off, then logged on using the new information. Presto! I was in.

Sixteen minutes.

I opened the documents folder. It held three files. One was a PDF—an onscreen manual for a printer. The second was titled *Dolphins,* the third *KD.* I chose *KD.*

The contents consisted of a list of email addresses. Most had suffixes indicating commercial providers. Dot-coms. I recognized Gmail, Yahoo, AOL. A few had suffixes indicating foreign countries.

Why store contact information in a document file? Some ill-conceived notion of online security? For easier printing or sharing? Seemed J. Kerr was less than a cybergenius. I considered sending the file to myself as an email, instead took a pic of the screen.

Dolphins contained the names and addresses of animal and nature charities. Humane Society of the United States. American Society for the Prevention of Cruelty to Animals. Greenpeace. Animals Asia. Alley Cat Allies. World Wildlife. African Wildlife Foundation. I closed the file, then went to Mail.

Nothing stored. Nothing in trash.

Nothing on Stella Bright.

Fingers clumsy, palms damp, I moved to the inbox. Four messages. All had landed within the past half hour.

Two emails were spam, one touting Belize as a tax haven, the other offering relief from erectile dysfunction. The other two were from senders calling themselves Trailblazer and Infidel. I opened the latter.

Godolphin Vintage Claret Beauty 05 05 06. FL1X: LM-inf /JC-GR/ B5-S2+4

Obviously code. I checked for Kerr's email address as the recipient: jhk07749@gmail.com. I entered it into the Notes app on my phone.

Using Safari, I found Kerr's Gmail account. Another box requested yet another password. I right-clicked on the six dots, selected Inspect Element, double-clicked on the command line containing *type* = "*password,*" and changed *password* to *text*. Instead of dots I was now looking at the password. Sweet Jesus in a romper. She was using her birthday.

Seven emails. All received within the past twenty-four hours. The two spam ads and another from a dear friend in Christ.

I opened the message from Infidel and checked the sender. Infidel567@gmail.com. I keyed the address into Notes below Kerr's.

Nineteen minutes, twenty seconds. I was sweating inside my jacket and wig.

I clicked on a tiny triangle to the right of the reply arrow, then chose the command Show Original from the drop-down menu.

A block of data appeared. At roughly midpoint was a line with the header Received. Embedded in the gibberish was a string of four numbers divided by periods, the sender's IP address. I took a phone shot of the screen.

Twenty-three minutes.

I returned to Gmail.

Trailblazer's message was succinct.

Confirmed.

I revealed the IP address of trailblazer745@gmail.com and entered it below the others. Tried a pic. Fumbled. Got it.

Twenty-six minutes.

The last two emails were from spearhead2021@yahoo.com and loyalc2020@aol.com. Both had sent the same one-word message as Trailblazer. I added both IP addresses to my list.

I poked around a few seconds longer. Photos. Calendar. iCloud. AirDrop. Found nothing. Clearly Kerr didn't maximize the Mac's potential. Or she stored all her files offline.

Twenty-eight minutes.

Out of time, I reversed all my changes, returning the Mac to the condition in which I'd found it. An expert hacker could ferret out my presence, but I doubted Kerr was that ferret. That hacker.

Thirty-four minutes.

A quick inspection of the apartment to see that all was pristine. To double-check for any indication of another occupant. For anything to suggest Stella Bright's presence. Negative on both.

Thirty-six minutes after breaking in, I slipped out, returned to my courtyard, and threw up. As though on cue, the rain resumed.

An hour later Kerr came slouching up the block. Or Latourneau. Or whatever her real name was. Looking neither left nor right, she climbed the stairs and entered her building.

I was settling in for a long, soggy wait when my mobile buzzed.

CHAPTER
15

"You want to see the video?"

"Detective Capps. Thank you for asking. My morning has been splendid."

"This a bad time? Maybe there's someone you need to shoot?"

"Give me the address."

"Western Avenue, just north of Belmont. Can't miss it. Place looks like Buckingham Palace."

"On my way."

"I'll alert the concierge."

I walked to Broadway and hailed a cab. I knew Opaline wouldn't want me to keep C-squared waiting.

Capps's description was dead-on. If the royals lived in a two-story brick box surrounded by pavement and billeting its own radio tower.

Most cop shops are basically the same inside. Some more so than others. The Area Three station was no exception. Dingy windows, scuffed floors, walls begging for fresh paint. The air was thick with the smell of cleaning products, wet clothing, and human discontent.

At noon, the lobby had only a light dusting of the usual characters. Two patrol officers were doing macho. A hooker in ass-baring shorts and neon makeup was protesting the injustice of her arrest. A geezer in coveralls and rubber boots was whining about a dead cat in his truck. A drunk, skin gray as curdled milk, was saying nothing at all.

I presented myself to a desk sergeant who appeared to be having an unrewarding shift. Her hair was bottle bronze, her eyes pointed at a copy of that morning's *Tribune*. Her name was Varga.

"I'm Sunday Night," I said, then bent the truth. "An investigator out of Charleston."

"I'll arrange a parade."

"Roy Capps is expecting me."

Varga checked a clipboard. "Violent crimes. Second floor, turn right, past youth division." Gaze already back on the paper.

I climbed the stairs behind a scruffy, stubbled dude who had to be an undercover narc. Or a crackhead unable to grasp the subtleties of the stairwell signage: POLICE PERSONNEL ONLY.

I found my objective precisely as promised. I'd underestimated Varga. The woman was at the top of her game.

Like the lobby, the violent crimes squad room held no surprises. Blinds on the windows and tile on the floor. Desks holding case files, phones, mugs, and Starbucks cups. Some had personal mementos—a framed photo, a joke trophy, an NBA bobblehead.

The room was buzzing with people taking calls, drinking coffee, clicking keys at computer terminals. One corner was hosting a debate about bite mark evidence.

I asked for Capps and Clegg and was directed to a window at the back of the room. Through the glass, beyond the concrete and another featureless, flat-topped brick structure, I could see a fragment of greenery bordering water the color of bean soup.

Capps and Clegg had their desks pushed edge to edge, facing each other. Capps was at his. Clegg was not. Probably out hacking my bank account. Good luck, Bernie. My dough is offshore.

"Room with a view," I said.

Capps was hunched forward, writing something. His shirt was avocado, his tie rust, a combo definitely not drawn from a Brooks Brothers playbook. A jacket hung from the back of his chair. It was brown herringbone and not a recent purchase. He looked up but didn't reply.

"What body of water is that?" I nodded at the window.

"North branch of the Chicago River."

"Nice spot." Except for the overpass and spit-ugly buildings. I didn't say that.

"Ever hear of Riverview?" Capps asked.

"No."

"The Bobs?" As though I'd said I'd never heard of cheese.

I shook my head.

"Only the most famous roller coaster of its time. Back in the day, every kid in Chicago hit the Bobs for cheap feels and giggles."

"You mention this because?"

"The park was razed in '67 and the city built this." Raising his arms to take in the room. "Ironic, eh?"

"How's that?"

"The kids coming here now aren't coming for laughs."

Capps hooked a chair with one foot, dragged it toward his desk, and gestured me to it.

"Any word on our tattooed friend in the morgue?" I sat.

"Negative. Not in the system."

That surprised me. "What about the tat?"

"Not in any database we checked. And Bernie floated it from here to Mars and back."

"How about the monk?"

Capps just looked at me.

"The guy from last night."

"John Scranton. Has a mama to prove it."

"Where does he live?"

"Mama's basement."

"Where's he work?"

"He's in transition."

"What was he doing at the Ritz?"

"Waiting for a friend when some lunatic jumped his ass."

"Did you run his prints?"

"He's not in the system, either."

"The guy was packing."

"He says the gun isn't his."

"I say it is."

"The Beretta was in your room."

"A hotel guest named Wryzniak saw him with it."

"All Wryzniak saw was a couple fighting in the hall."

"You believe Scranton's story?"

"No."

"You going to hold him?"

"There are reasons not to."

I lifted a brow.

"We plan to kick him, then stay close. Hope he leads us to the lair. If there is a lair."

"Is he sporting the double-*J* tat?"

"Nope. But he's got psoriasis so bad he looks like he's molting. Probably not into body art."

Behind us a phone rang. A guy answered. His name was Lopez.

"Brief me on what I'll see on this tape," I said.

Capps laid down his pen. Leaned back in his chair.

"It's monochrome. The detail's lousy due to distance and angle. And the fact that the setup was installed when the Bobs was still rolling. It's a VCR using time-lapse."

That didn't sound good. Most security systems now use hard drives. With a VCR on time-lapse, a tape can be programmed to run for as long as forty-eight hours. Slower recording speeds result in lower image quality. And loss due to quick turnover.

"Where was the camera?" I asked.

"Across the street and a little west of the school. Dov's Bake Shop. Dov had two—one outside aimed at the parking lot, one inside, aimed at the register. Both were wired to a video recorder in a back room. The one inside was dead. The one outside caught the street and the east end of Bnos Aliza."

"No cameras at the school or elsewhere on the block?"

"Nope." Capps pulled a tablet from a drawer down and to his left, flipped a few pages, scanned his notes. "The relevant parts were recorded on April 17, the day of the bombing. The loop starts at four in the morning. Shows a lot of nothing, then kids arriving, leaving. Cars going by. People walking.

"The footage that'll interest you begins at 4:16 P.M. Bowen, Stella, and Mary Gray Bright can be seen leaving the school with three other women. The women pause. Stella and Bowen walk west and disappear off frame.

"At 4:16 and 23 seconds, a dark-colored Subaru Forester can be seen traveling east to west on Devon. The plates are unreadable, either splattered with mud or intentionally covered. A woman and three men are inside. The blond guy you popped at the Ritz is driving. The woman is riding shotgun. The other two men are in back. The Forester passes the school and disappears.

"Mary Gray and two of the women walk off frame at 4:16 and 43 seconds. Debris is seen flying in from the west. Smoke. The woman who remained on the walk is thrown against the building."

Capps tossed the tablet onto his blotter. Its landing sent a little puff of air my way.

"That's it?" I asked.

"That's it. Seconds after the blast the camera goes black."

Sounded like the tape would be another dead end. I'd read the file, found nothing in it that others had missed. I debated. Tell Capps about my outing to Foster Beach? About Jasmine Kerr?

Capps and Clegg would get a warrant to toss Kerr's apartment. Kerr had passports. Contacts in other places. Enough burner phones to open a store. I didn't want her to panic and bolt. Not yet. Not until I pried free what she knew about Stella.

Full truth. I couldn't bear the burden of another death.

For some reason, Capps was actually talking to me. I decided to use that.

"Walk me through what happened," I said.

Capps's sharp little eyes crawled my face. Then, "A group of gutless bastards blew up a school."

"I meant first response immediately after the bomb."

"A billion people hit 911 on their cellphones. One woman reported a Subaru Forester speeding west on Devon. She thought she'd seen the same SUV cruising the area earlier in the week. She provided a fairly good description. Since the 911 calls came in so quickly, hope was the bombers were in the Forester and the Forester was still in the area. Units within a half mile were ordered to proceed to the scene. Units a half mile or more away were ordered to lock down a perimeter. Other than first responders, no vehicles or pedestrians were to get in or out. The goal was to find that Forester."

"And the kid."

"At that point no one knew she was missing."

"But you didn't find the vehicle."

Capps made no comment.

"So the group didn't go in blind, they did recon." I was thinking out loud. "Did you collect old tapes from the bakery? Check to see if the Forester appeared at other times? Earlier in the week? The month? If anyone was loitering near the school?"

"Yes, Ms. Night. We did. Unfortunately, Dov is a thrifty guy. He programmed the VCR to rerecord in a continuous loop, so there was little to check." Capps stood. "The tape is long. The van is visible for a few seconds. You want to view the whole thing?"

"Yes."

"Waste of time."

"Probably."

Capps shrugged.

I followed him to a windowless room with a video player, a monitor, a table, and two chairs. For the next several hours I watched vehicles enter and exit a small patch of pavement outside the bakery. An endless parade of traffic on Devon. The eastern half of Bnos Aliza. The school's lawn, walks, the barrier posts intended to keep it safe.

The heat in the building was going full blast. At first I didn't mind. I was sodden and chilled to the bone from my hours in the courtyard. Eventually, the cloying warmth took its toll. A headache kicked in. I began to sweat. I hit fast-forward more often and for longer stretches.

Between seven and 7:30 A.M. staff and faculty began to arrive at the school. Shortly thereafter, the girls, some from a carpool line at the curb, some on foot. They wore navy or blue plaid skirts modestly fitted to cover their knees. Sweaters or light jackets. Polo shirts with the BAS logo embroidered on the left breast. Some had breasts. Most did not.

The girls gathered in twos and threes, occasionally larger groups. Their hair blew free or was bound in ponytails or braids. Backpacks draped their shoulders or hung from their arms. They laughed and gossiped, unaware of the atrocity about to take place.

I felt the acid taste of bile in my throat. Swallowed.

By 7:50 the last girls had disappeared up a walkway leading off frame toward the west. I assumed toward the building's student entrance.

Throughout the day people came and went. A mother dropping off a forgotten book. Another picking up her daughter. Cars. Trucks. Buses. Shoppers. Workers. Cyclists. Joggers. I hurried and slowed them in a skittery panoply of jump starts and slo-mos.

At one P.M., a small group passed east to west in front of the school. Two men, four women, three kids. Among them were the Brights. Stella's hair gleamed like a newly minted penny in the afternoon sun.

Bowen and his mother had just over three hours to live. Stella?

A hollowness spread from my stomach to my chest. My throat tightened.

I dug a thumbnail deep into the flesh of my wrist. Inhaled.

At 3:27 P.M. girls started trickling into view. By 3:45 the walk-way, lawn, and sidewalk were clear.

Capps was right. At precisely 4:16, Mary Gray, her children, and three women came into view, two from the earlier group, one new. The Bright kids walked off frame.

Bowen and his mother had 43 seconds to live.

At 4:16 and 23 seconds the Forester crossed slowly from east to west.

At 4:16 and 43 seconds, Mary Gray and the two women with whom she'd arrived followed Bowen and Stella. The new woman lingered.

In less than a second, a half starburst of smoke and matter ex-ploded across the front of the school. The woman on the walkway flew backward and slammed into the stone. Her body was crum-pling to the ground when the screen went black.

I rewound, froze the image, and stared at the faces inside the van. Blurry. Shadowed. They could have been anybody.

I replayed the sequence over and over. Forty-three seconds that changed lives forever.

Capps was right again.

Watching had been a complete waste of time.

Nine Days

This house has no cellar, so she's back in the box. It's long and shallow, with a row of heavy clasps to secure the lid. Like a coffin.

She refuses to let that word into her mind. That image.

At first she could see light through the ragged perforations at her feet. She watched the outside world fade from amber to charcoal to black.

In her agitation, she became careless, was caught walking alone toward the alley. She was put in the box to meditate on her wickedness. Her commitment to the cause.

All she can think about is her tiny prison. The nail holes that are her sole source of air. The steel around her that will soon grow cold.

She listens. Hears only sounds coming from inside herself. Her racing pulse. Her ragged breath. She fights to slow both. To conserve her oxygen. Her sanity.

Outside the box, only silence.

She peers into the blackness. Sees nothing. Not even the sneakers she has bleached snowy white.

She smells oil. Something musty, like old drapes stored in an attic.

She runs her fingers along the metal below her. Feels shallow channels separated by parallel ridges. In the channels, particles, maybe soil, maybe rust.

She raises her hand. Her palm meets the lid inches above her face. She knows that. Isn't sure why she tests.

She has no idea how long she's been in the box. Has made no effort to measure the passage of time. She wants to disconnect. To anticipate nothing. Not food. Not light. Not freedom. It's easier that way.

She dozes. Or not. The sensory deprivation blocks her ability to know what is real and what isn't. What is waking and what is sleeping.

She sees the Leader. He is observing her, face still and cold as ice.

That's a dream. The Leader is not there. For a moment she's glad of the walls that separate him from her. From his scrutiny. His Testing. His pain.

The Leader's words ricochet into her mind. Or is she imagining that, too? Is her memory betraying her, turning reality into a nightmare too frightening to be true?

A calf muscle cramps. She tries to straighten her leg. The space is too small. She can't lie flat. She can't turn.

Suddenly she feels the walls closing in.

A tiny sound distracts her. One that wouldn't register but for the absolute stillness. An almost inaudible scritching, like a Lilliputian snail dragging across sand.

More darkness.

More nothing.

She is at the top of the stairs. The Leader rants below. Death. No exceptions.

Bad things are happening in her gut.

A feather tickles a path from her wrist to her elbow. Or a million tiny feet.

Her heart beats so wildly she fears it will burst from her chest.

Vivid images elbow out those of the Leader. Hairy legs. Venomous fangs.

She yanks her arm hard. Her elbow cracks steel.

She pushes toward a corner, tucks her chin to her chest and makes herself small.

She will not think about the spider. Centipede. Roach.

She will not think about the Leader.

She will not think about the past. The future.

She will focus only on not going mad. Nothing else matters.

Every nerve ending prickling, she tries her new trick.

She escapes to the canvas stored in her mind.

CHAPTER 16

After leaving Capps, I'd returned to my courtyard blind. The rain had let up, but the bench was soaked. Pro that I am, I'd snagged newspapers from a trash bin along the way. I'd watched, derriere cushioned by articles Varga had been reading hours earlier.

At eight the light in the back bedroom had gone on. At ten it had gone off. At 10:30 I'd returned to the Tremont to shower, rebandage, and sleep. I was staying another night. Risky business. But I was cold and wet and my shoulder hurt like a bitch.

I'd considered phoning Beau. Instead sent an email. He'd have posed a million questions. I'd have had few answers. And I didn't want to talk about the shooting. Or my fisticuffs with the monk. I'd also checked the social media and email accounts I'd set up before leaving Charleston. Nothing.

It was now nine A.M. Five days since my meet with Opaline Drucker. I was no longer a guest at the Tremont. And I was no longer watching from the bench. Pro that I am, I figured another day parked in the same spot was pushing my luck. I was around the corner, backpack on one shoulder, blond wig and explorer hat on my head, *Tribune* tucked under one arm should additional camouflage be needed. Not a wet copy, a brand-new morning edition. Oldest trope in the book, but I wasn't feeling particularly creative.

The wind was sharp and a layer of bruise-colored clouds was hanging low. If nothing else, I could use the paper to fend off the upcoming rain.

The angle wasn't perfect, but from where I stood the entrance to Kerr's/Latourneau's building was visible. For hours no one entered or left. There was little movement on Argyle. A few people going to or leaving parked cars. A few walkers. No one who looked like he or she might be packing a Beretta. But it was Chicago. According to the headline under my arm, fourteen people had taken lead on the mean streets overnight.

The lack of forward motion was making me crazy. But I had nothing but Kerr. I'd decided to call her that for now. Easier to spell than Latourneau. To pass the time, I made a mental list of things I knew about her.

Kerr was probably in her early twenties, had auburn hair, brown eyes, and a honker she could have changed but didn't. I liked that.

Kerr bought pricey health foods, cheap cosmetics, dressed mostly in black. She liked animals, or at least animal charities, and the White Sox. Or the cap could have been a gift. Or stolen.

Kerr wasn't interested in home decorating, believed in dry cleaning, rode buses. She wasn't afraid to walk alone to and from Foster Beach in the middle of the night. If she'd been alone.

Kerr used the Internet but kept few document files on her laptop. She had friends around the world. At least she had their email addresses. She cleaned her browser history and mailbox frequently, perhaps after every session. Otherwise, her concept of cybersecurity appeared to be patchy.

I'd found nothing to suggest Kerr had knowledge of Stella Bright. But I knew in my gut she was the link.

Kerr came out at 1:15. I followed her to a small art gallery on Clark. A sign above the door said DANCING DOLPHIN and pictured a performance by a member of that species. Artful.

I couldn't chance going in, but checked the offerings from across the street, through the plate glass window in front. The walls held mostly large abstracts. Some were okay. Some were just large. I was certain each painting was deeply meaningful.

Odd lady, Ms. Kerr. Not interested in home décor but a lover of art.

I wondered if the gallery visit had to do with the coded message. *Godolphin Vintage Claret Beauty 05 05 06. FL1X: LM-inf /JC-GR/B5-S2+4.*

Might Godolphin be a directive to go to the Dancing Dolphin? Might the sender be associated with the shop? Might he or she know something about Stella? Might the owner? A clerk? An artist?

Kerr emerged ten minutes after she'd entered. Her hands were empty. She strolled south on Clark and went into a restaurant called Café Raw. I held back, then walked past. She was seated alone, at a two-top to the left of the door. I crossed to the far side of the street.

Kerr loitered over her tofu. Or carrot puree. Or whatever vegan slop she was ingesting.

I watched and played with Google on my phone. Booked a room at the Warwick Allerton on North Michigan. It had a bar called the Tip Top Tap. I liked the sound of that.

I was just finishing when the thing buzzed in my hand. Caller ID indicated an unknown number. I answered with no greeting.

"Chilling in the lobby," a voice said.

"On my way," I said.

I took a taxi to the Ritz.

He was sitting in the same chair I'd chosen to read the note from Kerr, observing discreetly from under a cream-colored fedora with a black band. One foot was on a Tumi hardside roll-aboard, the other outstretched on the carpet. It wasn't much of a stretch.

His eyes swept over me, moved on. Expression neutral, he shifted from the chair to an unoccupied sofa set off by itself.

I checked my surroundings, then crossed to him. His head never moved. But I knew he was tracking me through the copper-tinted lenses hiding his eyes. Maui Jim Hang 10s. I recognized them from my outing to the Sunglass Hut. Not my style, but on him they worked.

Except for the shades and fedora, he might have blended in. Had he been on a veranda in New Orleans or Savannah. The fawn pants were probably Tommy Bahamas, the long-sleeved mint polo some high-end silk blend. No guess on the white belt. A tan jacket lay across his lap. Ralph Lauren? His loafers were made of leather that had once *capito*ed Italian.

"I follow you on the Golf Channel," I whispered, dropping onto the far end of the sofa.

He lowered the shades and regarded me from under the felt brim. His eyes were the same jade green as mine, the lashes wasted on one of his gender. His skin was caramel, freckled darker across a nose that was broad and flat, like an upright anchor pushed tight to his face.

"You have a problem with my threads?" Though hushed, his voice was smooth and rich, not unlike his clothes.

"I'm really looking forward to your next PGA stop."

"Forever the smart-ass." Sliding the shades into place and looking straight ahead.

"Always trying."

"Extremely. New stylist?"

"It's a wig," I said.

"Blond doesn't work with the chicken-white skin."

"Did you bring a gun?" Ignoring the fashion advice.

"I don't check luggage."

"Shouldn't be a problem scoring a piece."

"You have only one?"

"Long story."

A woman passed close. Her hair was overpermed and overdyed. Her makeup only served to amplify her wrinkles. We fell silent until she was out of earshot.

"You've bagged one so far." Tinted lenses constantly roving the lobby.

"Of the four on the video," I said.

"Meaning?"

"Later." I opened my paper and feigned reading.

"What do you want me to do?"

"Get a room here."

"Where are you staying?"

"Around."

"Drucker too cheap to pop for the Ritz?"

I lowered my voice even further. "I have a suite. I don't sleep in it."

"Of course you don't."

"You have credit cards?" I asked. "ID?"

"Several sets."

"When you check in, don't ask about me. Don't mention that you know me. They made contact here. They tried to kill me here."

"You'd rather they not see us together."

"You're quick."

"What if they're watching us now?"

"They're not."

"You're sure?"

"I'm a pro."

"I can tell by the wig."

A guy in a trench coat walked toward us, paused to verify something in his hand. Reversed.

"Get a suite, you say?"

"Sure," I said. "Call when you're in it."

I went to the Warwick Allerton and registered for one night. Sixth floor. The décor featured shiny black furniture and a fuzzy blue chaise. I was glad for the chaise. The hotels were starting to blend in my mind, the different floors and room numbers. The bold lounger would keep me anchored.

He rang as I was changing into dry clothes. While answering, my eyes fell on a magazine with a restaurant featured on the cover. I told him to meet me in an hour at the Italian Village on Monroe.

"How do I find it?"

"They have a sign."

I landed first. It was early and the place was largely empty. I got a booth upstairs in back, one probably favored by the naughty not wanting to be seen.

I'd just ordered a martini when Gus arrived, still head to toe in Tommy and Ralph. No shades. I was now sans hat and wig.

Gus slid into the booth. Gently placed the fedora to his left.

The waiter appeared, a bald, slouchy guy who'd probably been serving spaghetti there since opening day in the twenties. Gus ordered JB on the rocks.

The drinks and menus came quickly. I asked for osso buco. Gus went with cacciucco. I'd no idea what that was. Gus queried the wine options. The waiter suggested Chianti. They settled on a choice.

"I'll make some calls about a piece first thing tomorrow," I began when the waiter had gone.

"Done," he said.

"You have a gun?"

"I will. Explain again why I'm here."

I briefed him on everything since my meeting with Opaline Drucker. The bombing at Bnos Aliza. The disappearance of Stella Bright, the unrequited ransom, and the recent run at the bank account. The Subaru Forester. C-squared. The note at the Ritz. My outing to Foster Beach. The tattooed guy at the morgue. My romp with the monk, John Scranton. Jasmine Kerr/Jennifer Latourneau. My B&E on Argyle. The useless video. The crime scene photos.

Our food arrived as I spoke, engulfing the booth in a bubble of garlic. The cacciucco was some kind of seafood stew. The osso buco was good, the Chianti spectacular.

"So you think Stella is alive." Gus talked around a mouthful of fish. Genteelly. A feat I could not pull off.

"I do."

"Why wasn't she killed by the blast?"

"She was protected by a boulder the students use to paint their names, or the team mascot, or whatever."

Gus thought about that. "Why would she stay with the people who killed her family?"

I pictured Stella Bright on a sunny beach boardwalk. The void in the spatter.

Trigger flash.

A hot summer night. Twisted bodies, facedown, arms entwined. Charred clothing I knew as well as my own.

The familiar icy fire sparked in my chest. I squelched the images and the anger with a few deep breaths. Laid down my fork. Straightened it.

"I doubt she has a choice."

Silence in the booth. Garlic.

"That's why you've agreed to look for her," Gus said softly.

"It is."

"That's why I'm here."

"You're here because of my irresistible charm."

"And because I'm a silver-tongued devil."

I rolled my eyes. But it was true. Where I'm all bluster and sharp edges, Gus has a calming demeanor that draws people to him. You know the type. The guy who's listening only to you.

"Drucker knows our story," Gus guessed. "That's how she persuaded you to take the case."

"She's a sly old crone."

"How'd she connect?"

"Through Beau. I'm assuming there's history there."

Gus performed a meaningful lift of both brows. Which wrinkled his forehead. Which sent his scalp-buzzed hairline sliding north. I raised mine back.

Another hiatus as we both chewed on the past, the present. The known and unknown. The possibilities.

"Where does John Scranton fit in?" Gus, always pragmatic.

"No idea."

"Besides the passports, some toiletries, and clothes, Kerr's apartment held nothing personal?"

"Just the laptop," I said. "Which was purged regularly. She saves few documents, erases her browser history following each online session, deletes her emails right after she reads them."

"And uses burner phones."

"She does."

"Any pics?"

"No."

"Anything to suggest Stella had ever been there? Any link to her at all?"

"No."

Gus finished his food, dabbed his mouth, and leaned back, wineglass elegantly balanced in one hand.

"So far you've seen Kerr with no one other than the figure by the underpass. And there's been no further attempt to contact you."

"Correct."

"She aware you broke into her place?"

"I was careful."

"Maybe she should know."

"What if they're serious about burning Stella?"

"The note wasn't specific."

"Who else could they mean?"

"You want to keep watching Kerr."

I nodded.

"And you want me to cover your back while you do that."

"Yes."

"Is Kerr the woman in the SUV?"

"I doubt it."

"You're hoping she'll lead you to the kid."

"And the bombers."

"Say she does. What will you do with them?"

"Hand the pricks over to Capps and Clegg."

"They may dislike being handed."

"They may."

"They may resist."

"They may."

"And if they do?"

"My twin brother will have my back."

Eight Days

S he has made a decision. She will find proof. More than just overheard words.

That night the Leader takes her into the office, a dingy room off the kitchen furnished with nothing but a folding chair and gray metal desk. Cardboard boxes line the baseboards, dumped upon arrival and never opened.

He smells of male sweat. His face is arranged in the way that says he is anxious.

She knows the Testing will be bad. It is. Two hours of kneeling. He uses random tools from the kitchen drawers. A potato peeler. A fire starter. Skewers meant for kebabs.

The pain is so intense she can't escape to the canvas she's prepared in her head. She focuses instead on the boxes. Each is labeled only with the logo of the product it once held. Del Monte sweet peas. Alpha-Bits. Nestlé Quik.

She clamps her teeth. Composes a silent mantra.

Sweet. Bits. Quik.

Sweet. Bits. Quik.

Sweet. Bits. Quik.

At two she is set free.

Though the house is quiet, she waits a full hour. Counts it out, sixty times sixty. Adds another ten sixties for safety.

She lifts the covers and eases from bed. Another woman is sleeping in the room. She doesn't know why. Doesn't know what name the woman is using.

She stands in the dark, heart going ninety.

The woman snores softly.

She's tested the floor. Avoids the boards she's learned will creak. Feels like she's known these details forever.

Millimeter by millimeter, she turns the knob, cracks the door, and slips out into the hall. Pauses. Creeps to the stairs and scuttles down.

Luck is with her. Or fate. Or God. Though she wants no part of deities now. The night is moonless and the house is dark as a crypt.

This time she has a backup plan. If caught she will say she's had a nightmare and has come for milk.

She starts in the office. Rock salt still litters the floor, the white scatter darkened in patches with her blood.

She searches the desk. Finds only the routine: tablets, paper clips, pencil sharpener, pens. One glove in a bottom drawer. Nothing threatening. Nothing to explain how the upcoming horror will unfold.

She views the boxes. Each is sealed with tape that has discolored and begun to split. If peeled back it will never restick. She has no idea how to open them without leaving evidence of tampering.

She moves through the pantry. The kitchen. The dining room. The house seethes with quiet. With a darkness composed of black and pockets of denser black. She strains to see but dares not turn on a light.

She fears the Leader won't believe her story. Knows it won't matter. He will use the infraction as an excuse to torture her. She is certain now. He enjoys witnessing her agony.

She's in the parlor when a tiny noise slips into a gap between the heartbeats in her ears.

Riff!

Every hair goes upright on the back of her neck.

Her head whips toward the sound. She sees nothing.

Her eyes sweep the room. The old green lounger hulks in the gloom, a throne facing wooden chairs arranged like benches in a Roman coliseum. A satchel slumps abandoned beside it.

She knows the satchel. Knows its owner.

She moves to the bag and picks it up. The leather smells of hair oil and palm sweat. She takes it to a small end table that has a lamp. She risks the light. Pulls the zipper. The whrrp *is like a scream in the stillness.*

Boxes of Remington bullets. Multicolored pages tucked to one side. She tugs the papers free and, fingers trembling, rifles through them.

Order forms, invoices, receipts. She strains to read the print, makes out little but headers. One company name turns her gut to ice.

She skims the invoice. Another. A third.

The ice sends tentacles slithering through her core.

She knows how the tragedy will unfold.

CHAPTER 17

We followed Kerr all the next day. She bought groceries, visited the Dancing Dolphin, dropped the black boots off for repair, had lunch at a vegetarian sandwich shop. She met with no one. No one joined her at the apartment. A singularly solitary existence, with no hint as to how she supported herself.

As I trailed Kerr, Gus floated around behind, ahead, or across the street. His outfit was more innocuous, less country club chic. He had a Luger .22. I didn't ask how he got it.

We saw no one from the surveillance video. No one with a double-*J* tattoo. No one with a Beretta bulge in one pocket.

Late in the day, Capps called to report that John Scranton was out. We didn't see Scranton, either.

By dusk I was radioactive, my thoughts jumping in a thousand directions at once. I suggested that we grab Kerr and beat the truth out of her. Gus talked me down.

At our final rendezvous Gus told me to act sane for once in my life, his exact words, and stay at the Ritz. Reminded me about the "having my back" thing. About the Luger.

Reluctantly, I agreed. His room was on nineteen, five floors below mine. I had the motion detector and the Glock. My shoulder was healing well and no one had tried to kill me of late. And hotel hopping was getting old.

That night, Gus and I had dinner in my suite. Gyros from the food court. Heineken from the minibar. Kerr was asleep on Argyle. Or walking around in the black boots with their brand-new heels.

"They may be lying low," I said.

"You think?"

"They don't appear to be watching me." Ignoring Gus's sarcasm.

"You shot one of them and maimed another."

"Scranton isn't maimed."

"He won't be playing mandolin for a while."

"You may be right," I said. "They may be wary."

"Wary? They're scared shitless."

"If there is a 'they.'" Hooking finger quotes. "And 'they' are the 'they' who bombed Bnos Aliza."

"Right."

We both focused on spiced meat, tzatziki, and pita. Gus got us two more Heinekens from the fridge.

"You think Kerr knows I'm spying on her?" I asked after a long pull of beer. It could have been colder.

"I think she's clueless."

"They could have checked to see if I'm still registered here. You know, phoned and asked to be connected to my room, asked to leave a message, something like that."

"Have you had any hang-up calls?"

I shook my head. "But until you arrived, I was rarely in the suite, never at night."

"Okay. Say there is a 'they.' Say they're still in Chicago, maybe even planning another attack. They know you haven't left town. They've gone to ground until you do. I'm talking worst-case scenario."

"Or best." I flicked Groucho brows.

Maybe it was the beer. Or the long day of tedium. When Gus spoke again his words were fringed with something close to anger.

"Beau's right, you know. That make-my-day attitude is going to get you killed."

"Or paid."

"Not funny."

"Not intended to be." It was.

A few seconds of twisting silence. Then, "Don't underestimate these people, Sunnie. They want you dead."

"So have others."

"Because you provoke it."

"I should do what? Sit on my ass and get this kid killed? Hasn't our ineptness caused enough death?"

"We didn't know."

"We should have." Sharp. So much history clashing over the same issue.

"There are others who can find her."

"Really? Then why haven't they?"

"Stella may be dead," Gus said quietly.

"Or she may be alive and taking hits with a rubber hose."

Gus's eyes bored into mine, dark and clouded with frustration. I held his gaze. He looked away first, dipped his chin, and put his index finger to his right temple. The familiar little gesture went straight to my heart.

Wordlessly, Gus bunched and shoved his wrapper into the bag. I added mine. He raised his empty bottle. I nodded. He got two more Heinekens and handed one to me.

"After these it's Bud," he said.

"As I told Opaline. The job is rife with hardship."

Gus stretched out on the sofa and crossed his ankles. When he spoke again it was as though the timeworn quarrel had not resurfaced.

"This is their turf. They could wait you out a very long time."

"They could. Or they could send me Stella's ear in a box." The image kept my stomach in a rock-hard knot. Still, the current course of action was getting us nowhere.

"I say we goose Kerr," Gus said.

"I like it." I did. Action. "We spook Kerr, she bolts, we follow to see where she goes."

"Maybe she leads us to 'they,' " Gus said.

"Maybe."

Maybe she'd lead us to Stella's bullet-riddled corpse.

Overnight, a new front barreled into the heartland. The morning dawned clear and sunny. Temperatures were predicted to leap into the fifties.

I dressed in jeans and boots. Added the Charleston jacket and the Glock. Shades, no wig. Ready for combat, I descended to the Starbucks on level two.

Gus was drinking a latte and eating a muffin that looked like compacted weeds. I got coffee and joined him. We went over our plan. Then we rode the Red Line north and walked to Argyle.

I sat in the courtyard. Gus went somewhere. Kerr came out at 12:40 with a large tote hanging from one shoulder. She walked west toward Clark. I crossed the street and broke into her apartment.

This time my approach was different. I was tidy but left a few hints to suggest she'd had company. A rug corner kicked back. An improperly closed drawer. Signs of a careful but sloppy intruder.

I noted that the laptop was gone from the desk. Thus the tote? I didn't take time to ponder the significance. I was in and out in about six minutes.

My time in the military scored me training in surveillance, tracking, intel gathering. Sergeant Edwin A. Maddux was my first recon instructor. Sadistic little prick, constantly berating our mistakes and cussing us out. But a hell of a spy. Legend had it Maddux could materialize up your butt and you'd never see him coming. Never learned what the *A* stood for. Maybe asshole.

I thought of Maddux. Asked myself, What moves would he scorn?

Kerr returned at 2:15. I was across the street, half-hidden by a tree, but in her sight line as she walked east. Gus was somewhere behind her.

As Kerr drew near, I turned my face and pretended to fumble in my purse. I wanted her to see me but couldn't overplay my part.

If she noticed me, she gave no indication. When she'd entered her building, I moved from the tree to the courtyard. I stood behind the fountain, didn't sit on the bench, considered using the old newspaper ruse. Decided that would definitely classify as overacting.

I wondered if the staged B&E would work. If Kerr would be smart enough or observant enough to pick up on the clues. If so, would the ploy spook her?

No need to wonder long. Minutes after Kerr went through the door, a drape flicked in the bay. And I was worrying about Hollywood clichés?

I was behind the fountain, face discreetly pointed down. I stepped into the open, turned toward Kerr's building, and looked up at her second-floor window. Old Sol was shining with gusto. No way she couldn't spot a six-foot redhead with a scar crawling one eye. And recognize me.

Kerr had reason to worry. Or Latourneau. At least one of the passports in her possession was a fake, probably stolen and doctored. Forgery of a passport could get her up to fifteen years in a federal prison, maybe a quarter-million-dollar fine. If a prosecutor really wanted to play hardball, a zillion other statutes cover counterfeiting and identity theft.

But phony passports weren't enough. I didn't want just Kerr. I wanted the cold-blooded bastards who'd blown up a school and yanked a kid from her life. Maybe killed her. Maybe imprisoned her to suit their purpose. Kerr was my bait. They were my prey.

The curtain fell back into place. Time passed.

I knew Kerr was in there weighing her options. Which were few. Sit tight. Rally the troops. Run.

For the next two hours I shifted from the courtyard to the tree and back. Kerr stayed in her apartment and watched me do it. In between curtain peeks, I suspected she was making calls, sending emails, firing off texts.

Maybe there was no one else out there. Maybe, as Gus said, I'd scared them shitless. Maybe Scranton and the guy at the morgue were all the muscle they had. Maybe they were cutting Kerr loose. Maybe Kerr had arranged a meeting place elsewhere.

Maybe they were dumping Stella's body into Lake Michigan. Whatever the explanation, no one showed up.

Kerr should have stayed put. Either she couldn't bear the stress of waiting or she didn't know that. She chose option three.

At 4:25 she came out the front door wearing black pants, a black lightweight jacket, the Sox cap, and shades. The tote was on her shoulder. A large floral duffel was in her right hand.

I was at the tree. She passed me, walking west on Argyle, carefully avoiding eye contact. I fell in behind her, far enough back to be believable, close enough to allow her to be aware of my presence.

I thought of the sarge. Asked myself, What would Maddux disparage?

For forty minutes I tailed Kerr as she traversed Chicago's near North Side. West to Clark, north to Foster, east to Broadway, then south, making pointless diversions onto smaller side streets. Always, she could see me behind her.

At Gunnison and Marine, Kerr ducked into the main entrance of the Chicago Lakeshore Hospital. I stuck with her through the crowded lobby and back out a side door. Everywhere she went, there I was.

Throughout our travels I spotted Gus only once, at a covered bus stop across the street from the hospital. I was pleased with his look. Tan cargo pants, black windbreaker, no hint of the Luger. Did little to settle my nerves.

At Lawrence and Ravenswood, Kerr climbed the stairs to an "L" station on the CTA Brown Line. I held back, for effect, then followed.

A dozen people were on the platform, taking various approaches to waiting. Some were reading, either newspapers or books. A few wore headphones or earbuds and were grooving to their own personal concerts. Most were looking at or speaking on cellphones, or thumbing in emails or texts. One old guy was preaching loudly about Jesus. Or talking to him.

I positioned myself at the far end of those gathered. Kept my face averted. Two minutes after our arrival, the train clanked and whooshed into the station.

Kerr got on and stood just inside the door. I got on one car away and did the same. At the last second, as the doors were closing, Kerr hopped off. I watched her go.

Kerr raced down the stairs leading from the platform. As the train pulled out high above, I caught a flash of her floral duffel on the sidewalk below. Gus was behind her, a grin curling his lips.

One Week

S he stares at her bowl, stomach curdled with shame.
    Not shame.

Fear.

The Leader notices her untouched food. Admonishes her. They must be strong.

She takes a spoonful. The oatmeal is a cold gelatinous glob in her mouth. She swallows. Feels the glob rise into her throat.

She looks up. Surreptitiously searches the faces circling the table. They are tense. Closed. They tell her nothing.

There is only one person she can truly trust.

She must warn him. But she can't do it with others around.

Her knees quake so hard against her chair she fears they will notice. Her skin crawls. She resists the urge to check her clothing for bugs. Places her hands in her lap.

She makes a decision. She will share her secret place.

She finds a chance while reshelving plates in the pantry. They are alone.

He listens, apprehension apparent in his eyes. She tells him about the clearing. Says it's urgent they meet there.

He refuses. She presses, using a stern church-whisper voice. He finally agrees.

She says the meeting must be at night. Admits to her nocturnal adventure.

He gives her the dropped-jaw face. The one she despises. She says things she will later regret.

Not a budge in his opposition.

She has to convince him.

CHAPTER
18

I returned to Argyle Street to stake out Kerr's building. She never showed, and no one else went in or came out. Oddly, I was hearing nothing from Gus.

I thought of burgling Kerr's place again, decided it was unnecessary. Given the large tote and the duffel, I figured she was headed for new digs. Good. Any movement was better than none. Unless I'd signed a death warrant for Stella Bright.

I called it quits at seven, bought solvent at a sporting goods store, cotton swabs and a new burner at a Target, was back at the Ritz by eight. I cleaned the Glock, set up the mobile, finally fell asleep just past two.

I was chasing someone down tracks, or being chased, when a whistle shrieked. The train was close and barreling right at me.

Every muscle and neuron went from zero to sixty. My eyes flew open. Heart pounding, I shot upright.

The room was dark, the shriek coming from the bedside table. The old Walmart phone. Caller ID told me it was Gus. Of course it was. Only he and Beau had the number.

"What's happening?" Struggling to bring my voice up to speed with my adrenals.

"Did I wake you?"

My eyes flicked to the digits at the top of the screen. "It's three in the morning."

"Not here."

"Where are you?"

"Land of fruit and nuts."

That took me a moment. "California?"

"L.A. City of Angels. Thinking of setting up some auditions."

"Where's Kerr?"

"She's here."

"Can you be more specific?"

"The Marina Seven Motel in Venice. Free cable and parking. No ocean view."

"You're there, too?"

Gus gave me his room number. And Kerr's.

"Why haven't you called?"

"Battery issues."

Seriously?

"I'll catch the first flight out. Did anyone meet Kerr at the airport? The motel?"

"She got a cab, bought take-out Mexican en route, checked in here, hasn't left her room. Her window's been dark for twenty minutes now. I'll stay up and keep watching."

"Life in the fast lane."

"Wish I had a Whopper."

"I'll bring you one."

"Wish I had the Luger."

"Where is it?"

"Assorted trash barrels at ORD."

"I'll get you—"

"It's covered. I like this town."

"Yeah?"

"I think I saw De Niro at LAX."

"Everyone thinks they see De Niro at LAX."

"Can you collect my clothes? Bring what you can, have the concierge ship the rest to Beau?"

"The hotel will do that?"

"It's the Ritz, baby. I'll call with instructions."

After disconnecting, I got online. The first flight with availability departed at 9:50 A.M., getting me into Los Angeles at 12:23. Row twenty, middle seat. First class was chock-full of the wealthy and the lucky upgraded.

I tried to sleep, didn't really pull it off. At six I gave up and descended to the front desk. Gus was right about the service. For a fee, the hotel was delighted to FedEx his bag to any destination of his choosing. A bellhop let me in to gather his things. Which were abundant. I couldn't imagine how he'd gotten so many garments into such a small suitcase. And still managed to look unwrinkled. I wondered if he actually spent time ironing. Or why he bothered.

By 7:30 I was on my way to O'Hare. In the taxi, I phoned Layton Furr, explained where I was going, and asked him to clear the two bills at the Ritz. I also asked him to tell Roy Capps. And Peter Crage in Charleston.

Though tired, I never dozed off on the flight. Or absorbed much Tolstoy. I was wedged between an old man who snored wetly and a woman who sneezed and blew her nose for seventeen hundred miles.

At LAX, I collected my bag, rode a shuttle from terminal four to terminal seven, then took a cab to the Motel 6 on Century Boulevard. After checking in and paying cash for one night, I went to my room and phoned Gus. He reported that Kerr was having a salad at the Venice Ale House. He was watching her eat.

I reassembled then repacked the Glock. While I didn't need a permit to carry concealed in Los Angeles, I wanted no hassle. And I was certain I hadn't been followed. Then I took a taxi to Venice. On the way I bought two Whopper meals.

The Marina 7 looked like half the motels in America—a two-story L, with entrances off a sidewalk bordering a parking lot below, off a railed balcony above. I asked for a room for one night, you know the drill. The geezer at the desk had leathery skin, a long gray beard that he'd braided, puka beads, and a Grateful Dead tee. Unlike some of his Magnificent Mile counterparts, he didn't question my desire to pay in cash.

My room was on the upper level. It had faux Early American furniture and a sink outside the bathroom. The window was covered by short blood-red and pea-green floral drapes. The bed had a pea-green spread and fuzzy red blanket draped across the foot. The attention to decorative detail went unappreciated.

I unpacked my jeans and the undies and sweaters I'd brought, left Gus's clothes in the case. I hung the holstered Glock on a hook in the closet, set up the motion detector. Then I phoned room 207.

No answer. I considered dialing Gus's mobile, decided against it. He knew I was coming, would contact me when he could.

Antsy, I looked out my window. Scanned the street. The parking lot. The ground-level rooms. Kerr's drapes were closed. I cracked the door and looked in both directions along the balcony. Gus's drapes were also closed.

The room was thick with the smell of charbroiled burgers and oil-soaked spuds. I ate one of the Whoppers and all of the fries. Looked out the window some more.

California's State Route 1 runs from Mendocino County in the north to Orange County in the south and goes by many names. Pacific Coast Highway. Coast Highway. Shoreline Highway. Since the pavement navigates some of the most primo scenery in the land—the Golden Gate Bridge, Marin County, Big Sur—it's designated an All-American Road.

It was not so picturesque where I was standing. Here the PCH was called Lincoln Boulevard. Lots of traffic, car rental joints, strip malls, a car wash, Venice Boulevard off to the left. Didn't matter. Nothing had changed since the last time I looked.

The carbs and lack of sleep were slamming me. I yawned. Rolled my shoulders. Checked my watch. 3:10. 6:10 East Coast time.

I transferred the Glock to the bedpost and stretched out on the pea-green spread. For once, sleep came hard and fast.

The phone rang at 3:49.

"You got the Whoppers?"

"Yes."

"Fries?"

"Long story. Where are you?"

"My little slice of paradise, to the left down the balcony."

"Come over." I told him my room number.

One minute later there was a knock on the door. I squinted through the peephole. Gus was wearing the fedora, a lavender polo, and jeans. In his hand was a six-pack of Beck's.

I undid all the locks and Gus came in. He reached up to give me a hug. Fighting the reflex to stiffen, I hunched down to return it.

Gus stepped back. His eyes went to the white paper bag with its red and yellow logo, the bunched wrapper and two empty packets beside it. Slight frown, but he said nothing.

"The burger might still be warm," I said. "The Coke's probably not great."

He removed the Fedora and set it on the bed. We talked while he ate.

"After checking out here, Kerr went to an apartment on Rose Avenue, half a block off the boardwalk." Through tidy mastication, "We should move to a place with an ocean view. Maybe Shutters on the Beach."

"Any sign of Stella?"

"No."

"What's Kerr been doing?"

"Busy morning. A trip to a pharmacy. A walk on the beach. A visit to a place that'll teach you to surf. Lunch."

"You just left her there?"

"She's a slow eater."

"You couldn't call?"

"I forgot your new number in my room. Life would be easier if you had a permanent phone like normal people."

"Or shorter." I pointed. "You have sauce."

Gus swiped a napkin across his chin.

"Well then," I said.

"Yes," he said.

"That's it?"

I waited while he chewed, swallowed, sipped one of the Beck's. "We aren't the only ones watching Kerr."

"What?"

"We aren't the only ones watching Kerr."

"I heard you. I'm questioning your meaning."

"Someone other than ourselves has Kerr under surveillance." Overly precise.

"What?" To clarify, "Why do you say that?"

"There's a guy hanging around. Thinks he's slick, but he's obvious as a hooker at Mass."

"How so?"

"He either trails Kerr or hangs out at the top of the block, in the public parking area. Never goes to a car, just stands watching her building. Talks on a cell. Everyone else is in tees or tanks. Or bikinis. I like this beach."

"Gus."

"It's eighty degrees. This douche is decked out like the Marlboro Man. Stetson, boots, suede jacket."

"He packing?"

"Oh yeah. Shoulder rig. He keeps adjusting it. Probably sweating like a pig under all that cowhide."

"Describe him."

Gus tugged his phone from his pocket, clicked to a photo, and handed it to me.

Stetson was standing on a narrow strip of grass, arms crossed on his chest. Behind him stretched a wide expanse of pavement. Beyond the pavement, sand. I used my thumb and forefinger to enlarge the image.

I couldn't tell the guy's age. Not young, not old. Long and lean. Dark Oakleys. Under the hat, his hair looked dirty blond.

"He one of the bombers in the Forester?" Gus asked.

"I don't think so. Does he look dangerous?"

"He looks like he thinks so."

"Did he spot you?"

Gus leveled his eyes on mine.

"Right." I gave him the phone.

We both fell silent. I spoke first.

"Why tail Kerr?" I asked.

"They want something from her."

"Why not just snatch her off the street?"

"Huh."

"Maybe Kerr's not the target," I said.

"Then who is?"

"Me."

"Makes sense." Speaking slowly, as though reviewing footage in his head. "She goes in and out all morning. Short trips, open places. Stetson follows but hangs back. He's watching to see if someone is tailing her. They're a team. He's the hunter, she's the lure."

"How about we join in the chase?" The adrenaline was already humming. "I watch Kerr. Stetson watches me. You watch him."

"What if their strategy is to kill you on sight?"

"They did try that once."

"Twice."

"Good point," I said.

"Neither attempt went well for their side."

"Another good point."

"Maybe this time they'll bring more to the game."

"As have I."

"Meaning me?"

"Meaning you, twin bro."

CHAPTER
19

Gus took the suitcase and returned to his room. After phoning the office to say I was checking out, I placed my key on the dresser, strapped on the Glock and slipped into my jacket, and left the motel.

Following Gus's suggestion, I went left on Lincoln, left again at Rose Avenue. The sidewalk was narrow and, where palms struggled up from small dirt squares in the pavement, piled with feces, both canine and human.

Some blocks were trying hard for hip—Whole Foods, trendy eateries, a chic yoga studio. Others hadn't given a damn since the sixties—a dollar store, cheap top shops, a Hare Krishna temple, a barn-style restaurant offering buffalo wings and sushi.

Brooding over the northwest corner of the Main Street intersection was an enormous clown, half ballerina and half hobo, stuck above a CVS pharmacy like a bug on a pin. On seeing it, my heartbeat became a war engine. Ridiculous, I know. But my subconscious has its own take on the world. One it rarely explains.

The last stretch was a mix of low-rise apartments and Craftsman-style bungalows. The Venice on the Beach and Rose hotels took up most of the north side.

Kerr's address was on the south side, toward the Pacific Avenue end. I walked past it to the boardwalk and bought a visor from the first vendor I saw. It featured a dog in sunglasses and said, fittingly, VENICE BEACH.

Wearing my new visor and my Maui Jims, I went to the Venice Ale House and asked the waitress at the outdoor podium for outdoor seating. She gestured at a collection of picnic tables, some occupied, most empty. Help yourself. I settled in a spot near the street. Ordered an Anchor Steam. Continued making myself obvious while pretending to act sly.

Kerr's address was a two-story calamity with mustard-colored siding and a front porch stacked with a mind-boggling array of junk. In front was a rectangle of pavement big enough to accommodate one car. The rectangle was empty. A lone palm threw a needle of shadow over the whole.

A larger paved area butted up to the structure's east side, parking probably shared with the neighbors. Occupying three of the slanted spots were a red Honda Civic, a silver Lexus, and a black SUV, maybe a Nissan Pathfinder, all empty.

I watched Kerr's building. The traffic on Rose and Speedway. The pedestrians clogging the street in front of me and the boardwalk behind me. The surfers and sun worshippers wore little but skin. The tourists, dog walkers, Rollerbladers, and skateboarders a bit more. Though that was variable. I didn't see Gus.

I was nursing the Anchor Steam when I noticed a white Volkswagen Jetta cruise by slowly, make a U-turn, and head back up Rose. No biggie. Opposite where I sat, the street dead-ended into a beach parking area. Either lost or unwilling to fork over the cash, other drivers were making the same about-face.

Seven minutes later the Jetta was back. A man was at the wheel, one elbow jutting from the open window. The elbow was pasty white. The man had a bulldog neck. That's all I could tell. He drove to the kiosk, paid, and parked in the lot. He didn't get out.

Another ten minutes passed. I finished the beer. The waitress asked if I wanted another. I told her I'd switch to lemonade. She gave me a sad look. I returned it.

The waitress had just delivered my nonfestive beverage when a Range Rover pulled into the single space in front of Kerr's building. Two men got out. One was Stetson. He went inside. The other man strode in my direction.

I looked over my shoulder. Bulldog had left the Jetta and was smoking toward me. The plan was obvious. A fast ambush with *moi* caught in the middle. The plan was also moronic.

Ahead, Rose Avenue was busy but manageable. At my back, the boardwalk was crowded to the south, empty to the north. Beyond the boardwalk were the parking lot, sand, and a whole lot of ocean.

I had cover, room to maneuver. A tangled neighborhood with many streets barring vehicle access. Easy, if I wanted to get away. I didn't.

Leaving money under my glass, I wove my way through the tables and stood on the sidewalk with my back to the restaurant. Feet spread, arms loose at my sides, I waited. Relaxed but ready.

Forced to confront me face-on, my attackers stopped three feet away, shoulders inches apart. They probably called it the wall formation.

Bulldog was toned, but not as tall as his collar size had suggested, five ten tops. He had a hawk nose, small eyes, sensationally bad acne scars. I suspected he was one of the men in the Bnos Aliza SUV.

Looking at Bulldog's pal was like looking at a gorilla sans African majesty—darkly shadowed orbits, oversize chin and jaw, no lips. Body like King Kong.

Both men wore gaudy Hawaiian shirts that wouldn't have worked anywhere in our fiftieth state. The reason for their choice was quickly apparent.

Kong pulled a Beretta from his waistband and leveled it at me. A double-*J* tat decorated the base of his right thumb. "Don't try anything stupid."

"Really?" I said. "No aloha?"

"You're coming with us."

"No." I smiled.

"We're all going to walk up the street, nice and slow, friends enjoying a day at the beach." Soft accent. Lowland gorilla?

"I'll bet you guys dig Iz. I can never spell his last name. Starts with a K, has a kicky little 'okina that says clear your throat."

"Turn around." Kong gestured with the Beretta.

"Don Ho? Maybe you're 'Tiny Bubbles' guys?" Heat sizzling in my chest.

Still Kong ignored me. "Mitts out where I can see them."

I started to raise my hands.

"Out from your body! Not up." Eyes darting to see who was taking an interest.

I extended my arms. Bulldog stepped forward and frisked me. Found the Glock. Took and slid it under his blue and orange parrots.

"*Hawaii Five-O*? I know. You're playing McGarrett." Pointing at Kong. "And you're Danno." Pointing at Bulldog.

"Move."

It appeared the two didn't like island culture. It appeared they didn't like me. Kong shoved my left shoulder so hard with his free hand I almost screamed. My torso twisted and he slipped around me, close at my back. I forced myself not to flinch at his touch.

Bulldog moved to my side. I could have disabled them both with very little effort. A kick to the groin. An elbow to the head. Would have enjoyed it. Instead we shambled in a knot to the mustard-colored building.

Kerr's apartment was on the ground floor in front, to the left of stairs with open spaces between the treads. The door gave directly onto the living room. She was in it, sitting on a large green pillow on the floor, knees drawn to her chest. No surprise, she was dressed in black.

Stetson was on the couch. He was wearing jeans, a pale yellow shirt with piping and snaps, no jacket. The boots were snakeskin, the toes reinforced with steel. Up close his face appeared almost

KATHY REICHS · 162

boyish—plump cheeks and chin, arched brows, bangs fringing across his forehead. But not boyish in a good way. In an evil master *Doctor Who* way.

Kong gun-muzzled me forward. I heard the door slam behind us but not the click of a latch.

Stetson's eyes rolled to Kong. His chin dipped slightly and he intertwined his fingers. Long fingers. Long thumbs. At the base of one was a double-*J* tattoo.

"Why are you harassing our friend?" Directed at me. Kong was trying for tough to impress the boss.

"Am I?"

Before Kong could follow up, Stetson placed his hands on his knees and pushed to his feet, all the while appearing to study his boots. He crossed the room slowly, gaze still down. He had long limbs, took long, unhurried strides. When he was two steps from me his arms shot out and his fingers wrapped my neck. Strong fingers. Vise fingers. I raised my hands and clawed at them. They tightened. Their owner's eyes drilled mine. Ice-blue eyes. Mean eyes.

I tried breathing through my nose. Failed. Tears ran down my cheeks. My vision started to blur, my thoughts to splinter.

I was fighting panic when Stetson released his grip and stepped back. I gulped air. Bent at the waist to clear my brain. Wiped my face with my palms.

Kong was beside me, the Beretta aimed at my head. Bulldog was between Kerr and the couch, gun drawn and pointed at my sternum.

I straightened. Stetson pulled a hanky from his back pocket and held it out. I ignored the offering. Something in his eyes sent a chill down my spine.

Stetson pivoted and, catlike, returned to the sofa. Crossed his legs.

"Why are you harassing our friend?" Never looking at Kerr, still watching from her pillow.

"I believe she helped blow up a school in Chicago."

"Why do you care?"

"People were killed."

"Why do you care?"

"I've been hired to find those responsible."

"And then?"

I just looked at him.

"I see." Examining what I hadn't said. "Why didn't you abduct her when you first found her? Or shoot her? You seem skilled at that."

"I'm a softie."

"And you hoped she would lead you to bigger game."

"And that."

"Did she?" he asked.

"Did she?" I asked.

A few seconds of tense silence. I broke it.

"Nice tattoo."

"Let me ask you something," Stetson said. "You have killed one person, disabled another. You are a keen observer and an expert tracker. You eluded our people in Chicago. You found us here."

Down a hall to my left, a door opened. A woman's voice floated out. I couldn't catch her words. Another woman spoke, sharper. A different door opened and closed. The room hiccuped softly, as though alien air had puffed in from outside.

Stella? I kept my breathing steady, my eyes unreadable.

Stetson had paused, distracted. Or listening.

"Is there a question in there?" I asked.

"You are good at your job. Why so slovenly today?"

"I was drinking beer."

"You're a clever woman. It's a pity I have to kill you."

"You're a clever guy. You can think of alternatives."

"Yes." Smiling with zero warmth. "You are smarter than most with whom I am forced to associate."

"And they would be?"

"Idealists who have led clean lives." He studied me, fingers pressed together under his chin. "You are no stranger to violence."

I said nothing.

"You can think and you can handle yourself," he went on. "Such a shame I can't recruit you to my cause."

"And that cause would be?"

"Defending our way of life."

"Against whom?"

"Those who would destroy it."

"A fifteen-year-old kid?"

The blue eyes narrowed ever so slightly.

"Where is she?"

The narrowed gaze held.

"What's the *JJ* stand for?" Cocking my chin at the hands with their long, strong fingers.

"Jihad for Jesus."

"Nice alliteration."

"We are crusaders for Christ."

"You Galahad or Gawain?"

"My name is Bronco."

"Yippee ki-yay."

"You are a very disrespectful woman."

"I try my best. Who are these evil destroyers you fear?"

"Outsiders who threaten our religious freedom. Our country. Our very civilization."

"You talking vegans?" Buying time. Where the hell was Gus?

"I'm talking those who believe in Islam and its repressive anti-constitutional Sharia law. Those who kill in the name of Allah. Those who oppress women. Those who bully the world with their suicide attacks, honor killings, stabbings, hijackings, kidnappings, beheadings—"

"Bombings."

"Bombings."

"Crackpot extremists don't define a religion." Straining to hear what was happening down the hall.

"That's how you see these jihadists? These terrorists who wage holy war to force the world to conform to Sharia? I fear you underestimate the gravity of the situation. Islam is not just a religion. It has become a global and political military offensive."

I didn't respond.

"Taliban. Islamic jihad. Al-Qaeda. Boko Haram. Al-Shabaab. ISIS. Shall I go on?"

"The radical fringe." Silence in the back of the house.

"Muslim immigration to the United States is growing at record rates. Muslim leaders are relying on our own First Amendment rights to build mosques and Islamic centers, then use those centers to recruit and indoctrinate jihadists. To promote violence against nonbelievers. Against the descendants of the authors of that very Constitution. A charter created to protect the Judeo-Christian principles upon which this country was founded. Familiar with the term Wahhabism?"

"The Saudi wing of Islam."

"Did you know that an overwhelming majority of these centers are under Wahhabist influence? Ever hear of the Muslim Brotherhood? Civilization jihad?"

I let him rant on.

"Muslim Brothers are worming their way into positions in business, government, the schools, the military. Their plan is to destroy Western civilization not with bombs and beheadings but from within."

"How's that going?"

Bronco studied me a long time before speaking again. "We share a lot, you and I."

"I don't blow up schools and abduct young girls."

"You know nothing."

"Help me out."

"The school wasn't the target."

A reel of CSU photos unspooled in my mind. The school. The painted boulder. The bicycle rack spiraling skyward. The vacant lot to the east. The food market beyond the lot. Synapse. "You were going for the Muslim grocer next door?"

"Don't let appearances fool you. The owner of that grocery donates enormous sums of money to Muslim causes worldwide. And he had plans to expand into a national chain. Expansion is the cornerstone of their scheme for civilization jihad. Slow growth, business by business, property by property, country by country."

"You're saying you bombed the wrong place?"

"Unfortunately, I don't have the luxury of working with people as expert as you and I are. The luxury to choose. That will not be the case in the future. But, to be fair, the error in Chicago wasn't totally their fault. The backpack was left near the store as directed. A child spotted it, perhaps decided to be a Samaritan. Sadly for him, the bomb detonated as he was returning the pack to the school. You know the old saying?"

"May you rot in hell?" Feeling a warning twist in my gut.

"No good deed goes unpunished."

"That child was Bowen Bright." Fury crackling through me. I wanted to kick the bastard's nads up into his brainpan. Or worse. "He was twelve years old. They scraped his face from the pavement, tweezed his brain from the trees. The blast also killed his mother."

Bronco shrugged.

"What happened to Stella?" Heart thudding.

Bronco gave me a blue-obsidian stare.

My breath quickened. My fingers curled into fists.

"We're done here." Bronco looked to Kerr. She got to her feet. He rose, and together they started toward the hall from which the women's voices had come.

A fuse blew in my brain. I wanted this scumbag.

Fast as a heartbeat, I dropped below the angle of the two Berettas and jackknifed toward Bronco's ankles. He yanked one foot free of my grasp and kicked out. The steel-tipped toe connected with my cheek. My head flew back and my ass slammed the floor. I rolled.

Stunned, Kong and Bulldog hesitated that one critical second. Kong recovered first and got me back in his crosshairs.

The door flew open. Gus thundered in, a Luger two-fisted at his nose, a spare magazine clamped in his teeth. Kong and Bulldog whipped toward him as one. Kong fired. Missed. Gus shot him. Kong went down with a thud and a soft little grunt.

I scrabbled behind a chair. Bulldog crouched and began working his way along the sofa. Gus fired at him from the cover of the doorjamb.

Life and death can intersect in the blink of an eye. Reaching the end of the sofa, Bulldog half-rose for a better angle. In the same instant, Kong levered up on one elbow and fired blindly from the floor. His round caught Bulldog halfway up his spine. Bulldog hit the hardwood with a sound like meat slamming ice. Kong fell back and lay still.

Silence exploded into the room.

Gus and I stared at each other, wild-eyed, panting. Scrambling to my feet, I pointed at the archway through which Kerr and Bronco had gone. "Be careful. There may be others back there."

As I recovered my Glock from Bulldog, Gus disappeared down the hall. When I joined him, he was standing in a small kitchen, tense as a leopard ready to spring. Across from the kitchen were a bedroom and a bath, both empty. The kitchen was empty. The back door was open.

Our eyes met. Still jittery and pumped with adrenaline. Nothing stirred.

We lowered our guns.

Legs like rubber, I dashed to the living room, pulled out my burner, and took pics of the two men lying on the floor. When done, I searched for a pulse on each. Felt a murmur in Kong's carotid. Maybe. It could have been the trembling in my fingers. Neither man seemed to be breathing. Bulldog's parrots and leis were going dark fast.

Quick scan of the apartment. No Stella.

Using the landline, I dialed 911 and reported a shooting.

"Time to haul *okole*," I said to Gus.

"Hawaiian ass?"

I nodded.

We hauled.

CHAPTER
20

We legged east, weaving the maze of streets paralleling Rose. Slowly our heart rates eased. My right cheek was purple and swollen, but no one seemed to notice. Or find it unusual.

By 8:15 we were back at the Marina 7. Gus's presence was reassuring, so I registered for another night. If we stayed longer in L.A., I'd insist we relocate. Maybe go oceanfront. Gus would like that.

While downing warm beers in Gus's room, we studied the blurry faces printed from the Bnos Aliza video. I told Gus the Forester's driver was the mustachioed John Doe at the Chicago morgue. We agreed that one of the pair in back was probably Bulldog.

"That's two," Gus said.

"We didn't exactly catch this guy."

"You've got pics. You called 911. It counts."

I said nothing.

"Look, these asswipes didn't grab you to have dinner at the Ivy." Gus finished his Beck's and wiggled two more cans from the plastic six-pack rings.

"How did you know I was in that apartment?"

"Followed the plan, baby sis."

"We're twins."

"I'm six minutes older," he said.

"And six inches shorter."

"I ain't no shorty. I'm a straight-up ghetto brotha." Gus did gangsta. Badly.

"Seriously. How did you find me?"

"You pretended to tail Kerr. I tailed you. I was on the boardwalk when Dumb and Dumber made their move. I admired your restraint, by the way."

"Thanks."

"I followed you into Kerr's building—"

"Showing restraint."

"While concealed behind the staircase, I noted that the door hadn't latched. Used that to my benefit."

"And mine."

"Who's the dude boogied with Kerr?"

"Calls himself Bronco. White supremacist, revolutionary type. Wants to save the world from Muslim domination."

"By blowing up little Jewish girls?"

"The intended target was the grocer across the vacant lot."

"Jesus Christ."

"That's their man." I explained the meaning of the *JJ* tattoos.

"Islamophobe assholes."

"And Bronco's the head asshole. He's smart, obsessed, and willing to use violence. That's a deadly combination."

"He give anything up on Stella?"

I shook my head. "But I heard female voices."

"You think they're planning something else?"

"Bronco as much as said so."

"Soon?"

"I got that impression."

"What?"

"I don't know."

"Here?"

"I don't know."

"What's our next move?"

"I don't know."

I got to my new room around ten. It had two double beds. The theme was grape jelly and algae salad.

I tossed my backpack onto the chair, dug out and set up the motion detector. Then I removed my jacket and took off the Glock. While undressing, I remembered the visor. Couldn't recall losing it. Felt bummed. I really liked that dog.

Gun on the edge of the sink, I showered and did my evening toilette. Then, dressed in a clean tee and panties, I slid my MacBook Air from the pack and carried it to the bed opposite the TV. After removing the quilt, transferring extra pillows, and locating the remote, I stretched out, back propped by a double set of synthetic foam.

I found the local ABC station. A medical or police drama was winding toward the credits. Lots of sirens. Lots of angst. Since connecting with Kerr, I hadn't checked my email or social media. I muted the TV, opened the laptop, and got online.

I'd lost all but two of my Twitter followers. Still, no one had liked me on Facebook. Overcoming the sting of rejection, I logged into the Gmail account I'd created before leaving Charleston. My inbox contained a lot of spam and one message from TNT82 @yahoo.com. I opened it.

You're both dead.

I stared at the words, heart beating steady and hard. Not fear. Eagerness. An anger-fueled desire to nail the dickwad who was threatening me.

Both dead? Who else? Gus? Stella?

"Bring it on, chickenshit." To the empty room.

As in Kerr's apartment, I clicked the tiny triangle to the right of the reply arrow, then chose the command Show Original from the drop-down menu. A similar block of data appeared.

I copied TNT82@yahoo.com's IP address, and then I went to ipTRACKERonline.com. A keystroke combo pasted the series of digits into the empty box. I hit enter and a Google Earth satellite image appeared. On it was a red circle with its root stuck into the ground.

Below the map were data organized into three categories. Provider. Country. Time. I skimmed the middle column. Country. Region. City. Metro code. Postal code.

TNT's email had been sent from Los Angeles.

I thought about that. On TV, an ER team was trying to save a kid who'd arrived by ambulance missing a leg. The kid wasn't responding and the docs and nurses weren't taking it well.

I lifted my burner from the bedside table, opened Notes, and went to the list of IP addresses I'd created from the emails received by Kerr shortly before my spin through her Argyle Street pad. The only four she hadn't erased.

I repeated the process of geolocation with trailblazer745 @gmail.com.

Trailblazer had sent his missive from Corydon, Indiana. Infidel567@gmail.com was in Louisville, Kentucky.

The other two messages were from spearhead2021@yahoo.com and loyalc2020@aol.com. Both had been tapping the keys in our nation's capital.

When I'd considered doing PI work, I'd learned of services that allow reverse lookup of email addresses. If you're lucky, you get names, addresses, photos, blogs, family background, online profiles, social networks, neighbors' addresses, etc. I subscribed to several and ran the names. Got nothing.

I thought about that. Not a single hit for any of the five. I suspected the accounts were created for short-term use and abandoned quickly. My MO.

Next, I checked the other photos I'd taken while in Kerr's apartment. The passports. The delivery label from the capsules.

When I glanced up, the evening news had come on. A reporter in a flapping poncho was braving a downpour in a gale-force wind. Behind him, waves hammered a seawall. A crawler stated that Tropical Storm Atticus was barreling toward Mexico.

Really? Atticus?

The scene cut to a somber-looking anchor. Immobile hair, capped teeth, salon tan. His lips formed words, then a graphic appeared above his left shoulder. The headline SHOOTOUT ON VENICE BEACH was superimposed above a shot of the mustard-colored building on Rose Avenue.

The anchor spoke earnestly, then handed off to another journalist live on location. This one was female. She was outside, behind a police cordon surrounding the entrance to Kerr's apartment. Gawkers lined the tape. Other reporters flanked her. She spoke silently but solemnly for a moment, then the picture shifted to footage of a body bag being wheeled to a coroner's van.

As I groped for the remote, the action jumped to a police official with very severe eyes. Or maybe his squint was due to the camera lights. Microphones hovered close to his mouth. A gaggle of reporters circled him. A crawler gave his name as Alves.

I found the remote. Searched for the mute button. The ABC reporter shifted her mic to her own face and spoke. Even without sound I knew her question. Alves ignored her.

"—received a 911 call at approximately 7:10 this evening. The responding officers entered the home and found two Caucasian males. Both men had been shot. One was DOA, the other remains in critical condition."

"Have the victims been identified?"

"Not yet."

"Do you know who was living at that address?"

"I'm not at liberty to go into detail at this time."

"Are the murders gang-related?"

"Were drugs involved?"

"Do you have a suspect?"

"I'm not at liberty to go into detail at this time. But rest assured there will be a full and thorough investigation. We will find the person or persons responsible. Thank you."

Alves stepped away from the scrum. As he climbed the steps and disappeared through the door beyond the mind-boggling junk, shouted questions followed his retreating back.

The ABC journalist turned to her cameraman.

"This is Emily Mattimore-Green reporting live from Rose Avenue in Venice."

I dialed Gus.

"I saw it," he said in way of greeting.

"Kerr and Bronco sure as hell aren't going back to that apartment."

"I have a feeling you're about to explain our next move."

I reminded Gus about the four emails I'd found on the Argyle Street laptop. "I did some IP geolocation. Two people were contacting Kerr from Washington, D.C. Her passport lists her place of birth as Alexandria, Virginia."

"Just outside the District."

"Yes."

"Six million people live in the Washington metropolitan area."

"I found a bottle of Brahmi–Gotu Kola in her kitchen."

"Kerr must feel stressed. Or fatigued. Brahmi is supposed to boost energy and calm the mind."

"Does it?"

"No."

"The point is, she bought the stuff online. The Amazon mailer was still in the drawer. Delivery was to J. Kerr at an address on Mount Pleasant Street in Washington, D.C."

"Looks like we're heading to our nation's capital."

"I'll book a morning flight."

"Text me the info."

"I suggest you travel, how shall I put it? Unencumbered? Some ME's probably digging lead from Bronco's pal as we speak."

"I have contacts in D.C."

I didn't ask.

"I'll miss this place," Gus said.

"You've been here a total of two days."

"Lots of sunshine, naked people."

"It's spring. The cherry trees will be blooming."

Gus blew out a breath. "Think we should contact this guy, Alves?"

"Not yet."

"How about Capps and Clegg? Explain the *JJ*, the organization, that the grocer was the intended target?"

"Yes, they should have that. But by text from a suitable phone. I don't want Capps grilling my ass."

"Have you reported our Left Coast adventure to Drucker?"

"I will. She owes me another twenty-five K."

"I hope the old gal's still happy with you."

"Why's that?" I asked.

"Keeping me armed is getting damn expensive."

Six Days

They are moving again.

All day the house sizzles with preparations. The others trade glances, tense lines between their brows. No one will say where they're going. Or when. Perhaps no one knows.

She is largely ignored. She uses the rare pocket of freedom and, in the afternoon, finds a flashlight in the basement. Hides it under her bed.

She hasn't told him what she overheard. What she found. There's been no chance. No time when they were alone long enough. Just snatches. Passing moments when she could plead with a word or a phrase. Sometimes only with her eyes.

But her persistence has paid off. He has agreed to meet her in the clearing.

He shares a room with three other men. She hopes he's following their plan. Doing exactly what she's doing.

Fifteen minutes before the agreed-upon time, she tiptoes to the bathroom. Sits on the toilet. Smells mildew, Clorox, and soap. The lid feels cold through her jeans. She counts out ten sixties.

Satisfied that no one is awake, she sneaks downstairs and into *the kitchen. The ladder is gone from below her window. The roof is no longer an option.*

Out the back door. A quarter-moon throws some light, not much. Standing there in the chill, she wonders why the moon affects her as it does. Wonders why she wonders that.

She runs, not exhilarated now. Terrified. Of discovery. Of what she has learned.

Over the grass. Across the alley. Into the trees.

Her heart stops.

He isn't there.

She calls out, barely a whisper.

No answer.

A fresh kind of fear rears up inside her.

He is loyal. It's his nature. But to whom? What if he has betrayed her to them?

She refuses to believe that.

She pulls the quilt from the hollow in which she conceals it. Sits cross-legged. Indian-style, they called it as kids. Moonlight through the branches stripes her legs.

He'll come.

Minutes pass. She's unsure how many. Is way too wired to count.

She lies back. Closes her eyes. Hears voices in her head. Soothing, from when she was little. Mama. Speaking of love. Of bravery. Telling her not to be afraid of anything. Not spiders or snakes, or monsters or bogeymen. Now voices cajole that she not fear death. Demand commitment, courage. Promise a better world.

An old tune. But now she understands the lyrics.

A twig snaps.

Her lids fly open. Adrenaline fires through her.

She listens, motionless, fighting hard to muffle her breathing.

She wants to scream. She can't scream.

A blackness shapes up in the trees to her right. Moves toward her.

CHAPTER
21

Our flight left at 7:45 A.M. It was dark when I woke. It was dark when the taxi dropped us at LAX. I wasn't in the mood for conversation. Nor was Gus.

We got our boarding passes. I checked my bag, then we cleared security and went to the gate. Gus strolled off, reappeared wearing a tan windbreaker he hadn't owned before.

Our first full sentence was exchanged at thirty-four thousand feet.

"You really think Kerr and Bronco are in D.C.?" Gus asked.

"I don't know about Bronco. But two emails, a passport, and an Amazon mailer suggest D.C. might be within Kerr's comfort zone."

"Hmm." Gus had his seat tilted back, his eyes closed.

"On the other hand, Kerr bolted Chicago and that didn't work out for her. She could still be in L.A."

"Or Paris. Or Cincinnati. Or San Juan."

"Admittedly, it isn't a dream lead," I admitted.

The Stella voice in my head had echoed all night. The pull to her was now so strong I could feel it in my marrow. She was out there, calling to me. From a closet? A shallow grave? I shared none of this.

After a pause, Gus said, "Lots of targets in Washington for Islamophobic pricks."

"The Islamic Heritage Museum. The mosque and cultural center on Mass Ave."

"Certain members of Congress or the Senate."

"The Supreme Court, the Joint Chiefs of Staff—"

"Et al. Where are we staying?"

"The Morgan Inn."

"Not the Ritz?"

"Not the Ritz."

"Why?"

"The inn's website described their rooms as unfussy."

"Unfussy?" Rolling his head to raise skeptical brows.

"Understated."

"Meaning cheap."

"The Morgan Inn is close to the address on the Amazon mailer."

"Do I get my own bath?"

Before I was forced to acknowledge the possibility that might not happen, a flight attendant reached our row to query our happiness and thank us for flying American. His name was Justin. Justin also asked about our breakfast preferences. I ordered the omelet. Gus went for the healthier yogurt, fruit, and granola option. Justin noted our choices on his clipboard and moved on.

After attempting to eat the rubbery yellow lump Justin served, I tried reading, ended up watching an old Bond movie until I dozed off. Gus slept most of the flight. God bless first class. God bless Opaline Drucker.

We landed at DCA just before four. Split up and headed for separate taxi stands.

My driver was a dandruffy guy named Moses. Not a talker. Another blessing.

Moses took the George Washington Parkway. While skimming along the shore of the Potomac, I saw the top of the obelisk built to honor the first of our founding fathers; closer to the water, the Roman pantheon designed as a tribute to Jefferson. Crossing Memorial Bridge, I admired the Doric temple created for Lincoln. I thought about architecture. I thought about dead presidents. I thought about Stella Bright.

Eventually, we wound through the urban canyon known as Rock Creek Park. Wooded banks, tunnels, and jogging trails flashed by outside the windows. I thought about Chandra Levy. I thought about Stella Bright.

Like many American cities, the District of Columbia is a crazy quilt of quartiers, each with its own history, name, personality, and style. Capitol Hill. Dupont Circle. Georgetown. Mount Pleasant. Columbia Heights.

Moses pulled to the curb at a double-wide three-story in a row of three-stories on Lanier Place in the Adams Morgan neighborhood. Except for the hotel and a fire station, all red brick, the block was entirely residential.

Out front, two short staircases rose through disinterested landscaping to side-by-side porches enclosed by white picket railings and outfitted with chairs and potted plants. Rusty AC units jutted from windows on all three floors. A quaint-as-hell sign hung by chains to the right of the main entrance.

I paid my fare, got out, and scanned the street. The curbs were lined with vehicles parked nose to tail in both directions. Before climbing the steps, I did another visual sweep. No vehicle was occupied. No aloha-shirted thug was hanging out behind a lamppost or shrub. Or Stetsoned.

The hotel's interior lived up to its sign. Lots of knotty pine and collectables. A globe. A wall-mounted pay phone. Overstuffed sofas and chairs. The wood-paneled dining room offered family-style seating conducive to making new friends. That wouldn't happen.

The desk was manned by a nice old fella in need of breath mints. I asked for a room with a bath for two nights. Gus was bringing out the daredevil in me.

As the nice old fella assessed availability, I read the screen upside down. It appeared no one else had checked in that day. He concluded that only one en suite remained unoccupied. I left it for Gus.

After raising his wire-rims to glance at the ID giving my name as Susan Bullock, the nice old fella accepted cash, entered a few keystrokes, then took a large brass key from a hook at his back. Smiling, a decidedly bad idea, he explained that Wi-Fi, breakfast, and snacks were free. Then he told me not to smoke.

"I have rules, too," I said.

The nice old fella's mouth popped open, clamped shut. His brows floated high enough to clear the wire-rims.

"No one goes into my room. Ever. Not for any reason."

"Maid's gotta clean."

"I'll do it myself."

"Not sure we allow that." Laying his open palm on the counter. Seemed the nice old fella was up to his halitosis in greed.

I pulled two twenties from my purse and placed them on the glass. He scooped them into his fist and smiled.

"Hang the sign on the knob, your room is Fort Knox."

"Thank you."

The nice old fella wished me a pleasant day.

I ascended a broad staircase that made a hard left from a landing five treads up. My room was at the end of the hall on the second floor. It had yellow walls, white trim, a fireplace and radiator painted white, a crooked white sink with a mirrored medicine cabinet above. The bed had dark head- and footboards probably carved during the Great Depression. The single chair was wood and needed repair.

I ran my usual check. The lock worked. The phone worked. Filmy white curtains covered a window overlooking a tiny yard at the back of the property. No fire ladder or rope. No tree branch within reach. Though far from secure, it was acceptable.

After removing my jacket, I sent a text. Got no answer.

I set up the motion detector, then went through the routine of arranging my few belongings and reassembling the Glock. That done, I Googled directions to the Amazon mailer address. Then I waited, certain of the errand that was delaying my twin.

My mobile buzzed at 6:15. The text said: *37*.

Gus's room was grander than mine. It had two queen beds, red walls, black furniture, and a bath large enough to share with a very small pet. I was envious.

There was no need to ask where Gus had been. He was in shirt-sleeves and a shoulder holster housing a Glock 17. Twin siblings. Twin guns. Snap!

"Ready?" I asked.

"Ready." Gus slipped on the airport windbreaker and we headed out.

The trip took less than ten minutes. Lanier to Argonne, then left on Mount Pleasant. Dusk was settling in and the temperature was a pleasant sixty-something. It was nice to be outside.

As we walked, I watched everything. The pedestrians. The bikers. The cars and buses. The doors, windows, walkways, and roofs of the buildings around us. So did Gus.

Argonne was lined on one side by well-kept row houses with postage-stamp yards. Lots of trees. Lots of brick. Facing them was a 1920s-era low-rise apartment complex.

Where Hobart T-boned into Mount Pleasant, we went by a church and a small park. Beyond that, the street was largely commercial. We passed stores offering coffee and tea, booze, groceries, paint. An auto repair shop, a dry cleaner, a laundry, a nail salon. Many restaurants. Thai. Vegan. Dos Gringos, Haydee's, and El Pollo Sabroso were serving up salsa close enough to one another to tango. That and the snippets of Spanish I caught suggested a robust Latino presence.

Bigger complexes stretched along the sidewalk opposite the one Gus and I were on, most with rental units above and businesses below. Kerr's Amazon herbs had been delivered to an address with this arrangement. Situated near the intersection of Mount Pleasant and Irving, its upper two floors were residential. At ground level were a unisex hair salon and a used-clothing store.

Gus and I stood a few moments studying the setup. Directly in front of the building was a covered bus stop. Affixed to the Plexiglas walls were WMATA route maps and a poster advertising a production at the Kennedy Center. Two women were in the shelter, one standing, one sitting on the metal bench. Both wore black jackets embroidered with brightly colored flowers, mid-calf floral skirts, white cotton socks, and sneakers. Both carried double-handled woven bags that looked heavy.

The building entrance was through a centrally positioned door directly behind the bus stop. Flanking the door were picture windows covered with bars. The unisex salon was on the left. It was called Rosa's. Behind Rosa's bars were Styrofoam heads with wigs cut into styles that might have been big in the eighties.

The resale shop, Ginny's Gently Used, was on the right. Behind Ginny's bars were three torso-only mannequins. One wore a blue polka-dot tank, one a pink sweater, the third a red sundress with its skirt spread around it like poppy petals.

"You got an apartment number?" Gus asked.

I pulled my phone from my pocket and checked the photo of the Amazon mailer.

"206."

We both considered the top floor. The building ran deep but was narrow on Mount Pleasant. I guessed that one of each pair of upper-floor windows facing us belonged to a separate unit.

The sky was fading from dirty yellow to charcoal. Street- and store lights were coming on. Traffic on Mount Pleasant was bumper-to-bumper and creeping. The faces behind the windshields seemed tired and cranky.

A woman passed pushing a kid in a stroller. Both had long black braids. The kid was screaming. The woman looked exhausted. I felt for her. A dirty diaper and an uncooked meal probably awaited her at home.

"We going 24/7 on this?" Gus asked when the woman was out of range.

"How about we start with days?" I said. "See how it goes."

"Kerr's no night owl."

"My thinking exactly."

"Allows us time to enjoy all the amenities at the inn." Gus, king of sarcasm.

"Your room has a bath."

"Yours doesn't?" Gus shot me a look of genuine surprise.

"It's fine. You need more prep in the morning than I do."

"You say that because I always look bona fide."

"I say that because it's true. We should move."

"To the Ritz?"

"From this spot. Surveillance is going to be trickier now. Kerr knows us on sight."

"And she knows we might shoot her."

"A fact that probably has her on edge."

"If we loiter too long, D.C.'s finest might also have questions for us. Maybe not you, definitely me."

"That's racist."

"It be," Gus said.

I scoped out options. Irving Wine and Spirits sat diagonally across the intersection from Kerr's building. Maybe Kerr's building. At our backs were a Chinese restaurant called the Mayflower and another Latin eatery called Ercilia's.

"How about this?" I said. "You get a window table in Ercilia's. Order. While you eat, I'll rotate between the bank and the liquor store. When you finish, I'll go into the Mayflower and have some lo mein. You move to the bus stop, then shift to the stretch of Mount Pleasant north of Irving."

"Why can't I hang at the corner liquor store?"

"Don't force me to say something racist."

"That's racist."

"We keep rotating, never going to the same place twice, never staying the same length of time. If Kerr comes out, one of us will have eyes on her right away."

"If she's in there."

"If she's in there."

"If she's even in D.C."

"If she's even in D.C."

"Take a peek inside the foyer?"

"Don't want to risk that yet. Maybe later."

"What if she makes us and slips out a back door?"

"Good point. Revised plan. While you enjoy your tacos I'll poke around the building, see if there's a rear or side entrance. Then, depending on what I find, I'll take up position at the bank or elsewhere."

"What if I spot her while you're elsewhere?" What Gus was saying but not saying was he wanted backup.

"If Kerr comes out and I can't reach you or you can't reach me, the tail stays with her, finds out where she's going. Then we meet back at the hotel."

"Sounds solid."

I found a street-level entrance in back. The metal door was secured by a chain looping the handle and connecting to a bolt in the exterior wall. I guessed the improvised arrangement violated every fire reg in D.C. I also guessed the building's residents had endured one break-in too many. Didn't matter. Kerr wasn't coming out that way.

Gus and I tacked and jibed until midnight, then returned to the hotel. Uninterested in amenities, I showered in a bath two doors down from my room. It was clean and had a tub enclosed by a plastic curtain with black fish and bubbles in a rosy-pink sea.

Five Days

I t hurts!
   It hurts!
It hurts!
Too much.
She loses control and begs him to stop.
A few seconds. A few more. The Leader lets go and steps back.
Tears run down her cheeks. Her scalp aches where his grip has knotted her hair.
An image slices through. A different face in the dark of the woods. A kind face. The memory triggers a tug in her gut.
She hears the whisper of fabric. The Leader's agitated breathing.
She looks up.
The Leader is watching her, smiling that hideous smile.
I'm sorry, she says.
You must prove yourself.
How?
She can't imagine she hears him right. Stares, disbelieving.
The Leader says it again, voice louder. A sheen of sweat now coats his forehead.

She is not mistaken.

Blood thuds in her ears.

A sudden terrifying thought. This is all wrong.

I can't, she says.

The Leader's eyes go dark. His hands ball into fists.

Blind with tears and terror, she backpedals away. He follows, close.

Her shoulders slam a corner. She presses herself into it, cringes, waits for the blow.

The Leader's fingers wrap her throat. His thumbs dig into the hollow at its base.

He says it again.

He wants her to die.

CHAPTER 22

My alarm went off at six the next morning. Too early for our free breakfast, Gus and I got coffee and croissants at Flying Fish on Mount Pleasant, were circulating by seven.

We spent our time shifting from one vantage point to another. Observing Kerr's building. If it was Kerr's building. Or Bronco's. Or spearhead2021@yahoo.com's. Or loyalc2020@aol.com's. We stayed out of sight in case anyone was watching from a third-floor window. Difficult not knowing the exact location of the apartment.

Mount Pleasant Street was relatively calm until mid-morning, busier throughout the rest of the day. The crowd seemed local and multiethnic. Diligent and conscientious. Lots of eco-friendly bags, dogs, long hair, Birkenstocks. D.C. cruisers patrolled frequently. No one hassled Gus or me. Kerr never appeared. Nor did Bronco.

Throughout the long, tedious vigil, my heart beat a rhythm faster than normal. Stella sat center stage in my consciousness. Was I below her prison? Waiting to spot the monsters who held her? Who'd killed her?

By evening I wanted to storm the place. As usual, Gus persuaded me of the folly in that.

At eleven P.M. I was in the laundromat. A young woman with sallow skin and questionable hygiene was running three loads simultaneously. A cooking competition was playing on a small TV high up in one corner. She was watching, blowing bubbles that popped and clung like pink jellyfish to her face.

The woman had sneakers in two machines, and the thrumming and banging had my already jangled nerves on edge. Not to mention the gum. I was also hungry, despite a day of boredom munching.

I texted Gus, begging that we take action. He suggested we meet at a place called the Diner on 18th Street. It served late and was close to the Morgan Inn. Reluctantly I agreed.

The Diner had outdoor seating under square blue umbrellas, at that hour folded and belted tight. Inside, booths ran along the left, tables filled the center, and a counter ran down the right side of the room. Tiny hexagon tiles formed black-and-white patterns on the floor.

Gus and I chose a booth. A waiter appeared with water and menus.

I ordered the grilled cheese and a Heineken. Gus went with the patty melt and a Sierra Nevada Pale Ale.

I watched the waiter retreat. He looked good in his jeans.

Gus's burger came with Swiss and sautéed onions. That seemed okay. On rye. That seemed wrong.

I tried but couldn't force myself to eat. Gus watched me lift the sandwich, replace it on the plate again and again. I waited for the lecture, but he said nothing.

The waiter and his jeans took forever to deliver the bill. Bored, I played with my phone. Noted an anomaly that goosed my pulse.

"The motion detector's dead."

"Since when?"

"I'm not sure."

"Batteries?"

"I replaced them yesterday and checked to be sure the thing was working."

"Could be nothing."

"Right."

Gus slapped bills on the counter and we bolted.

The nice old fella wasn't working the desk. No one was. We flew past it and hit the stairs running. Stopped on the second landing, both breathing hard. Gus at my back, I craned around the corner.

The hall was empty. The DO NOT DISTURB sign was hanging on my knob. The wood beside the lock appeared freshly gouged. A sliver of yellow oozed from below the door.

"You leave a light on?" Gus whispered.

I shook my head.

We drew our guns and crept forward.

Gus went shoulders-to-the-wall on the right. I went left. We both listened, breath suspended. The hotel was absolutely still. Too still?

I leaned in and put my ear to the wood. Heard no muffled conversation. No running water. No squeaking floorboard.

I turned to Gus. He tipped his free palm. Now what?

I'd put in my time staking out hotel corridors. No way I'd do a repeat of my stint at the Ritz.

I circled a finger in the air. Gus gave a thumbs-up. As I drew back, he stepped forward and dropped to a crouch, Glock double-fisted beside his nose.

Staying to the side of the jamb, I inserted and turned the big brass key, twisted the knob, and pushed. The door swung inward. Gus remained low, knowing an assassin would expect a vertical target and go for the kill shot—torso or head.

"Jesus flipping Christ." Gus rose slowly, Glock still aimed into the room.

I peeled from my position to peer past him.

The old wooden chair had been repositioned. Kerr was in it, ankles duct-taped to the front legs, wrists cuffed to pipes looping under the sink. She was gagged with a length of black and white fabric that looked like a scarf. The motion detector lay shattered at her feet.

With the restricted movement her bindings allowed, Kerr had

twisted her head toward the door. A red furrow on her forehead suggested hours facedown on the edge of the basin. Her eyes were wide and dark with terror.

Kerr was wearing a long black skirt, a black tunic, and the newly repaired black boots. On seeing us, her lips flattened against her gums and a keening whimper escaped her throat.

I circled Gus and entered, gun and gaze sweeping the room. He followed, mimicking my actions. I heard him kick the door closed with one foot.

I checked under the bed. The room offered no other cover. No closet, no bath. The window was closed and latched. No figure lurked in the yard below.

"Clear." Holstering my Glock.

Gus kept his weapon drawn and trained on Kerr. She was moaning and yanking the cuffs as high as they'd go, then letting them drop. Repeating the action again and again. Her wrists were bruised and abraded. I crossed to her but maintained a safe distance.

"I'll untie the gag," I said. "But any loud noise or sudden move would be a bad idea."

Kerr moaned and overnodded. Air was moving in and out of her nostrils in short wet sniffles. Her cheeks were slick with tears and snot.

Gus stepped to my side. I frisked Kerr. She didn't object. I found no hidden weapon, and she wasn't wired with explosives. I untied the knot and removed the scarf. It was soggy with drool and blood. I let it drop to the floor.

"The caminet." The corners of Kerr's mouth were angry and raw. She was having trouble with consonants. "—lease."

The keys to the handcuffs lay on the top shelf of the medicine cabinet. Using a tissue from my pocket, I lifted them down.

While freeing Kerr's wrists, I noticed a dark flash on one of the bracelets. I straightened to inspect it. Black lettering, probably made with a Sharpie.

"—lease." If not hysterical, Kerr was close. "I've —een like this all day."

I handed the tissued cuffs to Gus and squatted to release Kerr's ankles. A whiff of urine suggested she'd peed herself.

"Don't leave that chair." Pointing a stern finger.

Kerr brought her legs together and gingerly straightened her spine. I rose and turned to Gus, dreading.

"Hurryhome407@gmail.com," he read aloud.

"It's the Gmail account I set up before leaving Charleston."

"Check it," he said.

I did.

The mailbox held a single message, from a sender whose username I hadn't seen before. Included with it were seven attachments. I opened the email.

It was unfortunate that our meeting ended so abruptly. Particularly for my colleague who is no longer with us. Were I at liberty to follow my own path, I would find and kill both you and your dark little partner. It would be challenging, but I would succeed. You are skilled, but not as skilled as I. Sadly, for the present, my mission demands my undivided attention. But who knows what the future will hold?

I have sources. Through them, I have learned what it is you want. And, truth be told, I am disappointed to find your motivation so base. Money, the great corruptor. In the end, human nature is what it is.

A price has been put on the head of each member of the Chicago team. To date, you have killed two. To save both of us time and energy, I am delivering the remaining individuals to you. One is my own personal gift. Credit for the other must go to a malignancy of the pancreas. These deaths should satisfy the requirements of your contract. I have left the young lady in your room as a bonus. Do with her what you will. She knows nothing, means nothing to me.

I hope this will suffice. And that I can now continue my mission unmolested. Should that not be the case, consider yourself warned again. I have been merciful to this point but will not

hesitate to carry through on my threats. I have retained my little
"bargaining chip" for just such a possibility as this. Thus, in good
faith, I include the final photo.
   Sorry about your little toy. Really. So amateur.
            — Bronco

Barely breathing, I right-clicked to open the attachments. Each
was a jpeg file. The images appeared one by one, unfurling slowly
from the top to the bottom of the screen. The colors were vibrant,
the details disturbingly sharp.

The seventh photo froze my respiration altogether.

"What?" Gus's voice seemed to come from a long way off.

Skin prickling, I displayed Bronco's message, then held out the
phone.

Gus read. Kerr sat in her chair, shoulders slumped, gaze on the
hands that had landed palms-up in her lap.

"Dark little partner?" Brows floating as high as they'd go.

"Jesus, Gus!"

"That's racist."

"Look at the pictures."

Gus scrolled. Then his eyes rolled to mine.

"Sonofabitch," he said.

"Sonofabitch," I said.

CHAPTER 23

The woman was sitting on a concrete floor in a corner, slumped like a rag doll against one wall. She was wearing a pink hoodie, black leggings, and pink high-top Chuck Taylors. Her jaw was slack, her legs extended, right knee twisted at an impossible angle. A sneaker lay upside down at her right hip. Propped on it was a copy of the *Chicago Tribune,* front page purposefully displayed.

The woman's forehead had a single hole directly above her nasal bridge. Blood darkened her face and hoodie. Gore spread from a point on the wall where her head had once been. A smear led down to where it had ended up.

The woman's expression showed nothing. No anger, no fear, no surprise that her life was about to end. I saw no signs of rigor or livor. Save for the bullet hole, the blood, and wrenched leg, the woman might have been sleeping. Deduction: The photo had been snapped immediately after she was shot. The newspaper documented the date on which that had occurred.

I studied the lifeless face, the slim neck, the snarled hair. Had no doubt. The woman had been the front seat passenger in the Subaru Forester outside the Bnos Aliza School.

The second image showed the woman lying prone. The hoodie was a war zone, the back of her skull a yawning cavern. I knew the missing bone and brain matter were the gore spraying the wall.

The third picture was a close-up of the *Tribune*'s front page. The date roared up and slammed me like a fist to the chest. The woman had been killed the previous day. The day Gus and I arrived in D.C.

Fingers ice, I scrolled to the next shot. Centered in it was a headstone. Inscribed in the rose granite was the name BRIAN LEE HARKESTER. Below the name were the dates 1973–2015. Beyond Harkester's plot, I could see other graves, one with a tall monument sculpted in the shape of a vine-wrapped tree.

The fifth photo captured a castle façade, the architectural style similar to that of the Chicago Water Tower. Chiseled above the drive-through entryway were the words ROSEHILL CEMETERY.

Next was a head-and-shoulders portrait of a man in camo cap and fatigues. The camouflage pattern said he was army. A Velcro patch said his rank was sergeant. Another patch on his breast said his name was Harkester.

Harkester's brim was low and skimming his brows, his chin cocked with a defiance that also showed in his eyes. A line drizzled from the base of one ear onto his cheek. I stared at the scar, thinking of my own.

The seventh image showed a girl with bound wrists and a leather belt wrapping her throat. Her head was tilted, her features half-hidden by tangled red hair. Still. I recognized the face.

Hot lava was erupting in my chest.

"I need to —ee."

The whiny voice broke through. I looked up.

I'd shown Gus the boardwalk photo of the Brights. His eyes told me he recognized Stella, too.

"You don't know when that picture was taken." Understanding the fury short-circuiting my thinking. Talking me down. "It could be a bluff."

My mouth was a desert. I couldn't speak.

"Focus on the present." Indicating Kerr. "What to do here?"

My mind kept swapping Stella's face with that of the woman in the hoodie.

"Sunnie!" Sharp. "Breathe."

I did.

"For now, let's hold Kerr in my room," Gus said.

"Why?"

"I have two beds."

"Why bother? Why don't we just—"

"She might prove to be *our* bargaining chip."

"He says he doesn't want her."

"She knows them. She can help lead us to Stella."

Deep breath. Another.

Of course Gus was right.

I nodded. Wordlessly dug out spare jeans and panties, and slung my purse strap over my shoulder.

"Move," I said, leveling the Glock at Kerr.

Gus's room was one floor up. As we climbed, I noticed that Kerr was limping. Being shackled had taken a toll. Or maybe she was playing for sympathy. I didn't care.

When Gus's door was closed, I handed Kerr the clothing. "We don't want to smell your stinking pee."

She scuttled to the bathroom and locked herself in. I heard a flush, then the sound of running water.

"The last two bombers?" Gus cocked his chin at my phone.

"Yes," I said.

"Think the pics are legit?"

"I'll run them by Capps. But, yeah. I do."

"Why give up Kerr?"

"To make us go away."

"Risky," Gus said. "Though he claims she knows nothing."

"Pol Pot claimed he was saving a culture."

"He's threatening to kill Stella if we don't back off." A beat, then, "Why would they have kept her alive this long?"

"Leverage. The man is an animal." I heard the squeak of faucets, then the steady purr of a shower. "I'll take first shift."

"You sure?"

"Yes." No way I'd be sleeping.

Gus removed his windbreaker and shoulder rig, freed the Glock, and laid it on the bed nearest the door. Stretching out, ankles crossed, he closed his eyes and rested his arms on his chest.

I slipped off my jacket and holster and placed my gun on the black desk. Sitting in the black chair, I dug Capps's card from my purse, checked his mobile number, and forwarded the email and images to him. It was 1:27 A.M.

I'd just finished when Kerr turned off the shower. I heard no movement in the bathroom. When enough time had passed that I was growing concerned, the door opened and Kerr came out. Her hair was wet and she was wearing my jeans, the legs rolled so many times the hems looked like doughnuts around her ankles.

Kerr glanced at me, quickly away.

"Want to tell me how you got here?" I asked.

No response.

"Did Bronco chain you to the sink?"

Kerr said nothing. A few seconds passed. She drew a juddery breath, ran an index finger below each of her lower lids, observed the wetness. I noticed that her hands were trembling.

"Hit the rack," I said, struck by a sudden, irrational splinter of pity.

"I'm hungry."

"Can't help you with that."

Kerr limped to the bed. Lying supine, she settled her arms atop the covers and laced her fingers over her belly.

When Kerr's breathing fell into a steady rhythm, I crossed to the coffee machine and made myself a cup using two packets. Didn't really need it. Every nerve in my body was raw.

I spent the next four hours fighting my personal demons and pumping caffeine. Fortunately, the inn was generous with amenities. Or Gus had stockpiled.

I watched a cobweb dance on a grate as the furnace kicked on and off. Clouds run the moon outside the windows. Shadows shape-change in the wake of the clouds. I found the moon, if not calming, at least reassuring.

The bedside clock hummed. The old hotel played a soft serenade of tics and creaks and thrums, silent witness to the wee-hours secrets of its occupants.

At six, the sky was deep purple-gray going light at the edges. I was about to wake Gus when my phone vibrated. Recognizing the number, I answered.

"You're up early." Keeping my voice low.

"What the fuck?"

"Top of the morning to you, too."

"Where are you?" Capps demanded.

"D.C." Kerr was snoring softly. I moved to the bath.

"Explain the meat show."

"I was hoping you'd do that. Rosehill Cemetery is in Chicago, right?"

"So?"

"Day before yesterday, field any 911 calls about a woman with her brains on a wall?"

"Could be." Wary.

I'd never gotten around to texting Capps. Okay, I'd never bothered. So, keeping an eye on Kerr through the cracked door, I briefed him on all that had happened since I'd left Chicago. Gus. Bronco. Jihad for Jesus. The bungled bombing on Devon Avenue. The shootout at Venice Beach. The clues pointing to D.C. The stakeout on Mount Pleasant Street. Kerr's appearance in my hotel room.

There was a long silence as Capps arranged facts in his head.

"So your twin capped one of the goons who grabbed you on Rose Avenue."

"Yes."

"Then the goon's partner capped him."

"He didn't mean to." Kerr's skirt was hanging over the shower rod. I touched the fabric. It was damp. I looked around, saw wadded white panties in the trash basket.

"This Bronco character calls all the plays," Capps said.

KATHY REICHS · 198

"Yes."

"He and his group want to wipe out Muslims."

"He'd put it more elegantly, but yes."

"And he's now in the wind."

"It was *High Noon* in that apartment."

"So you've said." Pause. "He's not the only one."

"Meaning what?"

"The goon that caught the bullet took a pass on long-term treatment."

"He left the hospital? Didn't the LAPD have a guard at his door?"

"That moron won't be enjoying a promotion real soon. Is this guy Bronco in D.C.?"

"Haven't seen him."

"I don't suppose you caught his last name."

"I was hoping you'd clarify that detail. By the way, the dead goon in Venice was one of the bombers."

"You're sure?"

"He was one of the four in the Subaru Forester."

"His name?"

"I was hoping you'd clarify that, too. A guy named Alves is handling the investigation. LAPD."

"I should do this so you can score another twenty-five bills?"

"I want names for personal reasons. Drucker only asked for proof of capture."

"Or death."

"I try to avoid that."

"Seems to me you're all done. You shot the guy in our morgue and the guy in Venice."

"I didn't shoot the guy in Venice."

"I'm guessing he counts. Bronco killed the woman in the photo. The fourth bomber, Harkester, died of cancer." Empty air, as though Capps was running back through the photos. Or rereading the message. "You're thinking this bargaining chip he's threatening to kill is Stella Bright."

"You saw the seventh image. He has her."

"Or had her. The pic could be old. Why include a date marker in one shot and not the other?"

I'd thought of that. Didn't believe it.

"I know you're good at your job, Detective. And I know you're busy." Doing humble. "But you're also frustrated. I was hoping we could help each other."

"What are you talking about?"

"You want to close the files on Bnos Aliza and Stella Bright. So do I."

"Or maybe you're playing me. Maybe you're thinking this Bronco might be good for a bonus."

"Bronco's not on Drucker's list."

"Lucky for him."

"The man's a terrorist, Detective. Homegrown, but just as deadly as any foreign jihadist." I let that lie for a second. Then, "I don't know the target, but Bronco's planning something big."

"When?"

"Soon."

"He said that?"

"You read the email."

Nothing but humming silence.

"How about you do me a solid, I do you a solid."

"Ms. Night." Capps spoke when he felt I'd grasped the depth of his aversion to dealing with me. "I will make no deals, no promises."

There was a "but" in his tone, so I said, "I need you to background Harkester. Verify that he's dead. He was army. Start there. I doubt he's got a jacket."

"Why?"

"Bronco said his movement only recruits people with clean records. Have you ID'd the John Doe in your morgue?"

"No."

"Makes sense now he wasn't in the system." I had a sudden mental image of Capps in pj's and slippers, frowning but listening.

"Do the same for the woman in the hoodie. Who was she? What's her story? Where was she murdered? Who's leading the investigation? What's the thinking on motive? A doer?"

"If your theory's correct, that investigation is only one day old."

"The first forty-eight."

"Information relating to a homicide will be strictly confidential."

"Last I knew, you were a cop."

"I am. You're not."

"But I'll need facts if I'm going to pitch the story to *Dateline*." Stupid. But stress always brings out the sarcasm.

"You can't do your own digging because . . . ?"

"I can. But you're local. And your access to certain resources will speed the process."

"And what's the solid you'll be sending my way?"

"I share anything I get. And I keep looking for Bronco." And Stella.

"I'll think about it."

Capps disconnected.

The flood of coffee was making itself felt. After peeking out at Kerr, I eased the door shut and used the toilet. Flushed. Washed my hands.

When I emerged Kerr's blankets were on the floor. Her bed was empty.

CHAPTER
24

M y brain screamed a five-alarm crisis alert.
"Gus!" Eyes darting the room.

He was on his feet without seeming to go through any intermediary stage. The gun was in his hand.

Then I saw her, crouched between the radiator and the wardrobe.

It took a mind-bending effort not to rush forward and grab her. "What the hell are you doing?"

Kerr gaped as though I'd just ripped the heart from a baby. I realized I was pointing the Glock at her chest. Good. I'd use her fear.

"I ought to knock you into fucking tomorrow!" Feigning rage. Or not.

Kerr stared, eyes Frisbees.

"No. I should put you out of your goddamned misery. Right here. Right now."

"Easy." Taking my cue, Gus slipped into good-cop mode.

"What's your problem? It's what I was hired to do."

"She's not on Drucker's list."

"I don't like her."

"Doesn't mean you should kill her."

"She tried to kill me." Eyes blistering Kerr. "Foster Beach? The underpass?"

"They made me." High and quavery, a terrified sparrow trapped by a cat.

"Who made you?"

Kerr said nothing. I knew her mind was racing, testing for right answers.

"Maybe she really doesn't know," Gus said.

"She knows. And she knows Bronco would fry us if he wasn't tied up planning to murder more kids. Or is it old ladies this time?"

"You could be right," Gus said.

"She probably knows where the bastard is. Right. This. Moment." Air-jabbing the gun at Kerr's face.

"I know nothing." Pleading. "You have to believe me."

"No. I don't." To Gus, never taking my eyes off Kerr. "Do I?"

"Not really."

"Bronco keeps me out of all that," Kerr said.

"You being his loyal jihadist."

Tears trickled down Kerr's cheeks. She raised trembling hands to wipe them away.

"That why he left you cuffed to my sink? Like a dog you don't want anymore. Tie it to the tracks and walk away."

"Does seem cold," Gus said.

I stepped closer to Kerr. "Who are they, cupcake?"

Her head wagged slowly.

"You going to tell us what we need to know?"

Kerr glanced up, just a flash of brown. Her lashes glistened. They were long and heavy with tears. Then she looked down again.

"That's it," I said. "She's wasting my time."

"Maybe if we feed her," Gus said.

"I'm not feeding her."

"She must be hungry."

"Why don't you take a walk?" Tightening my grip and sliding

one finger into the trigger guard. "Get breakfast for two. When you come back all this will be resolved."

"Resolved like in Atlanta?"

"Up to her."

"You really want names that badly?"

"Go."

"No!" Kerr shrieked. To Gus, "Don't leave me with her. She's psycho!"

"She won't like you saying that," he said.

"Psycho?" With a hint of insanity in my voice.

"Oh my God!" Kerr now sounded like a scene in a teen slasher movie.

"Well, shit." Gus crossed to Kerr and reached down a hand. She recoiled, shoulders turtled in, arms hugging her knees.

"What in the name of sweet Christ are you doing?" I demanded.

"Get up," Gus ordered Kerr.

"She'll shoot me."

"I won't let her."

"She'll hurt me."

"I won't let her do that either."

"Really?"

"Unless there's no other option."

Kerr moaned and tightened the pressure on her legs.

"You're a pussy," I said to Gus, mean as I could.

Gus used an elbow to nudge me sideways. Pointed to Kerr, then to the black desk chair. "Sit there."

"I don't want to," Kerr whimpered.

"Shall I go out for doughnuts?"

Kerr unwound and hobble-crawled to the desk, eyes skidding between Gus and me. Gus dragged a chair from the windows and dropped into it, facing her. I sat on the end of the bed, Glock still in my hand.

"Let's start with your name," Gus said. "Is it Jasmine Kerr?"

"It is right now."

"Fine. We'll go with that. Tell us about your group."

"It's Bronco's group."

"Jihad for Jesus."

"I'm not a member."

"That why you tried to ambush me at Foster Beach?" As menacing as I could.

"I didn't try to ambush you."

"That's not my recollection."

"Bronco told me to deliver an envelope to the Ritz. Then to be at the underpass to point out the person who picked it up."

"You always do what Bronco says?"

"Yes."

"Why?"

"Everyone does."

"Why you? You're not a disciple?"

Pink mottled Kerr's cheeks. She focused on the desktop. Ran a thumbnail along a groove in the wood.

Sudden insight.

"You're banging him," I said.

The pink went crimson.

Jesus Christ.

"What's Bronco's last name?" I snapped.

"Nagurski."

"Seriously?" I wasn't sure which was stronger, my revulsion or my pity. "How did you and lover boy meet? You kick off your Hanky Pankys to pick him up in a bar?"

"Bronco doesn't go to bars."

I snorted.

Gus tried to bring us back on topic. "Talk about Jihad for Jesus."

"Muslims plan to take over the world."

"Which Muslims?" I knew I should let Gus handle the questioning. Couldn't help myself.

"What?"

"Sunni? Shiite? Sufi? Wahhabi?"

"All of them, I guess. They want to force the whole planet to follow their rules."

"Which rules?"

"What?"

"Which rules?"

"They don't believe in the Bible. Bronco's going to stop them."

"By blowing up Jewish kids?"

"That wasn't supposed to happen."

"Why were you in Chicago?"

"I live there."

"Was Bronco in Chicago when the school was bombed?"

"No."

"Last week?" Hitting her hard, looking for a crack.

"No."

"Who planted the bomb?"

"I don't know."

"Who was the thug at the Ritz?"

"I don't know."

"Why did you go to L.A.?" Fast switch. An old trick to keep the interviewee off guard.

"Bronco told me to."

"Why?"

"I don't know."

"Does he live there?"

"He lives a lot of places."

"Who's the guy got killed in Venice?"

"I don't know."

"You never once caught a name?"

"I think I heard someone call him Jano."

"Is there a cell in D.C.?"

"I think so."

"Is Bronco here now?"

She nodded, eyes again down, thumbnail digging.

"Why?"

"He's organizing something." The hand came up, palm out. "I haven't a clue what it is, where it is, or when it is."

"You were staying at the address on Mount Pleasant?"

"Yes."

"Whose place?"

"I don't know."

"Who else was there?"

"Landmine."

"Who's Landmine?"

"He's disgusting."

"Tough to pick that out of a lineup."

"I'm trying."

"Try harder."

"His real name is Landon. He thinks he's a stud, gets off on being called Landmine."

For an instant I almost felt sorry for Kerr. She was so pitifully, pathetically lacking on so many levels. "Describe him," I said.

"Big. With huge muscles. Like he works out a lot. You met him."

"The other guy who got shot in Venice?" A feeling like smoke curling cold in my chest.

"Yeah. That's him."

"Someone spotted us yesterday on Mount Pleasant?"

She nodded. "Bronco did. When you left we all slipped out."

"Where did you go?"

"An apartment near Dupont Circle."

"Bronco brought you to my room while we were watching the building today."

Her cheeks flamed anew.

"How'd he duck the motion detector?" Not really caring. Mostly pissed at having missed its final signal, sent while I was prowling Mount Pleasant.

"He's good with gadgets."

"Where's the Dupont apartment?"

"They won't be there."

I waggled the Glock.

"Twentieth Street, near R. I don't know the address. There's a coffee shop in the basement."

I looked at Gus. He got up, slid his Glock into the shoulder rig, donned it and the windbreaker, and left.

"Now," I said. "It's just us girls."

Kerr's body seemed to curl in on itself.

"Until yesterday you were boning Bronco. I'm sure there was pillow talk."

"No."

"Nothing?" Not asking nicely.

"No."

"And you never got the teeniest bit curious about him and his pals? Maybe eavesdropped on a meeting or phone conversation? Peeked at a text? We know you're good with email."

Kerr looked at me with something. Wariness. Guilt. Fear. "That's not his way."

"What's his way?"

"Bronco never shares anything with anyone. When it's time, he tells people what to do. His instructions are always last-minute, never in advance."

I got my phone and scrolled to the photo of the woman with her brains on a wall. Laid it on the desk. Kerr glanced at the image. Her breath caught and her eyes cut away.

"Who is she?"

Nothing.

"Who is she?" Harsher.

"Tibby Icard." Dry swallow. "She lives in Chicago."

"Where?"

"No idea."

"What can you tell me about her?"

"Nothing. It's not like we hung out. I think I saw her once."

"Where?"

"With Bronco."

"Yet you know her last name."

"She must have told me."

"Bronco ordered Icard's death."

"I don't think so."

"I know so." Another quick swerve. "Who else was in the apartment in Venice?"

"What do you mean?"

"Don't play games. I heard women down the hall."

She gave me a long flat stare. I gave it back.

"One of them I don't know," she said. "The other was Selena."

Stella?

Sudden click.

"What did you mean, 'we all slipped out'? Who else was in the apartment on Mount Peasant?"

"Selena."

"Any others?"

"No." The flat stare turned away. "Anyway, I doubt they're still here."

"What's Selena's last name?" Pulse humming.

Kerr shrugged both shoulders.

"What does she look like?"

"Kind of pale and weird."

"Young? Old?"

"Young."

"You can do better."

"Maybe like me."

"Talk about Stella Bright."

Flash of something? "Who?"

"Don't mess with me."

Slight change in the curve of her spine. No response.

I scrolled to the last photo in Bronco's email. "That her?"

Kerr dragged her eyes to the image. Her breath caught again, held as she balanced emotions. Weighed. Made decisions.

"You can't even see that person's face."

"Could it be Selena?" Oh, so controlled.

"I don't know."

I found the picture of the mustachioed blond in the Chicago morgue. Again placed the phone in front of Kerr.

"Who is he?"

"That's Lew. His last name's Lewinoski. I don't know his first."

I hit her with another fast changeup.

"Why do you say Bronco's not at the Dupont Circle apartment?"

"He's way careful. He'll be long gone."

"Why did he leave you in my room?"

"It was necessary for the cause."

"Cuffing you to my sink will help foil Islamic domination?"

Kerr's hands came up and curled into fists. Her forehead dropped onto knuckles bulging white and bloodless in rigor contraction. A few seconds, then her shoulders began rising and falling in short little hops. Tears fell, glistened like tiny round moons on the smooth black wood. One. Two. A dozen.

"I know he was sorry." Barely a whisper.

Dramatic lunge to the bed.

She lost it.

CHAPTER
25

While Kerr blubbered, I went to the desk and dialed Capps. He picked up right away.

"Sweet mother of God. It hasn't been an hour."

"Got a pen?"

I heard rustling, then a heartfelt exhalation.

"I squeezed some names out of Kerr," I said.

"I'm listening."

I told him about Jano, Lew, Selena, Landmine. That Kerr thought Bronco's last name was Nagurski.

"Brilliant." Incredulous. "She able to ID his hit?"

"Tibby Icard. A Chicago girl."

"What's Icard's story?"

"Kerr claims she knows nada, says she wasn't part of the group."

"She screwing Bronco?"

"Yes."

"Think she's covering for the skank?"

"He cuffed her to my sink."

"Could sway her loyalty. I'll call when I've got something."

After Capps disconnected I spent a long time watching daylight bring the room into black and red focus. I thought about Stella. Were we closing in? Could she survive long enough for us to free her?

I thought about Tibby Icard. Somehow, knowing the woman's name made her more real. Not just a subject in two photos, one murdering, one murdered.

I wondered again about Icard's distress in the van. What she'd said to the driver as they disappeared off frame. Had she seen Bowen Bright pick up the backpack? Had she known he was about to be vaporized? Felt remorse? Panic that she and her friends would be caught?

My skin felt tight on my flesh. My heart raced in my chest. I was on fire to run these bastards to ground.

Why? I wasn't responsible for Icard's death. For the slaughter at Bnos Aliza. It wasn't my job to find Stella. To keep her alive. All this had nothing to do with me.

Oh, but it did. I'd failed once, way back in the grim dawn of my life. Failed to prevent a massacre. I couldn't let innocents die again.

By nine, I was sweating and pacing and my nail beds were throbbing. I decided to go back at Kerr.

"Come over here," I said.

Kerr peered at me through a tumble of hair. Checked to see if I still had the Glock. I did. Taking her time, she sat up, rerolled one pant leg, then walked to the chair vacated by Gus.

"Tell me about the passports," I said.

Kerr's eyes watched me, guarded, mimicked by an identical pair in a mirror to our right.

"Forging a passport buys you housing with a whole new set of friends," I pressed.

"So does breaking and entering. Besides, I didn't forge them."

"They had your picture and were in your possession."

"It wasn't my apartment. I was just crashing."

"Your name was on the mailbox."

"The landlord thought that was doing me a favor."

"Let's talk about the Mac."

"What Mac?"

"The one you wiped clean every time you logged off."

"I don't own a laptop."

"Bronco make you do that?"

No answer.

I opened the Notes app on my phone. "Jhk07749@gmail.com. What's the *h* for? Hotpants?"

All I got was a cold stare. By then she'd figured out I probably wasn't going to shoot her.

I read from the list. "Infidel567@gmail.com, trailblazer745 @gmail.com, spearhead2021@yahoo.com, loyalc2020@aol.com. Who was it popped Tibby? Infidel? Trailblazer? Spearhead? You banging one of them, too? Maybe the whole team?"

Kerr pretended she'd stopped listening. But a change in her breathing gave her away.

Sudden synapse. With all the shooting, and spying, and ping-ponging around the country, I'd forgotten about the email sent by Infidel the day I tossed the Argyle Street apartment. I opened the phone pic and read the first part of the message aloud. "Godolphin. Vintage Claret Beauty 05 05 06."

"Leave me alone." Covering her ears like a kid caught scribbling on a wall. "I'm not talking to you anymore."

"Suit yourself."

"I'm starving."

"Go do it on the bed."

Kerr flew from her chair.

What the hell was keeping Gus? To occupy my mind and stay sane, I began researching Godolphin on my phone. Found the following: a girls' school in Salisbury, Wiltshire, UK; a seventeenth-century English statesman; an eighteenth-century horse; an Australian Shiraz-Cabernet blend.

Vintage? Claret Beauty? Did the code refer to a vineyard?

I thumbed keys, working through loop after loop. Learned that Godolphin was produced by Glaetzer Wines, a small boutique vineyard in the Barossa Valley in South Australia. I felt a tick of excitement on finding an image of a bottle. Centered on the label was an ankh, the ancient Egyptian symbol of sunrise and regeneration. The vintage pictured was 2005.

I kept looping. Found a Glaetzer unfiltered Shiraz called Amon-Ra, in Egyptian mythology the king of all gods. Its label featured the all-seeing eye of Horus, ancient symbol of protection.

My mind started running possibilities. Could Glaetzer Wines be Bronco's next target? Did a foreign hit track with the MO of Jihad for Jesus? Might the group have a cell down under?

I skimmed the Glaetzer family history. The first members emigrated from Germany to Australia in 1888, established Glaetzer Wines a century later. Nothing on their website suggested they were Muslim.

In their distorted worldview, might these bastards interpret the Egyptian iconography as evidence the Glaetzers were Muslim? If not, might they view the symbols as pro-Islam? But Australia? Surely they could find something closer. And a winery? Not too many people there.

I was still poking at scenarios when Gus returned, a McDonald's bag in one hand. Kerr was curled under her quilt, back turned, doing nothing, saying nothing.

Gus looked at Kerr, at me. Placed his bounty on the desk. Shook his head.

I took a coffee and an Egg McMuffin. So did Gus. We crossed to stand by the windows. Roused by the smell of grease, and seeing we'd distanced ourselves, Kerr scuttled to the desk, helped herself, and returned to the bed.

"Empty," Gus said in a low voice.

"You managed to get into the apartment?"

He looked at me as though I'd asked if he knew how to breathe.

"Did they leave anything to suggest who they are? Where they've gone?"

"A boarding pass for a flight to Athens. Bronco Nagurski, seat three A."

"Really?"

Again, the look.

"Did anyone see them? A neighbor? A janitor? A mailman?"

"A guy across the street said he noticed three people leaving the building late last night. Wasn't sure what unit they'd come from. A hefty guy, a skinny guy, and a chick with bad hair. His words."

"Sounds like Landmine, Bronco, and Selena."

"Or Laurel, Hardy, and Sinead O'Connor."

"Where'd they go?"

"Got into a car and drove off. No, he didn't catch the make or the plate." Gus tipped his head toward Kerr. "She good for anything?"

I repeated what I'd told Capps about Tibby Icard, Selena, Jano, and Lew. About Bronco's alleged managerial style.

"You believe her?"

"She lacks the gray cells to follow through on a lie."

Gus considered that long enough to finish his muffin. "They managed to regroup here in D.C. after Venice Beach."

My conclusion also. "So there's a system for communicating in emergency situations."

We looked at Kerr. She was looking at us, coffee cup pressed to her lips.

"Where is he, Hotpants?" Ominous as I could.

"Don't call me that."

"Answer me."

"I don't know."

"Not good enough."

"He could be anywhere."

"Why did you all go to L.A.?"

"Bronco called a meeting. I wasn't at it, heard nothing."

"They're planning something big."

Kerr nodded.

"Soon?"

Kerr shrugged. I took a step in her direction. Gus raised a palm. "How does the group reconnect if disrupted?" he asked calmly.

"What?"

"If they're fucking busted by the cops," I snapped. "Jesus H. Christ, is anyone home in there?"

Above the cardboard rim, Kerr's pupils dilated with fear.

"Calm down," Gus admonished me softly. "He wouldn't have left her here if she knew spit."

I turned away in disgust. Whipped back and went at her from a different direction.

"Did Bronco score your passport collection?"

"I only had two."

"You're pissing me off."

"Bad idea to piss her off." Gus shook his head.

"Bronco has a lot of passports," Kerr said.

"You've seen them?"

"Yes."

"American?"

"Some."

"Issued in what name?"

"Huh?"

"More than one name?" Jackhammering, looking for that crack.

"I can't say."

"You can't read?"

"No. I—"

"You've seen your boyfriend's phony passports yet you don't know his real name?"

Caught in the lie, or in the realization of her own stupidity, Kerr flushed. "I can't remember."

I bunched my wrapper and winged it toward the bed. Kerr dodged, spilling what was left of her coffee.

"Let's try it this way." Gus, good-cop reasonable. "If Bronco has left D.C., where do you think he's going?"

"I don't know." Blotting the tunic with a corner of the sheet.

"Not good enough." Me, bad-cop mean.

More blotting.

"Did he ever talk about places he might like to travel?" Gus asked. "Places he'd been or planned to visit?"

"You just don't get it." Almost a wail. "Bronco told me nothing."

I stared at the mottled face, searching for signs of intelligent life. Came up empty, which puzzled me. Bronco was vile, but he was clever. How could he have tolerated such stupidity?

Then I remembered the laptop.

"Bronco had you perform tasks online," I said.

"Sometimes."

"Did you make travel arrangements?"

"I looked things up, but he never wanted me to book anything."

"Travel to where?"

"Like, cities?"

"No. Planets."

I saw question marks form in her eyes. Her brows dipped, then, "Los Angeles. D.C. Baltimore. New York."

I left space for her to continue. She didn't.

"That's it?" I asked.

"And Louisville. It's in Kentucky."

"Why Louisville?"

"I don't know." This time, a thread of uncertainty.

"Bullshit."

Brown eyes wide. Then she pulled her face back together.

Facts collided like protons in my head.

Fusion.

I knew.

CHAPTER
26

"Watch her!"

Brain throwing off sparks, I raced to my room, grabbed my laptop and the encryption device, and was back in under a minute. With pictures already forming in my mind, I got online to double-check my theory.

As I pointed and clicked and read, the pictures coagulated into something solid. Something real. When I sat back, electricity jazzing my nerves, they were watching me, Gus intent, Kerr blank-faced, working hard to reveal nothing.

"Talk about the tracks," I ordered Kerr.

"I don't know what you mean."

"Yes. You do." My Glock still lay on the desk. I reached out and wrapped my fingers around the butt. "We both know. Which means I don't need you anymore."

"Bronco wanted information on horse races." Eyes on the gun.

"Thus his interest in Baltimore, New York, and Louisville."

I rolled a look to Gus. His nod said he caught the link. The Preakness, Belmont Stakes, and Kentucky Derby.

"I guess. If you ask me, it's wrong to make horses run like that. They get hurt all the time."

"Bronco planned to go to a race?"

"Maybe."

"Which one?"

"I don't know. He asked me to price tickets way last fall."

Gus kept quiet. Curious but letting me work her.

"Who's Infidel?"

"Huh?"

"Your email buddy." I was asking about the IP address that had tracked to Louisville.

"How do you—"

"I know all your dirty little secrets, Hotpants."

Kerr's chin jutted out, going for defiant.

"One last chance." Meaningful lift of the Glock. "I'll be more specific. Did Bronco buy tickets for the Kentucky Derby?"

"He might have, all right? Gawd! It's not my fault."

With a theatrical flourish, Kerr flopped onto her side and rolled up in the quilt, larvalike. I signaled Gus to join me at the desk. He listened as I walked him through the components of my particle collision.

"This message was circulated in the thirty minutes before I tossed Kerr's apartment. Four recipients, one in Louisville. Those four were the only emails Kerr hadn't erased." Showing him the pic I'd shot with my phone. *Godolphin Vintage Claret Beauty 05 05 06. FL1X: LM-inf /JC-GR/B5-S2+4.*

"You think Godolphin could be the next target?"

"I do."

"What is it?"

"At first I thought it referred to an Australian winery."

Gus cocked a skeptical brow.

"There actually is a wine with that name. But that's not it. Look." Turning the computer to face him.

At the top of the screen, centered on a blue banner, were an Arabic symbol and a single word: *Godolphin*. Below the banner, a paragraph explained three things. Godolphin was a global Thoroughbred racing stable. The stable was founded by His Highness Sheikh Mohammed bin Rashid Al Maktoum. The sheikh was vice president and prime minister of the United Arab Emirates and emir of Dubai.

"Holy shit," Gus said.

"The Godolphin stable has horses entered in both the Oaks and the Derby."

"Those horses are named Vintage and Claret Beauty."

"They are."

"His sheikhness is Muslim." Still scanning the half-dozen photos displayed on Godolphin's homepage. "Bronco and his Crackpot Crusaders take exception to his presence at Churchill Downs."

I nodded.

Gus glanced again at the email captured by my phone's camera. "Oh-five, oh-six. Derby races are on May fifth and sixth this year?"

"They are."

"What's the significance of the final string of numbers?"

"We should find out," I said.

"We're going to Louisville," Gus said.

"We are."

"What about her?" Indicating the lump on the bed.

"She's lousy company." The lump had gone totally still. I spoke for its benefit. "And she knows zilch."

"She can ID us."

"Good point. She's useless *and* dangerous. Dead weight. I say—"

"I do know things." Clawing free of her blanket cocoon. "Not the things you were asking, but other things. And I'll remember more. When I'm not tired. Not scared."

"You scare her," Gus said.

"I don't like her."

"You said that."

"I told you Bronco was planning something. And I told you about Landmine. And Lew. And Tibby Icard."

"She did," Gus said.

"You can't leave me here." Eyes on Gus.

"Yes we can," I said.

"Noooo!"

"Why not?"

"Bronco will—"

"Bronco will be in Louisville."

"There are others. He's not really—"

I cut her off. "Give me something I can use."

A beat, then, "Bronco got tickets from some guy in New York. Two-day passes. Pricey seats."

"Where are they?" Gus asked.

"The tickets?"

"The seats."

Kerr didn't answer.

"The bitch would say anything to save her ass." Tightening my grip on the Glock.

"It's true," Kerr wailed. She was definitely a wailer.

"What's the guy's name?"

"I'll think of it. Chuck. No. Chip. No—"

"Give it a rest."

Kerr's mouth opened, but I scowled it shut. "Once more. Tell me what you know about Stella Bright."

"I don't know who she is." The intensity of the denial sent her eyes skidding.

"Don't screw with me!"

"Maybe I heard the name, all right? But I never met her."

"Heard the name where?"

"I don't—"

"*Where?*" Dragon fire.

"Chicago. Maybe L.A. I'm not sure. It was ages ago."

"Fucking hell!"

Deep inhalation. Settle down.

Could Kerr help find Stella? Maybe, maybe not. But what the hell, it was Drucker's dime. If there was one chance in a billion, I wanted her close. Under my control. But why did she want to stay with us?

Not optimistic, I got online to book travel. Yep. The whole world was going to Louisville. Using an airline industry search engine, I finally found a 2:12 P.M. flight on American with one open seat, another at 4:57 with two seats in first class. Grateful for what were probably cancellations, I grabbed them.

"I'll get my stuff." I held out my hand.

Gus gave his Glock to me.

When I returned, both guns disassembled and packed with my few belongings, Gus and Kerr were ready. Her eyes tracked me like one of those trick paintings that appear to follow your every move. I didn't ask what he'd told her.

We took a taxi to Union Station. As we walked around, killing time, Kerr kept stopping to hike the waistband or reroll the cuffs of the jeans. Spotting a women's apparel shop, I told her to choose something fast. Kerr flipped through a rack, disappeared behind a curtain, came out wearing baggy black pants. Wordlessly, she handed me my jeans. I paid, hoping she'd also been wearing my undies.

Another taxi took us to terminal A at DCA. We made the long trek to the American counter and got our boarding passes. I checked my bag. After clearing security, Gus and Kerr headed off in search of a restaurant.

It was standing room only at my gate. I stood. The flight boarded fifteen minutes late. My seat was in the middle of row eighteen. The aisle and window were occupied by blond belles wearing the full line of some designer's makeup. I wondered where they'd stowed their bonnets. Or if they'd shipped them ahead by ground.

Two hours after takeoff we touched down at SDF, Louisville International. I collected my luggage and went in search of a rental car. Forty minutes in line brought me to a frazzled-looking clerk at the Hertz counter. Another thirty and he'd managed to locate a red Nissan Maxima in some outer reach of the galaxy. Another twenty and I was finally behind the wheel. Or Susan Bullock was. By then it made sense to wait for Gus and Kerr.

Just before seven, my mobile vibrated. I checked the little screen, then answered, puzzled. Listened. Gave noncommittal responses. After disconnecting, the moths were jitterbugging in my chest.

Gus called ten minutes later. I told him what to look for, then drove from the cellphone lot to the arrivals area. A distance of meters that took a quarter of an hour.

Gus put his bag in the trunk, Kerr in back, got in next to me.

"Nice color," he said. "Shows restraint."

"My options were limited."

"Where to?"

"While waiting for the car I managed to find a room."

"I note your use of the singular."

"This place is a zoo. We're lucky to have that."

After exiting the airport, I followed signs to the Kentucky Exposition Center. Opposite the center's main gate, I hung a left on Phillips Lane, then a right on Crittenden. In less than a mile, the Four Points Sheraton appeared on our left. I pulled in.

"You sure this is necessary?" Gus, skeptical.

"You want to put a bullet in Stella Bright's head?" Too sharp.

Gus looked at me with an expression I couldn't decode. Did he think I was deluding myself? That Stella was dead?

"Twenty minutes." I got out and grabbed my bag. "In back."

Gus slid behind the wheel and roared off.

I entered the hotel and asked for a room. No reservation? Barely hiding his amusement, the clerk explained that they'd been fully booked for months. Derby week, you know. Sad smile.

I returned his smile. Silly me, what was I thinking? Then, wheeling my case behind me, I found a rear entrance and went back outside. Gus pulled up eight minutes later.

"The Hilton Garden Inn," I said. "Just past Central, on the right."

The hotel rose from a small island of green in a sea of black asphalt. Red brick walls, green roof and trim, covered drive-through, patios bounded by well-mannered hedges. It could have belonged to any of a dozen chains.

Gus parked around to one side, got out, and collected both

bags. I circled the hood and dropped into the driver's seat. Kerr did nothing until Gus signaled her to join him. Together they rounded the corner to enter through the main door.

I waited until my mobile buzzed.

"Six twelve."

I disconnected. Checked Google. Put the car in gear and drove off. An hour and a half later I was back with peanut butter, bread, and a new burner phone.

The room was clean, the décor unmemorable. The washcloths were pleated like little white tutus. Nice touch.

Gus was on one bed, catching a basketball game. Kerr was on the other, doing nothing. She was good at it.

We made sandwiches and ate in silence, Gus and I watching the hoops. Everyone was tired and hungry. At least I was. They'd probably munched and napped on the plane. When the game ended, Gus helped me drag a mattress off one of the beds. I tossed a blanket onto it and looked at Kerr.

"I need to use the bathroom." Sounding all of five.

"Go," I said.

While Kerr was doing whatever toilette she could sans unguents and lotions, Gus and I discussed strategy.

"Opaline Drucker called while I was waiting for your flight."

Gus's brows floated up in question.

"She wants to see me."

"In person?"

"Yes."

"Think she plans to shut it down? You've delivered what she paid for."

"Not her granddaughter."

"Stella may be dead."

"It's a possibility." I didn't believe it. "But Bronco ordered the Chicago bombing and he's still out there."

"You agreed?"

"Not yet. But I think I need to go."

"Work the old Sunnie charm?"

"Something like that. We've got three days until the Derby, two until the Oaks."

"If a race is the target."

"Yes. How about I do a quick hop to Charleston. You stay here, get a feel for the layout."

"What about Kerr?"

"Keep her with you."

"She and I just waltz into Churchill Downs?"

"Let me work on that."

I moved to the bare box spring and, back against the headboard, opened my laptop. A six A.M. flight through Atlanta would get me to Charleston by 9:38. Returning, there wasn't a seat to be had. I decided to worry about that later.

Kerr emerged as I was closing the Mac. Her hair was center-parted and braided. She was wearing the new black pants and the tunic in which she'd been chained to my sink. The latter didn't look good. Avoiding eye contact, she scurried to the floor mattress, dropped, and executed her cocoon maneuver.

Another pity-hate moment. I shelved both feelings.

After setting up the remaining motion detector, I phoned Gus so he'd have my new number, transferred everything from the old burner to the new, and blocked my caller ID. Then I dug a spare blanket from the closet and crossed to him.

"I'll leave my Glock with you."

"Yowza!" Dual-finger firing.

"Catch a ride to the airport?"

"When?"

I told him, then pulled five twenties from my pocket and held them out. "Take Kerr shopping."

"Why?"

"She needs things."

"Whatever. Drucker's money."

I waggled the bills. "Make sure those things include panties."

"What? I should check?"

"Your call."

Three Days

She has no idea where they are. Has ridden in the back of a panel van, wedged among suitcases, boxed linens, and the cardboard cartons from the office baseboards. The hours of bumping and swaying have made her sick. She's slept most of the way.

It's just past dawn when they arrive. The air is sticky warm and the hardwoods are in full leaf. The forest mix is different. She has studied her plant book. Can identify magnolia, sweet gum, and rhododendron. The pines seem to shoot straight up to the sun.

She hears the trilling of mockingbirds. The peeping of frogs. A complex recital by some unseen rooster.

The older ones go inside. Like ants, the younger ones begin hauling their possessions to the new nest.

When the office boxes are directed to the basement, she volunteers. Four trips. On the fifth, she is alone. One by one, she rips the tape and peers inside. A lightning glance into each.

Three of the boxes are filled with bundled cash. Lots of it. A fourth holds jewelry and a collection of mail bound with a rubber band.

Footsteps continue to thunk overhead.

She slips the envelopes from their binding and checks the front of each. All are addressed to a person she doesn't know, sent to a street and city she's never visited. Or has she? No letter is marked with a return address.

She opens a flap. The envelope holds a single snapshot. A Polaroid. She slips it out.

The image shocks her. The distorted mouth. The unseeing eyes. The flesh the color of bleached concrete.

She recalls the Leader's words. Imagines her own death portrait.

She feels she is about to unravel.

Heartbeat jamming her throat, she restores the terrifying photo to its place, sets her jaw, and turns all the breached tape to the wall. Adrenaline zinging, she hurries upstairs.

It's hard to get him aside. After their meeting in the clearing, he is dodging her again. In the late afternoon, she catches a break.

She lays it all out. He listens, eyes wary, index finger worrying a temple. She is tired of his wariness. What more does he want? The invoices. The corpse. The constant talk of death. The Leader's plan for her.

They figure the jewelry was surrendered by newcomers, the required yielding of worldly possessions. Neither of them can explain why cash would be hidden in boxes.

That night, lying in bed, she thinks she may truly be coming apart. But in some cool, undamaged recess of her brain, she is now certain. The Crossing is the product of an irrational mind.

Her fingernails rake her skin, turning her forearms into a battleground of angry red streaks. The death of children cannot benefit the world. It's all a monumental delusion.

A delusion that she must prevent from happening.

She pictures the dead woman. Was she a trial run? An impediment that had to be removed?

She pictures her mother. It's too late for Mama. But they must save themselves.

The next night, the Leader's rhetoric includes a terrifying new urgency.

Our once-free lives cannot continue. I can no longer do my work. We have killed. We cannot turn back.

The photo of the dead woman is passed around. When it reaches her, she shrinks from it, fearful lest such evil contaminate by touch.

Our children will suffer. Only one option remains.

Listening to the rant, she is certain they are all caught in a web of insanity.

Out of choices. Out of time. Saturday night.

The words jackknife into her chest.

The Crossing is upon us.

She has to stop the slaughter.

They have to escape.

CHAPTER 27

It was pitch-dark at 4:30 in the morning in Louisville the first week of May. The streets were deserted.

We were at SDF in a heartbeat. Gus dropped me with a mumbled comment I didn't catch. Kerr remained an inert shadow in the backseat.

Despite the upcoming equine lollapalooza, the airport was calm. At dawn, few people were leaving town. No one was arriving.

We took off late, landed so late in Atlanta I missed my connection. The next flight with availability was at one P.M. Fuming, I accepted a boarding pass.

I used the layover to phone Peter Crage at the mobile number on his card. He answered after seven rings, suggesting my call was probably kick-starting his day.

"I'm en route Louisville to Charleston," I said. "All four bombers are accounted for."

"I've been in communication with Layton Furr and the detectives in Chicago, so I'm aware of your progress. As is Mrs. Drucker. She was pleased to learn of the fourth. This encounter happened where?"

"L.A."

"The gentleman is . . . ?"

"Dead."

"Assuming all is verified, you've completed your task and we can cut you a check quickly. I'm sorry. Did you say Louisville?"

"Advise Drucker that I'm on my way."

"Of course." Glacial. "May I have your number?"

"No. I'll call again when I land."

During the hours that I paced and checked and rechecked the board at Hartsfield, a mongo weather system rolled over the south. Lots of delays and cancellations, lots of dejected passengers standing in lines. My flight finally took off at 2:15.

Bumping and rumbling at thirty-two thousand feet, I thought about Bronco, Selena, and Landmine. About the identity of Infidel567@gmail.com. Mostly, I thought about how to stop the bloodbath the bastards had planned.

To keep myself sane, I ponied up for Gogo and did some research. I learned the following.

The Kentucky Derby isn't a single happening. It's a bonnet, bow tie, and bourbon extravaganza spanning several days and many races. The Oaks is for three-year-old fillies and, that year, would be one of twelve races on Friday. The Derby is for three-year-old colts and fillies, though the girls rarely run. It would be one of thirteen races on Saturday.

The Oaks boasts the fourth-highest attendance of any horse race on the planet, roughly 112,000. The Derby packs in closer to 170,000. Godolphin Thoroughbreds were entered in both.

Would Bronco strike early, hoping for easier access, more maneuverability, better odds at slipping under the radar? Or would he wait for the main event, for what was labeled the greatest two minutes in sports? Would he hit when the carnage would be maximum and millions would be watching?

Would Bronco target Godolphin specifically—the horses, the trainers, the jockeys, the owners? That might mean the stables, the paddock, the track itself. Or would he focus on the fans? That might mean the stands, the boxes and suites, the clubhouse, the infield. Would the sheikh host his party in an owner's box?

The more I considered, the more convinced I became. Bronco and his freak show wanted maximum media attention. The Derby was the perfect opportunity to deliver their message of hatred and fear.

I debated contacting the Louisville cops. Heard that conversation in my head. Terrorists from Chicago are planning an attack on Churchill Downs? And you are? Sunday Night, a one-eyed ex-cop out of Charleston? The Jewish girls' school was a miscalculation? The group is anti-Muslim and opposes Arab-owned horses at American tracks? Thanks for your concern, Miss Night. We are always on 100 percent alert at Derby time. Stay out of our way.

Sounded wild, even to me. The cops were undoubtedly fielding dozens of crackpot tips. And they were stretched to the limit. I didn't want to stay out of the way. No. Gus and I would do it ourselves. Which meant we needed tickets.

Again and again, I thought about Stella. Was she huddled, alone and frightened, in some dark place? Was she broken, mind warped by abuse, isolation, and a constant onslaught of terrorist propaganda? Would she be in Louisville?

Was she dead?

As the wheels kissed the tarmac, I was already dialing.

"Mrs. Drucker has sent a car," Crage said. "She will receive you."

"Of course she will."

"You are a very confident woman, Ms. Night."

"Comes with the height."

After disconnecting, I phoned Gus.

"How's it going?"

"You're right," he said. "She's lousy company."

"I'll be meeting with Drucker in about an hour. I'm hoping she has the grease to get us Derby passes."

"And the inclination."

"That's where the charm comes in. In the meantime, you and

Kerr scope out the track. Hang around, check entrances and exits, watch for Bronco and his pals."

"Got it."

"Watch for Stella. And be discreet. We don't want to get her killed."

"Maybe I could score tickets from a scalper."

"Worth a try."

A man was waiting beyond security, holding a sign with NIGHT written in neat block letters. His suit, shoes, and cap were black. His eyes took in the scar, the ebony nails, but his expression remained impassive. He gave his name as Winton, then led me to a town car that matched his outfit. Kerr would have approved.

The drive took thirty minutes. Traffic wasn't bad, but fog was moving in off the harbor and drivers were taking it seriously.

At 4:20 I was passing the same bed of peonies I'd passed on my first visit. The stems were more bowed, the blossoms hanging lower, as though burdened by the heaviness of the late-afternoon air. Or prescient of the news I was about to deliver. Other than that, Poesie Court seemed as satisfied with itself as it had back then.

The same woman answered the door. Miranda? Avoiding eye contact, she led me to the same terrace. Drucker was on the same sofa. With the same dog. Same lap quilt, same petunias overhead.

Drucker looked at me but didn't speak.

"I tracked down your bombers," I said.

"Sit."

The dog opened its eyes, confused.

I sat.

"One succumbed to cancer," Drucker said. "One was shot execution-style. One you killed. The fourth died in a shootout in L.A., according to Detective Capps. I'm afraid all I have is his word on that one."

I showed her the phone shots of Jano in his luau shirt on the floor at Rose Avenue in Venice.

"Your work?"

"Indirectly."

"I suppose you expect to be paid for all four."

"Your call. But that can wait."

"Who is the black man traveling with you?"

"An associate."

"Perhaps a relative?"

I didn't reply.

"I know who he is," she said.

"So do I."

"Have it your way," she said.

"The bombing at Bnos Aliza was the work of homegrown terrorists," I said. "They're zealots and they're ruthless and they're planning more attacks."

"On Jews? On schools?"

"The school was a mistake."

"I don't understand."

I explained the real target on Devon Avenue. The backpack. Bowen's fatal good deed.

"These maniacs also killed my Stella?" Stony.

"Maybe."

"What is it you're not saying, Ms. Night?"

"I believe your granddaughter may be alive. That her life is now in danger."

"Because of my actions?"

"Because of me."

"What is it you want?"

"I want to stay on them. I want to nail their leader, a xenophobic psycho calling himself Bronco."

"Did this Bronco give the order to murder my family?"

"He ordered the bombing in which your family was killed."

I scrolled to the photo of the red-haired girl with her wrists and throat in restraints. Handed Drucker the phone.

At last, the ice shattered.

One gnarled hand fluttered to her mouth. Sensing tension, the Pomeranian stood. The other hand pushed the dog down. Both were shaking.

"This Bronco is holding Stella?"

"And threatening to kill her."

"Why?"

"To force me to back off."

"Merciful God in heaven."

I allowed a hiatus for Drucker to collect herself. She did. I think the dog helped.

"I want tickets to the Kentucky Derby," I said, when the window-glass eyes again met mine.

"That's an odd request."

"I think Bronco is planning to hit Churchill Downs."

I laid it all out. The Islamophobic fanaticism of Jihad for Jesus. The cells in Chicago, L.A., D.C., and Louisville. I described everything I'd done and learned since our last meeting. The ambush at the Ritz. The rendezvous at Foster Beach. Jasmine Kerr's flight to L.A. Bronco's allusion to an imminent attack. The shootout at Venice Beach. The bolt to D.C. Bronco's "gifts" of Kerr, Tibby Icard, and Brian Harkester. The message containing the name Godolphin and the dates May 5 and 6. Godolphin stable's entries in the Derby and Oaks. Infidel's email to Kerr from Louisville. Kerr's recollection that Bronco bought Derby tickets.

Drucker listened, fingers nervously stroking the dog.

When I finished, only canine wheezing filled the space between us. Finally, "Mary Gray and Bowen are dead. Their killers are dead. You say Stella may be alive. If so, I will do nothing to endanger her."

"Going forward, these savages won't be satisfied with Muslim grocers. They want to spread their message. To shock the world. To do so, they'll take as many lives, destroy as many families, as they can."

Drucker's eyes moved over me, hooded. A long, wheezing minute passed. Then, "Your obligation to me is concluded, Ms. Night."

"But—"

"You are to do nothing further to antagonize these people."

"Mrs. Drucker—"

"Do I make myself clear?"

"We may be able to prevent the deaths of other innocents." Chest fizzing hot.

"Do I make myself clear?"

"This is wrong."

"You're like a dog with a bone."

"You have no idea."

"If you disregard my wishes I shall alert the police."

"That won't improve your granddaughter's life expectancy."

"Rest assured." Reptilian smile. "My report will have nothing to do with Stella."

"You heartless witch."

"Is there anything else you require?" I was being dismissed.

"I've left my belongings in Louisville." Voice betraying none of the chaos in my chest. "I need to retrieve them as quickly as possible. Because of the Derby, every flight is full."

"My plane will be at your disposal."

"How generous." Frosty.

"We made a deal. I honor my commitments. Winton will transport you to Mr. Crage's office for payment. When the plane is ready, he will take you to the airfield."

Miraculously, Miranda appeared. I stood and followed her toward the door.

"Ms. Night."

I turned back to Drucker.

"I hope you understand. I prefer that my granddaughter not perish."

"As do I."

"I prefer that you not perish."

I said nothing.

"You have a twin, correct? August?"

My molars clamped tight.

"Inform August that in the event you do perish I wish for him to contact me."

What the hell? Did she suspect I had no intention of quitting?

Winton was at the curb, a dark upright beside a dark shape in the mist. During my brief visit, the fog had thickened and taken on the essence of a living thing.

Crage was waiting. He opened a large ledger and wrote out a check. Through the window, I could see nothing but swirling white. Far below, a blurred red point, maybe a traffic light.

Crage handed me the check. I put it in my purse.

"The fog is a problem," he said. "The pilot can't take off until visibility improves."

"When will that be?"

"I am not a meteorologist. They speak of inversion and dew points and water temperature, things beyond my ken."

"What about flying commercial?"

"Were seats available, which they are not, it wouldn't help. The airport is shut down."

My gut knotted. I felt trapped. Disconnected from Gus.

"Winton is at your disposal." Disapproving? "Mrs. Drucker has directed him to drive you wherever you wish. If you provide your number, I'll have him call when the pilot determines it is safe to fly."

Reluctantly, I gave it to him.

Winton was where we'd parted. He opened the door. I got into the backseat.

"Where to, Miss?"

Beyond the tinted glass, nothing but nothing.

"Sullivan's Island," I said, black nails gouging crescents into my palms.

Two Nights

S he catches his eye. Tips her head toward the shed at the end of
the drive. Raises seven digits. Five and two, a referee calling a
foul. A trembling referee.

He nods. At last she has convinced him.

He has promised to speak to her. To make her understand. To
convince her to go with them. He is much more persuasive than
she. More tactful. She doubts it will work. Still.

A light rain is falling when she slips out the back door. The air
smells rich, earthy. The woods pulse with the sound of a million
insects.

He is waiting when she arrives. 7:05 P.M.

They stand, heads together, the barest of shadows in the drizzly
dusk.

Voices hushed, they review their strategy. She fights back tears.
Denies the quaver in her voice. This is her doing. She must be as
tough as the game she talks.

But she is terrified.

What do they know? They've seen the random newspaper, forgotten or carelessly tossed in the trash. A Chicago Tribune. A

Charleston Post and Courier. *A Montreal* Gazette. *Nothing recent.*

They understand phones and television but haven't used technology for far too long. They possess not a single number. Haven't a soul they can call.

They don't know the distance or direction to the nearest town. Its name. They don't even know what state they're in. From the heat and vegetation they suspect it's Dixie.

They can't drive. Know nothing about renting a hotel or motel room. Buying a bus or train ticket. Purchasing supplies. Getting jobs. Surviving in the world.

But they're committed. They're doing this.

They have a plan.

First, the money. She's checked. It's still in the basement. He's found and hidden four backpacks. Three empty, one stuffed with food and water.

Phase one. Completed.

Phase two.

They will go that night, once everyone is asleep. They will meet in the cellar, grab as much cash as they can carry, leave enough so that, on a casual glance, the boxes look normal.

They have agreed upon signals. Green light. Abort.

Phase three.

They will travel by foot. While she's confident she could figure out how to drive, they have decided against it. Stealing one of the vehicles would be too risky, too noisy.

They will head toward the blacktop on which they arrived. She's sure they can find it by following the dirt track that leads from the house. They will walk the shoulder by night, stay to the woods by day.

They know about 911. They will call once they are safely away. Leaving tonight allows them a cushion. Enough time to get to a pay phone. Enough time for the cops to intervene and stop the massacre.

Phase four is vague.

They will not get caught.

CHAPTER
28

"W e've arrived."
       My head snapped up. My hand shot to my waistband. No holster. No gun.

"Poe's Tavern, miss. That's what you said?"

"Right." Heart banging.

"Shall I wait?"

"No." Blinking into the fog, seeing little with my good eye, nothing with my bad.

Winton started to open his door.

"I'm cool." I held up a palm.

"As you wish." He lifted a card from the console and handed it over the seatback. "My mobile number. Call when you need me."

"Thanks."

I got out, passed through the picket fence, and climbed to the porch, steps muffled in the warm, still air. Above me, a string of tiny white lights barely cut through the vapor. Behind me, Middle Street, normally buzzing at happy hour, was eerily quiet.

The door was wide open. I entered. Ahead, diners occupied wooden tables nicked and gouged by years of abuse, some of it mine. Poe's was the first bar to serve me. Fake ID, expression far older than my seventeen years.

To my left, high tables to one side, bar to the other, two stools empty at the far end. I took the last in the row, orienting so I could see the whole room.

The bartender, a guy wearing a Hornets cap, a red golf shirt, and an apron tied over butt-sagging jeans, finished drawing a beer, then moseyed over. I knew his name was Sean. Sean and I exchanged comments about the fog. We both agreed it was a real pea-souper. I ordered a Palmetto draft and a Pit & Pendulum burger.

Agitated, I kept scanning, checking faces, body language. I recognized some locals. They looked content enough. Other patrons less so. Having one week away from Toronto or Saint Paul, tourists resent dirty weather disrupting their quest for the perfect skin-shriveling tan.

My beer came. I sipped. Relaxed not a hair.

Poe's has changed little since my first adolescent suds. The smoky haze is gone, the perfume now a mix of stale booze, sweat, and salt air. The memorabilia remain—the knickknacks, portraits, posters, and framed letters. I know every kitschy piece. Over the years, I've spent hours on one barstool or another.

What keeps me coming back? Not Edgar Allan's literary genius. I've read few of his works. The man's personal story is the draw. In 1827, at age eighteen, Poe used an alias to join the army. Thirteen months at Fort Moultrie, then he left the island and cut short his enlistment to enroll at West Point. After one cadet year, he was booted with a dishonorable discharge. Not his first unglamorous exit from academia or authority.

Orphaned young, a screw-up his whole life, dead at forty. Oh yeah. I identify with the guy.

In addition to enshrining the master of the macabre, Poe's Tavern has two other attributes that assure my loyalty. Proximity to home, and a few regulars with whom I don't mind engaging.

I'd been there maybe ten minutes when one of them strode through the door. Six foot two, one seventy, shaggy blond-gray hair, couple days' stubble. Montgomery "Gum" Sweet, profession unclear.

I watched, not watching, as Sweet executed the same three sixty I do upon entering any new space. His gaze snagged on me briefly before completing its journey. I tracked him in my peripheral vision. To the stool beside mine.

"This taken?" Sweet wore hiking boots, faded cargo shorts, and an overlaundered tee that hinted at serious rippling beneath.

"Nope. Still there."

"Buy you a beer?" Voice dusky and rough, unused for a while.

"Got one." Lifting my mug.

"How's it hanging?" Sweet balanced his ass on the edge of the stool. A very fine ass. I knew. I'd seen it.

"Rosy." My anxiety-amped brain was offering inappropriate flashbacks.

"I can't complain." As though I'd asked.

"You never do."

"That a complaint?"

"Could be." Looking Sweet straight in the eyes. Which were gray flecked with green and cornered by pale starburst creases.

Before he could answer, my mobile buzzed. Roy Capps.

"Gotta get this."

"Suit yourself."

"You took your time," I said, once out on the porch.

"File a grievance. Where are you?"

"Charleston."

"I heard Louisville."

"Did you."

"What's happening in Charleston?"

"Fog." Which appeared to have rolled up its sleeves for a very long siege.

"Got some names," Capps said.

"I'm listening."

"Your boy Bronco's a loser from Milwaukee name of Kenneth

Noel Dickey. Failed minor league outfielder, failed motivational speaker, failed salesman—long list of flops."

"Dickey have a record?"

"Just a reputation. Nothing ever stuck, because the family has sauce."

"Yeah?"

"Ever hear of Ball and Dickey Tool?"

"You're kidding, right?"

"What? You in heat?"

"Talk."

"Dickey senior started the business with a guy named Sheridan Ball. The two played football together at Wisconsin, were a big deal back in the day. Long story short, Ball went on to become a city councilman."

"What's Dickey junior's story?"

"Five years back, Daddy canned him for decking an assembly line worker. The deckee declined to press charges, so little Kenny skated. No record of employment since. No permanent address. When Bronco left Milwaukee he went off the grid."

"To rely on the kindness of nitwits like Jasmine Kerr."

"Here's an interesting factoid. Dickey's older brother was killed in the Madrid train bombing in 2004."

"Al-Qaeda."

"Some suspected Basque separatists, but that was the verdict."

"Might explain Bronco's hatred of Muslims." Yeah. I'd stick with Bronco.

"Bronco's muscle is a guy named Landon Crozier."

"Landmine." The Hawaiian ape at Venice Beach. "The goon who boogied from the hospital in L.A."

"Former army infantry, did stints in Iraq and Afghanistan, said sayonara in 2012 after reupping three times. Another Milwaukee boy. Parents dead, no siblings, wife, or kids. No criminal record. The apartment in Dupont Circle was rented under the name L. Cozen. Landlord says Cozen looked like a mountain with legs."

"I'm guessing something bad happened to Landmine in the Middle East."

"Something bad happens to every grunt in the Middle East."

"Anything on Jano, the guy Landmine killed?"

"Jano's not in the system. LAPD is working on him."

"Selena?"

"Clegg's working on her. And L.A. And D.C."

"Kerr says the stiff in your morgue is named Lewinoski."

"You're telling me now?"

"I just learned it. Any progress with the monk?"

"Who?"

"The second asshole who tried to burn me at the Ritz."

"John Scranton. Still in Winnetka."

"Doing what?"

"Bingeing *Bones* with Mama."

"What's your plan?"

"Bust him the second he steps out and drops gum in the park."

"Did you toss the apartment on Argyle?"

"The place was rented furnished. Kerr left nothing but tofu, toothpaste, and toilet paper."

"No laptop or cellphone?"

"No crumpled receipt, no uncollected mail, no indent of a scribbled number or address. I did mention I've done this before?"

I said nothing.

"The lease was short-term, in the name Janet Kerr. The property manager said Kerr paid cash for six months, was there maybe two."

"Who owns the place?"

"A holding company. We're looking into it."

"Prints?"

"Billions. The old coot wasn't big on deep cleaning."

"What about the passports?"

"Both fake. No signature pointing to any known forger. I ran the names Janet and Jasmine Kerr, Jennifer Latourneau, variations on the three. Nothing popped. No one on the block remembers her.

One neighbor thought he might have seen a woman coming or going a couple of times. I'm thinking all three names are aliases."

"The gallery on Clark, the Dancing Dolphin?"

"Dead end. The owner and the clerk said she came in a couple times asking about dolphins, was disappointed they had only one fish painting and that was a trout."

"Dolphins aren't fish."

"You want to hear this?"

I waited.

"Both thought she was weird, neither knew her name. I take it you got nothing more out of her?"

"I will." Factual.

"She with you voluntarily?"

"Happily."

"How do you read her?"

"There's nothing to read. She's got the IQ of pencil lead and a personality to match."

"Think she's part of it?"

"If so, she's too dumb to know."

"Why you keeping her with you?"

"Comic relief."

"Why's she staying?"

"Astute question, Detective."

"You following anything else?"

I briefed him as I had Drucker, leaving out Louisville and my suspicions concerning the Derby. Risky, I know. But I was certain Capps would phone the Louisville PD the instant we disconnected. I was also certain that, when he did, I'd be sidelined, the cops would underestimate the threat, and Bronco and his horror show would again slip the net. Maybe kill Stella. I couldn't take the chance.

"Anyone try to cap you lately?" Capps asked when I'd finished.

"Not that I've noticed."

"Kick anything loose on the Bright kid?"

"No."

"What's your next move?"

"I'll think of something."

"Uh-huh." Tone saying he didn't believe me. "Keep your head up."

"Aw, see? You really do care."

Dead air.

I peeked through the door. Sweet was still on his stool. My burger wasn't yet on the bar.

I phoned Gus to tell him I'd be returning in Drucker's plane but that I was grounded by weather. He said Louisville was also socked in.

"Flying private. The charm worked."

"Not exactly. She cut me loose."

"So you're calling it?"

"What do you think?"

"Going rogue. I like it."

"How's Kerr?"

"Compliant."

I summarized my conversation with Capps. "Tell her I know about Bronco and Landmine, that life will be very unpleasant if I find out she's lying. As in using an alias."

"Will do. Where are you?"

"Poe's." A beep indicated an incoming call. "Hold on."

It was Winton. He'd been asked to inform me that the entire Southeast was affected and that conditions weren't expected to improve before morning. The plane was grounded until then.

Sonofabitch.

Frustrated, I clicked back and gave Gus the news.

"You gotta do what you gotta do," he said.

"The Oaks is tomorrow." Too sharp. "I have to get back to Louisville."

"Calm down."

"Jesus, Gus."

"You going out to Goat?"

"Yes. No. I don't know."

"What about Bob?"

"Good title for a movie."

"There's the old Sunnie wit."

"Bada-boom."

"Why didn't you ask the driver to take you to IOP?"

"Didn't want him to know where I live."

"He could have dropped you on Waterway, your usual MO."

"And risk stirring Beau?"

"He's going to be pissed that you haven't called."

"I'll call."

"No you won't."

"Will you do it?" I rubbed my neck, trying to work out the tension. "Update him, see if he has pull with Louisville should things go south? See if he can score us tickets for the Derby?"

A voice came through the open door behind me. "Beer's getting warm."

I pivoted and gestured Sweet away.

There was meaningful silence hundreds of miles to the northwest. When Gus spoke again his voice was starchy with distaste.

"You with that asswipe Sweet?"

"I'm not *with* anybody."

"I don't trust the guy, Sunnie."

"I'll be fine. I was a cop."

"Which almost cost you an eye."

"I can handle myself. I have a gun."

"No you don't."

Gus had a point. I'd left my Glock with him.

"We've had this discussion," I said.

"Why can't you ever be sane?"

"Meaning what? Screw the church deacon?"

"Pop a pill. Take a bath. Smoke weed when you can't sleep."

"Pot is illegal in South Carolina."

"Fine. But why that creep?"

"He's zipless."

"What?"

"No taking, no giving."

"What the hell does that—"

"See you tomorrow."

I clicked off and looked around. Saw nothing. Heard only the soft tinkling of a wind chime, the cawing of a stalwart bird.

I ran through options. Louisville was roughly nine hours by car. In this mess the drive would probably be double that. Ridiculously insane idea. No passenger train. There might be a bus. I don't do buses.

I was trapped. Acknowledgment of the fact goosed my angst even higher.

I returned to the bar. My burger was there. A fresh beer sat where my old one had been, a shot beside it. I raised the little glass. Sweet raised his and tapped my rim. We knocked back the booze. He watched as I downed my burger and draft.

When finished, I shoved my plate aside and put my elbows on the gouged old wood. Worked circles on my temples with my up-raised hands.

"I could do that." Sweet's breath was boozy and close to my ear.

"You could." What the hell? I was going nowhere. Going crazy.

I was gathering my purse when Capps phoned again. I considered ignoring him. Didn't.

"You sitting down?"

"No."

"John Scranton was just stabbed to death in his mama's kitchen."

CHAPTER 29

"What the fuck?" The drinks. The frustration. Not my snappiest.

"Yep."

"Where?"

"Two to the belly, one to the neck."

"Where did it *happen*?"

"Winnetka."

"Give me a clue."

"North Shore suburb. Porsches, Presbyterians, perpetual propriety. Neighbor heard shouting, called to complain. By the time the cops landed, Scranton had already bled out."

"Where was the mother?"

"Nowhere to be found. Guy who called says her Lexus gunned off right after the yelling. Says that isn't her style. I've broadcast a BOLO." Be on the lookout.

"Did the guy see who was driving?"

"He thought it was a man but couldn't be sure. Seems his eyesight isn't great."

"You thinking the perp stabbed John, then abducted the old lady?"

"We're thinking many things."

"What's Mama's story?"

"Longtime widow, semirecluse. Well-heeled. Neighbor says she kept large sums of money in the house."

"How'd he know that?"

"His kid cuts her grass, shovels her walks. The old lady pays him from cash she locks in a drawer. Kid told his dad it looked like a pretty big stash."

"That doesn't sound good."

"No."

"Any suspects?"

"Besides the kid?"

I was poking at that when Sweet ran a callused fingertip down my cheek. I batted his hand and shook my head. He reached out again.

"Knock it off!" I snapped.

"What?" Capps.

"Hold on." Pressing the phone to my chest, "This is important."

"Right now?"

"Right now."

Sweet drew back, brows raised in amusement. "You change your mind I'm there for your usual fifteen, chickadee."

"Another time."

"Maybe not."

"Screw you."

"You know where I live." The khaki shorts and nice ass went swinging toward the door.

"Yo!" Capps's voice came through the mobile, metallic, impatient.

"I'm here."

"Winnetka PD's working the scene. I'm en route now."

"Scranton's connected to Bronco and his jerkwad jihadists. I'm sure of it. Find something in that house pointing to their next move."

"Hadn't thought of that." Hitch of breath. "Ran the name Lewinoski."

"And?"

"It's not a common one."

"Try Warsaw." The adrenaline talking.

"There are a handful in the area. I'm following up. In the meantime, stay out of trouble."

I came within a skin cell of telling Capps about Louisville. Instead, "Hadn't thought of that."

I disconnected.

Counting out bills, I ran options in my head. I was doing a lot of that lately.

I tried calling a taxi. Got busy signals with three different companies. Stuck and discouraged, I was banging along like a moth in a jar. Imagining Stella inching through her last hours on earth. I needed to move.

I left the bar and started walking. Pushing hard. Taking long strides. Middle Street to Jasper. Over the Breach Inlet Bridge to Isle of Palms. Palm Boulevard north, past the connector. Through pockets lit by the eerie glow of streetlamps. Elsewhere, murky darkness.

The muffled silence was strange, an auditory black hole created by the dense fog. Now and then a car crept by. Far off, the ocean droned its steady advance and retreat. Close by, my heart thudded my ribs.

I was fifteen the first time I saw the Atlantic. I'd lived within miles my whole childhood, never walked a seawall or set foot on a beach. I was so different back then. So vulnerable. So naïve. Only Gus had kept me alive. Or had I saved him? Hadn't I forced him to accept that the others were lost? Hadn't the plan been mine? Hadn't its failure put their deaths square on me?

A humming rose from some dark corner of my skull.

Don't go there.

I walked even faster, eyes pointlessly probing, mind pointedly fixed on nothing.

In ninety minutes I was at the little house with the tilted mailbox and weathered gray siding. Every window was dark. The glowing digits on my watch said 9:47. Not unreasonable for Beau to be down for the night.

Relieved, I scurried to the dock, untied the boat, and pushed off. Once safely in the waterway, I cranked the engine.

While tying up on Goat Island, I glanced back across the water. No lights. No Sherman. I'd pay a price, but not tonight.

I let myself in, disarmed then rearmed all security devices, cracked the kitchen window. Bob didn't appear. No biggie. Extreme weather upsets his psyche. But not his appetite. I filled his bin, then went to the gun safe for a .357 SIG I keep for emergencies.

I'd barely lit the bedroom lamp when a small body shaped up at the window. I opened it. Bob scampered onto the dresser and regarded me with reproachful eyes. Or so I read them. I supplemented my apology with a stale macaroon. The squirrel seemed good with the offering.

Vowing to purchase a new burner in the morning, I phoned Winton, asking for an update. He said the forecast looked good, that the plane would be ready at a private facility behind the main airport at 6:30 A.M. Offered to pick me up. I asked him to meet me at the Harris Teeter by the IOP Connector at 5:45.

Next, Capps. He told me to fuck off. Hot damn.

My mind was running at warp speed. A cold shower didn't help. No way I'd sleep. I needed to do something.

I now had names. Jasmine Kerr, the round-shouldered woman in the White Sox cap. John Scranton, the gunman with the tonsure and scaly pink skin. Kenneth "Bronco" Dickey, the boy-faced zealot in the steel-toed boots. Landon "Landmine" Crozier, the Beretta-packing ape in the luau shirt. Tibby Icard, the woman in pink with her brains on a wall.

I also had a few locations. Argyle Street in Chicago. Twentieth

Street and Mount Pleasant Street in D.C. Rose Avenue in Venice. Shit. I hadn't asked Capps for Scranton's address in Winnetka. Phone him back? Not a chance.

I got online and began digging. First, I used a telephone database, www.masterfiles.com. My info was crap, just names and apartment complexes, so the results were crap. No surprise. Using the same site, I did reverse searches to see if any of my addresses had phones listed. I found several, probably tenants of other units, none in the names Kerr or Latourneau, Crozier or Cozen, Dickey.

Next I shot the names through the three big credit bureaus: TransUnion, Equifax, and Experian. Of course it was legal. I was thinking of hiring these fine citizens to my employ. Didn't matter, I got nothing. I had no Social Security numbers so couldn't run traces that way.

Disheartened, though not surprised, I turned to other databases, each drawing from a different mix of intel: telephone directories, magazine subscriptions, driver's licenses, vehicle and boat registrations, cellphones, book club lists, Internet search engine results, traffic accidents, criminal charges, social media pages, public notices of bankruptcy, foreclosure, nonpayment of taxes, fast-food delivery names, addresses, and phone numbers. The list is endless. And frightening.

Four hours and beaucoup bucks later, I'd learned nothing about Kerr, Latourneau, or Icard, certainly all aliases. I'd found zip on Kenneth Dickey or Landon Crozier dating to the past five years.

I did confirm that Bronco was employed by his father's tool company prior to slipping under the radar. And I learned that, after leaving the military, Landmine worked for a feed supply outfit in Indiana. I unearthed not a single hint that either of these men was moving toward terrorism.

Finally, I read everything I could ferret out about Churchill Downs, the Oaks, and the Derby. I checked Google Earth, studied photos and diagrams. Did a lot of printing.

At three I called it quits. My higher centers did not. I lay in bed wondering how, in the age of ISIS and iPhones, anyone could drop so completely off the grid. How, in the age of CSI and DNA, the dead could remain nameless for so long. Mustachioed "Lewinoski" in the Chicago morgue. Bulldog "Jano" on Venice Beach.

At four I got up and padded out onto the deck. Above me, palmetto palms swayed tall and shaggy-topped in the fog. No moon. I like having a moon overhead.

When sleep finally came, I dreamed of a copper-haired girl with a beach at her back. Of painted boulders and twisted bike racks. Of severed limbs and torn flesh and blood-spattered concrete.

Of dangling petunias and window-glass eyes.

Yet another day. I was up before dawn. Bob was gone. So was the fog. I stuffed the SIG and a few other items into a backpack, locked up, and crossed the waterway to IOP. Moving as quietly as possible, I docked and set out for the strip mall beside the connector.

The airfield was off South Aviation Avenue in North Charleston, set behind an acre of grass and a barrier of scraggly crepe myrtles doing their best. The terminal looked like a concrete bunker with a large glass bay wrapping one corner. Nice flags.

Winton escorted me inside. The lobby was done in the style of a concierge medical practice—cushy leather chairs, gleaming wooden tables, lots of hushed privacy. No robes, but tasteful and discreet.

Winton led me to a couch and asked if I wanted coffee. I did. He brought it in a nice china cup. Wordlessly, he crossed to a counter and spoke to a woman behind a sliding glass panel. She wore small oval glasses and John Hardy silver on her neck and left wrist. The check-in process took roughly five seconds.

Winton returned and whispered that the plane was ready. Of course it was. He led me out a side door, across a tarmac no different from any tarmac in the world, to a plane that looked big enough to transport a marching band.

The pilot and co-pilot were in the cockpit, checking flight plans, or fuel gauges, or take-out options in Louisville. The nine seats in back were empty. I took one on the right and buckled up. A magazine on the small table by my knee said I was flying in a Cessna Citation Excel.

Beside the magazine was a lidded silver dish. In a recess beside the dish was a matching carafe. Beside the carafe, a creamer. Beside the creamer, tiny bowls of sugar, both brown and white.

The Citation entered the runway and accelerated after a ten-second pause, quickly, confidently, fully aware of its privileged place in the universe. Feeling the movement, I pictured the takeoff in my mind, the plane rising then banking, wings elegantly glinting in the first light of day.

When the plane leveled, course set to the northwest, I helped myself to coffee. Then I lowered my seatback and closed my eyes. Opened them at wheels-down.

A Winton equivalent greeted me planeside, welcomed me to Louisville, and led me to a black town car waiting with the engine running. No security. No fight for overhead space. No wait at baggage claim. In life, many things are flawed. Flying private is not among them.

The driver's name was Leach. The guy in back was Nolan Schrader.

"Welcome to Louisville." Schrader resembled Peter Crage—trim, tanned, designer-gray hair. His attire did not. I attributed the blue and white seersucker suit, lavender shirt, and teal tie to Derby tradition.

"Thank you," I said.

"I represent Opaline Drucker." Schrader's vowels outsugared anything Charleston had to offer. "Mrs. Drucker requested that I meet your flight."

"The town car was the giveaway."

"Of course. Where might we take you?"

"The closest Target or Walmart, whichever is open."

Schrader relayed my request. Leach, now behind the wheel, tapped icons on a dashboard screen, then shifted into gear.

We drove past a terminal and down a driveway in an airstrip resembling the one in North Charleston. Schrader spoke as Leach merged into traffic. Which was substantial.

"My goodness." Refined chuckle. "I expected someone a bit fiercer than yourself."

"Yeah," I said, clearly sharing in his disappointment. "Maybe the Walmart can sell me some war paint."

Reflex smile but no comment.

The trip took less than ten minutes. The parking lot outside the big box held surprisingly few cars. Leach informed us that the store wouldn't open for another quarter of an hour.

"Shall we take you elsewhere in the meantime? A restaurant or coffee shop?" Schrader sounded less than enthused.

"I'll hang here." I levered the handle with one hand and grabbed my pack with the other. Leach was at the door like a shot.

"Shall we wait?" Schrader asked.

"No." I wondered if Drucker had tasked him with spying on me.

"You're certain?"

"I am."

"Y'all have a fine day."

Leach closed the door, circled the car, and off they went.

Ten minutes later an employee flipped the CLOSED sign to OPEN. I entered, purchased and activated a new throwaway mobile. Then I called Gus to report my location.

"New phone?"

"Yes." I gave him the number. Which I'd blocked from appearing at his end.

"On my way."

As I waited, two women parked, got out, and opened the back of their Volvo XC90. Inside was an astounding inventory of hats, each flamboyantly repurposed for Derby week. As I watched, the women draped the SUV's side panel with a banner stating that all proceeds would go to a shelter for battered women.

I walked over and, after a brief exchange, chose a red metal equestrian helmet outfitted with a lime-green band sprouting Day-Glo orange magnolias. I figured the look was all mine, the thing too hideous to be purchased by anyone else. At least anyone with color vision. And that Gus could easily track it. As an afterthought, I grabbed a feathery white cap for Kerr.

The gaudy red helmet would prove a lifesaver.

CHAPTER
30

Gus swooped up in the understated red Maxima. Kerr was in back. While he drove, we discussed strategy. Kerr said nothing, but her stillness suggested interest in the conversation.

Gus and Kerr had spent the previous day at Churchill Downs. Since no one was galloping for any goodies, and the weather was lousy, access had been easy.

"Thurby." Gus clearly liked the way the word rolled off his tongue. "On Thurby, twenty bucks gets you into the paddock, the plaza, and the first floor of the grandstand."

"I'm sure you restricted yourself to those areas."

Gus flicked me a mischievous wink.

"Any sign of Bronco or his goons?"

"No." Before I could ask: "Or the kid. And yes, we were very discreet."

"Did you talk to Beau about tickets?"

"We're all set."

"How's security?"

"Involves everyone but the colonel himself—Kentucky State Police, Louisville Metro Police, Jefferson County Sheriff's Office,

Kentucky National Guard. The track's interior, exterior, and all entrances are covered. The Louisville PD has the biggest presence, and only they work the outside."

"What numbers are we talking?"

"Six to seven hundred uniforms, fifty to a hundred plainclothes."

"Any chance of Bronco or one of his crew slipping an IED through?"

"Every gate has a cop, and dogs are plentiful. Post–Boston Marathon, coolers and backpacks are banned, and bags have to measure less than twelve inches. All belongings are checked, and at intervals more rigorous random searches are done."

"Cue the hounds."

"Yes."

"Impressive."

"It is."

"That you learned so much."

"Cruised for hours. Then I bought a brew for an off-duty cop."

"He shared all that over a casual beer?"

"She. Okay. Maybe I bankrolled several rounds. A lowly mall cop from Akron fanboying over one of Louisville's finest. The eighty bucks will appear on my bill."

"Where was Kerr?"

"At a corner table fangirling over me."

"I'm getting pukey," Kerr said.

"We'll be at the hotel soon," Gus said.

"No." Petulant. "We won't. I'm going to die in this car."

Kerr had a point. Traffic was moving at the speed of a dial-up download.

"There's good news and bad news." Gus braked to queue for a red light. "Tickets don't allow reentry. You leave, you're out. So a hundred and seventy thousand people won't be coming and going all day."

Three cycles, then we finally crossed the intersection.

"And the bad news?"

"Churchill Downs is lousy with gates."

"How many?" Though the diagrams I'd printed showed only a handful, I knew online information was for public consumption.

"Better I demo."

Thirty minutes later, Gus parked behind the hotel and we rode up to the room. Kerr beelined to the floor mattress and slipped into catatonia mode. She really had it mastered.

I pulled the facility map from my pack and laid it on the desk. Gus and I leaned in.

"You're kidding. There are twenty gates. This piece of crap shows four."

"Cut the commentary and brief me on the layout."

Using a hotel pen, Gus worked his way around the colored shapes representing Churchill Downs's track, seating sections, out-buildings, and parking lots.

"Number one is the main entrance, specifically for the grand-stand and clubhouse areas." He drew a small circle at that gate, one of the four marked on my piece of crap. "Gate two, used for deliv-eries to the Derby Museum, is closed and guarded on race days. No access there." He drew a circle with a 2 inside. "Two-b is a fire gate for the grandstand." Circle, 2b. "Three, the Central Avenue gate, allows access to the infield."

"The cheap seats." I knew that from my cybersurfing.

"Except there are no seats. Ticket holders aren't even promised a view of the track. But they're allowed to bring chairs through gate three, blankets or tarps through gates one and three. Most general admission spectators use three. A tunnel under the track gets them across to the infield." Pointing out the location.

"One tunnel?"

"Three. Two small, one large, which is closed to the public. Two lanes wide and twelve feet high, the big boy's used by semis to get rigging into the infield."

"Scenario one." My mind was already firing possibilities. "Bronco gets an IED through gate one or three rolled in a blanket or tarp. Or elsewhere, concealed in some permissible item."

Gus waggled a hand. Maybe yes, maybe no. "Four is a fire gate for the barn area." He drew another circled digit. "Five is a back-side gate for workers and vendors. It's also used throughout the week for delivering horses, feed, straw, and other supplies."

"I assume anyone using a vendor or delivery gate has to be vet-ted," I said.

"Entry requires a license, which is a photo ID issued by the track. Clearance involves fingerprinting and a database search to see if an applicant has had issues at other racetracks, felony convic-tions, the usual. Actually, all track workers undergo a background check."

"I'm sure credentials are little challenge for Bronco. The asshat buys passports like I buy soap."

"My beer buddy said it wouldn't take a genius to forge a track license. Making the badge involves entering the person's info into a computer, shooting a pic, and printing hard copy."

"The old DMV method."

"Exactly. Credentials are delivered early in the week, so there's plenty of time for copying and retooling."

"Scenario two." I traced a route from gate five to the grand-stand. "Bronco gets his bomb through in a beer keg or hidden in a case of pickles or popcorn."

"Or embedded in a feed sack or bale of hay."

Elbow nudge from my lower centers. What?

Gus resumed pinpointing entrances. "Six is an exit gate for ven-dors servicing the backside. Seven, eight, and nine are fire gates for the barn area." Four circles, then the pen came down on the nu-meral 10 inside a small red circle. "The Longfield gate allows direct access to the clubhouse."

"High rollers."

"Higher than the mopes in the infield. Eleven and thirteen are locked. Twelve is a bus and limo gate."

"Used by whom?"

"For the Derby and Oaks, only the governor and his party, the queen, ex-presidents, yada yada. Tradition."

"Not likely Bronco would try that."

"Not likely. All the media trucks set up at gate fourteen." Circle. "Fifteen is another entrance for vendor deliveries. Sixteen is an access point for the clubhouse and paddock. On Derby weekend, so is seventeen. Eighteen is another fire gate. Nineteen is for EMS and corrections vans." Five more circles. Churchill Downs was now looking like Swiss cheese.

"So five patron gates—one, three, ten, sixteen, and seventeen." I tapped each. "What's the story on the fire gates?"

"During my perimeter sweep, I asked about that. They're all locked, and only the fire department and track fire personnel have keys. One geezer said entry through a fire gate would be rare without an actual emergency. All his geezer cronies agreed."

"What are these?" Indicating a row of odd shapes rimming the grandstand side of the infield.

"Corporate tents. Visa, Budweiser, Lockheed Martin, etc. Some are three stories high. Eyesores in my opinion, but I'm not tallying the profits."

Again the elbow. What?

"Tell me about the barns." I pointed to a cluster of gray rectangles behind the green and brown oval representing the track.

"Folks in the barn area weren't as willing to chat."

"You got back there?"

Mouth hitched into a lopsided grin, Gus tugged a plastic rectangle from the pocket of his chinos. Encased in the plastic was a white card. A man with dark eyes and ragged black hair stared from a little square in its upper right corner.

Reading the name below the photo. "Hector Martinez could lose his job."

"Hector Martinez shouldn't leave his license lying around," Gus said.

"We'll send him something."

"We will."

"The barns?"

"They're all numbered, so are the stalls, and assigned to specific trainers. A trainer may work for one owner if it's a big operation, like WinStar or Phipps. More commonly, a trainer works with several owners and fills a barn with horses from different farms. Because of extra security, everyone backside knows the location of the horses running for the roses."

"Why extra security?"

"Can't have Joe Public messing with Whirlaway. Or Geraldo or Anderson Cooper. Apparently it's crazy backside during the Derby."

"You said the media trucks park at gate fourteen?"

Gus nodded.

"Scenario three. Instead of a track license, Bronco scores phony press credentials and drives a bomb through in the trunk of a car."

I began pacing, mind running the table with possibilities.

"Journalists, vendors, drivers, janitors, restaurant personnel, trainers, valets, hot-walkers, the guys who shovel shit from the stalls. The place is a sieve. Ticket entrances are the least of our worries."

"Hot-walkers?"

"Bronco could already have an IED inside. He could be taking one through as we speak."

Gus said nothing.

"Maybe camouflaged as a box lunch." I'd read about those online.

"Box lunches can be only eighteen inches square. And they have to be in clear plastic containers."

"Built into a stroller. Concealed in a diaper bag."

"To take either through you have to have a kid."

"Maybe he borrowed one."

No response.

"Or, forget forgery. Maybe he or one of his pals stole a track license. You managed. How hard can it be?"

"Thanks."

"You know what I mean."

"Stop pacing."

"When?" Rounding on Gus so fast he started. "When would you strike? Today? Tomorrow?"

"You kidding? The Derby, no question. Maximum crowd, maximum media presence."

"But when?"

"I've been thinking about that. He could hit during saddling up. The jockeys are mounting, the cameras are rolling, the world is watching. And logistics would be easier in the barn or paddock area than out on the track."

"Say Bronco has gotten a bomb in via a backside gate. Or he gets one in today." Darting back to the desk, I traced a route with one finger. "Through the tunnel to the infield and across to the tunnel under the grandstand. He plants it there. The bomb goes off, the tunnel collapses, people are packed shoulder to ass on the infield with no way out."

"First responders would direct survivors through the large tunnel."

Again the subliminal nudge. What was I forgetting? Missing? The sheikh and his party?

"Show me where the Godolphin horses are stabled."

Gus tapped a gray rectangle on the right side of the cluster of gray rectangles. Made an odd noise in his throat.

"Say it," I said.

"Bronco's been planning this attack for a year. Maybe longer. I doubt he'll settle for some workers and a bunch of dead horses."

"Where do the Godolphin folks sit during the race?"

"Jockey Club, second-level suite. Should his horse win, his sheikhness has to haul cheeks fast to the track."

"Thus a low floor."

"Yes. He brings his own security, so they'd be tough to target."

"But not impossible, with a plant on the inside. Say a waiter or a bartender. Someone who could roll a cart into the suite. Or leave one outside the door."

"Not bad. But think about it. Bronco wants breaking news.

CBS, ABC, CNN, BBC, Al Jazeera. To grab that kind of attention I'd hit as the horses cross the finish line. Cameras are rolling, fans are cheering, hooves are thundering. Ka-boom! Bloodbath on the track and infield, panic in the grandstand."

"What did you say about dead horses?"

We both turned.

Kerr was sitting up, expression that of a terrified child.

"Your boyfriend plans to bomb the Derby, Hotpants. To kill and maim as many horses and people as he can." Knowing we'd hit a nerve, I hammered hard, playing on her fear for the one thing that seemed to matter to her. "You know what happens to an injured Thoroughbred?" I pantomimed shooting myself in the temple.

"He can't do that!" Frightened eyes jumping between Gus and me.

I pulled the trigger again. "Poom!"

"Don't! That's so mean! Horses are innocent creatures. They have thoughts and feelings like we do."

I just looked at her.

"You have to stop him!"

"How?"

"Are you a witch?" Eyes locked on my ebony nails.

"Never felt the calling."

"Gus said you're a cop."

"I was." Gus? First names?

"Why?"

"Why what?" Letting my arm drift down, my fingers uncurl from the make-believe gun.

"Why were you a cop?"

I slinked a glance at Gus. He nodded, encouraging me to humor her.

"I was a grunt. Coming back civvie, law enforcement felt like a fit."

"Why'd you quit the military?"

"Long story."

"Why'd you quit being a cop?"

"I was injured."

"That how your eye got messed up?"

"What is this, Truth or Dare?" Out of patience, hearing a ticking clock in my head.

Kerr's head dropped. Her fingers raked her hair like bony white claws. A full minute, then her chin leveled.

"My name is Denise Scranton." Answering the question she'd been stonewalling for days. "I'm from Winnetka, Illinois."

CHAPTER
31

"Any relation to John Scranton?" I'd forgotten all about him. About the stabbing.

"John's my brother."

It was Opaline Drucker with a twist. Dead sibling, missing mother. Christ almighty, do I tell her?

For a long moment I could only stare at Kerr. Scranton. No, I was used to calling her Kerr. For now I'd stick with that. Her grieving, if that's what she'd do, would have to wait. I needed her functional. And I needed to get to the track.

"Give it up, Hotpants. What's Bronco's plan?"

"I don't know. I swear."

"Don't dance me around."

"He bought tickets for the race. If I knew anything else I'd tell you. Cross my heart." She made the sign on her chest. "I would never do anything to hurt an animal."

Her anguish seemed so genuine, the gesture so childlike, I believed her. I was also struck by a sudden realization.

"How old are you?"

Her lips parted to answer. Too quick.

"Don't lie to me. I'll find out anyway."

"Twenty." Mumbled.

Nineteen when Bnos Aliza was bombed. Fuck a duck.

I looked at my watch. 9:25. Churchill Downs had been open since eight.

I turned to Gus. "The first race goes off in thirty-five minutes."

"We taking Hotpants?" he asked.

"I still have the cuffs." A bluff. Gus knew I wouldn't leave her. Kerr could recognize members of Bronco's group that we didn't know. It was the main reason we'd kept her with us.

"Don't chain me up here! I won't run. I want to help you."

I shrugged, uncaring. Keep her scared. Later she'd be pliant, willing to explain John Scranton's link to Jihad for Jesus. Their connection to the bombing at the Bnos Aliza School. Scranton's reason for trying to shoot me at the Ritz.

"Go strapped?" I asked Gus.

He shook his head. "No way we'll get guns through security. And firing in that crowd would be too risky."

I pulled the SIG Sauer and spare magazines from my pack and handed them over. Hated it but knew Gus was right.

"Lock everything in the safe."

Gus nodded, then got an envelope from the bedside table, slid free three wristbands, handed one to me, tossed the other to Kerr.

"Delivered early this morning. These will get us full access to all areas. Discretion was requested since this category is rarely issued."

"To what lucky recipients?"

"Primarily law enforcement."

"Did Beau ask why we're at Churchill Downs?" As we all slipped on the bands.

"No. But I'm sure he's aware it has to do with Stella Bright."

"Think he'll go all paternal, tip the local cops?"

"Discretion was requested."

"He was good with that?"

"For now."

Snagging the Walmart bag, I removed and tucked the red riding helmet under one arm. Then I winged the feathery white cap onto the bed. "Wear this."

"Why?" Kerr was eyeing the hat as one might a dead slug on the porch.

"To blend in."

She lifted but didn't don the headgear.

"It'll be a mosh pit out there." Gus was moving from the safe toward the door. "I suggest we take a shuttle from the U of Louisville."

"Lead on," I said.

The pickup point was outside Papa John's Cardinal Stadium. The connection eluded me. Pizza, birds, football? I didn't ask. Was too jazzed to care.

We queued for an eon, found standing room only when we finally boarded. My stomach knotted as I forced a space among the perfumed and aftershaved bodies. The doors whooshed shut. I did a lot of deep breathing. Scowled at those I caught staring at me.

As we crept along, I tried scanning faces outside. Couldn't bend or maneuver my body to accommodate my good eye. The flashing glimpses I snagged showed streets clogged with pedestrians moving toward Churchill Downs.

The bus unloaded under the watchful gaze of a bronze version of poor dead Barbaro. No one looked my way.

On Oaks Day it's full-out war on breast and ovarian cancer. I'd expected a lot of pink, but the effect was dizzying. I took a moment to get my bearings. To let my heartbeat drop to normal.

To the left was the museum, ahead the grandstand with its legendary double spires. The plaza and paddock areas lay to the right.

Gus cocked his chin toward the largest part of the main structure. "The Jockey Club Suites are in there."

"Accessed how?"

He indicated a bank of elevators.

I reviewed the entrances in my mind. We were standing by gate one. Sixteen, seventeen, and ten were to the northwest, past the clubhouse. Three was to the southeast, just off Central Avenue, now closed to traffic.

"We'll enter through gate one, then split up." I indicated the area to the left of the spires. "You take the Jockey Club Suites, the grandstand, grandstand pavilion and terrace. Start low, move up by levels, then reverse and go back down." I pointed right. "I'll work the clubhouse, the elevators and escalators, the Skye Terrace, the paddock area. I'll start at the top and move down. After my first sweep I'll take the tunnel to the infield, check the Turf Suites, hospitality tents, the Fan Zone, whatever else is in there."

An amplified voice overrode the din around us. A subdued cheer followed the announcement. I waited out the noise before continuing.

"We maintain contact, share our positions every few minutes. If we spot either Bronco or Crozier, we stay on him, see where he goes, what he does."

"Who's Crozier?"

Gus and I both looked at Kerr.

"Landmine," I said.

"Easy peasy. Landmine's immense." Kerr raised and spread both arms, a little too enthused.

"Watch for Stella," I said. "Anyone with a *JJ* tattoo. And be careful not to get spotted. Bronco and Landmine both know what we look like."

"I be the dark little partner." Gus grinned.

We queued and crept forward, body length by body length, eventually reached the gate, showed our wristbands, and were wanded. Then we were inside.

Gus and Kerr went straight, I cut right across the plaza. Speed-reading faces, jostled by the throng, I felt naked, vulnerable. What if Bronco and his zealots really were here? What if it came to a showdown? I was unarmed.

Bronco and Landmine would be unarmed, too, I told myself. Myself scoffed. The assholes can get an IED inside and not a handgun? Myself had a point. The fact did nothing to assuage my anxiety.

Nor did concern for Stella. What if these butchers used her as a shield? What if she'd been brainwashed and resisted rescue? What if she was elsewhere, her whereabouts known only to her captors?

Fear twisted like a cold hard blade in my gut.

I rode an elevator that, surprisingly, allowed each passenger a few millimeters of breathing room. That because the rim-to-rim bonnets forced spacing between their wearers. My red riding helmet remained under my arm.

After exiting, I quick-scanned the corridor, then veered into a dining room. A buffet stretched across one end, tables filled the center. No Bronco or Landmine. No Stella. A glass wall at the back overlooked a terrace. I wove my way to it and stepped outside.

And got my first live glimpse of Churchill Downs.

The spires were to my left, glinting tall and silver in the morning sun. Their twin shadows fell across a grandstand painted in rainbow pastels, hatted heads like dots in a Seurat landscape.

The track was a russet oval looping a grass infield crammed with humanity. On the oval's near side, Turf Suites occupied prime real estate at the starting gate, the tunnel, the eighth and sixteenth poles, the finish line. The Winner's Circle sat dead center. Hospitality tents near the first turn and finish line bore corporate names. Humana. UPS. Lockheed Martin. Pepsi. On the oval's far side, the world's largest ultra-HD 4K Jumbotron loomed over all.

The place had a distinct aroma. I inhaled, testing. Flowers. Horses. Earth. Sweat. I tried but couldn't dissect all the components.

The Kentucky Derby. How often I'd watched on Beau's old RCA with the foil-wrapped antenna. We'd place fifty-cent wagers, argue the all-time greatest Thoroughbred. Gus steadfastly championed Citation, Beau stuck with War Admiral. Early May, the smell of grease and charcoal coming off the grill, June bugs already banging the screen.

My phone buzzed. I snapped back, blood humming in my skull

like wind in a conch shell. Exhilaration at actually being present? Fear of taking a bullet? Terror at the thought I might get Stella killed?

I gave Gus my location. Put my shades on my face and my hat on my head. Pulled the brim low and resumed searching. Section by section, row by row, dining room by dining room.

Each suite was named for a horse that had worn the rose blanket. Affirmed. Secretariat. Seattle Slew. Moving quickly, I skimmed faces, body types. I couldn't disagree with Kerr. Landmine would be easy to spot. Bronco was tall, but not tall enough to stand out in a crowd. Maybe if he wore the Stetson.

At one point, the bugle called "Riders up," horses entered the gate, hooves pounded, the crowd cheered. At another, a procession of pink-clad cancer survivors paraded the track. I ignored the action and kept my attention focused on the spectators.

It was an upmarket crowd, more golf and tennis than NASCAR or WWE. Lots of crested blazers, pearls, designer dresses their wearers probably called frocks. Lots of pricey technology—iPhones, binoculars, camcorders, GoPros mounted on selfie sticks. Lots of kids, many in sneakers that cost as much as my Glock.

Up and down, back and forth, through the tunnel, around the infield, I worked my assigned areas, regularly checking in with Gus. Our paths crossed occasionally. Each time I saw Kerr, she looked less enthused than the time before. By late morning she was wearing the feathered cap, probably fed up with carrying it.

Hours passed. The temperature climbed into the eighties. Now and then, perspiring, I paused to glance at the track. A black horse won one race, a brown one another. Both jockeys were liveried in royal blue.

It was past five when I decided to break for lunch. I'd just finished a sweep of the infield, not pleasant given the tightly packed bodies and the collective level of inebriation.

I maneuvered to a vendor and bought a barbecue, sans drink. No way I'd risk needing one of the trillion port-a-johns, each with a waiting line longer than the U.S.–Canada border.

Tables not an option, I ate my sandwich standing at the edge of the food tent. A few feet from me, a beluga in an Ole Miss tee struggled to maintain his balance while dancing on a rickety lawn chair. He'd just chug-drained a julep, clearly not his first, when Bronco passed within yards of my right shoulder. No Stetson.

I turned, dipped my chin, and hit speed dial.

"Bronco's in the infield, heading toward the tunnel."

"The one leading to the grandstand?"

"Yes." Plowing not at all gently through the mass of bodies. "I'm on him."

I was cutting around the beluga when gravity won out. He tumbled, elbows flying, and knocked the burner from my hand. When he landed, a dead hit, I heard the screen shatter.

"Move!" I booted the beluga's substantial derrière. Groaning, he rolled to his belly and threw up.

"Gus?" Snatching up my phone, eyes everywhere, looking for Bronco.

No answer.

I clicked off, tried to reconnect. The thing was dead. Bronco was disappearing into the tunnel.

Shit.

I drove forward like an icebreaker, obscenities following in my wake. I didn't care. I'd spent hours searching for Bronco, he walked right past me, and a boozed-up frat boy took out my sole means of communication.

Shit.

Bronco crossed the tunnel to the grandstand and climbed to the second level. I followed, continued past him, and stopped one section beyond.

Bronco stood gazing down at the track. I watched him from under my helmet and behind my Maui Jims. Tried but couldn't interpret his line of vision.

A long minute, then Bronco pivoted to peer up and to his rear. Maybe toward the clubhouse, where I'd started the day. Maybe the Jockey Club Suites. Reverse pivot for another long perusal of the infield, then he took out a mobile and spoke briefly.

I looked around, didn't see Landmine. Was good with it.

Bronco glanced left, right, then descended, moving with the same catlike fluidity I remembered from Rose Avenue. I held back a few beats, then fell in behind.

The Longines Kentucky Oaks, the eleventh race of the day, was scheduled for 5:49 P.M. Soon the jockeys would mount their fillies. More than a hundred thousand juleped spectators would be pumped and ready. Had Bronco phoned to signal showtime?

Bronco wormed through the flow of people moving toward their seats. Or toward the rail for a better view of the track. On the ground level, he walked back toward the tunnel, seemingly in no hurry. Once through, he began working his way east across the infield.

Elbows winging, I cut through the jam of bodies, staying close enough to see Bronco but far enough back not to be seen. That worked until the bugler sounded the call. The crowd cheered and surged. In the commotion, Bronco disappeared.

I sped up as much as possible. Kept angling on the same course, curses again following my not-so-courteous progress. Bitch. Asshole. Worse.

Five minutes later I found myself at gate three. Bronco was nowhere to be seen. Nor was he in the street outside. I'd lost him.

I stood a moment, mind racing, blood pounding in my ears. Return to the track? The race had ended. No bomb had exploded.

I had no way to contact Gus. Knowing he'd be frantic, and confident the Oaks wasn't the target, I decided it would be wise to regroup.

I walked to the hotel. No point going nuts crammed into a shuttle.

Once in the room, I lay down on the box spring to think.

One thing was certain.

It was time to loop in the Louisville cops.

The Crossing

A glitch. *No one sleeps that night. They must delay and hope fatigue works in their favor.*

It does. The next day everyone drags. That evening the Leader orders early bed. All is dark and quiet by ten.

They meet in the cellar, make the transfer, slip out the back door. Hunkered behind a bush at the house foundation, they hear only the wind and their own pounding hearts.

She asks, fearing his answer. Yes, he has spoken to her. She won't divulge their plan but refuses to leave.

Memories fire in a single unending synapse. She knows there is nothing they can do to fix Mama. To save her. Still, she feels hollow.

The sprint down the dirt track is vicious, a twenty-minute ankle-twisting nightmare. Behind them, no window casts sudden light through the trees. No engine revs up.

They reach the road, a black strip of asphalt shooting in both directions. They pick one. Begin their slow trek north or south. Or east or west. They have no way to know.

She counts sixties to the rhythm of her footfalls. No reason.

He walks ahead, hunched under the weight of the overloaded packs. His dark skin glistens like moonlight on water.

Sixty sixties. They pass the mouth of a trail marked by a hand-lettered sign. DOCK. *She wonders. A family name? A pier?*

Now and then, they see the double white shimmer of an oncoming vehicle. Scramble for cover. Watch the headlights expand, whip by, twin red eyes recede to pinpoints and vanish.

The straps hurt her shoulders. Her tongue sticks to the roof of her mouth. Still, she trudges on, pulse doing its own forced march in her ears.

She is wearing her white sneakers. She watches them, pale in the gloom. Counts.

Another six-pack of sixties, then a riff of warning from her amygdalae. She raises her eyes.

The horizon is pulsing like an electric flag.

He notices, too. His gaze darts like that of a wild, frightened bird.

They belly-flop over the shoulder. Crab-claw swivel to face the road.

Seconds later, three cars race by flashing red and blue.

Her skin is fizzing.

He's blinking like a tic.

We're okay, she says.

We're okay, he says.

They sit, an adrenaline-wired pair, all wide eyes and sweat.

He tells her to stop scratching.

She rolls to her bum, every sense hypersonic.

She smells moss and stagnant water. From the shoulder, petroleum and dirt. The air is thick with pollen and spores.

She hears murmurs all around, insects among the leaves. Or snakes. Or predators with sharp yellow teeth.

She sees a clump of pink flowers swallowed in shadow. Pines, tall and black.

She scan-sweeps the road.

Her heart catapults into her throat.

Lying on the blacktop is a tentacled creature. Not tentacles. Straps.

She gropes, frantic. Not hers. She has two.

She grabs his arm. Points.

His hand flies to his back. His mouth reshapes into a silent O.

She's off before he can object. Is crossing the two-lane when the light show reappears, diminished but moving like a bullet, retracing its path.

She grabs the backpack. Dashes. Lands beside him.

The unthinkable.

The cruiser brakes. Arrows to the shoulder directly opposite.

They lie paralyzed, not breathing.

The driver's door opens. Static floats out. Music. Rock and roll.

A man unfolds, a dark silhouette against the strafing red and blue. He pauses, body blocked by the door. His head rotates slowly.

The man isn't tall, but tall enough. And powerful. The arm she can see is thick as a sapling.

His head stops. He straightens. Braces. His voice booms.

Come out of the trees.

They go graveyard still.

His voice booms again. Sharp as a knifepoint.

Frantic, she whispers in his ear. Bury the money. She will distract with a story.

He refuses.

She insists.

No.

Again, she acts before he can stop her.

Shrugging off her load, she shoots from the trees and across the pavement.

The cop tracks her from behind his car door barricade. Wary.

She stops at the yellow line.

The cop speaks into a radio mic, gets a buzzy response, approaches, tense, careful. She raises her hands above her head. Slowly.

The cop frisks her. Steps back.

She stands, blank-faced, prepared to give away nothing.
You know anything about these dead folks yonder?
Her body goes numb. She fears she'll collapse.
Name? *he demands.*
Sunday. *Mumbled. Mind flying apart.*
Sunday what?
Just Sunday.
Come on, kid. You got a last name.
Pavement at her feet pulsing red and blue. Heart banging. Mosquitoes whining high and hungry in her ears.
You listening to me, girl?
Lyrics drifting from a radio far off.
"Hot August night, and the leaves hanging down . . ."
Give it up here, or give it up in jail.
Night. Sunday Night.

CHAPTER
32

Gus and Kerr arrived at 7:40, having circulated until the end of the last race. Though outwardly serene, I noted a subtle loosening in his shoulders upon seeing me. Not so the brows, which stayed unnaturally tight. Body language only I can read.

"It was definitely Bronco." Wanting to sidetrack Gus's lecture about failing to maintain contact.

"Landmine?"

"Didn't see him."

"Where?"

"He took the tunnel from the infield, then went to the second level of the grandstand. Scoped out something behind and above him. And the track. Then he went back down, crossed the infield, and left through gate three. That's when I lost him."

"Shit."

"Yeah."

"I'm hungry," Kerr said.

Gus ignored her. "Why didn't you call back?"

I told him about the dancing beluga.

"You need a new phone." To Kerr. "I'll order room service when she goes out."

An Academy Award eye roll, then Kerr flopped onto her mattress. Gus and I moved to the far side of the room.

"Time to dial in the locals," I said, voice low and even.

"Beau gave me a name. Major Bertie Hoebeek. He's working as an onsite commander for the Derby."

"Hoebeek is solid?"

"Beau must think so."

I realized that, in my haste to get to the track, I hadn't told Gus about John Scranton's murder and Scranton's mother's possible abduction. Did so.

"What's the latest from Capps?"

"I've had no phone for the past two hours."

"Right. Think events in Winnetka are coincidental?"

"Damn big coincidence."

"You have to tell her." Tipping his head toward Kerr.

"Food first."

"It improves her very little."

"Was she helpful today?"

"Is tapioca helpful?"

I glanced through the window. Below on the street, traffic seemed to be flowing.

"While I score a phone, you call Hoebeek. I'll get an update from Capps, then break the news to Kerr."

The drive took a while, but the purchase was quick. Once the burner was activated, I dialed Capps's mobile, fingers crossed he'd answer an unknown caller. I wouldn't. He did.

"Where are you now?" Capps, noting the new number.

"Louisville. Any news on the Scranton front?" As I hurried toward the Maxima.

"John's still dead, Mama's still missing."

"Kerr claims her real name is Denise Scranton."

"No shit. Neighbors said there was a daughter." I heard a voice in the background, maybe Clegg. "Here's a tidbit. Shirley, that's the mother, is a 9/11 widow. When the planes hit, John senior was on the thirty-ninth floor of tower one."

"And thus a domestic terrorist was born."

"John junior would have been twelve or thirteen."

"Tough age to have your father murdered by al-Qaeda."

"Tough age to have your father murdered by anyone."

I did more math. Jasmine Kerr/Denise Scranton would have been four in 2001. Images rushed me from a past life. I blocked them.

"What did Scranton do?" I asked.

"Money management. Left the family loaded. By all accounts his death also left Shirley pretty screwed up. She worked briefly with organizations aiding the families of terrorism victims, gave that up, and became a recluse. According to one neighbor, when the kids were young she hardly let them leave the house."

"Find anything interesting in there?"

"Lots of cash."

"Anything linking John junior to Bronco and his Jihad for Jesus?"

"No."

"To any of the email addresses on Kerr's laptop? The Bnos Aliza School? The addresses in L.A. or Wash—"

"No."

"A mobile phone? Computer?" I *wheep-wheeped* the lock.

"Wow. Maybe we should have looked for those things."

"Bronco's here in Louisville."

"You saw him?"

I told him everything that had happened since last we'd spoken. Said Gus and I were contacting the Louisville cops.

I expected to be blasted for going solo so long. Instead, "Landon Crozier works for Old Capital Feed and Supply in Corydon, Indiana."

I grasped the significance, not the geography. "Supplies would come to Churchill Downs from that far away?"

"Corydon's maybe thirty miles from Louisville, just over the state line."

"That's it. Landmine's hidden IEDs in hay bales or feed containers." I yanked the door open and threw myself behind the wheel, mind seething with gruesome images. "Someone on the inside has retrieved and planted them."

"I want you to—"

"Gotta go." Tossing the phone to the dash, I palmed the gearshift and tore from the lot.

Gus had carried through. Back at the room, two uniformed cops filled the open doorway. He stood facing them. Behind him, Kerr was eating a BLT on her mattress. Two covered plates and two bottles of Stella Artois sat on a cart.

The first cop spoke while scanning to see if I was armed. His name tag said GOMEZ. He was younger than his partner and had a curiously aerodynamic nose. "Hold it there, ma'am."

I raised my hands, palms out, indicating I meant no harm. Down the hall, a door opened.

"I suggest we take this inside," I said.

Gus stepped back.

Gomez looked at his partner, whose name tag said O'ROURKE. O'Rourke nodded.

Right hands not so subtly cocked at their hips, Gomez and O'Rourke followed me into the room, eyes circling, resting a second on Gus, Kerr, the bed, the open bathroom door.

"I couldn't get through to Hoebeek," Gus said to me.

"One of you want to explain the 911 call?" O'Rourke had an explosion of tiny vessels in each cheek, features that looked straight out of Killarney.

I told him that I'd been on the job in Charleston, and that I'd come to Louisville in connection with work for a client.

"Inspiring. So why are you and your brother claiming terrorists plan to blow up the Derby?" Sounding mildly irritated.

"We think terrorists plan to blow up the Derby."

O'Rourke's face remained steadfastly impassive.

I explained Jihad for Jesus, the group's anti-Muslim agenda, the pipe bomb at the Bnos Aliza School, the coded message referencing the Godolphin horses.

"You know Major Hoebeek?" O'Rourke asked when I'd finished. I nodded.

"I assume you have firearms." Addressing both Gus and me.

"Real beauties."

"Where are they?"

"Locked in the safe."

"Keep them there. And yourselves available. Contact info?"

I gave him my new cellphone number. Which I had to check. Which caused his brows to twist like suspicious little worms.

"We'll be in touch."

"That's it?" I wasn't really surprised.

"Y'all have a good night."

With that they were gone. To report up the chain, I hoped.

Bertie Hoebeek called twelve minutes later. I answered and put him on speaker.

"You're Beau Beaumonde's kid?" Low, raspy. I guessed Hoebeek perpetually smelled of tobacco.

"Yes." Close enough.

"How is the old goat?"

"I believe IEDs have been smuggled inside Churchill Downs."

"Go on." All business.

Figuring O'Rourke or Gomez had relayed my personal creds, I skipped that part and shared everything I knew, beginning with the school bombing and Stella's disappearance, continuing with Kenneth "Bronco" Dickey, Landon "Landmine" Crozier, and John Scranton, Chicago, Venice Beach, and D.C., ending with the intel I'd just gotten from Roy Capps and my theory about explosives being smuggled in supplies going to the barns. I didn't mention the guys Gus and I shot.

Hoebeek never interrupted. When I stopped talking, he asked the spelling of Crozier's name, a few more details, as though checking quickly jotted notes.

"You got pics of these guys?"

"I can send them by email." No point explaining the loss of every image on my late burner. "Landmine won't look good."

"You said the Chicago investigation is out of Area Three, violent crimes?"

"Yes." I gave him Capps's number.

"Thank you, Ms. Night."

"I hope I'm wrong."

"I hope you're wrong, too." I detected strain in Hoebeek's voice. Maybe exhaustion. "This is my private number in case you think of anything further. In the meantime, you and your brother sit tight."

I said nothing.

"Are we straight on that?"

"We look forward to hearing from you." I disconnected.

"Think he's blowing us off?" I asked Gus.

"Could be he listened out of professional courtesy to Beau, but I doubt it. I think he's feeling what you said, pulling in all the extra security he can manage. Rallying the bomb squad."

"Either way, we sitting tight?"

"Not a chance in hell."

We slapped a high five. Childish, but we did.

Gus cocked his chin toward Kerr. "You have to—"

"Okay. Jesus."

I redid the binder holding my hair. Took a deep breath. Cleared my face and went to sit on the edge of the box spring. Kerr kept her head down, her eyes on her empty plate.

"Denise." As tender as I could manage. "I'm sorry. I have some bad news."

No reaction.

"There was a break-in at your home. In Winnetka. Your brother was stabbed." Blunt. I could think of no buildup.

Still holding the plate with one hand, she drew the quilt up and over her head with the other.

"Your mother is missing." I felt awful. Knew she had to be feeling worse. "John died."

She didn't ask when or where. Or who. She didn't ask anything.

"I know you must be devastated."

Silence.

"You can help catch the animals who did this."

Nothing.

"John was one of Bronco's followers, wasn't he?"

More nothing.

"After the failed ambush at Foster Beach, Bronco sent John to kill me at the Ritz."

No response.

I glanced at Gus. He was eating his BLT but listening.

I tried again.

"What happened to Stella Bright?"

I felt like I was talking to myself.

"You need to work with us, Denise. To have any hope of finding your mother. Or saving the horses."

I heard a hollow little laugh. "You don't have a clue."

"Help me out."

She looked up, quilt encircling her head like an Inuit hood, plate still clutched in one hand. I noticed it was trembling.

"John was nothing." Cheeks moist, face oddly blank. "We're all nothing."

"Stop playing the fucking victim."

Too harsh. The plate smashed the wall with such force it shattered. I jumped. Gus shot to his feet.

Kerr dropped to her side and curled into a quilt-wrapped ball.

I looked a question at Gus. "Tomorrow" was all he said.

As I booted my Mac, Gus got his Glock from the safe and laid it on the nightstand. After hitting the head, he stretched out and, in seconds, was snoring. I envied him. His ability to sleep anyplace, anytime was a skill not coded in our shared DNA.

I searched through images, thankful of the transfers I'd made from earlier phones. Found Gus's shot of Bronco standing lookout on Venice Beach. Mine of Landmine bleeding through his luau shirt on the Rose Avenue floor.

I paused at the image of the laptop screen in Kerr's Argyle Street apartment. Read the cryptic email that had sent us hurtling down the path to Louisville. *Godolphin Vintage Claret Beauty 05 05 06. FL1X: LM-inf /JC-GR/B5-S2 +4.*

Vintage, owned by Godolphin stable, had run in the Oaks that day. Claret Beauty was entered in tomorrow's Derby. For the zillionth time, I strained to crack the final sequence in the coded message. For the zillionth time, I experienced no breakthrough.

Frustrated, I sent the images to Hoebeek, then tried my sandwich. The toast and bacon were cold and soggy, the lettuce limp as pale green tissue. I chucked it and drank the Stella. The bedside clock said 10:20.

I plugged in my phone and settled on the box spring.

10:40. 11:00. 11:20.

Hoebeek didn't call.

Just past midnight, Gus sat up and grunted something I took to mean I could rest. I closed my eyes, but sleep didn't come.

12:17. 12:32. 12:45.

Finally, fatigue had its way. I dozed fitfully, drifting in and out of familiar dream fragments.

I'm sitting in shadow at the top of a staircase. My heart is pounding. Something bad is going to happen, but I don't know what. I'm afraid. For me. For Mama. For Gus.

I'm running through woods, branches clawing my hair.

I'm crouching in darkness, too terrified to slap mosquitoes sucking my blood. Someone is with me. I'm afraid for them.

I see circled corpses, black as briquettes. Feel Beau's hands on my shoulders, strong and solid.

I woke, fists clenched, face damp with sweat. Moving quietly, I got up for water, then lay back down. All was dark save for the glowing digits on my phone.

Maybe dreaming about Beau. Maybe being at the Derby with Gus. Those gatherings around the old RCA replayed in my head. The disputes about the all-time finest Thoroughbred. One year I argued for Genuine Risk, one of only two fillies ever to win the roses.

Sudden synapse. A grenade exploding in my brain.

Dear God. Could that be it?

The idea swelled and filled every inch of the room. I turned it this way and that. Grabbed the Mac and rechecked the puzzling cipher.

Pulse racing, I reached for my mobile.

CHAPTER
33

Hoebeek didn't answer. I left a ten-second message. Ten seconds later, he called back.

"Explosives already inside the track? What in the name of sweet Christ are you talking about?"

"Along with the pics of Bronco Dickey and Landmine Crozier, I sent you a screenshot of a coded email. I think the final sequence refers to potential or actual bomb locations. LM-inf. Lockheed Martin has a hospitality tent on the infield, right?"

"Smack-ass on the finish line."

"JC-GR. One of the Jockey Club Suites is named for Genuine Risk. I'm guessing the Godolphin contingent has it this year."

"Go on."

"B5-S2+4. Barn five, stalls two and four. Godolphin horses?"

Hoebeek didn't answer.

"Doesn't Lockheed Martin do business in the Middle East?" I asked, meaning the company has ties up the wazoo.

Tense breathing. Then, "You come to Louisville planning to spoil our party?"

"No."

"Well, you got lucky."

"I wouldn't shut it down yet." Hoebeek's words had just unlocked the last missing piece.

"I won't have people blown up on our watch," Hoebeek said, meaning his watch.

"The middle of the code. FL1X. Finish line, first crossing." Hiding the adrenaline rush I was feeling. "Does that make sense?"

"The track's a mile long. The Derby goes a mile and an eighth. The horses cross once after the bell, again when they finish."

"I'm guessing the first crossing is when Bronco plans to pull the trigger. It's 1:20 now. The Derby is scheduled to go off at 6:24 P.M. That gives us more than seventeen hours to find and deactivate the devices."

"The track opens at eight."

"So we work fast."

Hoebeek thought about that. Or reread the email.

"I've got the bomb squad and ATF onsite. You say it's terrorism, so the feds will want in."

"And on our end?" Meeting Gus's eyes. Which were sparking like mine.

"Keep the guns in the safe and your ass in that room."

"Not a chance."

"That's an order."

"You can't order me."

"I can have you detained."

"For what?"

"Questioning."

He could. "Find the bombs, lose the bombers," I said. "Not a headline to be envied."

"We'll get the sons of bitches."

"You talk to Capps?"

"Your point?"

"Bronco and Landmine are slippery as hell. My brother and I can ID them."

More breathing. A lot. I was about to push harder when the rusty voice rasped again.

"Might be you could contribute in some limited way." Meaning, do exactly what I say, nothing more.

"You're the commander." Meaning, that flies at Churchill Downs.

"I'll send a cruiser."

It took ninety minutes. By the time the squad car arrived, driven by Officer M. Albee, I was almost nauseous from the anxious energy swirling inside me. Unthinking, I snatched the red helmet from the bed and hurried downstairs.

Albee pulled to the curb near the point where our shuttle had dropped us the previous morning. The plaza, paddock area, and grandstands were dark and deserted, a scene starkly different from that of Oaks Day.

Albee led us up a VIP elevator to the fourth floor of the clubhouse, our footsteps echoing loud in the stillness. My restless instincts shrieking that the serenity would soon be shattered.

The command post was an ordinary room with two desks, a couple of laptops, and a bank of monitors. Bland horsey print on one wall, ugly carpet on the floor. I hoped money saved on office space was going toward Louisville Metro Police Department muscle. And bomb-sniffing dogs.

Unlike the post, the commander was far from ordinary. Bertie Hoebeek had skin the color of rind inside a lemon, ruddy cheeks, hair morphing from wheat to gray. She kept it buzzed on the sides, long enough on top to flip forward onto her forehead, perhaps to divert attention from the fact that only half of her ear remained on the right.

Yeah. She. The major's first and last names were inscribed on a brass plaque riding her ample left breast. Huberta Hoebeek. I guessed her family legends involved a lot of tulips and windmills.

I also guessed no one asked about the AWOL ear. Bertie Hoebeek stood six one and looked like she could bench-press three
hundred pounds. Maybe bend crowbars with her bare hands. Think
the Pillsbury Doughboy toned and on steroids in full cop attire.

My eyes did their usual scan, ending with the monitors. The
screens displayed a glowing montage of empty rooms, deserted
tunnels, unoccupied bleachers, and abandoned parking lots. The
two techs wore polo shirts with LMPD patches. Soft uniforms.
Not-so-soft weaponry. Like their boss, each carried a great big gun.

Hoebeek was at the end of the row, elbows on spread knees,
viewing a monitor with a man to her left. He had salt-and-pepper
hair and wore a navy windbreaker with the letters FBI in bold yellow on the back. Though both were seated, it was obvious Hoebeek had five inches on the guy.

In the gap between their heads, I could see action on a screen.
Figures in helmets and fatigues, a dog on a leash, the inside of what
I assumed was a horse barn.

"Ma'am."

Hoebeek turned at the sound of Albee's voice. Eyes bluer than
delft took in our foursome.

"I assume you're Night." Studying me.

"I am."

"Nice when an outsider embraces local traditions."

Blushing, I winged the tricked-out helmet onto a folding chair
pushed to one wall. Didn't recall bringing it from the hotel.

"This the guy dimed 911?" Hoebeek indicated Gus.

"It is."

"Thought the caller was your brother."

"You thought right."

"I'll be damned. Name?"

"Gus."

"Two Nights. Ain't we blessed. Who's this?"

"Denise Scranton."

Hoebeek's brows dipped in annoyance. "Why's she here?"

"She can ID members of Bronco's group that we don't know."

"No way I involve civilians."

"I'm a civilian," I said.

"You were on the job."

To cut off further discussion, Hoebeek cocked a thumb at the empty chair to her right. "Sit." Pointed a finger toward the desks. "You two, park there."

I sat. Kerr sat. Gus remained standing, arms folded, feet spread. Albee retreated to stand guard in the corridor.

Pivoting back toward the screen, Hoebeek made introductions by stating our names. "Special Agent Jordan Millet. Sunday Night."

Millet and I exchanged nods. He had small, close-set eyes the same French roast as his skin. They didn't look pleased with my presence.

"What's happening?" I asked, focusing my attention on the monitor in front of Hoebeek.

"First off. Don't misconstrue your being here as meaning you'll take part in any action."

"Your confidence in me is uplifting."

Hoebeek motioned with a slight tip of her head. "We found one. Barn five."

"This is bullshit." White heat flaming my chest. "You let us cool our heels until you had proof?"

Hoebeek fixed me with hard blue eyes. "You got a problem with the way I run my command?"

"Did you notify those in charge?" Forbidding the anger to scorch my words.

"I'm in charge."

"Of the track."

"They know." Swiveling back to the screen.

"They didn't ask to close shop?"

"Quite the opposite."

"Did you give them a deadline?"

"I did."

A few moments of morgue-chill silence. Millet avoiding eye

contact. Then I refocused. The last thing I needed was a face-off with either.

"Bomb type?" I asked.

"Pressure cooker."

"They've upped their game." I didn't know if either had been briefed on Bronco and Bnos Aliza, wasn't about to do it. "Disguised how?"

"In a feed sack."

"Same as the Tsarnaev brothers at the Boston Marathon," Millet said unnecessarily.

"Except for the feed sack." I felt hostile eyes hit the side of my face. Didn't care. "Has it been disabled?"

"We deployed a robot outfitted with an XSR." Hoebeek referred to an X-ray scanning rover, an apparatus providing high-resolution scans in real time. "Then we blasted the bitch with a water charge."

"What about the other two locations?"

"Teams are working the Jockey Club, the Lockheed Martin tent, the grandstands, the vendor areas. Got EDCs sniffing every square inch of this place." Explosive-detecting canines. The woman liked acronyms. "So far, nothing."

And so we waited. Paced. Stared at screens. Downed coffee that tasted like old stool specimens.

At 4:37 and 20 seconds, Hoebeek's phone rang. She checked the number and clicked to speaker function. The room went absolutely still.

A dog named Pickle had alerted on a case of Fritos.

"Where?" Hoebeek asked.

"A food storage area servicing the Jockey Suites."

"Send in the robot."

"Moving."

"And maintain voice contact."

As though sucked forward by a vortex, everyone present drew toward the monitors. Preoccupied, or not caring, Hoebeek didn't object.

On monitor six, the robot entered the frame, positioned itself on one side of the corn chips, and extended its X-ray arm around the back of the carton. A pause. Then the voice came again through the speaker.

"The scanner shows a pressure cooker bomb inside."

"Take the son of a bitch out." Hoebeek, steely.

We heard a confusion of voices and barking and running. Then a muted pop as, far down the line, the box, the Fritos, and the bomb were blasted by water powerful enough to blow them to bits.

"We got her," the tinny voice said.

"Well done. Now, let me remind you. The special agent sitting beside me has a huge throbbing hard-on for every speck of trace at that scene. Got it?"

"Yes, ma'am."

"And get the dog a Milk-Bone."

Then we waited some more. The techs and Millet scouring pixels. Gus scowling. Kerr snoring. Hoebeek wearing her pin.

5:14.

5:19.

At 5:30 Hoebeek asked me to join her on a walk. I thought it odd but followed out into the hall. When safely distanced, she stopped and thumb-hooked her belt.

"You appreciate why I had to check things out."

"Check things out?" My eyes level and steady on hers.

"Before bringing you here, I dimed Beaumonde."

I said nothing.

"He told me about the kid you're trying to find. Explained why you're intent on nailing these turds."

"Did he."

"I remember the rash of murder-suicides back in the nineties. Branch Davidians. Heaven's Gate. Solar Temple. Don't recall your particular coven, maybe because of the no name thing."

Her words sent a high-voltage impulse into my brain. Hoebeek had probed the holy hell that was my childhood.

"It'll stay between us, of course."

I didn't trust myself to speak.

"Apologies if it's insensitive, but I'd like your take on what's going on here."

"Take your apology and stick it right up your ass."

Hoebeek's cheeks flamed as though she'd been slapped. Looked like blood spreading on snow.

Knowing my reaction was out of proportion, I went into control mode. Deep breath. Another. Then I turned and strode back to the command post.

5:45.

5:54.

The tension in the room was thick enough to roast on a spit. I sat, paced, palms damp, mouth dry. A flash storm raging in my head.

A summer night. A breathless sprint through dark woods. Charred corpses. Blackened lips that had once kissed my cheek. I hated Hoebeek for poking down the snake hole and setting the images free.

But who was I kidding? It wasn't Hoebeek. I'd lived this before. And failed. Everyone. My own mother.

One night. Not two.

He'd lied. I'd missed it. In his voice, his body language, his animal eyes.

The Leader. The Monster.

Feeling powerless, I got up, dropped back down, chewed my shiny black nails.

Wondered, where the fuck was Stella? Would she also die because of me?

Churchill Downs was scheduled to open at eight. How late would Hoebeek go before ordering that the gates stay closed? If I was wrong, how much revenue would be lost? If I was right, how many lives would be lost?

Did another bomb exist? Had the third been deleted from Bronco's plan? Placed elsewhere? If so, where? I knew so little. I'd fail again.

The doubt and fear began to devour the space in my brain I'd reserved for clear thinking. To undermine my capacity for logic.

At 6:10, Hoebeek's phone rang again.

An ATF dog was alerting on a box of plastic drink cups in the Lockheed Martin tent. The first sweep had missed it.

Hoebeek ordered in the robot. The scan showed a bomb.

The adrenaline cleared my head quickly. "We should be leaving decoys. In case Bronco checks."

"You think so, lollipop?"

Attributing Hoebeek's dig to ire at my earlier comments, I let it pass. Gus didn't.

"Yes, cupcake." Anger simmering below the civility. "We think so."

Hoebeek twisted in her chair. "Sir, long ago I told you to sit. Yet there you are standing."

"Here I am." Belligerent.

"Don't get smart."

"One of us should."

Blue eyes locked with green. Hoebeek blinked first. "We're leaving decoys."

Within the hour, the third IED was disabled.

With a promise to me of an upcoming interrogation, Millet hurried off to oversee the processing of the final scene. Maybe to pee.

Everything from my stomach to my throat was in restless turmoil.

"The track opens in forty-five minutes," I said. "Bronco and Landmine will be coming for their big show."

"We're on it," Hoebeek said.

"How will you know them?"

"We have your pics."

"That won't be enough."

"We'll nail the cocksuckers."

"You haven't so far."

Maybe remorse over her lollipop crack. Or her tactless incursion into my personal nightmare. Hoebeek didn't bite back. "Bronco's not inside now. I've had teams looking all night." Rising, she jabbed a finger at me. "I'm about to spread joy to a gaggle of seer-suckered jackals. Your cheeks stay glued to that seat."

They did. Briefly.

I looked at Gus. He tipped his head toward the door.

Grabbing my flowery helmet, I bolted.

CHAPTER
34

Lines were already forming outside. When the gates opened, spectators streamed in. A trickle at first, with increasing volume as the sun climbed. Figuring Hoebeek would focus her efforts on the bomb sites, Gus and I split the territory as we had the day before.

By mid-morning, the place was sweating room only. The crowd worked in our favor and against us. The press of bodies helped us to blend but also provided cover for our quarry.

By noon, we'd not seen Bronco, Landmine, or Stella. We'd also not seen them by two P.M.

At 4:17 I spotted Landmine exiting a men's room near the grandstand end of the infield tunnel. He was wearing a white shirt and black pants, all size elephant. Dark Ray-Bans covered his eyes and a straw panama hat rode low on his brow. A track employee ID hung from his neck.

I donned my headgear, turned a shoulder, and allowed him to pass. Then, gaze fixed on the panama, I dialed Gus, who was circulating with Kerr.

"Landmine's here," I said, walking fast enough to keep him in sight, slow enough not to draw his attention.

"I'll need more than that."

I gave him my location. "Looks like he's dressed as a vendor or waiter."

"Think Hoebeek's dogs will spot him?"

"In those shades and that hat? I almost didn't."

"Alert her."

"I will."

As I disconnected, Landmine pulled out a cell and answered a call. We'd both arrived at the infield. A click of a conversation, then he circled to a point opposite the Lockheed Martin tent. Pocketing the phone, he turned and peered into the swarm of humanity covering the grass.

I called Hoebeek. Got voicemail. Left a message.

I could have taken Landmine. I wanted Bronco. And Stella, wherever she was.

Five minutes. Ten. A voice warbled from the PA system. My eyes jumped to the Jumbotron screen. Race ten, the Woodford Reserve Turf Classic, was about to roll.

I watched Landmine. Landmine watched his surroundings, head moving in slow little arcs. He didn't look quite as gorilloid as I remembered. Maybe the hat. Maybe his canines didn't really interlock.

More amplified announcements. Jolly. Unaware.

More arcing scans.

When Landmine's head froze, I followed his sight line.

Bronco was worming through the crowd. The dark suit, curly-cable earbud, and newly shorn hair suggested he was costumed to look like security. Unabomber aviators hid his face. The loathsome steel-toed boots covered his feet.

Bronco joined Landmine. Words were exchanged.

A bugle sounded the "Riders up" call.

Without warning, a hand clamped my shoulder.

I spun as though hot-wired.

"Goddammit!" Heart thudding. "You scared the shit out of me."

"Sorry." Gus's fingers were contritely raised and spread.

Kerr watched with her usual vapid expression.

"There." I indicated Bronco and Landmine.

Gus appraised them from behind his Hang 10s. "What's Hoe-beek's plan?"

"No idea."

The bronze-tinted lenses swung to me. "Jesus Christ, Sunnie."

"I left a message." Defensive. "Let's just hope she doesn't go all Rambo. Bronco's our target and the asshole *just* showed up."

"*Our* target? Who put us in charge of priorities?"

I said nothing.

Down the track, horses were led to their gates.

Down the infield, Bronco and Landmine stood mute.

The starting bell trilled. The horses fired out, thundered past, leaving the scent of torn grass in their slipstream. The crowd noise congealed into a murmurous swell. One loop and a bit, then the winner trotted off for his flowers and photo ops, the losers for their rubdowns. The next race would be the big one.

Still, Bronco and Landmine stood.

"What the hell are they doing?" A single finger worrying Gus's right temple.

"The devices were too far apart for a single detonation. I'm guessing they'll use signals from three separate mobiles."

"They're waiting for other JJs."

"That's my guess."

Counting the clock, minute by minute. Eventually, a woman sang the national anthem. Not bad, not great.

We watched and waited.

A man urged spectators to raise a glass of Mumm in the world's largest champagne toast. Not a hit on the infield.

We watched some more.

Suddenly adrenaline began making the rounds.

A woman in a yellow pantsuit and yellow-banded bonnet was arrowing straight toward Landmine and Bronco. Her chin was down, the hat's wide brim shadowing her features.

Following Pantsuit was a woman in an ankle-length gray skirt

299 · TWO NIGHTS

and a white tunic similar to the one Kerr had worn when chained to my sink. A pink floral scarf wrapped her head, hiding her hair and lower face. She kept her shoulders hunched, not making the most of her height. Which was unimpressive.

Tunic looked thinner than the girl in Opaline Drucker's photo. Still, my heart beat faster. Was I finally laying eyes on Stella Bright?

Hearing a sharp intake of breath, I turned. Kerr's eyes were saucers. One hand was pressed to her mouth.

"Who are those women?" I asked.

Kerr shook her head slowly, gaze riveted on Pantsuit.

"Is the woman in the tunic Stella Bright?"

Nothing but the terrified stare.

The heat. The inactivity. The all-night vigil. The familiar anger switch tripped in my brain.

"Who are they?" I yanked Kerr's hand from her lips.

"You don't know." Mumbled.

"No shit." Fury was melting the world into a cumulous blur. "Who are they?"

Kerr thrust her chin to one side, desperate to escape my wrath. "Let me go."

Through the white haze, I sensed eyes on my back. A man offering help. A woman asking if she should phone the police. Gus, chuckling, sisters, too much bourbon.

"Tell me!"

Kerr refused to engage.

My eyes cut to the women. Pantsuit had pivoted, and light now sculpted her features. They were gaunt, the hard roots of jaw and cheekbone evident, the nose spiky as vertebrae inside a desiccated corpse. Bronco, the target of her glare, seemed to shrink into himself.

"Who! Are! They!" Savage. Shaking Kerr hard.

"My mother." Sobbing. "She's my mother!"

Stunned, I released Kerr's arms. She rocked a bit, steadied herself. I watched her intently, forgotten scraps exploding into my forebrain.

Bronco on the Rose Avenue couch. *I don't have the luxury to choose.*

Kerr on the Garden Inn floor mattress. *You don't have a clue.*

Bronco's email offering Icard and Harkester. *Were I at liberty to follow my own path.*

Capps's description of a missing widow. A recluse, warped by the terrorist murder of her husband.

Female voices down a hall.

The hidden clues that had been sending up flares from my id.

"Is the other woman Selena?"

Tearful nod.

A hint of breeze caught the edge of the floral scarf. A flash of copper sparked in the afternoon sun.

I swallowed. Inhaled. Inhaled again.

"Your mother runs the whole twisted mindfuck. That's what you started to say back in D.C. There are others. Bronco's not really in charge of Jihad for Jesus."

Kerr nodded, face a death mask. "No. It's"—maybe fear, maybe love, maybe hatred, she stumbled on the word—"Mama."

All I saw was Stella. The pale skin. The intense eyes. The scarf I knew was hiding rowdy red hair.

Suddenly, the full horror struck. The stooped shoulders. The crossed arms. The shadows falling wrong among the folds of the tunic.

My heart accelerated so fast I thought I would vomit.

"Jesus Christ. She's wearing an IED."

"Sonofabitch." Gus started thumbing keys on his phone.

Bronco checked his watch, a sharp, quick dip of the head, then said something to Scranton. She pivoted and pulled Stella into her arms.

A stiff embrace, then the women separated. Stella raised a fist and brought it down hard on her chest. Turned and began weaving toward the finish line.

In my peripheral vision I saw uniforms clotting up on the infield, materializing like storm troopers out of a mist.

Beside me, Gus was barking into his phone. Suicide bomber. White tunic. Pink scarf.

A vicious claw clamped down on my heart. I knew protocol. Knew that in seconds snipers would focus their crosshairs on Stella's brain stem and fire.

The next few moments flashed by like blurred images outside the window of a speeding train.

Ignoring Gus's shouted pleas, I lowered my head and muscled my way to the edge of the track. Once there, I sprinted toward the finish line. When Stella emerged from the crowd, ten feet up, I checked for one critical detail. Almost cried with relief. Clutched in her right hand was a triggering device.

Body still acting without permission from my higher centers, I rushed up behind her, fingers death-gripping the chin strap of the red equestrian helmet. Sensing danger or hearing movement, Stella spun.

For a blink, our eyes locked. In that heartbeat joining I recognized a passion I knew only too well. The fire in the brain that blocks reason. The flame in the heart that allows only blind compliance.

And I saw something else. Inked on Stella's right cheek were two interlocking J's.

Conflicting emotions blast-beat a death metal cadence inside me. Fury. Loathing. Pity.

Stella had succumbed. Had become the very thing I'd battled my whole childhood.

Still.

I didn't want her dead.

Acting on instinct, I slid my left leg forward, bent my knees, and swung the helmet with all the strength I could muster. The rigid outer shell struck Stella's right temple with a sound like a rock hitting concrete.

Stella's head snapped sideways. Her brain sloshed right, slammed hard, then ricocheted left and collided with the opposite inner surface of her skull. Tiny vessels ruptured at both impact sites.

Stella's lids fluttered, then her eyes rolled up. As her body crumpled, her hand went limp.

The detonator fell free. I kicked it across the ground.

"Move away!" A voice bellowed at my back.

"She's out cold!"

"Move away!"

"Don't shoot! She's a sixteen-year-old kid!"

"Now!"

I stepped back, gaze whipping from Stella to the trio she'd just left. Landmine remained huddled with Shirley Scranton. They hadn't yet noticed all the blue closing in. Not so Bronco. He was gone.

Fuck! Which way?

Eyes skidding, searching, I began plowing toward gate three. Twenty yards, then, to my right, curses and catcalls, a ripple of outrage snaking fast.

Bronco was moving like a buck caning tall grass. On his head was an Irish flat cap. The aviators had been replaced by black plastic frames holding clear lenses. Reading his direction of movement, I swung the same way, cutting the angle.

Never slowing, Bronco yanked off and tossed the suit coat and tie. He was fast for a guy in steel-toed boots. But not fast enough. When we hit the tunnel I'd drawn to within thirty feet.

The narrow cavern was wall-to-wall revelers. Bronco skimmed along one side, knees and elbows pumping. I followed, breath sounding like thunder in my ears, footfalls like buckshot bouncing off cement.

At one point I heard a series of pops topside. Gunshots? Had Stella resumed consciousness and attempted to rise? An amplified bugle made it impossible to interpret the sounds.

Bronco hooked right at the end of the tunnel and drilled through the jam on Central Avenue. I bull-charged the same path. Those we knocked aside took us for two more rude drunks.

Until Bronco pulled a Kahr P380 from his boot.

People screamed and scrambled to get out of the way. I was glad for their scattering, if not for the gun. The extra space allowed me to kick into high as I fired onto Fourth Street.

The years of jogging twenty miles each week were paying off. My legs were staying strong. Still I felt like I was running through one of my nightmares. Like my feet refused to move fast enough.

Eventually, Bronco veered left and skirted the side of a pharmacy. A few loping strides, then he charged across the street and disappeared into an armada of RV big rigs moored in a vacant lot. I was seconds behind.

Rounding the outermost Winnebago, I saw only amber sun slashing the narrow passages intersecting at right angles between the rows of trailers. No Bronco.

Panic hit me like a rockslide.

I pulled out my burner and dialed Gus. Got voicemail. Pant-whispered, "RVs, Oakdale."

Disconnected. Stood motionless, face flushed, shirt soaked and stuck to my skin.

From inside Churchill Downs, an announcement, then music, the lyrics muted by distance, but familiar.

The sun shines bright in the old Kentucky home. . . .

Far off, crowd noises. People rushing in panic? Nearer to me, a car engine. A cat. Gasping.

Quick scan. A tire iron lay on the Bago's back bumper. I lifted it and, moving gingerly, crept forward. Two lines of campers, then, shoulder blades pressed to an Airstream the size of cruise ship, I peeked around to check the laneway to my left.

Bronco was doubled over, back to me, so close I could hear the phlegm in his throat, smell the noxious mix of his sweat and cologne. The black specs were gone, the cap. But the long spider fingers still gripped the pistol.

Clutching my weapon two-fisted, I cocked my arms high, a batter at the plate. I was tensing, imagining the soft flesh behind Bronco's knees, when his torso came around like a snake on a branch.

Straightening fast, chest still heaving, he pointed the Kahr straight at my head.

We will sing one song for my old Kentucky home. . . .

The tire iron sliced the air with a high-pitched whir. Landed on bone with a sickening crack. The gun flew from Bronco's hand and bounced off the orbital rim above my good eye.

Tears blurred my vision. Blood. I ducked sideways. A second too late. The spider fingers wrapped the iron, yanked, and twisted. The shaft slipped through my grasp. One end kissed the side of my head.

A roaring filled my ears, overpowering all sounds but those inside my body. The scene that followed played to an internal symphony of inhalation and pulse.

Bronco wet his lips. Before he could strike again, I stepped back and kicked out. Connected. The iron winged up, then joined the gun on the gravel.

Bronco's mouth went feral with a silent cry. He came at me swinging wildly, one hand a fist, the other a useless collection of bones and tissue inked with two *J*'s. Trembling and heaving, he locked both arms around me and squeezed. I felt a pop, air explode from my lungs.

Twisting hard, I broke free and brought my elbow up against the side of Bronco's nose, felt it shatter, saw the pain register before I hit him again, this time below the nostrils with the heel of my hand. He staggered back against the Airstream, head torqued, blood spurting.

There were people around now. I saw mouths move, maybe goading me on, maybe admonishing me to stop.

Adrenaline and caffeine had me wired from hell to tomorrow. Ignoring the gawkers, and the agony in my rib cage, I hit Bronco again, so hard his skull slammed and dented the metal.

Suddenly, like synchronized puppets, the heads circling us whipped toward Churchill Downs.

Toward the sound of an explosion? Sniper fire?

I kept hammering.

Bronco's head lashed from side to side, whipping blood and saliva across his face and mine. Trails gleamed on the outer panel of the Airstream, dark and shiny. I hit him again. Wrapped his throat in a death grip as he had once wrapped mine.

Time passed. Seconds? Eons?

Then Gus was dragging me away, one hand on each of my shoulders.

I tried to shrug free. Gus held me like a vice.

"Stop!" Just a movement of lips.

No one circled us now. The onlookers had vanished.

I let go. Bronco slid to the ground, hands cupping his nose. I looked down at him, hate-fueled, half-grabbing my breath.

Slowly, inevitably, the fire began to cool, leaving a nasty burning low in my gut.

"Landmine and Scranton?" I shouted to Gus, too loud.

"—FBI—" A fragment of his reply broke through.

"Stella?" Palming blood and spit from my cheeks.

Gus took my arm, eyes full of something I couldn't read.

Legs shaky and unsteady, I allowed myself to be led.

CHAPTER
35

The air was muggy and filled with the sounds of traffic, birdsong, and frond rustle. I could smell honeysuckle and fresh-cut grass, taste salt on my upper lip.

Because I was sweating inside a long-sleeved black jersey shift. Bad choice, but my only dress.

Not yet June and the low country was in full summer mode.

I was doing my perspiring outside Charleston's First Baptist Church. Beyond the curlicue iron fencing, Church Street stretched as a still life in Southern genteel—shuttered windows, balconied courtyards, overprivileged geraniums bubbling from window boxes and pots.

Inside the three sets of doors at my back, the memorial service was winding to a close. Gus was in a pew. Opaline Drucker. Peter Crage. Others I didn't know.

I tried but couldn't go in. Call me heathen, or damaged, or plain old nuts. I spent my youth with people under the influence of zeal. Or whatever.

Organ chords leached out into the day's glare. Voices warbling "Amazing Grace." They were swinging into a second chorus when

Roy Capps exited, stepping quick, like a guy trying to beat the parking lot rush. On seeing me, he stopped short, surprised or embarrassed.

"Ms. Night."

"Detective."

"How's it going?"

"I've spent merrier afternoons."

"You're telling me." Nodding toward a gravestone propped against the wall to my right.

We both took a moment to study the epitaph. The engraving was fresh, like white bone carved into the dark gray marble. Names. Dates of birth and death.

My gaze lingered on the final line.

Knowledge comes, but wisdom lingers.

"Would have helped if Drucker had reported the con right off," Capps said.

"A lot of things might have helped."

My words hung between us in the humid air.

"Shirley Scranton talking?" I asked.

Capps snorted. "The old harpy's got stone cojones. Actually, she's fairly young. Fifty-four."

"Bronco and Landmine?"

"Turning on each other like hammerheads on blood."

My eyes drifted back to the headstone. "How'd Stella end up with these mutants?"

"She was injured by the blast and blundered into the street. The woman riding shotgun in the Forester—"

"Tibby Icard." The murder vic in Bronco's photo. The woman whose reaction had troubled me.

"Yeah. Icard planned to drop the kid at an ER. Not sure her motivation. Anyway, it didn't happen. Shirley Scranton saw Stella's capture as a ticket to fame and glory. Shock the world with footage of a nice middle-class kid blowing herself up for the cause."

"What's the story on Jihad for Jesus?" Feeling a wave of anger, thick and tangled.

"The group wasn't large, maybe a few dozen. Those with criminal records need not apply."

"Just God-fearing Christians willing to kill." I swallowed. "What was Harkester's story?"

"He and his brother enlisted in the army straight out of high school, did that buddy thing, served together five times in Iraq and Afghanistan. Three years ago, the brother was killed in a suicide bombing at a checkpoint north of Baghdad. Harkester chose not to re-up, dropped off the grid. Last August he was diagnosed with pancreatic cancer, died thirty-four days later at Northwestern Hospital in my fair city."

Four months after bombing a Jewish girls' school. I tried to muster sympathy. Came up empty.

"Was the target always Churchill Downs after the Bnos Aliza fail?"

"Scranton was considering several options, thus the dispersed troops—Chicago, D.C., L.A. You know what swayed her?"

I shook my head.

"American Pharoah. She read about the horse, assumed Egypt, assumed Islam."

I could think of no response to such stupidity. Such insanity.

"Scranton kept each group in the dark about the others," Capps went on. "About the target."

"Except Bronco."

"Yeah. Bronco was her go-to guy."

"Landmine must have wondered why he was shunted to a feed store in Indiana."

"Landmine's not a deep thinker."

A carriage clopped by, guide yakking history, tourist faces pointed our way. The horse was brown and looked hot and bored.

"Scranton bankrolled everything," Capps said. "Owned the building on Argyle Street."

"Generous. Provided housing and her daughter." I pictured a Sox cap lit by the moon. "Where's Kerr now? Denise?"

"Locked up in Louisville."

"What's she facing?"

"They could hit her with accessory, aiding and abetting, conspiracy, the list is long. And there's the matter of the passports. But I doubt she'll be charged. Apparently her IQ barely claws out of the seventies."

"And she was raised by a lunatic."

"And that."

A match flamed in my chest as the parallels slammed home anew. Kerr had been shaped by childhood forces beyond her control. I'd missed the signs.

"Scranton stabbed her own son?" I knew the answer.

"She denies it. But the knife was from her kitchen and John's blood was in her car. We'll get her."

There was an undercurrent to his voice. I believed him.

"Have you ID'd the fourth bomber? The guy Landmine capped on Rose Avenue?"

"Janois Thomas. Jano. His uncle died in the U.S. embassy bombing in Lima in 2002."

Capps's gaze slipped to the courtyards and geraniums and retreating buggy. Up the block, an old man in a bow tie and suspenders was encouraging his poodle to pee on a hydrant.

"How did Scranton rope people into her lunacy?" I asked.

Capps's eyes came back to my face.

"Her kids had no choice. The others she recruited through an organization that helps the families of terrorism vics. By the way, it was Scranton who spotted your online posts. And this is rich. The dog hair found in the Forester came from her Rottweiler. We're thinking a bomber was in her house, picked it up, and transferred it to the SUV."

"Nailed by your own pooch."

"His name's Infidel."

"One of the email handles on Kerr's computer. Brilliant."

Capps nodded.

"Who sent the threatening email to me in Venice? TNT82 @yahoo.com?"

"Bronco."

"Bronco also made the original ransom demand?"

"At Scranton's direction. They figured why not score a little cash, maybe send the police down a blind alley. They forced the quote out of Stella, at that time living in a little funhouse in the crawl space of Scranton's house."

"She willingly posed for the pic Bronco sent with his email?"

"Wrapped the belt around her own throat."

An image began to shape up. I quick-slashed it into oblivion. Changed direction.

I knew how they'd gotten their explosives into Churchill Downs—faked credentials for the vendor area, and Landmine planted inside at a feed store supplying the barns—but not the final plan.

"How was the Derby supposed to go down?" I asked.

"Triggering by signals from three different cellphones. Scranton was to handle the Lockheed Martin tent from the far side of the infield, near the tunnel."

"For a swift exit."

"Landmine was dressed as a waiter. He was to get the second bomb up from the food service area hidden in a cart, stay close enough to the Godolphin suite for detonation, far enough out for a safe getaway. Bronco was dressed as security to get access to the horse barns. Stella was to stand on the finish line."

"Four bombs, not three."

"Apparently Stella was iffy until the last minute, and mere frosting on the cake. After detonation of the Lockheed Martin bomb, with news rats broadcasting their close-ups worldwide, she was to blow herself up, taking out survivors and immediate first responders."

"Good thing we were there for the go-down." Too pumped.

Capps took a moment. Then, "You have a chip on your shoulder, Ms. Night. And an aversion to authority. That combination will not serve you well."

"I—"

Capps cold-checked me in mid-retort. "Going lone wolf was reckless and irresponsible."

My throat clenched.

"Thank you."

That caught me off guard. Unsure I'd heard right, I said nothing.

Moments later, the center set of doors swung open. With the organ exhaling something appropriately uplifting, people filed out.

Leading the exodus was Gus, in a pin-striped black suit over a black silk tee. Shiny black loafers, white socks. A flicker in his expression, then he crossed to us.

I made introductions. "My twin brother, August Night."

"Gus." Extending a hand toward Capps.

Capps reached out. They shook.

"Literally?" Eyes ping-ponging between Gus and me. "Twins?"

"Spit don't lie," said Gus.

Years back, home on leave and overserved, I'd agreed to an online DNA test. Gus's idea. We'd gotten our pie chart and bazillion-in-one probability statement confirming the story we'd been told while growing up. I suspect Gus took it further, maybe talked Beau into running samples through CODIS, looking for a cold hit on dear old dad. Didn't ask. Didn't care.

"Note the green eyes." Gus widened said eyes.

"Irish mother," I said.

"I'm black Irish," Gus said.

"That's not what the term means," I said.

Capps had the confused look of a man whose cable has gone out in the middle of the game. He opened his mouth to comment. Reconsidered and closed it.

Mourners crossed the broad front stoop, descended the three shallow steps, and disappeared around the corner, returning to the Meeting Street parking lot. A few headed up the sidewalk on foot. No one smiled. No one laughed. Very few spoke to one another.

The last to leave the church was Opaline Drucker, Miranda pushing her in an old-fashioned cane-back wheelchair. The Pomeranian dozed in her lap.

Opaline flapped one knobby hand to indicate her desire to join us. Her dress was gray patterned with lavender flowers. Her maid was dressed entirely in black.

Three feet out, the gnarled hand rose to signal a stop. Opaline's lips were curled down at the corners, the lower one sucked in over her teeth. The clear-water eyes showed none of the emotion revealed by her mouth.

Drucker nodded to Gus, ignored Capps. Lifting a small silk purse from beside her hip, she squeezed the tiny bird whose wings formed the clasp, withdrew an envelope and extended it toward me. My name was penned on the front in no-nonsense script. Blue ink. It smelled of roses.

"You disregarded my wishes. Still, I owe you, Miss Night."

"I'm sorry the outcome wasn't—"

Drucker flapped the envelope, impatient. I took it, now understanding Peter Crage's warning. Erratic. Oh yeah.

"My granddaughter is alive. For that I thank you."

The red riding helmet had done its job. Seeing that my roundhouse blow had knocked Stella unconscious, Hoebeek had ordered the snipers to hold fire. Her team had managed to remove the vest and deactivate the IED. Mercifully, the RV gawkers had reacted to sirens, not to gunfire sending lead into Stella's brain. I'll never know what caused the pops. Firecrackers? Motorcycle backfires? My overwrought neurons?

"She will have the very best legal representation available."

I said nothing.

"The finest psychiatric care money can buy. If the doctors make her whole again, God be praised. If not, I will embrace whatever these monsters have made of her."

I recalled that one moment when my gaze locked with Stella's. And, later, after her arrest, I'd observed some of her interrogations. Defiant, she'd admitted to the attempt at accessing her grandmother's bank account. I'd heard the loathing in her voice, seen the hatred in her eyes. While pessimistic about a recovery, I wished her the best.

"Do you like my new memorial?" Indicating the stone at our backs. "The Tennyson quote was once Stella's favorite. One day she will approve. Mary Gray and Bowen will rest in peace knowing it lies above them."

"It's lovely." What people say at such times.

"I wish you peace, Miss Night." Eyes crystal-clear nothing.

I nodded.

"If you need help managing the money, Mr. Crage can advise you. It's what he does. He does it well."

"My brother helps me with financial matters." A glance at Gus. "He does it well."

CHAPTER
36

A week later, Gus motored out to Goat Island. Though I wasn't running marathons, my wounds were healing—the concussion, the bullet hole in my shoulder, the cuts and bruises on my face. I still looked like hell. That morning I'd received the mother lode of cheese from my goatly neighbor. I said thanks. I think it frightened her.

I'd walked down to the dock. Gus had produced a six-pack of Coors from the cooler on his boat. We'd talked it all out, watching the dusk slowly wither into night. Now we were just sitting, bare feet dangling, toes working the warm salt water.

The sky was dark, the waterway a deep strip of shimmery black. The silence felt comfortable. Until Gus grabbed my inner child by the throat.

"Would it help you to go back there?"

"Back where?" Unsuspecting.

"The house where everyone died. Where Mama died."

My skin prickled and my breath started going glitchy.

"I saw a documentary on Jonestown—"

"They didn't *die*." Words snapping sharp before I could stop them. "They killed themselves. They killed one another."

"Yes."

"The sick son of a bitch stockpiled cyanide." So many years, and still I couldn't utter the name he'd chosen for himself. "I saw invoices, remember?"

"Yes."

"They lay in a circle and drank poison because he told them to. They used syringes to squirt cyanide down kids' throats."

"Yes."

"They torched themselves because he said it would purify their souls." I kicked out at a tangle of seaweed floating on the current. "And we let it all happen."

"No, Sunnie. We didn't let anything happen. Our plan was solid."

"It was stupid."

"Naïve, yes." Gus, patient. We'd hashed this over so many times. "We should have had two nights. He jumped the schedule by a day to catch everyone off guard. To eliminate any window for second thoughts. We couldn't know that. We should have had time to alert the police."

"But we didn't."

"We never had the chance."

"So they made the Crossing." Waggling my hands in the air. "Crossing to what? Drawers in a morgue."

"Rise above your storm, girl."

"He used to put me in a box, Gus. Burn me. Make me kneel on salt until my knees bled."

"You had it the worst." Gus was watching me intently, assessing my level of crazy. Or letting me vent.

"I was his red-haired miracle. His little Immanuel." More finger waggling. "I doubt the fuckwit even knew what that meant."

Gus waited for me to go on.

I didn't.

A boat putted by. An owl hooted high up in the trees. A fish breached the surface, channel marker glinting red on its scales.

"Sorry." After a lot of deep breathing. "I know it was torture for you being powerless to help me. And I know you mean well. But I can't."

"Okay."

More silence, now not so comfortable. This time I broke it.

"How long have you been thinking about this?"

"Awhile."

"Have you ever gone back?"

"Just once, right after, to dig up the money."

"How's that going?"

"Exceedingly well."

"Bahamas?"

"Don't ask."

A beat, Gus's words boiling in my brain. One image.

"Do you remember the snapshot of the dead woman?" I asked. "The picture I found in his satchel?"

"Yes."

"I think he had her killed because she had doubts."

"I think so, too."

"I asked questions."

"You did."

"He wanted me to die first. To set an example for the others."

"We had to leave, Sunnie." After a pause. "Reconsidering?"

"No."

My past is like a snare. It allows me to move some, but never break free. No way I'd risk granting my childhood any more power.

"You know what really bothers me?" Gus asked after another long gap.

"What?" Guarded.

"American Pharoah. It's spelled wrong."

"The name was submitted like that in an online contest. The misspelling made it onto the horse's registration form." Bothered me, too. I'd looked it up.

"And the rest is history."

"Busy week at the marina?" I asked.

"A few charters." Gus drained the last of his beer and stood. "One of which sets out at dawn tomorrow. I'd better head into town."

That night, lying in bed, hoping to dream of nothing more menacing than a squirrel at the window, my thoughts spiraled down a white rabbit hole into a maze of riddles.

Was Gus right? Would going back help me face what had happened? The bizarre life I'd lived before Beau took us in? Would it help calm the rage? Help keep the monsters in check?

I saw three faces floating in the dark. Stella. Kerr. My own pale oval with its serpentine mark.

How had I survived? Sure, I'm damaged. I live alone with no permanent phone or Internet account. I have a scar I refuse to fix. I dislike being touched and have a temper that's my own worst enemy. I use icy showers and grueling workouts to escape stress and trick my brain into making me feel strong. To kick-start endorphins or whatever the current psychobabble is. Yeah, I have my crazies, but I've managed to cling to my identity. To not lose myself.

Kerr also lived a childhood overshadowed by madness. Like me, she resisted being sucked into the sick vision of others. Into her mother's delusion. Was her resilience a product of low intelligence? Of passivity? I ran away. Had Kerr endured by retreating into her own small world?

Stella traveled the opposite path. She broke. Succumbed to the brainwashing and embraced the creed of Jihad for Jesus. Why did Stella lose herself while Kerr and I did not?

Could time heal the girl who'd stood on a sunny boardwalk with her mother and brother? Could doctors resurrect the person she'd been? Or was hope of resurrection unrealistic?

Why had I felt such a visceral pull to Stella? Memories of the searing anguish caused by fanaticism? The fact that she had no daddy? Kerr and I had grown up fatherless, too. The flaming red hair?

Or had Stella been the attraction at all? Was Beau's take on me closer to the truth? Had I been drawn by the lure of the adrenaline rush? By the thrill of the hunt?

Like Alice, only puzzles. No solutions.

Sergeant Edwin A. Maddux, USMC, taught that life is a rat's nest of noise and chaos and chance. No logic. Just one single steadfast truth. Screw up and there's no way back.

I believed him.

My monsters still tug. But Beau's prediction was spot-on. Searching for Stella has changed me.

I'm no longer certain the sarge had it right.

ACKNOWLEDGMENTS

As usual, I owe many thanks to many people.

Major Donald F. Burbrink II of the Louisville Metro Police Department patiently answered endless questions. Tom Schneider was my go-to expert on everything Chicago.

My sincere thanks to my agent, Jennifer Rudolph-Walsh, and to my meticulous and skillful editors, Jennifer Hershey and Susan Sandon.

I also want to acknowledge all those in the industry who work so hard on my behalf. At Random House in the United States: Gina Centrello, Kara Welsh, Kim Hovey, Scott Shannon, Susan Corcoran, Cindy Murray, Debbie Aroff, Cynthia Lasky, Beth Pearson, and Anne Speyer. Across the pond: Aslan Byrne, Glenn O'Neill, Georgina Hawtrey-Woore, and Sonny Marr. At Simon and Schuster, north of the forty-ninth: Kevin Hanson. At William Morris Endeavor Entertainment: Sabrina Giglio, Erika Niven, Tracy Fisher, and Raffaella De Angelis.

I appreciate the support of my tireless assistant, Melissa Fish.

Any errors in the book are all my fault.

To my readers, I hope you enjoy reading about Sunday Night as much as I enjoyed creating her. Thanks for making the effort to find me at my signings and appearances, to visit my website (kathyreichs .com), to share your thoughts on Facebook (kathyreichsbooks), to follow me on Twitter (@KathyReichs) and Pinterest (kathyreichs), and to tag me in your photos on Instagram (kathyreichs). The stories I write are all for you. Thanks so much for allowing me to do what I love.

ABOUT THE AUTHOR

KATHY REICHS is the author of eighteen *New York Times* bestselling novels and the co-author, with her son, Brendan Reichs, of six novels for young adults. Like the protagonist of her Temperance Brennan series, Reichs is a forensic anthropologist—one of fewer than one hundred and fifteen ever certified by the American Board of Forensic Anthropology. A professor in the Department of Anthropology at the University of North Carolina at Charlotte, she is a former vice president of the American Academy of Forensic Sciences and serves on the National Police Services Advisory Council in Canada. Reichs's own life, as much as her novels, is the basis for the TV show *Bones,* one of the longest-running series in the history of the Fox network.

kathyreichs.com
Facebook.com/kathyreichsbooks
Twitter: @KathyReichs

ABOUT THE TYPE

This book was set in Sabon, a typeface designed by the well-known German typographer Jan Tschichold (1902–74). Sabon's design is based upon the original letterforms of sixteenth-century French type designer Claude Garamond and was created specifically to be used for three sources: foundry type for hand composition, Linotype, and Monotype. Tschichold named his typeface for the famous Frankfurt typefounder Jacques Sabon (c. 1520–80).

TURN THE PAGE FOR AN EXCERPT
FROM KATHY REICHS'S

A
CONSPIRACY
OF BONES

COMING SOON FROM SIMON & SCHUSTER CANADA

"It is far harder to kill a phantom than a reality."

— Virginia Woolf, *The Death of the Moth and Other Essays*

PROLOGUE

Reactions to pressure vary. Some people are ductile, able to stretch. Others are brittle, powerless to bend. Physicists talk of stress-strain curves. One thing is certain. If the burden is too great, or the loading too rapid, anyone can snap.

I reached my breaking point the summer after my boss was murdered. *Moi.* The igneous rock of emotion.

To be fair, Larabee's death wasn't the immediate or sole trigger. Slidell's retirement. Moving in with Ryan on both the Montreal and Charlotte ends of our geographically complex relationship. Katy's posting in Afghanistan. Mama's cancer. A world of stressors was chafing my personal curve.

Looking back, I admit I was out of control. Perhaps going rogue was an attempt to steer unsteerable forces. A bird-flip to aging. A cry for Ryan's attention. A subconscious effort to drive him away. Maybe it was just the goddamned Carolina heat.

Who knows? I was holding my own until the faceless man finally sent me over the edge. His remains and the subsequent investigation punched a big black hole in my smug little world.

Mama spotted the changes long before the enigmatic corpse

turned up. The distractedness. The agitation. The short temper. I denied it, of course, knowing she was right. I was ignoring emails, the phone. Declining invitations in favor of solo bingeing on old Hollywood flicks.

And the dreams. Twisting montages filled with dark figures and vague dangers. Or frustrating tasks I couldn't complete. Anxiety? Hormones? Didn't matter the cause. I was sleeping little, constantly restless and exhausted.

It didn't take Freud to recognize I was in a bad place.

So there I was, after midnight, jogging in the same park in which Larabee had been gunned down. Ole Sigmund might have offered a comment on that.

The weather was beyond Dixie summer-night warm. The air was muggy and hot, and my Pro Cool tee was pasted to my back. It had rained as I'd eaten my microwave pizza dinner at ten, and moisture still hung thick in the air. Puddles glistened black on the pavement, went yellow as my fuzzy shadow and I passed under streetlamps blurred by mist.

The lake was a dark void, woolly where the water met the bank. Murky shapes glided its surface, silent, aware of their tenuous state. Park officials fight an endless, often creative battle. No matter the deterrent, the geese always return.

I was passing a black Lego form I knew to be a picnic pavilion when I sensed more than heard another presence. Pulse pumping faster, I squinted hard.

A man was standing in the smear of shadow below the pavilion's roof. His face was down, his features obscured. Medium height and build. I could tell little else about him. Except one thing.

Despite the stifling heat, the man was wearing a trench coat. When he raised an arm, perhaps to check a watch, the fabric winked pale in the gloom enveloping him.

One nervous glimpse as I jogged past.

Eight more strides, then I slowed and glanced back. The pavilion was empty. I stopped, breathing hard, checking in both directions along the jogging trail. The man was gone.

The mist began to morph back into rain. Listless drops tested for a foothold on my face and hair. Time to boogie.

I turned. And caught a flicker of gray. There then gone.

Shot of adrenaline. Was Trench Coat targeting me after all? If not, what was he doing in a park in the rain in the middle of the night? And why so elusive?

Or was my wariness a product of paranoia, another gift from my overburdened stress-strain curve. Either way, I was glad I'd shoved pepper spray into a shorts pocket when leaving home.

Unbidden, images of Larabee's last moments unspooled in my head. The gray-green pallor of his skin. The eerie glow of the surgical trauma ICU. The impartial pinging of the monitors recording their bloodless peaks and valleys. The screaming silence when the pinging stopped. Later, in an interview room smelling of sweat and fear, the slouchy indifference of the brain-fried tweaker who'd sent the bullets into Larabee's belly.

Stop!

Aloud? Or just in my mind?

I lengthened my stride, footfalls pounding loud in the stillness.

A full minute, then a trench-coated silhouette, far up where the trail emptied into a small parking lot. The man was walking slowly, his back to me.

Suddenly, noise seemed to ricochet from all around. Rustling leaves. Shifting branches. Snapping twigs. Night creatures? Trench Coat's geeked-out pals looking to fund more meth?

I had no valuables—carried no money, wore no watch. Would that anger them?

Or were the sounds just overwrought nerves?

I patted the pepper spray at my right hip. Felt the canister. Pink and nasty. A molecule of the price I'd paid had been donated toward breast cancer research.

Momentary indecision.

Veer off and cut through the tangle of shrubs and trees enclosing the park? Stay on the path and time my pace in order to pass the man in the parking lot? There were streetlamps there, overwhelmed, but trying their best.

I slowed. Trench Coat was now just ten yards ahead.

My brain chose that moment to unreel a blockbuster tableau.

As I passed, the man would pull a knife and slit my throat. Our eyes would meet. His would be hard and cold as death.

Jesus!

Why was I letting this rattle me? In my line of work I encounter far worse than a dude dressed like Bogie in *Casablanca*. Outlaw bikers who chainsaw the heads and hands from their murdered rivals. Macho pricks who stalk and strangle their terrified exes. Drunken bullies who wall-slam fussy infants. Those thugs don't dissuade me from focusing on my job. Quite the reverse. They inspire me to work harder. A journalist once described me as the Queen of Cold Flesh.

So why the drama over a guy in a belted coat? Why the sense of threat to my person?

Yes, I'd hit a rough patch of late. Personally. Professionally. The latter self-inflicted. I could have been more diplomatic. Or kept my mouth shut. Who knew my comments would come back to bite me in the ass? Right. Don't they always?

So, here I was, out in the woods, not home in my bed. With a psycho? Or a harmless geezer overly sensitive to damp?

Screw it. The route would take longer, but I decided to cut out of the park then weave through neighborhood streets, eventually to Queens Road West, then home.

Before leaving the trail, I paused for one last look.

The man was in the empty lot, standing under one of the struggling lamps. His chin was raised, his features vaguely discernible as dark blotches on a smudgy white rectangle.

My breath froze.

The man was staring straight at me.

Or was he?

Heart thumping, I pivoted and plunged into an opening in the shrubs and trees at my back. The tunnel was narrow, barely there, or not there at all. Twigs and leaves snagged my arms and hair, skeletal fingers clawing me back into the park.

My breathing sounded louder, more desperate, as though fighting entrapment by the thick vegetation. The air was heavy with the scent of wet bark, damp earth, and my own perspiration.

A few yards, then a new odor slithered into the mix. A familiar odor. An odor that triggered a fresh wave of adrenaline.

I was catching whiffs of decomposing flesh.

Impossible.

Yet there it was. Stark and cold as the images haunting my dreams.

A minute of scrambling, then I detected a thawing in one slice of the darkness ahead. Within the slice, angles and planes of shadow shifting and tilting.

Trench Coat's minions lying in wait?

Paranoia playing parlor games with my sanity?

I was almost to the opening when a rip-your-face-off snarl brought me up short. As my mind struggled to form a rational explanation, a high-pitched scream sent every hair upright on my arms and neck.

Hand shaking, I pulled the pepper spray from my pocket and inched forward.

Beyond the tree line, on a narrow strip of brush, two dogs were locked in winner-take-all combat. The larger, the scraggy consequence of some lab–pit bull affair, was all hackles, bared teeth, and gleaming white sclera. The smaller, probably a terrier, cowered tense and timorous, blood and spit matting the fur on one haunch.

Unaware of me, or not caring, the lab-pit braced, then lunged for another attack. The terrier yelped and tried to flatten itself even more to the ground, desperate to reduce the amount of mass it presented to the world.

The lab-pit held a moment then, confident that rank had been established, pivoted and trotted toward a dark mound lying in the scrub. As the terrier slunk off, tail curled to its belly, the lab-pit sniffed the air, scanned its surroundings, then lowered its head.

I watched, spellbound, needing to know the cause of the fight.

A flurry of thrashing and tugging, then the victor's snout rose.

Clamped in the dog's jaw was the severed head of a goose, ravaged neck glistening black, cheek swath winking white like the smile of an evil clown.

I watched rain fall on the bird's sightless eye.